*To the sound defeat of
personal burdens and all those who have
chosen to embolden others as they dream of
bigger things, like we've been called to do, I
dedicate this novel. As to my own life
journey, you know who you are—the shots
in the arm, the allegiance, the staying
power—none of it went unseen.*

Winner of the Hawthorne Prize, 2024

Ada waited for a lull then summoned the town like a prophet:

"Quiet, scalawags! I have a message for all you fine citizens of Bellwether!"

The crowd still roared. Someone shouted, "Let's hear the devil woman!" and they quieted to a low rumble.

Ada saw the furor in their dimly lit faces, but she wasn't afraid. Not anymore. She glanced at Elinor—the black cowl atop her pretty head and her legs trembling, a puddle on the planks between them—then turned back to the crowd, quickly searching for her talisman one last time.

Their eyes locked.

A wide sneer formed on the boy's round face while his father whispered in his ear. As if Satan himself was the puppeteer, the child drew a tiny hand across his throat, slow and easy.

Ada gasped, then stiffened. "My news is brief!" she shouted. "And it's coming straight from the afterworld." She spoke from outside herself, from some other place, some other time. She could feel her eyes filling up, could hear the lack of feeling in her words. "Just as you've taken the light from my Elinor, God will take yours. You'll hurt for this. Your children's children will feel the ire. That's a promise." Then a hood was pulled over her head, too. As one deputy tightened the loops around both women's necks, the other yelled, "Release!"

The Fall
of
Bellwether

Also by Chad V. Broughman

the forsaken… a collection of stories by Etchings Press, 2018, winner of the Book Prize

slighted. by Etchings Press, 2022, Editor's Choice Award

Write Michigan Short Story Anthology, On Loss, and *Scribes Valley Anthology*

Short fiction available in journals and anthologies worldwide, such as "Carrier Pigeon," "Pulp Literature," "River Poet's Journal," "Burningword," and "Sky Island Journal," and many more.

The Fall of Bellwether

CHAD V. BROUGHMAN

Anamcara Press LLC

Published in 2024 by Anamcara Press LLC
Author © 2024 by Chad V. Broughman
Cover art and photograph by kokinnwakashuu
Adobe Caslon Pro, Pulpo Rust, Berlin Sans FB

Book Description: In the small town of Bellwether, where prejudice and judgment prevail, the harrowing journey of all who are jolted by the citizens' original sin unfolds—a tale of survival, defiance, and the unyielding human spirit.

ANAMCARA PRESS LLC
P.O. Box 442072, Lawrence, KS 66044
https://anamcara-press.com/

Ordering Information:
Quantity sales. Special discounts are available on quantity purchases by corporations, associations, and others. For details, contact the publisher at the address above.
Orders by U.S. trade bookstores and wholesalers. Please contact Ingram Distribution.

ISBN-13: 978-1-960462-16-9 eBook
ISBN-13: 978-1-960462-15-2 hardback
ISBN-13: 978-1-960462-14-5 paperback

FIC027050 - Fiction / Romance / Historical
FIC008000 - Fiction / Sagas
FIC019000 - Fiction / Literary

Library of Congress Control Number: 2023939816

CONTENTS

There you'll find the place I love most in the world. The place where I grew thin from dreaming. My village, rising from the plain. Shaded with trees and leaves like a piggy bank filled with memories. You'll see why a person would want to live there forever. Dawn, morning, mid-day, night: all the same, except for the changes in the air. The air changes the color of things there. And life whirs by as quiet as a murmur... the pure murmuring of life.

—*Juan Rulfo, Pedro Páramo*

PART I

The Fall of Bellwether

1841 - 1858

Chapter 1
God Sees You

It was in 1841 when the damp winds lashed at town square, tipping hats and rustling papery leaves against the scaffold. Ada saw Elinor's bonnet lift and a lock of reddish-yellow hair spill over her eye. She watched her trying to reach for the ringlet, to tuck it away, forgetting that her hands were bound. Surely the rope bit her skin.

"Don't let 'em see you hurting," Ada said.

Elinor leveled her shoulders and blew at the loose curl.

"That's my girl."

Ada knew Elinor was confused. Her only child stood blank-eyed, the shackles heavy as headstones on her wrists. She thought, my daughter will die the same way she lived, her simple mind unable to grasp the evils of the world. Perhaps her daftness was a blessing after all.

Ada surveyed the crowd of pinch-faced hypocrites. Brown smoke hung over their heads. The ghostly remnants of dynamite blasts from Bellwether's copper mine layered the air like sediment. She looked from face to face, marking the wrath in the onlookers' eyes. The same good people who sat next to them at church just a few months before, nodding while her husband preached from the pulpit with fire and flair. These same upright folks who said, "Hello, fine ladies," whenever she and Elinor crossed their paths at the postmaster's or the mercantile.

Today, they were judge and jury. Executioners.

Though Ada had managed to shield her daughter from the town's fury for months, ultimately, she had failed. And Elinor would pay with her life. Ada's instinct was to cover her girl's eyes to hide the cold-bloodedness. Her muscles ached that she couldn't as her hands were tied, too.

"Heathens!" someone shouted.

"Swindlers! Crooks!" Deacon John cried, raising his fists in the air.

Others cast their eyes to the dirt, unwilling to spur on the rage, yet not brave enough to stop it.

Ada looked just in time to see the deputy slip the noose over her daughter's head then pull it snug. The fat knot bulged at Elinor's dainty neck like a tumor on a rose.

But Elinor merely looked up at the deputy and smiled. "Ma says I'm going home to be with God."

When the coarse hemp rasped against Elinor's jowl, Ada saw her twitch, bow out her chest and stand taller. "Never stole anything," Elinor told the deputy, then looked to her mother for approval.

"No you didn't, baby," Ada called out, working past the swell in her throat.

The deputy yanked a hood over Elinor's head.

"Mama, I can't—I can't see!"

* * *

She called her husband to mind, how he'd abandoned them the year before, as well as his congregation, taking all their money with him and six-month's worth of tithing. In his wake, he left the church with a leaky roof, a half-renovated belfry, and a penniless wife and daughter. The people of Bellwether couldn't face the certainty that their man of the cloth could do such a thing. So they turned a blind eye to a desperate mother and her defective daughter, freezing them out of the church for their "selfish ways" and for "pushing away the Reverend like they did."

Ada and Elinor Williams survived on the goods they had canned from the summer season and the few meat chickens they kept. Soon enough, though, they had finished the last of the tomatoes and squash and were down to a puny-breasted egg layer. Ada never learned to hunt or fish, and it wouldn't have mattered anyway, as her husband had taken the rifle and poles, too.

Ada held steadfast that they could survive on the food store until God's grace came to pass, either the Reverend returned or their neighbors' hearts softened. But she brought out the last of their provisions from the cellar and placed them on the table: two canisters of beets and a dozen or so potatoes. The sparseness glared at them as sure as the nights turned colder. When she looked at the dwindled reserve, the house closed in on her. And the air drew out. She wanted to run for help, scream for mercy. Anything to save her daughter and herself. But her feet felt nailed to the floor, her tongue tied. She knew Elinor was watching, deep-blue, vacant eyes, wondering what to do, how to act.

That's when instinct took hold. Ada calmed her breathing, sucking in through her nose then blowing it out through pursed lips. She scooped several potatoes into her apron, then dropped them in the wash bucket, nodding at Elinor to do the same. As they rubbed the dirt from each spud and cut the tubers with dull knives, Ada said evenly, "Come tomorrow, we'll beg for money."

At the break of dawn, Ada made her way to the grove in front of the house, ax in hand. Though she struggled to garner a food source, she knew how to gather firewood and did so with a vengeance. *I'll be damned if I'm gonna be idle while our bodies wither away,* she thought. *At least they'll find our bony carcasses amidst cords of hardwood.* She cleaved into a fallen oak. As her joints stiffened, her swing grew fiercer. *They'll never be able to say those Williams women were weak.*

Oscar and Ruby Lee came clanking toward her, the falling-top of the carriage folded down, their two young sons in the back. Ada figured they must be headed to St. Ignace, in need of supplies for their dairy farm. This was her first face-to-face brush with the family as a spouseless mother, especially in such close proximity. They were friends. The week before the Reverend left, their families had eaten supper together. Inside, the men smoked pipes and talked about William Henry Harrison's sudden death and John Tyler coming to office while the women added ingredients to the cake batter—stirring in the suet, carrots, flour and baking soda—taking turns trying each new mixture then either shaking or nodding their heads. Outside, the boys showed Elinor their milking cows, ever patient and kind with their slow friend. But today, when the boys waved to Ada, Oscar said, "Hands down, lads."

After they passed, Ada's inclination was to chase after them, rein in her disgrace and shout a response. Though she did try to catch up to the carriage, the lack of nourishment took its toll. She fell in a few steps behind, close enough to hear the eldest boy ask, "Why Pa?" and Oscar to respond, "'Cause she's lost the Holy Spirit, son. Rumor is she's cursing folks, and it's all coming true. Told Mr. Turner that she hoped he got the trots. Poor man couldn't leave the privy for hours on end. And when Mr. Wilkinson told her she'd been acting like a witch,' Ada didn't say no. Instead, she said, 'This damned village will make me into whatever it wants.'"

To hear Mr. Lee, of all people, say the words that she could only guess were being muttered about town was like a knife through her brain, slowing everything around her, blurring it together. Her breaths were quick and sharp. She backed herself against a hemlock tree to rest, the uneven ridges of the bark poking into her spine. Arching her neck rearward, Ada tapped the crown of her head on the trunk, gentle at first, then a bit harder. The emptiness in her stomach grew heavy, making her legs light, her arms more tired. She thought about the spongy, withering potatoes on the table, white sprouts coming out of the tops and sides, then rapped her head once more and slid down the tree.

By then, Elinor had made her way to the grove, too. Having seen her mother break, she stepped to her and with searching hands, found the sore place on Ada's head. She held her fingers there a while before opening her mother's legs at the knees and settling in her lap, her head against Ada's chest. Both of them looked out over the road, and Ada could feel Earth's gravity pulling at their cheeks, their eyes, their hearts.

* * *

For two days, the Williams women trekked to the houses of old friends, Ada leaving her dignity outside with her coming-of-age daughter while she pleaded. But the conversations were always the same, as if the town had rehearsed them. Ada started each exchange, getting right to the point by explaining that she could now see Elinor's ribs when they readied for bed. Then she'd add, "It was the Reverend who left. Why is Bellwether forsaking us?"

"You ran him off! Your faith is weak. And the dimwit's, too. That's why you've fallen to conjuring and such things."

Ada bit down on her tongue, the tinny taste of blood flooding her mouth. Being accused of meddling with black magic was startling. But more stunning, were the disparaging words used to describe her daughter, and the ease with which they were hurled. She could never get used to it. "That's not the truth," she'd say. "I held my husband up. It was his faith that wavered, not ours. Not until now."

"You're a liar, Ada! The good Reverend out and said in his last sermon, 'If wives don't lift up their husbands, faith can be shaken.' And God knows you've probably been convening with the incubus all along. That's why you were given a fool child. May the devil damn you!"

Though Ada suspected folks might blame her for the Reverend's double-cross, hearing it out loud was overwhelming, stopped her mind from working. Finally, she was able to blurt out, "But we're starving. We'll surely die soon if—"

"That's your penance!"

* * *

On the third day, after every household had turned them out again, Ada and Elinor made their way home. The sun had gone down and the sky was blue-black, the soles of their shoes wearing through, their feet aching and swollen. A voice shouted out from somewhere in the village, "We see you Williams girls, out there scampering with the Prince of Darkness!" followed by a deep thump. Ada felt the hollow in her stomach and quick as the winds of an arctic northerly, her grief turned to anger. "Tomorrow, we'll beg in the street," she said. "We'll make our brethren have to see us every day."

So they did. Each afternoon, Ada and Elinor sat in the village's tiny marketplace—legs folded under, hands out—reminding their brothers and sisters in Christ how they were deserting those in need. After days of the townspeople walking by, wordlessly, Ada and Elinor traipsed to the front steps of the church where their husband and father should have been presiding. They sat on the church stairs in their best bonnets and tugged at their petticoats to make them smooth, greeting each family with the kindness of a loved one. Only to be slighted. The service began and the parishioners started to sing the opening hymns: the ones Ada knew by heart, the ones about grace and glory and blessed assurance as someone closed the doors upon the women.

"Burn in hell!" Ada roared, pounding on the wood slats. When she heard the muffled sound of Mr. Wilkinson, the deacon chosen as interim minister, trying to preach, she pushed her mouth into the crevice where the doors came together and shouted, "Sinners! Praying in the house of the Lord then turning your backs. That ain't our God in there!"

Below her, Elinor mimicked her mother, putting her lips against the dark slit, yelling, "I hate you!"

That night, as Ada crept into the Wilkinsons' barn, she prayed. Not for forgiveness, but courage. Don't know what God this town's turning to, she thought, but Lord, MY Lord, give me strength. Let me feed my girl. One of the cows started to grunt, and Ada quickly moved to it, stroked its back lengthwise until it quieted. Her heart beat fast, but she grounded herself, saying over and over again, you have to be here.

She tiptoed to an empty stall where two barrels sat side by side then plunged her hands into the first one, a heaping mound of feed. She couldn't stop from letting the corn kernels slip through her fingers a couple of times before shoveling some into the burlap bag around her waist. Then she side-stepped to the second barrel, plucking out apples until the bag was nearly full. She felt a rush of emotions—excitement, relief, fear.

But no guilt.

At the edge of her neighbor's property, just past the split-rail fence, Ada bent over a row of hardy radishes, grabbed several stems at the base and twisted them upward with a snap. With each stride toward home, she could feel the heft of the full bag against her thigh. She dusted off a radish and bit into it. Her face puckered at the tang then a smile broke across her face.

* * *

As autumn drew to a close, the Williams women continued to hunker down in the town square during the day, an empty basket between them and a coal-gray blanket covering their legs and feet. As the passersby shuffled to their destinations, heads high, Ada searched their faces, clearing her throat or calling their names until they looked her way. Elinor looked up at them, a fourteen year old's body, a toddler's smile.

Though many had complained to Sheriff Thompson, often right in front of them, telling him to "Rid the town of such rabble," his response was always the same—"They haven't broken any laws."

Then, come nightfall, Ada would sneak through Bellwether, pilfering neighbors. With each theft, she grew more confident and daring, swiping loaves of bread from a window set out to cool and from another, a pumpkin pie. Jars of honey from a porch and a salted down ham from a smokehouse. Though the Williams women were not overfed, the hunger pangs had abated some.

Talk began about the pillaged goods. Folks started bolting their barn doors against Ada and out by the county line, farmer Richardson set a leg-hold trap in front of his icehouse. Had a cricket not let out a leathery squeak, Ada might not have looked down in time to see the metal snare. Its sharpened teeth would have gnashed her foot. The heyday was coming to an end, Ada knew that. And once again, hopelessness thundered through her, louder than ever.

One night, as Ada was scampering through a backfield into the village, she told herself to take what she could as time was running out. Don't feel or think, she told herself, just keep moving. She looked this way, that way, then fixed her eyes on Mr. Turner's house, set back from the road a bit. In front, several big maple trees stood tall; out back, between the slanted outbuilding and chicken coop, there were several more. With all that cover, Ada had already robbed the old man's icehouse weeks before—a slab of jerky and some rock mouth bass. But this time, she prowled around the coop like a fox, looking for traps before unlatching the wired gate. Most of the chickens were in the shelter; some were stirring, ambling across the straw strewn earth. A couple of them clucked at her approach but quieted, bustling out of her path as she slid each foot forward slow and steady, never changing pace. By design, Ada moved more stealthily now.

She glided between the nesting boxes and up to the outside roost then lifted up a fat hen, held it upside down by the feet. Though it spread its wings in protest, Ada held them down and coolly backed out of the coop. It only clacked a few times before she was in the yard again, away from the rest, and could wring its neck without an uprising. She gripped its head, pulled down hard then jerked upward, fast and fierce. The body flapped wildly, but she held on tight, creeping backwards a few more steps. Under the moonlight, the blood was dark, gushing in one steady stream, like a pitcher pouring water. She took another step back, thumping against Mr. Turner's round, stiff belly.

"Give it to me, Ada." His voice was low, husky. Ada's mind whirred. In her fright, she clenched the hen's hocks with all her might, as if she'd fall into a fiery pit should she let go. But Mr. Turner gripped it by its breast with the same ferocity. It was his lifeline, too. They yanked the draining bird back and forth, stretching its cape and thighs like bread dough. Hackle feathers flitted down around them.

"You're a thief!"

"And you're a fraud."

Both shanks pulled loose and Ada tumbled back. One of the spurs had pierced her palm and she cupped her fingers over the cut as she dashed away from Mr. Turner.

"God sees you, Ada!" Mr. Turner called after her.

"God sees you, too! And all you twisted, hateful souls!" she yelled back.

* * *

Ada hadn't slept much in the three nights since Mr. Turner caught her looting his coop. She paced in front of the window for hours at a time, waiting for someone to come, deliver their doom. Then, late that Saturday night she saw the lanterns bouncing down their narrow lane, heard the jittery voices of the two young deputies and shackles jangling against each other. The motion and noise were strange in the prevailing stillness. No one ever visited. By the time they approached, Ada was standing on the porch, gathering her thick tresses into a bun.

"Been expecting you."

"Taking you to the town hall, Ada," the first deputy said. With each word, his pitch rose and fell, his eyes on the chains as he fumbled them from his belt loop.

"Well, get on with it." Ada finished pushing another hairpin through the black thatch that rested on her nape then held out her hands, wrists up.

"Where's Elinor?" The second deputy's voice was higher, more agitated.

"My girl's whereabouts don't matter none to you." Ada was matter-of-fact, holding still as she was fettered.

"We've come for her, too."

"But she's done nothing."

"Folks say she's been stealing right along with you."

Instantly, her face went slack. She felt weightless.

"And blaspheming the Lord," the second deputy added. Then he shook his head and said under his breath, "That girl don't seem like the ransacking kind, though. Let alone, a heathen." He clicked his tongue a couple of times. "Hell, never thought you to be that way neither, Ada."

"Well remember what the Reverend said, Lucifer means 'morning star.' And he was God's favorite before turning into the Devil."

"But Elinor ain't even smart enough to—" The boy didn't finish his sentence. He just strode past Ada and pulled the door open but never entered. Instead, Elinor stepped from the archway, her eyes on Ada and her wrists turned skyward, too.

After both women were bound, the four of them began walking to town. Ada felt the anxiety burning her skin from the inside, but she had learned to swallow the nervousness, hold it low in her guts so her mind stayed fresh. She needed to be alert, ready for whatever came their way. She badgered the callow deputies, prodding them for particulars, anything that would help her warn Elinor of the coming onslaught. But the men had already said too much, so they whispered to one another, careful to lag a few steps behind.

With her head kept straight, Ada steered Elinor the best she could. "Honey, listen—" Elinor turned to look at her mother.

"No! Don't look at me." She paused, then started in again. "They're gonna ask you a bunch of questions when we get there. Try to answer with just 'Yes' or 'No.'"

"They're gonna be mean to us, ain't they?"

"Yes," Ada said. In the scant light of the lanterns behind them, she glanced to see the bewilderment on Elinor's face, and her heart broke open. But Ada had learned to swallow her sadness, too. There was no time for grieving Elinor's guilt-lessness. Or her dull mind. Instead, Ada talked faster, angry now. She knew Elinor would listen harder if she heard angst in her mother's voice. "If you don't start listening, they'll fine us money we don't have. Or even jail us. Now, when they ask if you've been taking things, you say 'No'. Every time, you say, 'No.'"

"You're mad at me."

"Damn it, Elinor, don't talk. When they ask if you love God, you say, 'Yes.'"

The deputies paused their conversation, and Ada quieted again, trying to time her dialogue with theirs. Soon enough, Bellwether's town square came into view. The hunter's moon was high, looming over the village like a giant blue eye. Ada slowed her pace, desperate to buy more time, but the deputies didn't follow suit.

They approached the town hall, and voices of all different timbres sifted out into the street. The deputies stood on either side of the big doors and pulled them open, both nodding for

Ada and Elinor to enter. As they did, the clamor inside halted. The citizens were assembled in tall, rigid chairs, row upon row. They filled benches against the far walls, too. All of them were turned, watching with wild wonder, as though awaiting a bride making her way to the altar.

Lining the center aisle, lanterns lit every face like the moon outside, each in a different lunar phase. The smell of kerosene was acrid. The deputies veered them to the front of the building and seated them in the two straight-back chairs behind a long table. The first one stared them down like everyone else, insisting with a nod of his head that their arms stay in plain sight, bound or not. The second just stared at the ground.

The room grew strangely quiet while Mr. Turner plodded to the podium. He carried the mangled remains of the hen with him, plopped the carcass on the end of the table and wagged his finger at Ada. The putrid stench of rotting poultry wafted through the open room, overtaking the fuel oil. He turned to the villagers and spoke in his gruff tone, but fiery now, talking about the Williams women as if they weren't there.

"These women tried stealing my biggest hen." He pointed at the rumpled mound of feathers, and the pronouncement let loose the crowd's restraint. The townspeople shifted in their seats, grumbled to themselves, to one another. Then Mr. Turner shouted, "And those two been cursing God all over town!"

The room boiled over. Ada spoke to Elinor out of the side of her mouth, loud enough so she could hear over the grousing. "There's gonna be more yelling, Elinor, but never you mind that. Just remember, you didn't take nothing and you love the Lord."

As she finished the last word, a mealy apple glanced Ada's ear. The sting made her yip, and she lifted her shoulders to guard against any more that may come. She felt herself wincing and twitching as if a gun were pointed at her forehead. Most in the crowd hailed her cowering, yet some looked away. Even in her duress, Ada noticed Ruby Lee hastening out the door.

Knowing the bedlam would only build, she stood up. Her face and neck were taut, waiting to be hit by another hurled apple. Clenching all over, she screamed, "I stole from all of you!"

The crowd jeered. But Ada yelled louder. "Had to! And you know why! This ain't about me and the Devil. And it sure as hell ain't about taking chickens or pies, that's all happened before." The horde quieted, some. "We all know this is about the Reverend. He's a deserter. And you can't dare condemn your man of God, that'd make you have to look at yourselves, too. Well, that's fine. Go ahead and blame me." She dipped her head toward Elinor, and said, "But my daughter is innocent. You know that, too! So give us our fine or bring out the pillory if you got to. Lock me in it all day! But let Elinor be!"

Mr. Turner was still at the podium, standing near them both. "Oh, you're sadly mistaken, Miss Ada. This meeting ain't about fines or making amends. This here's about hanging."

Ada's stomach dropped into her feet then fell right through the floor. Cold sweat broke out on her arms and legs. All the words and shouts blurred into a flat buzz, like the hum of a wasp. Though she heard Elinor ask, "They mean to hang us, Ma?" she couldn't speak. Then Mr. Murray traipsed to the front of the room, arm above his head, fingers spread, beckoning the Holy Spirit.

"In the name of the Lord," he ministered, "We gotta hang 'em! Rid Bellwether of their sins. Let there be no doubt, the trespasses they're carrying are more than just swiping some grub. They turned on the good Reverend. And she can deny it all she wants, but they've been desecrating the Lord! Folks see 'em tromping around at all hours of the night. And we all know Mr. Turner ain't been feeling well since he caught her thievin' in his coop. No room for any hoodooing in Bellwether."

Mr. Turner gave the rolling snowball a final push. "We do it now, before Sheriff Thompson returns from Marquette," he proclaimed. "Not much longer till the sun comes up! Now, I say. In the name of Christ!"

"What are we doing?" a man's voice sounded out. "This ain't right." But his resistance was quickly drowned out as the village heralded its charge. In one fell swoop, Ada and Elinor were lifted up on their backs by random hands, bore like litters atop people's shoulders. Someone gripped Ada's inner thigh, thickset fingers lodged in her crotch. She floundered in their clutches, trying not to fall. But they kept her steady, seized harder. She arched her body until her head fell far enough back to see Elinor.

"Hold on, baby!" she yelled. Elinor was still, a rigid plane. In the open palms of the mob, the lanterns jostled up and down like frenzied fireflies. Amidst all the boiling, Ada heard several women crying. Though the voice was unrecognizable, one woman constantly shouted, "Stop this madness!" But Ada knew the bloodlust was untamable now, no pleas for good sense could conquer the need to see harm done.

After reaching the grove behind the church, they were set atop the scaffold. The deputies held them by their elbows and the backs of their necks as the crowd gathered at the base. The gallows were slanted, tottering with every movement. They hadn't been used for a couple of years, not since the young Ojibwe woman was hanged after her baby girl died. She had brought it on herself, the church council said, hadn't tried hard enough to make it well. Didn't even bring the babe to the Reverend when it was sick, no healing hands upon its head. Ada knew better, though. She saw the way Deacon John always looked at the girl during church, sideways and quick, like he was sweet on her, but warning her, too.

The deputies were desperate to get things right, but even

more desperate to distance themselves from the grisly task of killing the Reverend's wife and daughter.

"Imps!" A wrinkled woman crowed, sparking outbursts from different pockets of onlookers:

"Pagans!"

"Scamps!"

The deputies hauled down the gunny sacks. The nooses that would crush the women's windpipes leaned into the hard wind. Together, the men dragged the burlap bags across the platform, but sand began to issue forth, slow and thick, sifting through the wood planks.

"Damnation," the first deputy murmured. "These bags have lost too much weight. Those ropes ain't gonna be stretched enough."

"You cussed fool," the second deputy hissed. He dropped to his knees and madly scooped in the gushing sand. "Brush it up, will you!"

Ada watched the graceless men, her mind still spinning. "Look at me," she called to them. "Look at my face." But she knew they wouldn't. The men scurried like rodents, turning their heads to glimpse the townspeople, adamant in avoiding Ada's and Elinor's eyes.

There were no options left. Ada knew she could only comfort her daughter now, make it less horrific. She watched Elinor straining against the shackles. As always, her countenance was tender, child-like.

The sun broke over the horizon and burned through the fog, casting the deputies' shadows across the scaffold. Ada took comfort when she saw Elinor close her eyes and sniff at the fragrant fall air like a puppy.

"The rope's been stretched good and plenty," the second deputy lied. "These bags have been stretching the line for years. Can't break, even when you're—" He fell silent. Then the young man wrenched up his face like he'd swallowed brine.

"You're sad." Elinor tried to comfort him.

She'd spoken in her matter-of-fact tone, making Ada's heart pound even harder. She was awed by her daughter's grace and kindness, even now. Her half-wit girl was closer to God than any of these pretenders could ever dream to be. Yet here they are, smearing her goodness like ink on twill. Dear Lord, hurry, she pleaded. The injustice. It's more than I can bear.

Mr. Turner threw the rotting hen onto the planks, snapping the young deputy back to the chore at hand. With jutted chin, he said firmly, "Like I says, this won't hurt none."

"Hang the shrews!"

"Don't listen to them, Elinor," Ada called to her. "Just focus on my voice!" Ada could tell from her daughter's bunched up cheeks that she was trying furiously to understand what was happening. The crowd grew louder. "Hear me, Elinor! Only me!"

The first deputy sucked in a breath and pulled a black hood from his pocket. Ada held steadfast. He turned to Elinor. "Anything you want to say?" he asked, making a downward patting motion for the crowd to hush.

"Never stole anything," Elinor said, looking to her mother.

"No you didn't, baby." Ada's throat swelled. Then the hood was pulled over Elinor's head.

"Mama, it's dark! Where'd the sun go?"

Holding the noose tight at her neck, the second deputy asked Ada if she had any words. In a single blast, she felt an entire lifetime. The blood drained from her, down into the wood, down into the earth below. She was hovering overhead, watching Elinor and herself and the savage swarm. Snippets of cruel scenes played out in her mind's eye. The Reverend in his new life, full of splendor and frills. She could see him clearly, a villainous smirk, standing tall and thumbing through a wad of the church's tithing, flicking bill after bill into the open hands of a faceless merchant. By his side, a comely woman stroking the billowy sleeves of her new silk gown, swaying back and forth so her skirt fanned out, the price tag swishing with it.

The day Elinor was born flashed through Ada's brain, too. Several women from the congregation gathered to help with the birth. Ruby Lee acted as midwife, brought the babe into the world then passed it off to be rinsed. In all the bumbling, someone slipped in the afterbirth. That simple bounce of Elinor's head against the floor, just that once, meant a lifetime of dull wits and heckling. Ada heard the thick, heavy words of her pious husband again when they found out their girl's mind stopped growing—"That child is damned!" he spat in a breathy, clipped voice. "Damned, I say!"

Ada looked out at her neighbors now. Loathing burned hot in her chest, crackling and sputtering. In the midst of all the rancor, she saw a child in the horde. From where she stood, it looked like the Miller boy. He and his Pa had always sat in the back of the church on Sundays, neither of them ever saying much. The flaming torch in his father's hand shaded his young face and in the firelight, the whites of his eyes were shiny. He looked bewildered, as if the lad didn't know what to do. Keep watching? Scorn her as the men and women did? Look away? Ada found the strength she needed in the boy's struggle. He's a talisman, she thought, sent by God to bolster me.

Though the hate still churned, a calm swept over, too, like the skillet was lifted from the fire. Ada waited for a lull then summoned the town like a prophet:

"Quiet, scalawags! I have a message for all you fine citizens of Bellwether!"

The crowd still roared. Someone shouted, "Let's hear the devil woman!" and they quieted to a low rumble.

Ada saw the furor in their dimly lit faces, but she wasn't afraid. Not anymore. She glanced at Elinor—the black cowl atop her pretty head and her legs trembling, a puddle on the planks between them—then turned back to the crowd, quickly searching for her talisman one last time.

Their eyes locked.

A wide sneer formed on the boy's round face while his father whispered in his ear. As if Satan himself was the puppeteer, the child drew a tiny hand across his throat, slow and easy.

Ada gasped, then stiffened. "My news is brief!" she shouted. "And it's coming straight from the afterworld." She spoke from outside herself, from some other place, some other time. She could feel her eyes filling up, could hear the lack of feeling in her words. "Just as you've taken the light from my Elinor, God will take yours. You'll hurt for this. Your children's children will feel the ire. That's a promise." Then a hood was pulled over her head, too. The deputies tightened the loops around both women's necks. One of them yelled, "Release!"

The trap door banged open. Both women plunged earthward.

Elinor caught, her neck snapping low and hollow like a carrot. But Ada hit the ground with a sickening thud. The throng drew in a sharp, collective breath, as if they shared a lung, inhaling all the rotten air. Like the flash before a tornado rips open, all went still.

Ada lay in a mangled heap, her arms still strapped. She shifted on the ground to soften the ache setting in, both her skirt and the hood having pulled up some in the drop. She could see the white of bone poking through the skin of her lower leg. And the town erupted:

"Oh Lord, the rope busted!"

"Her bones is sticking out!"

"The Devil's here!"

From the raised hood, Ada could see the lower legs of her neighbors as they fled in terror, but she could see a couple sets of feet still standing near. She must be a sight to behold, her body broken, bent at strange angles. She pulled herself up into a sitting position, bridged her neck so the bottom of the hood opened up even more. Though her arms were still bound, she could reach her wounds. She watched herself fingering the jagged cartilage but couldn't feel anything. Behind her, someone was retching.

The pain tore up her legs and into her hips. She cried out. For the agony. For Elinor. To her own ears, the wails were like an animal's, an injured hound far off in the woods.

Still, amidst the tumult and the cannonball firing through her lower half, Ada heard Sheriff Thompson's thundering voice. "What have you done?" he boomed.

She knew he'd be elbowing his way to the open space. She wondered what his face looked like when he saw Elinor swaying in the air like a pendulum, her head limp upon her shoulder, and she in a ball, head cloaked, bleeding out her shin. Ada felt him kneeling beside her.

"It's me, Ada. Sheriff Thompson." Putting one arm under her knees and another around her back, he gently lifted her, but the bone ends grated together, the pain like a triggered flintlock. "Shhh. It's done now," he said.

"Take off the hood, Sheriff! I have to see my Elinor."

"Can't do that, Ada."

"You will!" She tried to wrench herself free and swipe at the cloth with her upper arms, but the shackles were too tight. The pain in her legs made her fade out for a moment. But the spiteful hiss of a woman's voice brought her back around. "And God said, 'I will punish the world for its evil—'"

"Away!" Sheriff Thompson cut her off. "You're the malefactress!"

"'—and the wicked for their iniquity.'"

Ada's stomach squeezed like a sponge, then she blacked out again.

* * *

Once they arrived at the jailhouse, Sheriff Thompson unshackled Ada, laid a blanket over her legs and pulled off the hood. She gripped the bottom of his shirt and buried her face in it. He let her weep a few seconds before nudging her away. Like a wild man, he rummaged the room for anything that might work as a splint. He picked up his chair, smashed it against the wall and jerked the armrests free. Then he tore off his shirt and pulled a bottle of bourbon from under his desk. He handed Ada the hooch and told her to take a hearty swig.

As he straightened her leg and placed the wood pieces on either side, she hoisted herself off the floor trying to rise above the biting sensation. And from inside the cell came a faint snivel. Ada and the Sheriff turned to see the first deputy sitting with his back against the wall, head bowed and legs crossed at the ankles. The early morning sun shaded his profile so that only the side view was visible. Seeing him between the metal bars of the cell door where he'd detained himself, Ada thought him an apparition.

"Didn't mean for the rope to break," he said, eyes wide like a deer's. "Rope wasn't stretched like it should be. That was an accident. But—"

"But what?" Ada bawled from the floor. The deputy leaned forward into the dawn's low gleam and looked at her a long while, then the Sheriff.

"Well, answer her," Thompson said.

The deputy stood, stepped out from the cell to face them, eyes narrow now. "As the Lord is my witness, I promise you, we didn't make that rope bust." Then he pointed at Ada, the rest of his fingers curled under. "What I want to say is that you and Elinor, why, you're nothin' but Satan's handmaids. Whole town knows you lost your faith years ago, Ada." His voice grew hawkish, "That's why the Reverend ain't here no more. And that's why God made you bore an imbecile!"

"That'll do, deputy." Sheriff Thompson stood, too, nodding toward the door.

As the deputy made his way out into the stilted air, he turned back. "Williams women," he said, shaking his head, "mere stains on our village." Then he held his thumb up again, moved it up and down. "And you, Sheriff. You're just as bad, protecting her the way you do."

* * *

Sheriff Thompson moved Ada into his home to care for her, to save her. He taught her how to fish and fire a rifle, and how to clean or cure what she snared. Though he couldn't fix her limp, he healed her leg and helped her grieve. Then, one night, he told her that he wouldn't be in Bellwether much longer. "It was never my intention to stay. I'm getting on in age, and I don't want to live out my days here. There's a place not too far from here, over in Wisconsin. They call it the 'Green Bay.' Always sounded so pretty to me." He stopped, shook his head gently. "They've wronged you in every way, Ada. But I know you'll never leave. Your daughter's spirit lives here. And I know, too, that you'll never change your mind, too damn stubborn. So I'll earn my shrift by making you self-sufficient." Sheriff put down his head. "Forgive me," he said. "I played a hand in Elinor's death."

"No, sir. You didn't. A hundred or so righteous folks hurt Elinor and me. Folks with heads so swollen they think they're above all laws, man's and God's. No magistrates, no lawyers, no jury, just a bristling to kill the lamb that drove away their precious shepherd. If they cleanse this whistle-stop of the devil woman and her broken child, there'll be no holes in their finely chiseled doctrine, the one they don't even understand themselves."

"You keep telling me that I'm helping you toe the line between crazy and sane," Thompson said. "Truth is, Ada, you're the one whose right as a trivet." Then he yawned, started unlacing his brogans. "Should've told you that earlier, too, I suppose." He stood, boots in hand. "In the eyes of Bellwether, I'm convening with the wretched, and I fear it won't go unanswered for much longer. The church board won't ever let it stand."

Later, when all the hapless things occurred, Ada remembered the Sheriff's prediction, how he had hinted at the bad to come. The calf they kept was hewed open, its innards left in a pile by the barn. The breeching straps on their wagon cut in two, wheel hub cracked down the middle. Messages from scripture carved into the trunks of their trees—*works of the flesh are evil*—and in the skins of a stillborn piglet, *God hates sinners,* the gray, milky residue of farrowing still coating its body.

After Sheriff Thompson told folks he'd be leaving soon, Bellwether's system of justice stretched its long, probing arm once again, afraid that word of their transgression might spread beyond the borders of the village.

Early one Saturday, just after daybreak, when the sun's rays began to leak through the towering pines, the Sheriff and Ada stood near the side of the road. They were crouched over the snowshoe hare that Ada had killed with the single-shot, side hammer pistol he'd given her. She had pulled off the animal's white fur, and it hung down from her hand like a sleeping bat. The Sheriff said "Another perfect pelt" then scratched his beard with the knuckles of his gloved hand. "I may have taught you too many of my tricks. You're a better hunter than—"

"Well, well," Mr. Wilkinson called out as he approached, rifle pointing backward over his shoulder, field hat resting far back on his head. "Seems the student has become the master. Word is, Ada's quite the stalker now."

"And a solid angler, too," Sheriff replied. "Did you expect anything less? She learned from the best."

Mr. Wilkinson bluffed a laugh. "Oh, Sheriff. This high opinion you hold of yourself will come to an end soon enough."

Ada glanced at the Sheriff, then at Mr. Wilkinson. The cryptic message and deadened tone made her break into a sweat, even in the morning chill. She stared at the naked hare at her feet.

"You mind telling me what that means, Reverend?"

Mr. Wilkinson tipped his hat and began to move along, but not without repeating himself, "Soon enough, Sheriff."

* * *

It was early spring, and the parish was assembling for Sunday services. The little Miller boy called on Ada through her window, his voice pitched high with excitement. "Something's happened to the Sheriff!" He was a bit older now and took the lead, pulling Ada by the hand, past the church, into the familiar space behind it. Then he ducked inside the chapel with the rest.

Sheriff Thompson was drooping on the gallows. Ada limped her way to him, reached for his feet to stop him from swaying. She wanted to put his tongue back in his mouth, wash away the blue in his cheeks. It wasn't dignified. All she could do is put her face between his boots, press them against her temples until the seams marked her skin as if she'd been sewn together there.

Ada stood with the Sheriff long after the others had crept home, whispering and shuffling. She talked to him as if they were still drinking coffee on the porch, as if he wasn't midair, dangling like a clock bob, all the vessels in his face and eyes busted open, forking out like tree roots. "Are there any boundaries to their chiding, Sheriff? All the badgering? All the spite?" She wondered how they'd come for her. Break into the house while she slept? Nab her in the light of day? Or am I being spared? Not as atonement, but for fear that their hearts are too hard. A dread that their notion of righteousness is cockeyed and reckless. She thought about how beyond the edges of this misguided place, there must be truth and sound minds. But she could never leave Elinor. Besides, Bellwether would never let her go. She held too many secrets.

Now, with her gatekeeper suspended overhead, stripped of any honor with bleeding from the ears, his manhood gorged and pushing out his britches—Ada thanked him for teaching her how to survive on her own. How to slow cook a deer flank to make it more tender. How to angle the chisel so it cuts through the lake ice faster and makes a hole wide enough for a northern pike or a fat crappie. And how to burn any clinging fur from the squirrel before you soak it in buttermilk. Then, Ada hoped that God was, indeed, a vengeful God, so that this hateful town would surely face His iron-fisted wrath.

Chapter 2
Whispers of the Shenandoah

Hiram and his brothers grew up in the foothills of the Allegheny Mountains on the shores of the Shenandoah River where they spent the bulk of their days pulling up trout—Brook, Brown and Rainbow—and the occasional catfish. They lived in a one-story clapboard house with a cast-iron stove, an open hearth and two windows, set on a flat, shady clearing. In their younger years, the three boys shared a bed with a steel frame and overstuffed mattress. Because his middle brother, Leander, always splayed out like rabbit ears, Hiram was usually pinned against the wall.

Even though they were four years apart, Hiram was closest to Clint, his oldest brother, who had just turned sixteen. And on a crisp April day, cool breezes wafting up from the wide, gray river, Clint headed off to the mines of Kanawha County like so many young men before him, filled with hope and vim, feeling unbreakable.

"Cussed fool," Leander barked, cuffing the back of Hiram's head, "You don't cry till after he's gone."

Clint moved to Hiram, stroked his hair where Leander had mussed it then squeezed his little brother's jaw and lifted his face. "If you feel sad Hiram, why, you go ahead and cry. Seems sorta silly not to, don't it?" Turning to Leander, Clint said, "You should be protecting him, not poking at him all the time." He put a hand on his shoulder. "Stop being so mad all the time." Lastly, Clint moved to his father, looked him in the eyes while he shook his hand, firm and hardy. Ma blew a kiss and fanned out her fingers like playing cards across her chest.

As he backed away, Clint said, "Come here, boy," and motioned Hiram with his head. As he lumbered forward, Hiram felt his breathing getting harder, and his chin trembling. Clint swept him up by the britches, jounced him up and down like a ragdoll until they both laughed. "Love your brothers, Hiram," he said, then angling into his ear, whispered, "Both of 'em."

Before he turned to go, Clint looked at his family a long while. "I won't be turning back," he said. Then he bobbed his head and traipsed toward the road, nimble and tall. Ma stepped beside Hiram and tangled her fingers in his. They all watched Clint trot away in silence. Eventually, their father retreated to the river and Leander made his way to the outhouse. But Hiram and his mother watched until Clint's silhouette melted away behind the elderberries and dogwoods.

"Goodbyes are a part of life," Ma said. Hiram wasn't so young that he didn't know those words were more for her than him. He wiped his cheeks in the crook of his arm and broke away. Then he looked at Ma for a moment before sprinting downstream.

She did not call him back.

As if the ground were burning, he dashed past the first and second bends, then the third. When his legs started to give out, he slowed to a trot, then finally stopped. He bent over and put his hands on his thighs, listened to himself panting like a dog. After steadying some, Hiram veered into the woodlands to mourn in private. Deep in the thickets, he sat down on a rock—elbows on his knees, chin in his palms—and wept with abandon.

* * *

It was just days later that Ma started telling stories from the boys' younger years, started looking thinner, her skin turning chalky. "And Clint snagged that twelve-pound brook. You remember?" she asked. Her face flushed. Often now, she paused in the middle of sentences and grimaced hard while she swallowed as if passing pebbles through her windpipe. Hiram figured she was just bone-tired from taking on all the extra chores now that Clint was gone. But the weariness in her voice made him afraid. He sensed her need to revel in the past. So he pretended to remember her mistaken recollections and let her retell them her way, sore throat and all.

"Thought it was Leander, Ma, but I must be mistaken."

"No, no, honey, it was Clint." She scooted closer, stretched her hands wide. "That fish was twenty-five inches, easy," she said, looking from one hand to the other then reaching out even farther, "Or maybe more." Hiram saw the red spots all down her arms where her sleeves had bunched up.

"You're right, Ma. It was Clint," Hiram replied. "And holy cow, it was a big one. Maybe the biggest ever, you think?" Hiram prodded her on so she wouldn't see that he noticed the rash.

But she did.

As she continued to recount her tale, Ma pulled the sleeves down, avoiding Hiram's eyes. "Oh, and so beautiful. Dark greens and rich browns, like a shiny marble." She looked lost, even frightened. "Then your father sliced it open, a slim, long cut. The innards spilled out, all slick and mired." She pulled a coin from her pocket, shiny and smooth. "You saw it first. 'Look Pa, there's a penny,' you hollered out." She flipped the coin over in her hand, admiring it, as if for the first time. "I aim for you to have this back now," she said, then lay it in Hiram's hand, closing his fingers around it.

Then, one day in early May, Hiram and Leander made their way to the breakfast table, and there was nothing. No oats. No honey. And no Ma. They found her in bed, a wet cloth across her forehead and Pa standing back from her. As they crept in, she turned her head to cough, and the deep red lines in the folds of her neck showed loud, distinct.

"You feeling alright, Ma?"

"Oh, I'm just mending from the scarlet fever is all. Need to steer clear of you for a while. No need to worry anyone about it. My tongue's red as a strawberry and I'm pretty tuckered. But nothing I can't handle."

There was a flutter in the pit of Hiram's stomach and he felt dizzy, like missing a step on the stairs. Before he could refrain, he said aloud, "God did this." The room went still. "And I curse Him for it."

* * *

By the time the snow flew, she was ailing again. It was a bitter season, the kind of cold that stings your lungs. And the fever found its way back in like a cold wind pushing under the door. Though Ma learned to fight the fatigue, the disease eventually broke her. She demanded that nobody call Clint home. "He needn't be worrying about me." And in the night she passed, Ma called Pa and the boys to her bedside, one at a time. She said to Hiram, "The light of God is in you, boy. Don't you let it go out. None of the bad things that go on are God's doing." Hiram wondered if she could somehow feel his doubts. "God's ways ain't your concern. That's what believing is all about, knowing that your Maker is doing you right."

But he didn't want to hear about the Lord being mysterious again, how life's questions will be answered when we die. What about today, this moment? That's when things matter. He nodded, told her that his faith was in order. "Just can't bring myself to praise God, not straight away."

"That's okay, Hiram," she said. "You can be confused. Even a bit mad if you have to be. True faith flickers sometimes, but the trick is to never smother the fire. That only sets you off course, leaves you scrambling to find your way back."

Hiram nodded, rested his head against her bed and fought back tears.

* * *

The ground wasn't frozen yet, so Ma was buried in a covert near the riverside. Pa said, "In this grave, my purpose and my will are buried," then scooped the dirt atop the pine box.

Hiram and Leander anguished in their mother's absence but did not talk of it. Until one day, months later, Hiram picked some great laurel and arranged it in a vase upon the table. At supper, Pa stared hard at the blush-colored blooms and yellow flecks.

"Who did this?" he asked.

"Hiram," Leander answered, head down.

"Why, boy?"

Hiram hesitated. So Pa asked again, louder.

"They remind me of Ma," he said. "They smell like her."

"Get rid of 'em," he said, not looking at him. "And don't do it again."

After that night, Hiram had a new understanding—they hadn't been alone in their suffering, just grieving with discipline. So that same spring, when word came that the City Point Railroad was reorganizing and needed men, Hiram knew why his father left.

"You boys look after one another," he told his sons. "I'll be back by month's end." It frightened Hiram something awful to be without both parents, and he had a sinking feeling that they'd seen Pa for the last time.

* * *

Leander and Hiram were no longer boys, but not quite men, either. Still, they learned to get by. What's more, they grew to care for one another. They fished and trapped come daybreak, weeded through high noon, then canned fruits and felled trees until dusk. And when Leander hewed off the top of his finger, Hiram washed it with cool water, bandaged it with pieces he cut from old knickers.

"Drink this," he said, handing Hiram a dusty bottle of their father's Old Crow. "I saw Pa do it after he slipped in the river, opened his shin on a rock."

Hiram took a swig, wrenched like a baited worm and sprayed it out his nose. Then Leander tried it. "Kinda tastes like piss, don't it?"

They chortled, quietly at first, then louder, until they worked themselves up to an all out whinny. Then the brothers took turns nipping the whiskey, whooping like herons. After a while, Leander declared, "Why, I do believe I'm slewed," his words garbled.

Hiram tottered out the door and returned with several laurel slicks. Having yanked them whole from the shrub, some of the waxy, oblong leaves floated to the floor, deep green against the timber planks. He set them on the table and both boys sat solemn, eyeing the pale pink clusters. Then Leander took a deep inhale, blew out through his nose and whispered, "Sorry."

"For what?"

"All these years, being a peckerwood."

Hiram pushed his lips together, dipped his head. "Another swash?"

"Give me that." Leander snatched the bottle and raised it to his mouth, pointing a finger at his little brother. "You know, you could've argued with me some about being a peckerwood."

* * *

Near the end of the summer, Hiram spotted his brother at the head of the trail, returning from the weekly trek into town. He scurried from the woodpile and through the open door, started washing his hands in the basin, waiting for any news, to hear about any encounters Leander might have had along the way. Anything was more exciting than chopping, plucking and canning. Hiram harried over his shoulder—"Any letters come?"—as he scrubbed the dirt and blood from his knuckles. "From Clint? Or Pa?"

Leander did not respond, just pulled back a chair and slumped down in it. The legs rubbed against the furrow in the floor, and the scritch turned Hiram's head. He recognized his brother's pressed visage, the beveled mouth and weighty eyes; he had seen it the morning they buried Ma.

"What is it?"

"They found Pa." Leander cleared his throat. "He was hanging from a tree."

"I don't—"

Leander shook his head, held up his hand. "Sit." In the opposite chair, Hiram lowered himself down. He could feel his nose begin to run, his legs bouncing wildly.

"Seems Pa was drinking too much, couldn't keep up as a crewman. So they reassigned him as a surveyor. Sent him to walk the tracks at sun-up, look for tree limbs, wash-outs and such." Leander stood, walked to the window then pushed his shoulder against the frame. "A summer gale had toppled the trundles over a nearby brook. Foggy Creek, I think they called it. Last week, Pa was told to head out, look for trouble. They found an empty bottle where he'd dozed off, leaning against a tree. They figured he came to when the boxcars crashed into the marsh." Leander slowed his words. "One by one."

"Then he isn't dead? Just drunk is all?" Hiram's heart skipped a beat.

"They said Pa probably wandered through the wreckage and seen what he done. That's when he found a yellow scarf in the ruins, made a noose of it and—"

"No more." Hiram's voice was calm but resigned. After a moment of stillness, he said, "Brother, I think we're damned."

* * *

The boys understood that they were men now, whether they wanted to be or not. And the work was tireless. Each week, they delivered firewood at the mouth of the river, first to Miss Avery, the well-spoken widow who had taught school in her younger years. She paid them each a nickel per load and asked pointed questions about the books she loaned them to read. A mile down from her was Reverend Thacker, who paid them a quarter per load, escorted them to and from services every Sunday at Holy Cross Parish and stopped by now and again with pies and socks and blankets from the congregation. The boys knew that neither Miss Avery nor Reverend Thacker needed that much wood.

* * *

Bluefield was a tiny village but held an open market in the town square that drew people from up and down the river. Hiram joined Leander on his hike to town whenever their harvest was overabundant, selling snap beans, cucumbers and sweet corn. Once in a while, if they snagged a mess of bluegill, they would barter with that, too. Coupled with their wood money, they afforded grain, flour, sugar and the town's newspaper, *The Blueville Herald*. Sometimes, they sat at a table near the edge of all the trading and small talk to wait for the mail, watched the young girls, fascinated by their movements and the shiny ribbons tied around their waists or clipped in their long, loopy hair.

After the postmaster, they would head to their final stop, Mr. Shipley's place, on the outskirts of the hamlet, just past Blue Stone ridge. The tumble-down dram shop sat amidst a clump of sugar maples, a rickety old place that leaned far to the right. Shipley was a lubber of an old man—crotchety as a wet hornet—and his spirits stung more than Old Crow. But a pint of his whiskey always did the trick.

On the walks home, if there was a letter from Clint, they took turns reading it, over and over. Each correspondence was accompanied by a five-dollar bill which the boys tucked in their Pa's wooden pipe box. When Clint came home to visit, they planned to hand it all back, show their big brother how they had made it on their own.

"You know, Leander, I'm going to the mines, too?" Hiram said.

"No you ain't. You're too young."

"Don't matter none. Clint will tell 'em I'm a hard worker. They'll take me." Hiram had already made up his mind, so any response was futile, which Leander seemed to know but poked at him like an ember anyway.

"You see that gal bending over by the fence today, the one pulling up her stockings?"

"Thought I was the only one." Hiram belly laughed. "Should've gone calling on her. No harm in that."

"I'll stick to looking for now. No time for sittin' any gals." Leander grabbed the moonshine from the day's wares and took a hearty swig. "Specially now that you're heading off to the mines."

"What's that mean?" In an instant, the blood pushed to the surface of his cheeks, his neck turning hot.

"Means what I said. You're headed to Kanawha, ain't you?"

"Damn right. Don't like the way you're saying it though. All sugary, like I'm some kind of featherbrain."

Leander grunted, took another swill.

"I swear, brother, you're about to get licked."

Leander grunted again, and Hiram bounded over the table, snatching him by the throat with one hand, raising his other open fisted. He didn't know what to do next, just sat there hoping Leander would lurch or wail or something. Instead, he covered his face and tears spilled from each eye, sliding beneath his fingers. The thorny truth lingered in the air. They had known all along which one of them was tougher, but now, it was in front of them—a conquered brother with a tear-stained face, trapped beneath the victor. Hiram slowly lowered his arm, climbed off Leander. He moved the tumbled chairs to the side and laid down next to his brother.

"Why do you gall me?"

Leander lay silent.

"Why, brother?"

"'Cause I know you're strong. And that you'll do all the things you say." He wiped the sides of his face.

"You think so?"

"I know so. You and Clint are thoroughbreds. Not me, though. Sometimes, when I think about you leaving Bluefield," he turned his face to Hiram, "I get—"

"Get what?"

"Scared. And mad. Both at the same time."

"But you can, too. You're smarter than me. Hell, Leander, the way you read through Miss Avery's books, you should—"

"I won't leave the Shenandoah." He turned to him again. "You know, Hiram, every spring when the water rises, I can hear it talking. How smart is that? But I swear, the currents speak to me, low and sweet."

The pecking order had shifted forever, and Hiram felt Leander's vulnerability. It pulled at his heart. "You ought to be courting the lass with the stockings, I tell you." He let out a cackle. "Did we knock over the lotion?"

"Hell no," Leander said. "I covered that up 'fore I covered my face."

Though sad for his brother, Hiram was bolstered by a new certainty, that he could beat anything, anyone. He put his hand on Leander's shoulder. "I hear the white-waters, too," he said.

"Yeah, well, I don't think we're damned neither." The brothers whittled away another night together, sharing their last bottle of Shipley's rotgut, sensing that change was near. They spoke louder, laughed harder. When the morning light broke through the foliage and spurred their spinning heads, neither of them was too surprised by Clint's bindle on the floor. They scrambled over one another to get outside, to see their eldest sibling, the miner from Kanawha Valley. Upstream, with a scrub brush in one hand and their nearly barren bottle of whiskey in the other, Clint stood naked in a ford, amidst the shade of several bowing aspens. A slant of light glanced his body. Hiram thought him bigger than life.

Clint turned toward his brothers and tottered to the riverbank. "Little shavers!" he called out. He sprung out of the water and chased them back to the house. Catching Hiram by the foot, he pulled him to the ground then brushed against him in all his rawness. Hiram squealed like a cornered pig. "Yep boy, them's my chitlins," Clint shouted, still rubbing up on him. They grappled in the dank soil until Hiram heaved out a roar, flipped him over on his front side and pinned back his arms. Clint tried to break free but couldn't.

"Alright, Hiram! I'm throwin' up the sponge," he shouted.

"Damn right!" Hiram cawed.

"Boy, you've gotten downright gritty these months. You're about ready for the mines." Hiram ballooned inside. This was it. His time had come. He felt the gladness in his chest. He tried to stay calm but the eagerness burned like a balefire.

"Give him a whack!" Hiram looked to Leander to join in, but he just dropped his head, made his way back inside.

Clint and Hiram untangled themselves and followed. Leander stood at the basin, breathing heavy. When they asked him what he was doing, he said, "I'm praying for the safety of my brothers, the lionhearted pitmen."

* * *

Several weeks later, Hiram got word from Clint that he could start mining as soon as he could get there. As a tenderfoot, he'd have to work as a barrow-man at the older mine first, many miles from Clint, just above Cheat River. So, without much ado, on a red southern morning, Hiram made his way through the late August haze. On his way, he wandered off-path into the thickets of western Virginia. He traipsed amid the towering trees and thought of Ma, knowing she'd make him loll a while. "Appreciate God's colors," she'd say. So he threw down his haversack and lay on the ground, fingers joined behind his head, elbows out. He told her about the skins of the trees as well as his fears. The poplar bark is coarse and bumpy; and the hickory's plaits are loose, flaky. And I'm too damn young to have no Ma or Pa. Don't know what the hell I'm doing. No time for grieving, though. Still can't pray, Ma, but I ain't turning my back either.

The sunrise bled through the trees, leading Hiram back out of the woods. A narrow clearing opened up, steep ridges on both sides and a dusty path running through the middle. In the distance, a row of lifeless, ramshackle shanties. As he neared, a hard wind blew down the hillside, bowing out the prairie schooners' pasty tops like bonnets. It was barren. He hadn't expected that. Still, he plodded toward the camp, the lean-tos showing rickety and colorless. The quiet was touchable, magnifying the sound of his boots crunching against the gravel. He found the galley and learned that he had missed the morning march to the pithead.

Master Hardy, the camp's overseer, bade Sarah, the reticent slave girl, to show him to his quarters. Hiram thought her beautiful in her own right—sleek skin, glinting like sunlight on gathered rain—and thin as a pointer finger. The two walked in silence down the row of shanties to the last one, butted up to a hillside and closest to the train-tracks. Hiram stepped inside his new hovel, looked all around, then poked his head back out the door to see Sarah standing nearby, hands clasped at her middle. He jabbered on about getting his own bed and his new independence, hoping his openness would make Sarah less afraid. Then he wanted to slap himself for not thinking things through, for talking to her about his freedom. She did lift her head but as soon as their eyes met, she looked back to the ground.

Though dispirited some, Hiram clambered inside again, reveling in his castle, grinning like a child. Then he thought, gotta look older than you are, and stifled his excitement. When he approached the only window, he saw Sarah dabbing at her forehead with her apron, trying to wipe away the garden dirt. She smoothed her frock then donned her headwrap and adjusted it just so. When she looked up this time, Hiram caught her gaze and held it, couldn't stop the smile forming on his face.

* * *

Master Hardy insisted the crew eat together. "Builds camaraderie," he said, "prompts loyalty, too." But the miners knew he was only trying to stop a coup. The talk of unions up north had trickled down the Ohio River, and Hardy had been gouging his men at the company store for years. On Hiram's first night, he found out why a revolution from these men would be terrifying. He was thrust into their dog-eat-dog world, scurrying amongst the miners at supper, catching on fast as the ravenous workers scrambled like suckling pups, banging into one another. And Sarah.

The air was sticky hot, and the men were irritable and aggressive, elbowing their way to a fair share. Ox, Master Hardy's chubby right-hand man, had bucked his way to the front again for seconds before all the men could reap their firsts. In the fray, Ox knocked a plate of stewed oysters from Sarah's grasp. "Stupid girl," he barked. And when Hiram knelt to help her gather the fallen mollusks, Ox shoved his boot into Hiram's backside and shouted, "Nigger lover!" His face struck the dirt, and the men yipped like a pack of coyotes.

Hiram stood, slow but tall, and spat the earth from his mouth. He knew the next move would decide his rank there. Before he could think too much, he said, "You ain't nothin' but a fat yak."

Ox turned on his heel, facing his unexpected rival. In the quietude, the two men stood nose to nose, swaying and flinching.

After a long impasse, Ox muttered, "Watch your bone-box," and snapped Hiram's chest with his middle finger. Then he headed back to the table, parting the crowd and stomping on several of the dusty, gray oysters. Through pursed lips, Hiram inhaled hard and blew out. Sarah remained on her knees, and he waited until the men began to graze and rib one another again before offering her a hand.

Later, Hiram stepped onto the bowed porch, filling his lungs with the night air. There, he found a handkerchief full of boiled hog maws, flavored with vinegar and red pepper flakes. He chewed them heartily but worried about Sarah's safety for bringing him the special vittles. He thought about his own welfare, too, but couldn't help shaking his head, pondering her brazenness.

* * *

At 5:00 a.m., the bell always sounded and camp crawled to life. Then through the purpling dawn, the miners trudged to the quarries and wriggled in the dank, craggy shafts like worms, day after punishing day. But another two dollars. Most nights, Hiram lumbered to his cottage after eating, skin still stinging from the furnace, and fingernails worn like paper, then wilted into bed. The straw poking through the wool mattress, felt good on his gnarled back. And other nights, he slept right through supper.

On those occasions, come nightfall, Sarah crept between Hardy's manor and shanty row, making her way to Hiram's hut. In her apron, she toted special feasts—a broiled pigeon breast dredged in eggs and sippets and mixed with rosemary, or thick slices of ham, marinated in cloves and brown sugar. Hiram knew by looking at the delicacies that she must have pulled the fattest breast off the counter or cut from the hank end for the ham pieces then hid them in the icebox all day.

* * *

Newbies at the Cheat River mine were made to work past sundown if quotas weren't met which meant slim pickings for supper but a bump in pay. Hiram was all too happy each time Hardy announced, "It's another late one, boys." The work was brutal, but he'd think about the Shenandoah, its cool, blue currents, and the honeyed smell of laurel washing over. He'd picture Leander felling a fat birch for Miss Avery. He couldn't wait to send his brother the extra money he'd make. He laid in bed staring at the wood planks overhead, and thought, it sure ain't easy, but I'm doing. I'm out here on my own, doing.

Chapter 3
Belly to the Ground

Her name was Sarah, but Master Hardy just called her "hey," usually when he was beckoning her to meet him behind the mess hall again, where he'd play out his devious cravings on her meager frame. Although her body belonged to Master Hardy, her heart already longed for Hiram, the miner with the moonstone eyes, she called him in her mind.

After learning of the wealth to be had on Cheat River—in the west part of Virginia, Master Hardy came down from Pittsburg and settled himself and Miss Hardy there. But not before buying a wagon full of slaves at an auction in Wheeling. It was there, amidst the boom of Virginia's capital city, that Sarah and her brother were split apart—$60 for Sarah and $85 for her brother who went to a plantation further inland.

Sarah used to say to God, "May as well of hacked off our limbs, would've been more merciful."

* * *

Even more than Master Hardy, Ox scared Sarah to death. He flinched at her whenever they crossed paths, making like he'd strike her. No matter how many times she promised herself not to duck, she always did. Then she'd curse herself for it. She already knew Hiram could never act nasty like the others, that's why she worried for him. Ox didn't take kindly to him for helping her pick up the spilled oysters. She remembers how he pulled himself up from the dirt, cheeks set, ice in his eyes. She didn't want to see all the wrangling, so she covered her eyes, put her head between her knees. And how after the ruckus, when she took his reaching hand, her heart beat faster, each pulse louder than the one before. Panic and thrill. She remembers looking over her shoulder. None of the miners were paying attention. Their fun with her was over, for the time. Ox was draining the last of his pork-corn stew, his face covered by the bowl and his back turned. A pang of defiance shot through her, and she wished one of them might actually see her hand in Hiram's. Big galoots wouldn't know what to do seeing a man of honor.

It was that night, after the camp was quiet, that she crept to the farthest cabin in the row and emptied her apron of the dressed-up pigeon breast on Hiram's porch. Later, as she lay in bed hoping he found her offering before the critters did, she remembers their first encounter. Hiram poking his head out of the shanty door, talking nonsense about beds and freedom, his voice easy, calming. How she tried dabbing at her forehead with her apron, praying she didn't smear the turnip dirt even more. How after she shifted her headwrap and looked up again, he was watching. How she fought the instinct to smile back at him.

And how later that night, Master Hardy came to her window, bid her to come.

* * *

Before daybreak, Sarah was mixing batter for the hotcakes and frying potatoes by the skillet full. Her breaths always grew shorter when she heard the men rousing for the day's labor, making their way to breakfast. Then, as they trudged toward the quarries to clamber underground, she could breathe easier, though still anxious. Before cleaning up the morning mess, she always watched them go, making sure none headed back her way to sport with her some more, corner her in the kitchen like vermin, flinch at her until she cowered.

* * *

A privileged life spurred Miss Hardy's plump physique and grew her obstinacy. "Rigid as a boxelder," the miners joked. Although wide bodices, domed skirts and full petticoats hid her girth, it took falling ill with consumption to finally soften her stubbornness, some.

In her final weeks, Miss Hardy called Sarah away from her duties to be her personal caretaker. At first, Sarah was terrified, and her thoughts ran wild. *Is this beastly woman aiming to make my life even more miserable? Will she lie to Master Hardy today, tell him I was sassing or being lazy, just to watch what happens? The way of the world is so upside down. It's all such a crying shame.*

The night she was told she'd start tending to Miss Hardy the following morning, Sarah sat cross-legged on the porch of her shanty, positioned herself so she could look at the sky but still see a corner of Hiram's place which always made her feel more rooted. She'd been fettered too long to know anything but powerlessness, every second of every day, yet keeping Hiram's quarters in sight helped her feel less alone. She often thought about what would happen if she died. *Would the camp even stop? Or would Hardy just assign a couple of miners to rustle up that morning's vittles and by sundown, when the men made their way to supper, a new scullery maid would be there. And as her substitute was doling out the poke salad and dumplings or cleaning up the mess of black-eyed peas that they'd spill out of the scoop, would they even notice it was a different girl?*

Miss Hardy lay in her big brass bed with silk coverlets about her neck. The hefty woman's greeting seemed sincere and within a half hour of Sarah's arrival, she was telling her private things, talking about the trials of marriage and the struggle to forgive. "Sometimes, a wife bends her will and worth so far, it feels like you might break in half." She told Sarah that she'd always felt silly surrounded by indulgences. "Such grandiose living is nothing but fluff, covering up the dirt and poo beneath it," she said, then let out a shallow laugh.

Mild winds blew down the hillside, stirring the white lace curtains. The woman's sadness was weighty in the room, like you could touch it with your hand. Sarah grappled with feeling like a liar, not telling the withering woman that Master Hardy calls on her, nearly every night now. Makes her face the mess hall as he pushes so hard against her backside that it feels like she'll pull apart.

Not too long after their first morning together, Miss Hardy told Sarah how to tame the miners some. "Mince pie, dear, with heaps of currants," she said, pushing up on one elbow. "That will satisfy those boorish ol' rips." Sarah was starting to trust her. Not completely, though. Even if she was opening her heart, Sarah was still leery. Not yet sure that a white woman's warmth could be anything but crafty, one last gibe before the consumption overtook her.

Sarah wrung the cloth in her hand, drew it over the woman's forehead then down the side of her sallow face. Miss Hardy clutched Sarah's bony hand, leaned in close.

"I'm sorry," she said.

"Ma'am?"

"Till a few weeks ago, I'd never even called you by your name," she said. Then she started to cough, low and dry at first, but the hacking grew loud and guttural and wet, until she choked up blood on her fresh nightdress. Both women stared at the deep red blight, and Sarah felt the grip on her hand tighten.

"You're in a family way," Miss Hardy said, matter of fact. Sarah scooted down off the woman's bedstead, started scrubbing the floor with the cloth in her hand. Her brain whorled as she scoured the wood planks like a rabid squirrel. The murky water spilled from the mop pail, soaking her petticoats.

"Come, child."

Sarah scrubbed harder, in all directions, like she was wiping up a murder. Miss Hardy began to pray out loud, asking the Lord for absolution and mercy. And Sarah began to hum, not a song, just the same three-note cadence, over and over, to blur the particulars of Miss Hardy's petitioning. But the weariness in her voice was clear and Sarah couldn't help feeling sad for both of them.

That night, Master Hardy bore into Sarah like an auger, grunting with delight as she whimpered. Though the penetration stung, having no say about it hurt even more.

* * *

Sarah followed Mistress Hardy's advice. Her mince pie became a favorite, though the men didn't tell her so. She just knew by the way they scarfed it down, licked their plates. She used extra brown sugar, sucking her fingers after she stirred. But as the child grew inside her, some smells began to make her gag, especially the gamey stench of mutton.

One morning, as she emptied suet into the mixing bowl, she retched atop the spices and meat. She looked down at her still flat stomach and touched her breasts, flinching at their tenderness. Resting her head on the rim, she began to cry, heavy tears soaking into the dreadful mush.

* * *

Sarah went to the water's edge to clean Miss Hardy's chamber pot. Through a row of trees between the shanties and the hillside, she could hear Ox and Master Hardy, their words weren't clear, but their voices were. She tried to pass by quickly but heard one of them utter her name. Something in her guts made her stop. She crept close to an unfurled white pine, needles poking at her arms and face, and held still as bone.

"What if I overshoot? What if the lash hits her belly?" She could hear the wobble in Ox's voice. Everyone in the camp knew that Ox had a fatter pocketbook on account of being Master Hardy's sidekick. And he wasn't afraid to boast about how he spent it: "The bawdy houses over in Bentley are getting pricey," he'd say, mouth full of okra. "And so's the whis-key." But now, his voice was whiny, soft.

"Folks find out we whipped a gal with-child, might turn bad." Sarah peeked through the limbs, still holding her breath. She saw Master Hardy cocking his head, looking Ox up and down. There was a tingle in seeing Ox squirm like a scorned child.

"Who's a person gonna tell? Me?" Hardy made a swipe at the air, a gesture of dismissal. "Sometimes I wonder why I put so much stock in a codger like you," he said. "Besides, you're getting too familiar." Hardy flinched at Ox just like he does to her and the younger miners, then he tapped his thick lips and pointed at him. "I can get rid of you, real easy. Remember that."

"Yessir."

"Now. I think it's best to dig a hole. Make her lay face down with her belly in it so you won't hurt the child."

"And what if she tells Miss Hardy? What if—"

"You let me handle that. Tell Sarah she's been too friendly with that Hiram fella. Tell her I said so. And as for him, just run him on outta here. Don't want to know how you do it."

Ox nodded, then beelined for shanty row. Sarah stood still, waited until the path was free. Her fear was too deep to take shape, to translate to thoughts.

That afternoon, she stayed by Miss Hardy's side as long as she could, afraid to leave. Afraid not to. Finally, Miss Hardy said, "Get on home, child." She remembered the stack of min-ers' socks that needed darning. Hide in the grove behind your shack, she thought, just mend and sew. And when Ox comes calling for you, say you didn't hear him. She knew it was only a bid for time, but she had to stall, clear her head. Socks in hand, she headed to the tree line, pulled a spool of thread from her apron and sat down on the ground, needle pressed between her lips. As she started stitching, she prayed hard for courage and clarity. Several ruby-throated hummingbirds flitted about the fire pink all around. But they darted away when Ox came traipsing through the high grass.

"You been fraternizin' with Hiram," he bellowed. "Come to whip you for it." He stopped in front of her, a grinning eclipse. His voice was mechanical, cool. Sarah's heart felt like it might burst through her chest, and no words would form. She kept stitching, head tilted down. She could feel Ox circling behind her like a hawk. Then she heard him unfastening his overalls, the buckles clinking together. She pulled back her shoulders and sucked in sharp. A breeze passed through and she followed it with her face, closed her eyes, readying for the assault.

"Uh huh, can't do it," Ox mumbled. Then he started to garble. Awkward lulls followed by bouts of fumbling and muttering. Stillness. Then a deafening yawp. He swatted the back of Sarah's head but quickly smoothed her hair back down.

"Dear God!" Sarah blurted out. For a split second, she wondered if it was really her who'd belched the words, so steep and low. She kept her focus straight ahead even as he slapped the back of her head again, sputtering behind her as if speaking in tongues.

"Get up," he snapped.

Before Sarah could obey, he clutched her hair in one hand, the knot of her apron in the other, and jerked her to her feet. She clawed at his meaty hands, kicked wildly at the air. She met his eyes. Terror burned her throat.

"Don't look at me," he wailed. Then he dropped her, trotted a few steps away. He turned around quickly and came back at her. Sarah watched him in awe, staring at the strands of her hair in his fist. He stopped a few inches from her, spread his arms wide and looked up at the sky. "Stop it," he shouted, bringing his palms and fingers together, pressing them hard against his forehead.

Sarah felt herself shuddering, begged God to halt the man's heinous rift.

"I heard you!" Ox shouted, head still angled upward. Then,

quiet as a mouse, he mouthed, "sorry, sorry, sorry" and peeked from behind his folded hands, licked his lips at her like she was a slathered brisket. And then, to Sarah's great trepidation, he punched himself hard on the side of his skull, teetering some before bending down to snatch up several pairs of socks strewn about the grass where Sarah had flailed. He balled up each one before flinging it at her face, one after the other. With each toss, he inched closer. Sarah never ducked, though, just stared at his wide, empty eyes as he closed in, holding a sock near her mouth. She resisted the yelp on her lips as he stuffed it in.

"Tell Hardy I done it," he said. "You hear me? Tell him I made you lay with your belly in the ground and whipped you good." Then he backed away, slow and steady, still panting. A knuckle-shaped red mark had formed where he struck himself. After several steps, he turned and ran like a little boy playing hide-and-seek.

Sarah felt the urge to pass water but squeezed her legs together until and lowered herself amidst the fire-pink and socks. She put her hands on her thumping chest and dreamt she had wings.

Chapter 4
Amidst Lions

It was cold the night Hiram finally caught Sarah in the act. In a kerchief, she placed several rusks that had been cut open and swathed in honey, as well as a wedge of spice pie. He had waited up for her, standing in the shadow of one of the stilted log posts that held up the narrow overhang. Nutmeg grew heavy in the air as she approached. He didn't want to scare her, so he waited until after she set down the special fare at his door and had started to descend the two wobbly steps. "And what should I do with your kerchief?" he said softly. Sarah jolted at the sound of his voice, but he kept talking, low and hushed. "I could wear it to dinner," he said as he untied it, emptied the contents and draped it over his head. "Wonder if Ox would think me pretty?"

Despite herself, Sarah sniggered. Her gladness made Hiram's pulse quicken, but she quickly covered her mouth, trying to halt the joy and the noise. When she turned to go, he jumped down from the porch, grabbed her elbow.

"Don't go yet," he whispered. He felt her clench. Instantly, he knew his mistake and loosened his hold. But Sarah didn't run like he expected. "Why do you do this?" he asked, nodding at the biscuits and pie. "We both know the wrath that would come if someone found out."

Though there were only a handful of slaves at the mine, Hiram had already seen Hardy take his belt to two of them for being late to the pithead, heard of another being branded for defecating in the woods, the man's pants still at his ankles as the hot iron burned between his shoulder blades.

"You're a nice man," she said. In the watery starlight, Hiram could see that her low-caste life hadn't dulled her eyes, they burnished like a fresh made key. "Bible says love your neighbor. Well, we're neighbors, right?"

Hiram kept his lips flat, trying not to look too excited that she'd spoken, nor too eager for her to continue. He said placidly, "But you got other neighbors?"

"None that'd pick oysters off the ground for me."

"Maybe not. But Hardy'll strap you good if—"

"He can't hurt me," she said. "Not any more than he has."

A dozing miner wheezed in the next cabin, pulling them from the cloistered space. They idled, held their breaths until a heavy gargling came from the same place, then a tootling exhale. When the man began to snore, loud and unquestionable, Sarah pulled up the skirt of her dress so it wouldn't swish then stole away home. Hiram watched her until he couldn't see her anymore, already thinking about seeing her in the morning, scampering about the mess hall. A lamb amidst lions.

That night, Hiram kept calling to mind Sarah's neck, where the clavicle stems from the sternum. Even her bones are delicate, arching out like little bridges. The sounds of his fellow digger grunting and puffing in his slumber came through the window, but Hiram held onto the muse, thinking how soft Sarah's skin might be, moist and slippery from another day's toil or maybe cool from walking in the autumn breeze. Did she smell rich like sweat and spices, or faint like butterfly weed. He pictured what they might look like stripped down together, she freed from the coarse fabric of her house-dress, too big and too plain, and he pressed against her, skin on skin. Brown and white, like a cattail broken open. He had thought about women that way plenty, though the guilt always pushed its way to the forefront, damming up his conscience like a muddy creek. It didn't feel like that now, not with her. These were wanton fancies for sure, that familiar warm prickling down below. But there wasn't a hankering to wipe his mind clean. He figured it was because the real pleasure was coming from envisioning Sarah reaching for him, too. It wasn't so much about their bodies coming together as it was her feeling safe in his arms. And telling him so.

The following night, Hiram waited for the groan of the porch as Sarah came to leave the next offering. He leapt to his feet, nudged a foot in the door, one hand on its outer edge, the other clutching the open space on the front of his nightshirt. Sarah was still squatting down, balancing on the balls of her feet, pralines and cornbread poking out the sides of another kerchief.

From under her arm Sarah pulled out a dark mahogany bible. The moon shone bright enough for Hiram to see the worn leather at all four corners. "I see you standing there," she said. Then she ran her thin fingers down the book's spine, spread them across her lips and chin and spoke through them, "I can't read."

Hiram bent down near her, resting on his haunches, too. "Ain't no shame in that." He leaned his head against his fist. "It's a nice bible."

"Master Hardy's wife give it to me. She slipped in paper scraps all over, like a thousand little tongues wagging at me, begging to speak. And she marked it up with her nib, too. Where she wants me to read it most, I suppose. She ain't thinking straight, about me being unlettered and all. Miss Hardy ain't well. Didn't do it outta meanness. I do want to read it though. Not just her inked up parts, but all of it."

Hiram steepled his fingers in front of him, nodding slow and easy. "So, that's why you've been bringing me food."

"Oh, you're wrong about that. I already told you why I do that."

He knew it wasn't true, not sure why he said it. He was all mixed up, reluctant and thrilled at the same time. "I wouldn't be a good teacher," he said. "When could we? I'm give-out at night. And if someone sees us, we're done for." The disappointment in Sarah's face was hard to see.

"You're right. Don't want you getting in trouble. I'll take all the blame. If they catch me here, I'll just tell 'em I let myself in. I'll tell 'em I was robbing you blind." The fervor sounded strange coming from her, but Hiram understood the burning she was having, wanting something so bad it hurts. Like working in the mines. Or wanting to talk to Ma just one more time, calling up her face by squeezing his eyes shut so hard that tiny white stars were shooting everywhere. Or the way he felt about Sarah right now, wanting to be with her but knowing the world wasn't a good enough place for that. Yes, he knew what she was feeling all too well. And he knew, too, that he'd help her, no matter how perilous.

"You're afraid of getting punished. You should be. You got something to lose. And the only thing I can give you is some cornbread and good meats, maybe a slice of pie now and then. But I want to read, Hiram. I want to know what the good Lord is saying. Not what a preacher or Miss Hardy tells me He's saying, but what I believe—"

"I'll do it," he said. Then he gave her a moment to let the answer sink in. When it did, he knew, because she smiled at him, her teeth straight and flashing in the night glow. "Everyone's got a right to read the bible for themselves." As he spoke, Sarah lay her hand on top of his free one. Her fingers were rough from tending to fifty belligerent men, weeding, shucking, hoeing and hauling rocks at the pithead. But it was the way she touched, velvety and slow.

"You're a good man," she said again. "I knew it right away."

There was a fierce urge to close any space between them, shield her from any more harm. She bowed her head, slid her hand to the side of his then kissed the back of it. In the thin blue light, he thought their blended bundle of fingers looked magnificent, and he savored the chill climbing up his arms.

* * *

When Sarah came into view the next night, Hiram focused on the task at hand, determined to teach her to read, to give her at least that scrap of freedom. He moved to the side for her to enter. Though she did, the hesitation was palpable. He had it, too. But there was no turning back. The plan was real, the consequences grave.

He lit the flat wick of the kerosene lamp, noticed the shadows casting on the wall and moved it to the floor.

"They'll still see it," she said.

Hiram pulled the thick wool blanket off his bed, draped it over his head and sat down next to the lantern. He held it up like a tent and motioned her to join him. He watched her chest heave as she sucked in and held it, then climbed into the shelter. He smelled the earthy odor of rutabaga on her hands. Next to her little body, the might of his size felt good, capable of guarding her from Hardy and Ox, though he knew the fight was much bigger than that. At least he could arm her with letters and words. He wriggled his finger between the pages and opened the bible to the first marked passage. Deuteronomy. He told her to follow along as he read; he used one of Miss Hardy's torn paper bits to guide them:

"'...in the field the man finds the girl who is engaged, and the man forces her and lies with her, then only the man who lies with her shall die. But you shall do nothing to the girl; there is no sin in the girl worthy of death—'"

"Show me. Where it says she won't die, point there." Hiram put his finger under the words, and she leaned across his elbow, looked at it a while then leaned back against the wall. He kept still, waiting for a sign to continue. Or not. "Ol' Miss Hardy. She knows things. And she's caring in a quiet way, like my brother. She'd love him if they ever met." Her voice had slack in it, as if she'd just untied a knot in her throat. "You would, too," she said, then rolled her head back and forth against the wall.

Hiram slowly closed the bible. "Tell me about him."

"Lord, the troubles that boy had." Sarah launched like a slingshot. "He was real small, so kids picked on him terrible. I remember one Sunday when Isaac asked if he could walk home from church with the Coleman brothers. Meanest boys in all the land. Like most kids living under the thumb, they had lots of rage, and they took it out on other slave kids, too young to understand why they were doing it. And boy, did those rascals dog my brother. Till then, they'd never laid a hand on him, just jabbed at him, sniggering when he'd tell him to stop. Come to find out, they only asked him so they could—" Sarah opened her eyes and searched Hiram's face.

"Well, go on then." He shifted some and let his arm down, the blanket fell over them like a hood.

"Suppose to be learning, not telling stories. This one ain't none too polite neither."

"You talking is a good start for learning. Helps me know you better. It'll make teaching easier."

Sarah stared at him for a short time, and Hiram hoped she could see the good intention. Though he couldn't help glancing over at her bare neck again. He had peeked while they were close but quickly turned away. She had shifted some, and now, in plain view, he couldn't help it. The blood started rushing through him like it had the other night, and his woolens started to stretch some, so he was relieved when she continued. He leaned back against the wall, focusing hard on her words, only.

"Well, turns out those little devils loosed their bladders on him. Way my brother told it, soon as everyone was out of sight, they circled around, pushed him down, then straddled his shins like he was a pony. One of 'em sat on his chest while the other piddled on him. He said the more he flailed, the harder they gripped. Tried screaming, too, but they piddled in his mouth. For years after that, I remember Isaac would just start gagging from time to time. We all knew why—" She paused, cocked her head like a foxhound catching a scent, and lifted the blanket, looking left, then right. The fear of a stray digger heading to the latrine was ever-present. The tiniest snap outside made both of them stiffen, hurling the ferocious consequences of their rendezvous to the forefront. Once the moment passed, and their stomachs stopped pulling as tight, Hiram gave the go-ahead with a quick nod. She continued, "I know Isaac waited till those scoundrels left to cry. My family holds dear to dignity. That's all we got." Though she kept her voice steady, fear from the noise outside had grown loud.

"Sounds like a lionheart," Hiram said.

"Sure is." Sarah sat up straight and inhaled hard, letting it out in a prolonged exhale. "Isaac was more ruffled trying to tell Grandpa he'd been disrespected than he was about getting piddled on. When he got home, supper was on the table. I remember him sliding into an empty chair, hair all caked and stiff. You could smell the sour. With his head drooping, it didn't take long for all of us to know. And for him to know that we knowed."

A heavy breath of wind pushed under the cabin door, into the lamp's chimney. And the flame shimmied and pranced. Shadows rose and fell upon the wall like grown men—stretching, jumping, reaching. Sarah tugged the blanket off her head and bolted upright as if something stung her. Before Hiram could get to his feet, she had stepped to the door.

"'Night," she said. "Got that bad feeling again, like folks are gathering out there, ready to snatch me up. Besides, I done too much talking. I shouldn't be jabbering on about private things. Next time, it's just learning. All right?" Hiram smiled as she gently pulled open the door, keeping one hand on the frame in case it squeaked.

"I liked hearing about your brother," Hiram whispered.

Though the lantern was still under the blanket, there was enough light for Hiram to watch her creeping away like a trespasser. He wished it wasn't this way, sneaky and dangerous. He wanted to just snap his fingers, make Sarah literate. Make everyone want good things to come her way, to come everyone's way. For no one to hold anyone back, not from reading or writing or laughing or loving. And he wished most of all that he could hear her tell more stories, every night, for the rest of his life.

Sarah came much later the next night. She winced as she entered, each step labored and short. Hiram knew her burdens were more than he could see and more than he wanted to think about. Sometimes, he hated being a man, having a common ground with beasts like Hardy—same parts, same fleshly thoughts. Even seeing the man's face now, he could feel his veins pinching down.

So, when their elbows brushed together and Sarah scooted away, Hiram stayed put, just held the bible out farther, keeping it in plain view. He read more of Miss Hardy's highlighted verses, this time from Samuel, where Prince Amnon violated his half-sister, Tamar, and her brother murdered him for it. He began circling the letters "a" through "f" as they appeared and repeated their sounds over and over, drawing them out like a metronome. He asked Sarah to do it, too. She parroted the consonants and vowels, fully sounding them out with her tongue and lips. Before they even made their way through the rape of Tamar, Sarah was pointing out letters herself, murmuring them under her breath. "You're a highbrow," he said. "Now, would you tell me more about your brother?"

She eyed him, as if his sincerity could be gauged in his cheeks. She took the bible from his hands, made sure the bit of paper was sticking out from where they had read, peered around the blanket before resting her head against the wall again.

"I ought not to. Sure was nice talking about him, though.

I can still hear him crying out, 'They sat on me, Grandpa! Piddle dripping down my face!' And I can still hear him sobbing till he was gasping for air. Mama put out her hands to comfort him, but Grandpa shook his head. So we sat there, listening as he sniveled himself sick. Then Grandpa said, 'You done?' and for the only time I can remember, Isaac raised his voice to Grandpa. He shouted, 'No, I ain't done. Why ain't you mad? You should be over there taking a belt to 'em.'" Sarah's tone lifted above a whisper. And she caught herself, stopped cold. They leaned forward, listened madly to the world beyond their cocoon—nothing.

Sarah apologized for having talked too loud but continued, her tone even more hushed. "Isaac bent toward the wash-bucket. He had made his hands into a scoop and was about to stick 'em in the water when Grandpa hollered, 'Don't you dare,' and swatted them away. Then he waved a spindly finger, 'Leave their bladders on you, boy. You hear me?'" Sarah explained how her brother tried to argue, pleaded not to make him stink something awful, but Grandpa didn't budge. "'You let it smell to Kingdom Come. Let 'em breathe in that stank till they can't take no more.'" She told him how Isaac's eyes glassed over when he said, 'Ain't no lesson they'll learn' and how his voice squeaked, 'They're gonna laugh.'"

There was another bout of quiet. Hiram figured she heard something that he didn't. He looked over both of his shoulders, then back to her. She had closed her eyes. "It's what he said next that I'll never forget." She deepened her voice like a man's, "He said, 'There's power in shame, boy.' Back then, I thought, it'll make sense someday. Just figured I was too little. But Hiram, I never did reason with it. Still can't."

The sound of his name coming from her mouth felt good. He stayed silent as she mulled things over a while longer. But soon enough, the quiet shifted from thoughtful to clumsy. So Hiram injected with "All due respect, Sarah, I don't agree with him either." And he hoped she liked her name passing through his lips, too.

* * *

Over the weeks that followed, Hiram read more verses, taught Sarah most of the alphabet, and listened to more stories, too. He tried to feel her every haunt, every bruise, every hope. And he could never stop stealing a glance at her when she wasn't looking, pondering the bloom of her skin.

The urge to kiss her becoming more fierce with every visit, and the fight to not act on it, too. Then, he'd stop himself—*it's not right; not here, not now*—and concentrate fully on her stories.

He learned that Grandpa took her and Isaac for walks along the crooked banks of the Maple River, especially when there was cheerless news to tell. He learned that Sarah was the one to find her Uncle Jerrick when he drank too much bourbon and tumbled face first into the wood stove. How she tried washing out the bubbling molasses from his eyes while he screamed, but they burned shut anyway. How her cousin Alice refused to bury her stillborn, just rocked it for days till the air smelled like skunk cabbage.

Hiram told her stories, too, about Ma and Pa and fishing in the Shenandoah. About sharing a bed with Clint and Leander. About finding a penny in the belly of a fish. And when he talked about the fresh scent of laurel, his eyes watered some.

On the last night that they would sit together under the scratchy, dark blanket, Sarah shared her worst memory. How some white fellas from the next county over had heard Grandpa talking in town, thought he was "too loud for a colored." How they filled an old ale barrel full of broken glass then stuffed him in it, rolling him back and forth across the prairie like a payload. How they laughed like hyenas every time Grandpa yelped. How they made Isaac watch, grabbed him up and told him to push the barrel, too. How Isaac said their eyes were hard and red and their breath smelled like okra and hooch. How, when Isaac said, "No sirs, I can't do that," Grandpa shouted from inside the barrel, "Do as yer told, boy!" How Isaac cried as he pushed the drum, too. How they made him keep pushing till his arms gave out. How after those fellas left, Isaac pulled Grandpa out and dragged him under a squat oak—his arms mushy as pone. How the old man finally broke, bawled like a baby through his bleeding fingers. How when Isaac finally got him home, he told them they must be the change they want to see in the world, and that wisdom and mercy were worth fighting for.

"Can't hold a man down without staying down, too," Hiram said. "This life is about quiet strength, nothing more." Then Hiram told her about the last conversation he had with his Pa. How he had asked, "What if I don't have courage?" When his Pa asked him why he thought he didn't, Hiram got shy, plucked at a clump of crispy grass from the hard ground, then finally said, "Cause I'm scared, all the time." Then he told her that Pa changed the subject—or so his young mind thought—and started talking about Heaven instead.

Hiram lowered his voice trying to emulate his Pa's, "Don't you believe them naysayers when they tell you those fluffy pictures of Heaven ain't real. When you hear folks saying Heaven ain't a place, that it's only in your heart? Why, that's a bunch'a cow plop. I know different 'cause I've seen it.' Then he told me it was only a dream, but that God showed him. Big buttermilk sky, and folks plucking on harps, eating blackberries and figs. 'It's all true,' he said to me. And I hope he's right. I hope the clouds are spongy and everything's frosty white, like fresh snow before folks go stepping on it. Kind of like cotton and crème. Then he said, 'We gotta be still. And brave. Have to teach our own children about quiet strength. Heaven will be waiting for us when we do.'"

Hiram wasn't convinced about the things he was saying, hadn't been sure of any of the things he was reading with Sarah in the bible. All of the holiness started seeping out of him the day Ma died and though he wasn't entirely drained yet, there was no reason to stop the runoff, to stop up the leak.

He only hoped he was pretending well enough for Sarah to believe him. He wanted her to bear fruit from all the sacred talk, even if he couldn't.

"Oh, I believe, Hiram. Never had a doubt. And I'm certain there's no room for hate on the road to heaven. Just not sure I can see things in a cotton and crème kind of way right now," Sara said. "Not yet anyway." Then, the thud of boots sounded out in front of the shanty, heavy and erratic—gravel grating underfoot, pebbles skittering in all directions. Sarah belched out a gasp. Hiram cupped her mouth in his fingers. The footsteps halted. And they held their breaths. Heartbeats clangored in dueling beats. The man began traipsing forward again. Hiram snuck to the window, watched his drunken comrade stumbling away toward the outhouse, heard him stammering, slurring. Only the cuss words were discernible.

Hiram turned back to Sarah, let out a breathy sigh to show his relief. But the rapture was gone. Even in the muted light, the fright in her eyes was crushing. She left without words, without turning back.

Chapter 5
These Wicked Mines

At night, the coal mine was raven black, still as a corpse. And it smelled silvery, like soot and soil, but sharp, too, like tin and limes. At the very bottom of the pits, hundreds of feet down, sat the sumps, murky from the lack of wind, dank as frying meat. Just before daybreak, the workers would lumber across the loam, their boots scuffing up dust; their voices dragging, still trying to purge the heaviness of morrow.

One morning, as the men trudged across the rock-bound mead—fog hanging low, gray—Ox tread through the middle of the pack and nudged Hiram's ribs. "Take a lead today, little nipper," he said. "Prove you ain't no hayseed."

So many thoughts ran through Hiram's head. They're already noticing, he thought. They're seeing how I work hard, even when some fellas start idling. He replayed a conversation he heard in the mess hall days before, two miners talking about Hardy giving a "greenhorn" a raise. One man said, "It's only 'cause he came from up north, knows about unions and such," and the other answered, "Nah, it ain't, you ol' bird. It's 'cause the kid works his tail off." Hiram knew the boy they were talking about. They were working the same vein one day when a fall of jagged coal sliced the boy's arm open. Hiram watched him tear off a piece from his shirt, tie it around the gash using his good hand and back teeth, then pick up his wedge and start hammering again. Never looking left or right.

Never missing a beat. And Hiram felt strong because he knew he'd have done the same.

Once they arrived at the pithead, Hiram made sure Ox could see him, then pushed his way forward and stood right behind the old regime. The veteran colliers gathered at the front of the line, an unwritten rule in the camp. After Hiram's show of backbone, Ox gave a quick nod of approval then turned to the banksman behind the crew. Hiram thought he saw him sneering but was too excited to ponder it long.

"All aboard!" As the seasoned miners scrambled into the cage, it bounced against the headgear then leveled. Ox called out each man's name, made a big red "X" on his roster as they answered. After those diggers were loaded, he made a downward motion with his chunky arm, and the banksman pulled the lever, jolting the pen into place. It rattled against the frame, jarring the passengers before disappearing into the narrow shaft. The longest-serving miners earned the privilege of working closest to the mouth, being able to use whatever daylight reached them rather than having to rely solely on kerosene to see. For all the rest, paraffin lamps suspended from the cribbing were the only light source, casting thin shadows on the broad wooden beams overhead and across the carbon-marred walls.

As the second group came forward, Ox bellowed for a leader to head down first, light the lanterns. "It's too damn dark this morning," he balked. Hiram raised his hand and Ox said, "Atta boy," then whacked him on the back. He made a wide sweeping motion with his hand, clearing an imaginary path. As soon as Hiram mounted the cage, Ox slammed the gate closed, the fence ringing out. The muttering amongst the groggy men halted.

Ox waved his hand high overhead then took a step back. Between the bars, Hiram could see the banksman pull something from his pocket—his heart stopped as the man clipped the cable.

For a blink, the metal hoist sat motionless. Then, it sank like an anchor. The cord zipped through the pulleys, whirring and rasping. Hiram couldn't open his mouth to scream, just plunged beneath the ground. He hurtled past the first burrow, wooshed by his fellow miners like a casted fisherman's line. The fall felt never-ending, like he might keep plummeting for the rest of his life. No thoughts could form, and his stomach was in his throat. Then he crashed through the thick balks of timber over the sump, slamming into the muddy pool.

Dead air.

Below the ground, baffled voices called out, "What's happening?" From those above, pure terror. They howled for their fallen mate. One man cracked, shrieking big and loud, "Dear God!"

Hiram tried to move but couldn't, his breaths cut short. Overhead, he could hear the men hailing orders, scampering for sheaves and, all around, the whinny of a pit pony bounced through the tunnels, shafts. Even though they browbeat one another, always strong-arming and badgering, he knew they wouldn't stop until they pulled him up. *One goes, we all go.*

* * *

The mine closed early. And the crew journeyed to Bentley to be by Hiram's bedside. Most of his ribs cracked, both lungs bruised and a busted hand, but a spared spinal cord. "Lord almighty," they all said. But the banksman never came. The men told Hiram that the poor man was blaming himself, asked Hardy if he could spend the day with his young sons. Hiram stayed silent, imagining the man fishing for brown trout with his boys, tousling their hair and saying things like, "my whippersnappers" and "fine as cream gravy." Come night, he'd make love to his wife and beneath their jostling cot, in a ramshackle tin box, the blunted pliers.

There was no sign of Ox either. But no one mentioned him. Hiram was glad of it. He couldn't win this fight, one man's word against another's. And if any saw, they would not speak up. He wouldn't expect them to. Hiram cleared the phlegm from his throat, and his back felt like it might split in two. He closed his eyes against the pain, pictured Ox on the other side of Bentley, crumpling a $5 bill into the bony hand of a harlot.

* * *

Several days had passed since Sarah eluded her beating. But she wondered if the waiting was worse than the actual thrashing might be. She jumped at every noise. If she heard a miner in the camp, her heart twittered and she'd flash hot and cold all at once. It was a matter of when she'd be whipped, not if. And she feared the wrath would be worse because Ox's pride was bruised, acting a fool in front of her the way he did.

She could feel the baby growing. Things were happening to her body that she'd never known. She was bringing up hot wind all the time, burning her mouth and making her gums bleed. Though she wasn't retching anymore, her bowels were always blocked, stomach clamping down and doubling her over. But she couldn't spend too much time in the outhouse or the anxiousness set in. Make supper. Draw Miss Hardy's bath. Get the children to the pithead by high-noon, now that Master Hardy had begun to pay all his little ones—a few pennies a week for picking up stray coal pieces—they were hard-nosed about getting there early, banging on the door of the privy, shouting her name.

Miss Hardy had started asking Sarah to take her for short walks. "Just a stroll to the hillside and back," she'd say, "that's all these crippled lungs can handle." With the disease climbing inside her, she was looking haggard, and she wasn't a comely woman to start with. Shaped like a slice of pie, thin shoulders up top and wide, fleshy hips below. A perfect circle rump. Her hair was thick as pigweed, a dull stew of blonde and brown, like the wings of a goose. Her eyes were gray and lightly hued, as if they could fade to colorlessness at any time. She had a high forehead and a narrow, straight nose that matched her bloodless lips. On this walk, Miss Hardy told Sarah that soon enough she'd be the one caring for the children. "They're a handful, I'll admit," she said, "but they'll be told to treat you more kindly." Then she asked if the morning sickness had let up yet.

Sarah's face burned. Miss Hardy asking about the child in her belly made her feel like a begrudged mistress.

"These walks are for you, too," Miss Hardy said. "Good for tempering your body to push out a little one. Nothing harder on God's green earth."

It was when they reached the end of shanty row that Sarah's world slid even further off course. Miss Hardy was eyeing Hiram's shack when she said, "What a shame that young men get hurt so bad in these wicked mines. It's a treacherous job. Getting cut open, breathing black air. And now, falling down the shaft." Miss Hardy spoke with compassion but distance, too, speaking generally.

Still, Sarah froze. Though she had become more comfortable answering Miss Hardy's questions, she never dared ask any herself. But now, she did it with a jerk. "Who fell?" she blurted. The inquiry sounded strange to her ears. To Miss Hardy's, too, as she stopped shuffling and turned to her, puckered face, sunken eyes, but a flash of life.

"Why, I believe his name was Hiram."

Sarah's hands balled into fists, and she held them hard at her sides. She focused on breathing in through her nose, out through her mouth, managing to shake her head when Miss Hardy asked if she knew the fallen miner. The weight of her lot in life had never felt so heavy. As the unknowns swirled through her mind, her chest grew tight, like someone was pulling it from both sides. A sob wedged in her throat.

On the way home, Miss Hardy talked about plantation owners fathering young ones with their slaves. She'd brought up the subject many times before, more times than Sarah could count. She always expressed disgust at reports that hundreds of mixed children were running all over the south. "Those poor wee ones," she said. "Must be confusing, wondering why their skin is fairer than their brothers', their sisters'. None of them certain who to call daddy. And for each one, there's an angry husband and a shame-faced wife, both wondering what they did to deserve such rap and lather."

Sarah couldn't cope with that now. She was trying to force all the hair-raising thoughts about Hiram from her mind. And then some mercy came her way, in two waves. The first was Miss Hardy saying that it will take a while for Hiram to recover; in jest, she said, "I wonder how my husband will cope, having to feed and house a flat-on-the-back miner." Sarah paid no mind to that, though, as the revelation that Hiram wasn't dead was too startling. She let out a breath, felt like she'd been holding it all her life, exhaling for the first time ever.

She gained her senses enough to hear the next bit of relief. Miss Hardy told her not to fuss with supper, that the mine had shut down. "Most of the workers are in Bentley tonight," she said, "some visiting the hurt man. Others carousing, no doubt."

Sarah didn't even try to hide her emotions. She felt the satisfaction beaming in her eyes, her face. No cooking for all those bellicose men. No cleaning up their messes. No corn chowder slopped on the floor. No hoecake crumbs to wipe away. No dirty dishes. A caged bird set free, for a night.

Though the idea of a night without duties brought a soft stir behind her eyes, Sarah knew the worry about Hiram would cloud much of the reprieve. She helped Miss Hardy eat the last of the mince pie then wiped the woman's face clean. She tried not to hurry through her routine—emptying the chamber pot, freshening the water basin, beating out the curtains and rugs—but inside she was giddy, a child let loose to swim in the river or just handed a candy stick on her birthday. When Sarah bid farewell, Miss Hardy told her to spend some of her night of leisure talking to God. "Thank Him for what you have," she said. "Ask Him to keep you strong."

Sarah nodded, holding on to the fact that the woman's intentions were good. But the objection must have been plain on her face, as Miss Hardy followed up with, "Easy for me to say, I know." Then she told her to get home, start her idle hours. As Sarah readied to go, Miss Hardy added, "I'll pray for Hiram. I'm thinking he might be one of the nice ones, given the worry you're trying to hide."

Sarah brought out her pine chair with the thin spindles for legs and thinner ones for the back rest, the patina a rich yellow-brown color, like a biscuit baked too long. She made herself a pitcher of sweet tea and sipped it right from the jug, perfectly sugared. At first, the ease was strange, the camp filled with birdsong and stillness. But then flares of alarm rose up, as if maybe she'd misunderstood Miss Hardy and at any second, the chaos of all the miners trekking home from the pithead would erupt. And she'd be running to the mess hall, scrambling to make supper, then scrubbing succotash off the tables well into the morning. Or maybe Hardy would come back early from Bentley. Or Ox might crash through the trees with his cat-o'-nine-tails reared overhead. But then, she'd take another swig of tea, swish the sweetness in her mouth and let it slide down into her belly. Soon enough, she'd dim the jitters, think of Hiram strong and healthy, sitting under the prickly gray blanket, holding it open for her to come inside.

After sundown, Sarah put her bible under her arm and made her way past the deserted shanties, all of them eerily dark. The windows were open in a couple of them, and the wind blowing through made clicking sounds against whatever it touched inside. She pressed onward to Hiram's place, scanning every shanty for movement before entering. She sat down on his lumpy bed. Such a rush of warmth to be amongst his things.

Hiram hadn't fallen on his own, she knew that. And that he was hurt because of the kindness he'd shown her. She looked out his window, then stood, paced between the door and the back wall, cracking her knuckles with her palms and shaking her hands like there were spiders on them. She tried to sound out some of the underlined words from the random page the bible opened to when she had set it down but couldn't get through the bigger words. She wanted him to know she was in his room, risking being seen by a stray miner just to be surrounded by the essence of him.

A ramshackle table was pushed against the side wall and even with wood scraps propped under the left legs, it still leaned. One of Hiram's helmets sat there, soft canvas cap with a rusty lamp bracket. Sarah pinched the leather brim between her thumb and middle finger, lifted it atop her head. The smooth, hazel-hued wood box that had been hidden beneath it was now in plain sight. She'd seen it before but never thought much of it, too busy learning, and the threat of being caught in Hiram's cabin always looming large. She wanted to write Hiram a note and told herself to only look inside the box for a pen, no snooping. She opened the lid, and dozens of bills unfolded like a triggered jack-in-the-box—ones and fives—so many that she gulped, reared back her head.

She shuffled them through her fingers, held them to her nose. At the bottom of the box was a pen and a single copper penny, the one he'd told her about, the one taken from a fish's belly. And last, an Old Crow label, folded over, so that the image of the black bird clutching stalks of wheat was facing out. She hoped that was a happy reminder of his brother, not a mournful one about his Pa. Sarah snatched up the bible again and scanned for specific words she needed. She found l-o-v-e and y-o-u, then slow and careful, scrawled them across one of the bills. Black ink smudged over Alexander Hamilton's nose and forehead. The pen was drying up, a fountain one, no steel point, no inkwell. So she simply made a big "S" and underlined it, placed the bill back in the box and smoothed it out with her thumbs. Then she shoved the rest of the money deep into her apron pocket and started praying for forgiveness.

Just after midnight, Sarah made her way to the kitchen, arranged it to look as if she was preparing the morning meal, setting out the mixing bowls and canisters. She decided to make some fry bread, set it out on the tables to buy herself just a little more time. While the men were chewing, waiting for the rest of breakfast to come, puffing on about the night's deeds—fistfights, working girls and Hiram's broken body— she'd be long gone. The thoughts of fleeing made her hands and knees shake. She dropped a bit of cornmeal on the floor, scooped it back into the batter, picking out a few brown blots of dirt but leaving some, too. *Maybe one of the ol' rips will get the trots from it.*

Put on the soft pedal, she told herself, just stir more coffee into the red-eye gravy, place it on the tables, too. Don't think about the furor of the miners when they realize the rest of their meal ain't coming, that she ain't even there. She had pushed the money into her shoes, buckled the notches tight, and the bills were pushing against her heels.

After staging the mess hall, Sarah sat in the corner of her shanty, knees pressed against her breasts, hands clasped at her shins. The first quarter moon was high, immersed in its own shadow. Sarah stared at it, waiting for it to settle between the two hilltops just above the cabins, so it would fully light her way. If the fear started to threaten her courage and she thought about sneaking to Hiram's and putting the money back, she pictured Master Hardy on top of her, heaving and wriggling like a tadpole. She'd make herself feel his fat thighs grinding against hers, chafing her inside and out.

After the moon moved into place, Sarah stole away to the pithead. Away from where the men would soon be shuffling about, coming home from Bentley, making their way to the latrine and carrying water from the well. Away from the creak of outhouse doors and the splosh of bouncing wash basins. Away from the Devil's house.

She wanted to start her journey at the place where every morning, Hiram tried to make his dreams come true, a little at a time. She approached the mouth of the mine, stood amongst the coal carts and tubs, the grey mounds of shale and all the fiendish looking tools. From below, the neigh and blow of some pit ponies rang out. Though they startled her, she was comforted by them, too. They made her sad, living the whole of their lives underground. But, she thought, at least they never have to see what's up here, all the bad stuff people do.

Seeing the empty frame where the cage always rested, Sarah was sacked by a moment of clairvoyance. It flowed through her like a wave. She saw the metal enclosure on the ground, bent and twisted. She saw Hiram falling. Felt the fear and dread, as if she were falling, too. The horror of hurtling through the cavern swept down her arms and legs and chest. She saw the darkness narrowing to a watery coffin, breathed in the dusty, black air. The fiery blasts swarming over, coal flakes sticking in his eyelids, lodged in his throat, nostrils.

And she came to see that now Hiram knew what it was like to be trapped, too, to be corralled in darkness. Still, even though he was constricted for the bulk of every day, it was his choice. He could crawl out at sundown, sleep sound in his own bed. He'd never have to feel Master Hardy's sticky milt draining from his private parts. But maybe he could relate to her existence on a small scale, feeling closed in, struggling for air.

She remembered him shifting under the blanket sometimes, letting out a low squawk and grabbing one shoulder, then the other. Once she glimpsed him rubbing camphor oil on his back, his sweat-dried shirt lifted midway. Where he couldn't reach to wash, there were black smears on his skin and down his spine, heavy scabs crusted over. She knew he must have scraped against the jagged rocks, but he'd never let on. Yet Hiram's pain was self-inflicted, and it led to opportunity, a gateway to something better. For her, the suffering was brought on by others. And when her walls were closing in and she wanted to scream, no one would hear. There were hands around her neck and they had seized her voice long ago. Sometimes she wondered if her mouth could still make sounds. And if not, did it even matter?

The air was soupy and hot, but a light wind passed through. If she spoke what she had come to say, said the words out loud, then the message would be more real, as if the shifting breezes would carry it to Bentley, through Hiram's window. She wondered how her heart could swell up the way it was doing, bouncing all around like a bunch of dragonflies in her chest. And she spoke to Hiram—

"See, there's a dream I keep having. And you're laid out across the mine tracks. There's a runaway cart full of coal, spilling over with every bump along the hard steel rails. There's craggy rocks all around. You're so out of place, sprawled across the tracks like a scarecrow hanging on a pole. Everything looks clumsy and cold against your face. I wanna put my hands under your head, soften things some. But I can't move. I'm all tied up, too. Then the cart comes barreling at you, just clinking at first. I push and pull, but whatever's holding me won't come loose, just tightens even more, making my wrists bleed. The cart comes faster, so quick it starts whistling. All I can do is turn my head so I don't see."

She broke from the reverie for a moment, began to wonder why God had spared them both, for a little while at least. She from a beating, and Hiram from dying. And she thought about how all of the bad things were simply because they knew one another.

"And I can't help thinking that maybe this life ain't about me. Maybe it's about the baby I'm carrying, how I'm gonna raise it to have all kinds of quiet strength. Maybe the day will come when its courage doesn't have to be quiet. That's when

I start feeling lighter, like the winds in springtime when the mine is closed on Sunday and there ain't no kerosene stinking it up. It's clean, full of phlox and chickweed. I look at the trees, not the saggy pines here in the camp, but the hardy dogwoods on top of the hills, the ones way up high, and I think, there's a big open space on the other side. And I shut my eyes, squeeze 'em real tight and remember that you're the reason I even want to see past this life."

She looked toward the hilltops, took a couple of slow, deep breaths—

"There's so many colors when I imagine it, Hiram. A sky as white as Miss Hardy's linens, flapping outside after I pin 'em up, the sun catching 'em just right. I see myself and my little one sifting our hands through the crisp water. You can bet our fingers won't look black when I do. Sure as hell won't look white neither. Why, they'll just be."

She paused, took a look around her, a glance over each shoulder—

"Sorry that I thieved you. You know why I done it. Just like I know that you won't be waiting for me. Not in this life or the one over the hills. We gotta be in a time when fingers is all the same, when they tangle up in the clear water all the same. And if you find yourself wondering about us, the youngster and me, don't worry. Why we're just past them trees, the ones on the sweeter side."

* * *

It was a week later when two fellow miners brought Hiram home from Bentley, the nearest place for medical care that called for anything beyond stitches and broken limbs. As they crossed the Cheat River, one of them told him about the slave girl going fugitive. "I think her name was Sarah," he said.

"Say it again," Hiram demanded.

"Sarah, I believe."

Hiram lay his head against the side of the carriage, arms out, trying to hold him steady, minimizing the impact of each bump in the road. He closed his eyes, pretending to sleep, listening hard for anything more about Sarah. Nothing. At camp, the men helped him into the cabin, drank from their hip flasks a while and talked about a slew of things, mostly how Miss Hardy was gonna die soon and how the new girl's mince pie wasn't as good as the other one's. But the men moved on to other things. Only then did Hiram tell them that he needed to rest. After they departed, he lay in his cot, trembling, sweating and ruminating on her whereabouts.

Sleep was thin, as he winced every time he inhaled too deep. Then, in the light of the kerosene lamp, he saw that his helmet had been moved. Though it took a long while, he drew shallow breaths, gritted his teeth and slowly shinnied to the table. He opened the empty box, picked up the penny and the single bill with l-o-v-e and y-o-u and "S" on the front, then the page that Sarah had torn from the bible, the one with a half circled passage from Deuteronomy: "... what does the Lord your God ask of you but to fear the Lord your God, to walk in obedience to him, to love him, to serve the Lord your God with all your heart and with all your soul."

Hiram wrapped the scratchy gray blanket around himself, fighting against the jarring in his chest. He thought hard about why Sarah chose that passage, wondered why all the people he'd ever loved kept being ripped from him. Then he told his Ma, "I'm still angry, but I've kept my promise. A fire for God hasn't gone out. It's burning hotter than ever. But I fear it's fueled by hate now. Or desperation. Doesn't seem right, holding onto something that keeps hurting me, something I don't trust. This can't be how God works? Beats you down till there's no choice but allegiance. And even as I'm thinking these things, I'm afraid I'll be struck down for my weak-kneed devotion." He read the passage again and again, searching for Sarah's intention.

After a day of contemplation, a realization unlocked. It didn't come as a mighty blow. There was no prophecy whispered to him by a lit-up wraith in a robe. Rather, he was staring at a struggling beetle on the windowsill, it had turned itself over, tiny legs madly chopping at the air, and the subtle awakening came: *If my faith is still wavering after all this time, why not dive right in. I'll study it, live it, test it. Either I'll find God for keeps or I'll surrender to the doubt for good.*

As soon as his ribs had mended enough, Hiram left for Ohio. When Miss Hardy found out he was leaving, she gave him money for the train, and a little extra. Though he didn't know her, he was grateful for the kindness, even more so for the mercy she showed Sarah. Years later, he learned that she died the same night he left. And in his first week at St. John's Seminary, when he was asked about the spiritual path that brought him there, Hiram told them about Miss Hardy's goodness and Sarah's bravery, in that order. Then he pulled the passage from Deuteronomy out of his pocket, unfolded it carefully and held it taut with both hands as he read. When he tried to tell them about Ma, how she encouraged him to look for God in the small places, something gave way inside. He couldn't stop the purge, and he sobbed with abandon, kept on weeping till it worked its way out.

Chapter 6
Look Small

Sarah fled the camp, just started running southward, scrambling through the thorns and brambles of the Kanawha Valley, looking for any of the signs Hiram had told her about Bluefield. She just kept climbing, scurrying until she heard the rapids of Cheat River. Then she walked along its rocky banks to a place that was shallow enough to cross. She took the money from her shoes and stuffed it deep into the satchel, then stepped in. The water like liquid mercy, flushing the dirt and grime from her feet, her ankles, her shins. She paused for just a minute, listened for anyone, then splashed some water on her face, hadn't felt so clean in all her life.

She walked all night and hid all day, sleeping at the base of trees, covering up with feathered out pine tree branches. And on one stretch, she was taken in by an older couple who spotted her traipsing through the backside of their property. They warned her about a slave catcher on the prowl and let her stay in their barn for two nights. On the third day, the folks shook her awake before sunrise, telling her to climb up on the roof, lay flat near the chimney. "Look small," they whispered. Sarah heard people talking in the front yard and she held her breath, tried melting into the shingles, the rounded butt wood digging into her skin. When she heard the voices heading around back, she rolled over the roof's peak to the other side. She could hear the man and his wife trying to warn her where they were standing by talking louder than they should, so she'd roll over the top again. Then a third time, a fourth.

* * *

Sarah knew the Bell house as soon as she came into the shadowy clearing. The sun was just breaking, the red-yellow streams were reflecting in the cabin's two windows. She hid behind a line of elderberry trees that Hiram had described to her, the cluster that Clint had stepped past as he headed off to the mines.

Leander came outside, and she knew him right away. He was wearing nothing but skivvies, the steam from his coffee wafting up from the cup in his hand. She waited just a bit longer before approaching him, figuring what to say and listening to the sounds of the Shenandoah, like it was murmuring something to her that she couldn't quite decipher. Then she reckoned that she need only say, "I know your brother, Hiram. We're good friends."

Chapter 7
In the Light of Our Own

Out of the deep of Ohio's backcountry then across the northern tips of Indiana and Illinois, Hiram eventually made his way north through Wisconsin. He stayed close to the western shores of Lake Michigan up to Manitowoc, then turned inland, traveled around Green Bay and landed in Michigan's Upper Peninsula. And when he finally entered his final destination of Bellwether, Ada Williams was the first villager he happed across. He watched from afar as she sidled up to each passerby then stepped around to the front of them, stealthy as a spider. She walked backwards, matching their stride. When they veered left, so did she. Then right. She stayed fixed on their faces while she wheeled and rambled. He couldn't hear her words; so after she had accosted several people and moved to yet another, he got down from his horse, moved nearer to the batty woman trying to be noticed.

Ada stalked up to a woman trying to get to the post—letters in one hand, a child in the other—and stared hard at her bowed head. Ada's hair billowed out on either side but was pulled into a loose bun in the back, stray wisps poking out on top and around each ear. Her dress was blue, the flounces undone at the bottom. The horsehair braids at the hemline were frayed.

What had sounded like drivel from a few yards away became audible now that he was nearer. He heard each word she spat, like they were putrid in her mouth: "You did this to me! All of you!" In a quick jerk, she tore at the baggy part of her bishop sleeve and clawed four straight lines in the flesh of her bicep. "There. Happy now?" She thrust her bleeding arm in the woman's face. "You satisfied?"

"Easy does it," Hiram called out. He took a few quick strides forward and with his hand, made a downward swoosh between the women. Ada snapped her head toward him. Her eyes wide and shiny. She studied his face as if reading a page from the herald. Hiram felt the scrutiny deep in his chest, felt her sadness, too.

As the woman and her baby hastened away, Ada leaned into Hiram, inhaled long and eager, sniffing him like a trout lily. Then she seized his ears, rolled the lobes between her thumbs and index fingers like dough.

"You ain't from here," she said matter-of-fact. Then she grabbed his chin, turned his head until it faced the empty gallows. "Look here, behind us." He tried to pull back, but Ada tightened her grip. "The fine folks of Bellwether hung my baby girl. Left her swinging like a clock's bob." She stood with him a moment, her hand still holding his chin, both of them staring at the empty platform. Then she let go and limped away speaking no more words, her head high. Just before veering into the shady woodlands, she shouted back at him, "They call me the bane of Bellwether! And I'm glad, too! You'll see!"

The next morning, Ruby Lee introduced herself to Hiram at the rectory door, told him she was chosen to welcome him to Bellwether. "Make Reverend Bell at home," the church board said. "Tell him we're a God-fearing bunch."

With a basket of honey-crisp apples and a few purple calla lilies, Ruby Lee greeted him, offering a slight bow. She walked him all around the village—to the well-tended town square, the golden lakeshore, and the splendid cliffs—talking of the village's holiness, the love they showed one another.

"For the elderly, we help with firewood, offer salted meat. The winters can be brutal," she said. "Come springtime, there are picnics and fish fries—"

"And the barmy woman? The one with the unkempt hair and tattered dress?" Ruby Lee stopped walking, looked to the ground. The sun lit up the rock-ribbed sea-stacks behind her. To see such a natural wonder, an unfamiliar gift from God, Hiram wondered how they had formed, how they must have come to be through violent sources, yet stood so straight, so tall, so rapturous. He thought about his faith, how fragile it used to be, so easily bent. And how centuries of furious storms could not put neither the stacks nor his journey with God asunder. And though wild winds may have ground each down, eroded the walls some, they only made the creation more beautiful, more custom-made. "The one limping through the village yesterday, asking folks to consider her, give her regard."

Ruby Lee's face pinkened and she looked at her hands as if they held the answer. The affection and shame were thorny between strangers, but Hiram needed to know. "What was more troubling than the poor woman's daftness was the way folks acted dull, couldn't be bothered. Not a drop of pity. And her eyes—" he shook his head "—so tired. She hobbled like a lame horse, muttering about her child, how the town had lynched her?"

After settling some, Ruby Lee said, "Let's head back to the rectory, Reverend. I've got more to tell you." Once there, she explained everything. How Ada and Elinor were hanged and that Reverend Williams was a bad man. "The church likes how much I do for Bellwether, and I like that they ask me to help. It's become who I am, the town do-gooder. But if I'm honest, I wish like crazy they'd have picked someone else this time." She cleared her throat. "You see, the town had to blame someone for stealing all the tithing, so they started calling the Williams women witches and thieves, trying to convince themselves they had to, that they was doing God's work. And it just kept getting bigger."

Ruby Lee let out a tiny squawk, and the tears spilled out as if they'd been waiting to for years. Then she confessed that just before coming over to greet him, the committee had circled around her with Mr. Murray issuing a warning: "Ain't no need for the new pastor to know our history. He might not see it the way we do," he commanded.

Hiram could see Ruby Lee's hands shaking as she said, "If they find out I told, I'll be in a heap of trouble."

"I can't allow Ada to be shunned from a church I'm leading. I have to address the spite and malice. But—"

"Oh, Reverend, please don't—"

Hiram put his hands over hers, marking the terror in her eyes. "You didn't let me finish," he said. "I assure you, there'll be no mention of you. How I learned of Bellwether's vicious secret is of no one's concern."

Ruby Lee said, "Thank you," but her tightly drawn face betrayed the panic. Both of them looked at their pile of hands, and Hiram pulled his away. Ruby Lee picked up one of the apples from the basket and shined it on her skirt then set it back down, pretending to admire the mound of fruit. She gave a full curtsy and said, "Welcome to Bellwether."

* * *

A day later, Hiram delivered his opening sermon. From offstage, he watched the congregation assembling themselves. Standing at the pulpit or greeting them at the door would have made him the center of attention, that's not where he wanted to be, not just yet. He needed to see the natural order of things, watch them interact without knowing he was there. First and foremost, he must be the protector of their souls, and second, a friend—that's what they taught him at Simpson Hall. He hoped it could be both, though condemning their banishment of Ada Williams was going to clog the chance for a mellow entrance. But he would not wait to condemn their errant deed.

Once his flock had settled, Hiram stepped from behind the east wall and strode to the pulpit with a straight countenance. Stake your claim, he told himself, just like at the mines. These first words will lay the groundwork for reverence or open the door to scorn. He stayed silent, looked into the face of every woman, man and child. He wanted them to shift in their pews a little, to wonder if somehow he already knew about the Williams girls, their bloody hands. The trepidation ticked in his heart, his nerves bristling and hot. It was the same stampede of emotions he felt when Pa died, wondering if he'd be able to do the things men do. It seems everything has been a test, leading him here, to this place, this moment.

Hiram had stayed awake most of the night before, pondering the seminary's mantra—reflect hard, then teach—to ready his sermon.

The seminary was in its first year when Hiram began, sponsored by St. Joseph's Parish, a tiny church in the wilds of Ohio. It sat atop a tree-laden headland with no footpath leading to or from it, just unfettered foliage in every direction. For the first few months, classes and meetings were held in the minister's cabin on the far end of the ridge. Though the divinity school was not yet associated with a college, there were two institutes in nearby cities wanting to educate pastors. Three of the four students in the inaugural class headed off to Columbus as soon as the opportunity arose. Hiram begged not to. Though he would have to travel to Canton now and again, then move to Columbus his final year, he was granted his wish to stay at the little church in the woods.

Most importantly, he was given permission to live under the tutelage of Reverend Harvey Caldwell, a wise man whose words were spare but sage. He listened with his whole body, that's what people said about him. One of Hiram's theology professors once said, "There are times when Harvey visits, and

I think his mind is wandering. But I know he's listening with all his might. That's why he looks all around while people are speaking to him, even steps away while you're still talking. He's trying to steep in their words like a ham bone in a pot of beans, trying to fully understand the moment. He is a godly man indeed."

The number of parishioners at St. Joseph's ranged between twenty and thirty, fewer in the winter as the trek was rugged for families living in the valleys. Hiram came to know each of them intimately—their hardships as hinterland people, their secrets, their struggles with faith and with each other. They were a family, for better or worse.

There was little David Campbell who wanted to help his Pa with the calving but got between the baby and its mother too soon. The newborn let out a bellow, and the heifer started thrashing, kicking at the stall. Young David turned his head just in time for the hard stump of her horn to strike his face. His upper lip tore open, a hunk of skin and fat hanging down. Mr. Campbell gave the boy a draught of moonshine and sewed his mouth shut with some fishing line. Infection set in the next night. The stitches branched out like the legs of a crawfish, pulled tight against the red, angry swelling. When David started heating up, they called on Hiram.

Mr. Campbell fetched him, then the two of them made their way back into the valley. When they stepped onto the porch, Mrs. Campbell met them at the door, pulled Hiram in by his shirt sleeve, shouting, "He's hot as coal!"

All three of them watched open-mouthed as David gasped then stiffened, hard as a board. His arms and legs twitched, fast at first. His trousers rubbed against the bedclothes making a clumsy scratching sound. Then, just as quickly as it began, the fit slowed, more and more, until the boy fainted.

Over the next few nights, Hiram sat at David's bedside. Soon enough the boy's lip started to leak a thin, milky fluid, and the smell was foul and pervading. Hiram dripped camphor into the mess and around the edges, he swathed a paste of garlic and onion. For hours, Hiram stroked the boy's hair with his knuckles, praying over him. On the fourth day, the swelling receded and Mr. Campbell fetched a horseshoe tong from the barn. Mrs. Campbell grabbed the boy's hand; Hiram took the other and said, "Take a breath, son."

The fishing line came out fast and clean, and they all let out a long breath. They weren't the hugging kind, Hiram could tell that, but when he saw Mr. Campbell give the boy a half-smile and Mrs. Campbell head to the stove, praising Jesus and offering slices of potato pie, he felt his full worth.

There was the Wheeler's stillborn baby, too. Hiram kept watch over Ma Wheeler well into the night, repeating the Mother's Prayer or the Father's Prayer, whichever seemed right at any given moment. For the would-have-been sister, young Lucy, Hiram made up his own devotion, wrote it from the baby's point of view, as if it was talking to Lucy. He called it, "For My Big Sister," and spoke of love and the afterlife and always being near. In between those prayers, Hiram asked God for strength, so the Wheelers could lean on him in their despair. And it was granted. Only after he was home alone did he break. Harvey had gone to Columbus for the week to help the theology professor with lectures and other academic matters. In the Reverend's cabin, Hiram dropped to his knees and wept until his chest ached.

Hiram ahemed, then introduced himself to the people of Bellwether as Reverend Bell, and it sounded strange to his ears. He briefly told them of his childhood years on the shores of the Shenandoah, and his time in the dark bellies of Virginia's coal mines. And he told them the reason he chose to enter the ministry, too. How he was tricked, how the wickedness of wayward men sent him tumbling head over feet to the bottom of a pit. How he laid in the swampy water with his insides smashed and mangled, looking up toward the light, wondering if his soul would rise toward it. How when the shock wore off and the pain took over that he bartered with God: "Let me live, and I'll be a soldier for Christ." And how a dear friend shared one simple passage that pushed him into motion. Then he stepped away from the pulpit and stood down center, scanning the audience again, more quickly this time, making certain not to pause on Ruby Lee any longer than the rest.

"I met Ada Williams," he said. The room stilled, even the colicky baby quieted. "Christ doesn't forbid us from judging sin, folks. But he tells us to do so in the light of our own." He made his way back behind the podium and opened Sarah's bible to the book of Matthew, held it up. And a single scrap of paper flitted to the floor. His chest was tight with the task at hand, but now his breath turned shallow and his skin tingled. Seeing a piece of Sarah in this place was staggering. Hope floated up, as if she might step onto the pulpit, amble through the front doors and take a seat amidst his new tribe. He swept up the paper with his free hand and glanced at it. The scrawl was untainted by wear and travel—*God bless yew.*

He folded it in his hand and held it tight and dove headlong into his sermon about grace, pity and charity. He raised his voice when he said, "The expectation I will hold for this parish is that we practice all three," and never rested his eyes on Ruby Lee for more than a second or two.

Chapter 8
A Blind Eye

Sarah could feel the brothers' devotion to one another. It was ever present. Leander didn't pledge his loyalty to Hiram aloud but showed it in the way he kept her safe from the moment they met. If the slave hunters ever came sniffing, he had a plan in place. The very day of her arrival and well into the night, Leander planed down wood pieces, flat enough to make a small tree stand. He walked her along the Shenandoah banks for at least a mile then turned inland, trekked another fifty yards to a cluster of fiddle trees. In the middle stood an older, wide one, a big trunk crotch and several branch-to-branch pockets as if God had made it just for climbing. Shouldering the flattened pieces—hammer in a belt loop, and a pocket full of nails—he scrambled up the limbs like a squirrel. Sarah asked no questions, just watched him work, mindful of the earnestness on his face.

It seemed that modesty was in the Bell family stock, too. A few minutes after starting the project, Leander slipped, crushing his thumb with the hammer. He let out a single yap then scaled down the tree as fast he had ascended it. He placed a wrought iron nail at the center of the purpling thumbnail, tapping until it poked through and the blood spouted out. He turned away shyly as he took off his shirt and wrapped it around his hand. Then he crawled back up the tree with nary a word, just a reassuring nod.

After the hideaway was finished, the two of them headed back to the house, then the talking began. Though strained at first, the conversation quickly turned to Hiram—his injury, his strength, his charm—then it felt much easier, opening the door to more grave matters, like the heartbreaks of oppression and the devilry that happens in smoke-filled rooms. Leander explained how Millard Fillmore came to be in office and the dangers of the Fugitive Slave Act. How northerners must give runaways back if they're found. "The Bloodhound Law, they call it, on account of all the tracking dogs."

Then he told her about a county in southern Michigan where folks were rebelling against discrimination. "Things are changing faster up there, it seems. Heard a bunch of planters from Kentucky tried raiding the area twice but failed. Heard there's cheap land they're selling to former slaves, too" he said. "Let's get you there, Sarah, north to Cass County."

She already knew he wasn't just saying things like most men do. He had that same purity of face as Hiram, like a starry-eyed child. She already knew that the baby would come into the world unharmed, that Leander would do everything in his power to deliver them both to Michigan. Or die trying. It was in his labors and the mild way he spoke about his brother.

Though the Shenandoah felt a million miles away from Master Hardy and Ox, the endless threat of being found was a tug of war between her nerves and heart. Not a minute passed that she didn't hear every little sound, fearing it was a slave hunter lurking outside, ready to bust down the door—crop and rope in his fist—to haul her back to hell.

A week after Sarah's arrival, Leander spotted her standing by a pile of Miss Avery's books. She was flipping through the pages of *Moby Dick* when he stepped inside for a ladle of water. Though trust had been born between them, boundaries were still being settled. She closed the book and apologized for snooping.

"Can you read?"

"Not yet. But your brother and me was working through the bible, a few passages at a time. Met in his cabin come nightfall. He was taking real big chances, I know. And he was a darn good teacher."

"I could help, too," Leander said. "Won't be near as good as my brother, but I'll give it a whirl." He glanced at the worn book in her hand. "That's a tough one. Not quite sure what all the fuss is about," he said. Then he took it from her and set it back on the pile. "I've tried reading it several times now. And I can't understand why that Ishmael fellow stays on with such a hare-brain. Makes no sense." He ran his finger down several other titles, searching, and still chiding Melville. "Too many big words, like he's trying to muddy things on purpose, make folks feel smaller than him just because he's a writer."

Then he stopped, pulled a book from the hoard. "*The Narrative of the Life of Frederick Douglass*," he declared, handing it to her. "This one's easier to follow." He told her it was about an American slave whose mother died when he was only seven. And that his master was called the "negro-breaker" but even so, "Frederick gave him a good thrashing of his own."

Sarah grabbed the book and opened the front cover. She studied the still portrait of young Frederick—his mass of hair and wide, silky cravat—then traced his forehead, nose, and chin with her thumb. "He wrote it himself," Leander said. Then he looked at the pile of books. "A lot of wisdom in that stack, there. We'll just have to keep at it."

Sarah faced him again with Frederick Douglass against her heart. "I'd be much obliged."

* * *

So the learning picked up where Hiram left off. Each evening, after chores, Leander read to Sarah and just like Hiram, he followed the sentences with his finger, repeating the harder words, the ones with tricky blends like "th" and "ng." Or with silent letters, like the "g" in fight versus the hard pronunciation in anger and hungry. Sarah told him that he was a natural teacher, even hinted he was better than Hiram.

Without a scratchy blanket to hide under, just a kerosene lamp on the table and glasses of sweet tea, Leander read through Frederick Douglass' triumphs while Sarah listened intently, trying certain sentences herself. After that, Leander tried some Edgar Allen Poe, but as soon as the main character plucked out the cat's eye with a penknife in "The Black Cat," Sarah said, "This man is out of his tree" and asked for a different author. Leander agreed then dug through Miss Avery's pile for a copy of *Civil Disobedience.*

Sarah loved Thoreau's boldness, marveled at his declaration that the government does more harm than good. And though she recognized they were mountains apart—Thoreau's freedom was like a storybook and hers was about survival—she was gladdened that his work was on her path to becoming a learned woman.

"It's all so backwards," she told Leander. "A well-read white man and me, thinking about the same things. How we all have to do what's right in our hearts, not just follow rules that the mightier half make. But when he tells folks not to be part of the bad stuff, like keeping slaves and starting wars, seems like horse sense. Don't get me wrong, I think a lot of him for saying such things, but then I get mad, too, wondering why he gets to write all his ideas down, get famous for 'em. And me, I gotta wait till sundown just to step outside." Sarah caught herself, took in a quick breath, the contrition showing in her fallen shoulders. "Shame on me. I shouldn't be—"

"Don't do that," Leander cut in. "Don't go apologizing for speaking your mind. Besides, Thoreau wouldn't like that much."

* * *

Sarah made her way down the riverbank to the wide fiddle tree. She stepped up into the big fork where the two main boughs separated and pulled herself up through the limbs to the wood shelf. She sat facing the water, legs hanging down like a child's on a swing. Though it was built as a hideaway, it became her place for thinking, praying. For guessing about the quiet times in others' lives as they, too, watched the white rays of day fade to shades of orange, like scattered yams and tangerines.

Right then, she made a wish for all those who had ever sought peace, no matter where they were—sitting on the muddy bank of a river, atop a mountain, on their knees in a jail cell—she asked God to lift them up, let them pull from those nights when they almost gave up. To look back and see that they are stronger than they thought. And for those resentful of their unfair share, she wished them stillness and hope, vowing to herself and them that she wouldn't let her child be caged by fear. She promised to never again let anyone like Ox or Hardy steal space in her head. Her baby would never know what it means to feel less than others, only endurance and dignity. Then she let herself imagine the folds and fields of Cass County, tasting the open air as it wrapped around her, so clean, so free.

* * *

It was during one of Sarah's and Leander's reading sessions that Reverend Thacker came calling, still feeling a fatherly obligation to check on Leander, now and again. He kicked at the door, beckoning Leander to open it, complaining that his hands were full of pie and venison.

Sarah covered her mouth with both hands, heart thumping like a drum. Leander whispered for her to keep still. When her legs began to shake, he held his palms against her bony knees. They sat motionless, eyes fixed on the unlatched door.

"I hear you in there, boy. Now stop fooling. I'm not leaving this pie on the porch for the coons to get."

When there was fumbling with the knob, Leander pointed to his room then made a walking motion with his fingers. But before Sarah could get to her feet, the door opened. The Reverend had loaded down one arm to free the other. In the crook of his weighted one were slabs of deer meat wrapped in a *Blueville Herald* and balancing in his upturned palm, a steaming pie.

He spotted Sarah. Everything slowed as if raw sap poured down over the house. Seconds felt like hours as the three of them gawked at one another, the only sounds were Thacker's heavy breaths and the high-pitched squeak of cicadas coming through the open door. The pie slipped from the Reverend's hand, and the tin upended, spilling its gummy contents onto the floor. The smell of pecan and vanilla flooded the room. Sarah felt removed from her body, sluggish and terrified at the same time. And with each passing moment, she grew more queasy.

"Well that's a pickle," Thacker said. He set down the deer meat then bent over the mess, scooping the filling back into the tin with his hands. "A better man would scrap a spilled pie, cut his losses. Though I'm not sure the good Lord made me strong enough for that." The Reverend licked his fingers, wiped his hands on his trousers and placed the heaping mound on the table.

Finally, he acknowledged Sarah with a quick smile. Even in her trepidation, there was a grain of comfort in the way his eyes twinkled, brown and clear. Still, her legs would not work. She stayed fixed on the burly man, his round cheeks, and bristly, silver beard.

"Brought you a couple of flanks from my ten-point," he said, nodding at the crumpled paper. "Been sitting in a cask of saltpeter and molasses for a week. Added a bit of cayenne pepper, too. If you smoked 'em in a day or two—"

"Say something," Leander snapped. "Prattling on about pie and brine?" He stepped to Sarah, waved his hand over her like a magician. "There's a fugitive in my house, Reverend.

She's right here. Her name is Sarah and—"

"Add brown sugar," Thacker said, his voice flat but strong. "If you don't smoke the flanks soon, salt them a while longer and add sugar right to the barrel. That'll honey the meat some, make it taste less like deer."

His turning a blind eye was jangling Sarah's nerves. The air around them felt hard and brittle, and she began to heave. Between huffs, she blurted out, "You're gonna tell!" The brashness made her heart skitter even more. She dug several fingers under her ribs to gain control of her short-winds.

"Not meaning to upset you, ma'am. Just taken aback is all." The Reverend stepped to a chair, ran his fingers across the top of it. "In Galatians, God tells us there's no slave nor free. And no male or female. That we're all one in Christ Jesus." He tugged on his beard then pushed his thumb into his chin and held it there. "And in Chapter Five, it says, never to submit to a yolk of slavery. So don't mistake my silence. My only discomfort is you having to hide at all. Any judgment from me is for those buying and selling women and children and calling it a right rather than a sin."

The frenzy in Sarah's chest melted some, but she still couldn't slow her breathing. Then the tears came. Her face felt hot and mottled, so she turned her back. That's when she heard Leander say, "She's pregnant."

Sarah knew the baby couldn't be any bigger than an elderberry but in that instant, she swore it was a giant. She kept her back to them, not wanting to see the man's reaction. Nor could she look at Leander. *Why did he feel the need to share that? Such a disgraced tone when he said it, almost sorrowful.* She hadn't thought about Leander's fears from that angle. She knew the danger of harboring a runaway, understood that he was putting his life on the line every day. But a new baby under a single man's roof? Why, of course he's scared about that, too.

"It isn't mine," Leander spat, quick and shaky, as if sitting in the witness chair. "Her owner, back at the coal mine—" He didn't seem to know how to finish the sentence. Or maybe he realized the bite of his trespass. He'd chipped at their unspoken regard for one another. Sarah's emotions were a boiling stew pot, her heart still thrashing from being found, and now this angst and ire, too. He didn't have to tell, made no sense. She flushed to hear the babe in her belly being talked about like it was something shameful, something to keep a distance from. And she was sad, too, for understanding why.

"I'm with my master's child," Sarah said, turning to face the Reverend.

"My heart aches that you were violated that way," he said. "Your master will answer for his transgression one day, I promise. But bearing new life, that's nothing to be ashamed of. Children are God's greatest gift. No matter how they came to be." He pointed at Leander and gave a command: "Teach her to read, son. Arm her with literacy. Though most southerners think we'll secede from the union someday soon, they're wrong. And if there's a war, we'll lose. Mark my words. So give her a fighting chance. I'll help in any way I can. Clothes, food, books." He waggled his pointed finger, "And don't add to her trials by thinking her unborn child a blemish." He dropped his finger, turned back to Sarah. "It's a crime that you can't roam free whenever you wish. Only Hell is made of such things."

The Reverend pulled out the chair and sat down slowly, legs the size of Sarah's waist, stretching the fabric of his pants until it seemed they might tear open. "Even as a messenger of God, my sway has big limits. I can't change the mindset of the masses, not about certain matters. Seems like folks' brains are like rocks when it comes to owning other folks. It's like they're only reading the parts of the holy book they want to hear, passing right on through the parts that shun slavery." He gripped the seat of the chair between his legs and pivoted with his feet until he faced Sarah directly.

Though it was hard, she faced him, too, only looking into his eyes for seconds at a time as he talked.

"One time, at the height of a sermon, I mentioned God's rebuke for slavery. I had been talking about Christ's hope for us, things like unity and goodness, and it just felt right, like I should set it next to captivity. Well, there were some sharp inhales and even sharper exhales. A couple of parishioners just up and walked out. And by the time I got home, both windows in my house were broken. All my chickens loosed from their pen. Later that week at the Blueville street market, a man I'd never seen called me a scalawag and when I asked why he presumed such a thing, he put his face near mine and said that over in Iron County, they don't like carpetbaggers none. Then he leaned in so close I could smell the eggs on his breath, and he whispered, 'Matter of fact, most of 'em wind up having real bad luck. Busted fingers. Gutted cattle. Hell, one traitor lost his tongue.' Then he backed away a little and said that a couple of them 'got gone altogether.'"

Sarah heard his words, but couldn't mull them over, not now. It was all too much—being found, feeling crossed by Leander, the baby growing inside her—but she felt obliged for what seemed to be his blessing, even if his story was rubbing salt in her fears. She was terrified every second of every day. Crawling under the window, holding her breath and standing frozen every time there's the slightest noise outside.

"I'm not the one calling the shots, haven't been for a while." His tone had lost its pitch, it was more tired now. "But I figure that as a clergyman, at least I've got a chance to make it known that in God's eyes, bartering folks is an abomination. The chips are stacked against me, and the ways to go about it are tricky. I must be clever and subtle. The bulk of ministers in the great state of Virginia are too scared to even try anymore. But I can't help them put out the light. I promise you, Sarah, that I'll never quit." He stroked the stubble on his cheeks, thumb on one side, fingers on the other.

Sarah marked the size of his hand, thinking, why can't he just wrap those big paws around every slave owner's throat, one at a time, until they beg for mercy.

"But I'm apologizing right now, for turning on you if I have to. If I'm gonna stay in this fight at all, try to gain some ground, I can't get myself dismissed. I want you to be free, Sarah, that's for sure. So I'll keep your secret and help the best I can. But if push comes to shove, my ministry—"

"I understand," Sarah said. And she did. She knew people were forced to make choices they didn't want to. That at the slightest test, some would drop their honor like a hot pan. Grandpa used to tell her, you'll never know if a person's truly loyal until they have to prove it. Sarah didn't hate him for his fair-weather allegiance. She felt bad for him, for anyone who had the power to rail against injustice, no matter how big or ugly, and chose not to.

Leander asked the Reverend to stay for a bit of mushed up pie. And with forks in hand, the three of them ate straight from the tin, silently agreeing to take a break from the bigger discussions of prejudice and morality. There was even some laughter, though muffled and cautious. Eventually, the conversation turned to Sarah's break to Michigan, but before they could delve too far into the plans, Reverend Thacker said it was time for him to go. "The less I know the better."

After he left, Sarah and Leander talked through the details of her disappearance, the routes, the timelines, the possible hitches. She would stay a month or two after the baby was born, long enough to nurse it to strength. And with much deliberation, they decided it would be easiest if she simply walked right out of town, stepped right through town—no disguises, no fan fair—just a servant sent from a neighboring town to shop the Blueville market. Leander had heard about escapes like this before. There'd be no raised eyebrows, just some curious looks at the unfamiliar face and newborn babe.

So, Sarah would simply load up her basket with fresh

fruits and beans, indulge in a pound of sugar, scooping some of the sweetness onto her tongue from time to time, letting it melt like snow. She told Leander that it would feel strange, buying goods alongside white folks, natural as could be. "But oh, it's gonna feel good, too," she said, "hoodwinking 'em right under their noses." She considered telling him about stealing Hiram's money, but it felt as if she couldn't explain her actions the right way, not in that moment anyway.

After the market, Sarah would just keep on walking, child and provisions in hand. They would sleep in the woods come daylight, then trek northward at night. She'd done it once before, though without a suckling babe, and not all the way to Michigan. There were connections Leander planned to make. Secret rides in the backs of wagons through Tennessee and parts of Kentucky, a couple of resting places in Ohio. She had heard about the underground railroad, but the thought of traveling through it herself made her head spin. All the crafting would take time. So until the departure, she would condition herself to calmness, learn to keep steady should the journey not go as planned, should she be too tired to take another step or the babe start wailing in the night.

Leander brought out a bottle of old man Shipley's rotgut, said it would soothe the strain they were feeling. Sarah remembered her Mama warning her shortly before she vanished forever in the middle of the night—one questionable yelp sounding out from the woods, and in the morning, a turned over chair and the front door wide open—that fire water was an evil broth. Satan made it himself, to mess up people's lives. She told her, too, it was really bad for babies growing in a mother's belly. But Sarah figured it couldn't be any worse for the wee one than her nerves still quivering from the day's events. And though it felt wrong taking nips of something that scorched her throat, she did it a few times, coughing and coiling with each swallow.

Before she knew it, the room was turning sideways and

her emotions split open like a milkweed pod, the cottony fluff floating every which way. She thought about her brother. How she'd be living in Michigan without him. How at least in Virginia, they were within reach. She could feel him. There was no chance they'd ever see one another, bump into each other at the post or market, catch up on old times, talk about the inclement weather. But it was reassuring to know they were in the same state. The nearness always made her feel less alone.

The room spun faster, like someone had set the house on a carousel, the ponies pulling harder every second. She gripped the armrests of her chair, put her feet flat against the floor. "I miss my brother," she blurted. The words sounded bumpy and slow, but she felt them fully. And she couldn't fight the sadness, tears poured forth as if someone had squeezed them from a baster.

Leander put his hand on her middle back, made a quick rubbing motion, left to right, then let it rest there. The touch was comforting at first, but it lasted too long, making Sarah's head whirl even faster. She felt an impulse to shift her hips, to turn away, but circumstances had taught her to fight instinct in times like that, to remain still. She was sobering quickly, her balance restoring.

Then, Leander dropped his hand, and her muscles loosened, some. She waited for him to move, to speak. When he didn't, she glanced back to read his face. Leander's lips were drawn together, his eyes stormy and expectant. He leaned in. She didn't have time to think. She just sucked in her own lips as if she had no teeth, closed her eyes tight.

Nothing.

Finally, she peeked. Leander had already about-faced and taken a step toward his room. She stayed still.

* * *

After that, the relationship was strained. Leander went about his routines—fishing, chopping, tending to the garden—and the conversations dwindled. But the reading sessions continued, though a bit austere. With each sitting, Sarah told him how much she appreciated his help. And she thought about telling him that what he tried doing that night wasn't really bad. That just like her Ma said, rotgut makes people do things they wouldn't dream of. That she had bigger grouses to bear, like ducking behind the table at the slightest click or snap, like waking up gasping, dreaming Master Hardy is pushing inside her again, grabbing at her throat and breasts, tugging and groping and saying nasty things.

Fall turned to winter, which turned to spring. All the while, the baby grew. Here and there, Reverend Thacker left necessary things on the porch, like a woman's calf-length cloak and a newborn layette with a long dress, a tiny nightcap and several baby napkins. While Leander worked, Sarah kept house and read books and then, come twilight hours, she'd head to her wooden platform, whispering to the river's current along the way.

On a brisk, April morning, Sarah stood to the left of the window, clear from view, staring through a clump of flowering dogwoods. Then, a popping sensation. A warm trickle down her legs. Her stomach hardened, and her spine began to grip. The baby was coming, faster than she ever thought possible. In minutes, the slow ache turned to twinges. No time to fetch Leander. And she didn't dare yell for him.

By the time she spread a blanket on the floor and wetted a cloth, the contractions cut her to the knees, recurring bursts of bone and muscle, a pain like no other. She wanted her Ma, asked for her through clenched teeth each time her belly seized. It ain't right, she thought, bringing a baby into this world without Ma wiping my head, telling me, "You're doing good." With the next surge, Sarah bit into the cloth, sucked on the water and cried, the reasons why all mixing together.

Sarah figured that baby Aaron was born in just under half an hour. He was tiny, six pounds she guessed. But he seemed healthy. She kept the window shut to smother his big, sturdy wail. Though she blundered her way through nursing the first time, soon he took to her breast like he'd done it in another life. And she found a way to bounce him that stopped the crying, in the crook of her arm and upside down, like he was treading water. That's how she showed Leander to do it when he came in that afternoon, the heavy smell of birth still in the air.

New life rushed over the house. For a couple of hours at a time, Sarah was able to push fear aside, revel in the baby's wandering eyes, savor the trifling puffs of breath on her neck as she patted his back. She thought the cheer that Aaron brought to Leander's face was sweet, and there was pride in knowing she was responsible for it. All traces of shame seemed to have withered with Aaron's arrival. They were a kind of family, a pretend one, even though bigotry and vice brought them together. For days, the house rang with harmony and even though danger shoved its way back to the forefront of Sarah's mind whenever Aaron let out a whimper, hope lingered.

Late one night, or early one morning, Sarah didn't know which, she woke with a start. Another haunting dream from the mine. Ox and Hardy cornering her in the mess hall, dropping eggs on the floor as they stepped toward her, grinding the shells, smearing the yolks, laughing and grabbing at themselves. She hadn't meant to fall asleep as Aaron usually fussed most at night. She shook the monsters from her head and looked toward the bassinet.

Leander was near the window, rocking Aaron in his arms, cooing and flapping his lips like a horse. He didn't notice Sarah, so she sat quiet, still calming herself from the terror of her dream. And then, Leander whispered, audible and positively,

"Aaron, my son."

Sarah waited until mid-morning to leave, after the dull thwack of Leander's axe was consistent. She packed light, stole the compass off the mantel and folded the map to Michigan in her apron, the one Leander had sketched her path on. Where he'd heard folks were helping runaways, there were big black X's. She thought of writing a note but figured it might make things worse.

So, she swept the floor, made a simple meal of fried green tomatoes and skillet bread. She set the table then headed out the door, bound for Blueville. Like they had planned—no disguises, and no mad dashes—just her haversack, a basket for the goods she'll buy at the market, and baby Aaron.

Though she forced herself not to turn back, she did wonder what Leander would do coming home to an empty house. Would he wonder if they'd been taken? Go looking for them? Or maybe he'd know she left early and just gnaw on the pillowy bread, taking swigs of that fiery moonshine to celebrate the quiet.

The market was full. She hadn't seen that many people gathered in one place since standing on a platform in Charleston, waiting to be stripped from her brother, folks pushing and poking and hollering. Even so, the size of the crowd made her rest easier. With that much bustling, no one would give her a second glance. Still, she kept her head down, only looking at the chins of people brushing by. As she was sifting through the bushels of tomatoes, baby Aaron squirmed in the woven baby sling Reverend Thacker had left one morning. His fussing made Sarah nervous, so she put a fingertip in his mouth as she bought the two tomatoes in her hand.

Then, she started walking north toward Huntington, head bowed, eyes on the road. The finger trick didn't work for long. Soon enough, only a feeding would soothe the baby. She hastened out of town and into the thickets. The trees were mostly bare, yet a few had started to sprout leaves, the heady smells of spring all around.

Aaron wouldn't take her breast, and his crying grew loud, bouncing through the mostly naked trees. She swayed him as she walked, gently at first, then harder, begging him to hush. "Please, boy. You're gonna get us in trouble." Then he began to cough. There had been some intermittent little barks before, quick and light, but now the cough had grown into a hard, sharp hacking. The fit was too much for his lungs and he choked. Sarah watched him writhing, his lips turning purple-blue. She patted his back, humming a tune that had no words or direction, more like a purring from her chest. After a few minutes, his breathing slowed again and his face lost some of the redness, but still, it wasn't the rich brown it should be.

Sarah bent her head back, took deep breaths as she rocked him, telling him that he was sturdy and brave like his uncle. And then, he started coughing again. This time, there was no building up to the frenzy. In a flash, he was whooping, red-flecked sputum on the fold of his long clothes. She kept the panic at bay for his sake, but her motherly instinct was wringing her heart. For the first time that she could remember, Sarah really didn't know what to do. Turning her mind to other things wasn't going to work now.

From the nearby road, the clang of a harness and breeching strap made its way to her ears. She pulled Aaron into her chest, hand on his head, the contents of her rucksack jostling as she headed deeper into the woods. A couple hundred feet in, she found a spot amidst some early blooming forsythia and spread her frock coat on the ground, nestled in it, gathering up the sides around them. Aaron had calmed and closed his eyes, his breaths labored and clicking but even. The air was chilly, and his body warm, dots of sweat on his forehead.

Sarah clung to him as if he was falling, held him so tight her arms went numb. Certain he was sleeping soundly, she turned onto her side and curled up like a bent finger, Aaron snug under her chin, his backside wedged between her breasts.

She fell in and out of sleep. Her dreams came fast, furious and fractured.

First, a blink of her childhood cabin, back in Norfolk County. Row after row of peanut plants, stretching to infinity. That was back when they worked for the kind-hearted folks, the ones her Ma called "the good ones." She sees herself walking hand in hand with her Pa after the workday is done, up and down the lines of green bushes.

Then, a flash of the lightning storm at the mines the night after she arrived. Shocks of white and blue ripping through the sky as if God was wielding a whip. The roof of the main house struck wide open, and Miss Hardy's screams shooting through the camp like gunfire.

Then an unlived scene hurtled through her sleep, vivid and real. A shadowy, unfamiliar place. A woman thrashing in dark waters, starless sky overhead. She can make out Leander and Hiram on the shore, both of them calling to her. And when she glimpses the drowning woman again, the dream closes in. She's nose-to-nose with herself, looking into her own eyes, wild and pleading. She goes under. Then, she thrusts herself upward and sinks down again, over and over. Her lungs like boiling pots, spilling over the sides, leaking down, spreading out. Before going under another time, she looks toward the brothers again. Leander is still on the shore, reaching out, shouting her name. But Hiram is halfway to her, swimming hard and fast, arching his arms in wide swipes like the vanes of a windmill, kicking his feet with abandon—

She wakes to Aaron gasping like he's being strangled, his tiny fists clenched and twitching in the air. Still groggy, Sarah held him up, looked into his eyes, trying to console him, give him a morsel of assurance. As she did, the violent coughing fit began to subside, turning into wailing again. Saliva had gathered in the corners of his mouth, frothy with more red flecks.

It was early morning, a thin light shone through the woods. Another slew of clanks sounded in the distance. And the next few minutes spun like a tunnel cloud, flitting be-tween a trance and the real world. She drifted over the scene like a shadow, watching herself run to the roadside, baby Aaron tucked deep in the sling, head against her chest.

Soon enough, she caught glimpses of the carriage through the trees. And then she was sprinting, floating. She watched her feet strike the ground but didn't feel it.

Everything happened in glimpses, her heart binding up, then pricking, stabbing. Aaron was hacking again, his lungs whistling in the struggle for air. Sarah ran faster, made sure she was far ahead of the approaching wagon. When she neared an open space and the flat earth of the back road, she darted toward it. She looked due south, spotted the travelers, still far off but coming, a slow-moving blur. She crept to the center of the lane, ducked under the sling and lay baby Aaron in the dirt then drifted back into the woods, the anguish too deep to feel.

Chapter 9
Teacher Man

It was 1854 when Basil met his wife at Hillsdale College, one of only a few colleges offering liberal arts degrees to women. And Stella was one of them. They shared Moral Philosophy class together in Kendall Hall, two nights a week. Basil filed in the first night, traipsed past his classmates then rounded back. He did this three times, making sure the prettiest girl in the room took notice when he plunked down beside her. She seemed to, but then quickly refocused on the "course of instruction" in her hand.

That night, their professor had assigned readings from Paley's *A View of the Evidences of Christianity* and come Thursday, Basil leaned over and asked, "Did you read?" When Stella did not respond, he tried again. "What in the world is tel-eo-lo-gy?" he asked, thumbing through the pages.

"I'm not certain," she said, scrunching up her cheeks and shrugging her thin shoulders. Her eyes apple green against her deep black hair.

Early in the session, the professor asked who could speak about teleology. He surveyed the room, appearing to enjoy the consternation. Then Stella raised her hand. "Yes, you, please," he said. Then he lifted a brow, intersecting his arms across his chest.

She stood, smoothed her Calico skirt, then spoke like a bard: "I understood it to be a philosophy of moral duty, sir."

The professor's face loosened, and he sat down on the edge of his desk. "It's about acting ethically and knowing there's a desirable end." She paused, glanced down at Basil, a wide cat grin on her face.

"Please, tell us more."

"Well, it seems philosophers differ as to the nature of the end," she began again. Though Basil squirmed at having been duped, he was captivated—the audacity, the poise. "For me," she tapped a forefinger against her lips, "for me, sir, it's all consequential. After all, virtue is the only true destination. Don't you agree?"

The professor made an *humph* sound and combed his mustache with his fingers. "And your name?"

"Stella. Stella Knight"

"Good, Miss Knight." He nodded. "Quite good indeed." He rose from his desk and approached the board. Stella turned up her palms and winked at Basil.

"Maybe I studied a little," she goaded. And Basil was hopelessly smitten.

* * *

Stella never finished her studies, as one year later, surrounded by droves of cotton-sedge, the white heads like tiny, low-hanging clouds, Basil proposed.

"Are you sure?"

"I fancy a wifely call," she said. "A maternal one, too." She nudged him with her elbow. "And I don't feel either are a misstep."

Basil shook his head. "You're intoxicating," he said.

Then, in the fall of 1857, Basil and Stella Brandt snaked along the rugged roads, northbound to Bellwether where they had heard farming was good and land was cheap. They borrowed against a fifty-acre plot and vowed to make it their own.

Two years after they settled, Miss Kauffman, the village's only schoolteacher, lost her brother in the battles of Bloody Kansas and returned to the prairielands to care for her ailing father. So, Basil vied for the role. On the morning of the interview, he donned his sack coat and white linen trousers and around his thick neck, Stella swathed a silk cravat, looped it into a fat knot. "I feel like a shell full of ice cream," he muttered. Stella grinned, pinning the tie through the puckered placket of his dress shirt with a smoky moonstone clip, the color of milk and plums.

"Well then," she slapped her hands on her knees, "better go before you melt." Though Basil smiled at her cleverness, it didn't come as easily as it had just months before. His belly still flounced whenever Stella came near, but not as hard. The love was strong, but there was resistance, too. He counted himself a blessed man and had to remind himself often that Stella wasn't to blame for their childless marriage.

Even dressed in all the fancy bauble, Basil felt the chinks in his armor. He knew that others saw him as two-fisted and virile. Somehow, he drew people in, though he wasn't sure why. He never fully understood his sway, like that with the Bellwether school board. It almost felt like cheating, as he knew he'd be offered the job simply based on his big-wheel air, none of them knowing it was a wall of gold bricks that he hides behind, only peeking over it once in a while.

"Due to your humility and wide skill sets, Mr. Brandt, we'd like you to teach our children," Reverend Hiram said, then stood, reaching out an open hand. "You're the huckleberry." He laid his hand on Basil's shoulder and added, "Hope you're good at patching shingles and making splints." Gentle laughter filtered through the room. A farmer and a teacher, Basil thought, it's a tall order. On the outside, he plumed like an eagle, but inside, he was already grappling, crumbling. He wondered if his number was up, if folks would finally see that he was merely a breathing powder keg.

* * *

Arriving home from the interview, Basil saw the full washtub. He knew Stella only washed clothes on Saturdays, unless she had bled into her pantalettes. She was busying herself at the hearth while proof that her menses had started again steeped in the corner. He knew the charade all too well. When he told Stella he'd been offered the job, she replied softly and without looking at him, "You'll be great."

"Once again, you have more confidence in me than I do." He sat down at the kitchen table, hoping his comment would steer her thoughts from infertility.

"Everyone does," she said. With the back of her hand, she brushed stray ashes into the fire pit. Basil let her words linger, knowing she'd feel the need to fill any silence. "I wish you could see yourself as others do." She turned toward him, a loose smile on her face. "People want to know you. They want to earn your respect. It's in the way you speak, the way you move." Basil eased some, hopeful that her sorrow might not take hold this time. He glanced at the tub, felt his own disappointment creeping in.

Stella moved to the basin, dipped her hands in and pulled up a heap of sopping clothes. Basil watched her face harden, listened to the water splash against the floor. She stood stone for a moment then stepped to the door—a thin trail of suds behind her—and lifted the latch with her elbow.

He knew he should tell her right then, confess that it was likely him who was sterile. Tell her about the winter before he left for Hillsdale College, how he'd just turned seventeen, and the season was more frigid than most. How he was chopping away at a dense log, swinging the maul hard, and then, the density tumbled him backward. How after tripping over the mound of uncut wood, he landed on the splitting wedge. And something burst in his groin. A dull ache spread like wildfire to his stomach and kidneys. An invisible fist gripped his insides, clamping down and pulling in every direction. How he curled into a ball and retched into the snow. And for days after, whenever he used the outhouse, there was blood and throbbing. How each time he had to go, the pressure mounted like a brimming dam, and he'd clinch and groan until there was release, then fight back tears.

But he didn't. Instead, he listened to her agony. "I know I'm broken," she said. With her back still to him, her voice flattened, "The way you look at me calls it to mind every day." She looked over her shoulder and Basil raised his eyes to meet hers. "We shouldn't be suffering alone." And the door clicked behind her.

For an instant, he was spurred to go to her. But he stopped short, like he knew he would. At the window, he watched her drape wet clothes across the fish line that bowed between the house and a hardy dogwood branch. His eyes followed her the entire time she worked and even after she tiptoed around a burgeoning firethorn, rolling out of sight.

Chapter 10
Ten Thousand Tongues

Although northern Michigan winters had hammered the walls of Bellwether's schoolhouse and sagged its roof, behind the big wooden door, beneath the leaning belltower, there was refuge. Every morning, the plodders' children sat at their desks, greeted with routine: one *McGuffey Reader*—perfectly angled in the upper corner—two freshly whittled nibs, and Mr. Brandt, ready to light them up. For a few cursory hours, the cropping, the weeding and the toil were put aside, and the boys and girls sat erect and wide-eyed, hair brushed or curled or slicked over a stubborn cowlick, immersed in the tutelage of their earnest teacher.

As the younger kids practiced their soft strokes, pushing up then pulling down, slanting their quills for the perfect 'S', Basil read aloud to the upper grades. With a special, leather-bound collection of poetry and prose perched in his hand, he paced and paused like an apostle, the words ebbing like the tide:

> *There is a sacredness in tears. They are not the mark of weakness, but of power.*
>
> *They speak more eloquently than ten thousand tongues.*

"These are the words of Mr. Washington Irving. Anyone care to guess what he means?" After a few seconds of blank stares, Basil called on mild mannered Uriah.

The boy rose like an ambling fawn then cleared his throat and said meekly, "I think he's talking about fellas mostly. Telling them that crying ain't so bad."

"Is he right?"

"I'm not sure that—" Uriah's voice trailed off, and he stood silent. The boys sitting next to him laughed.

"Ignore them," Basil said. "Just look at me, son." Uriah angled his head upward. "Go on. Finish."

"I think he's right, sir. My Pa says crying is for lady folk. And I've seen him trying not to, like when his own Pa died." Uriah swallowed hard as if there was a rock in his throat. "Looked like it hurt, trying to hold back the tears. Seemed kinda silly to fight it."

This lamb of a boy is steadier than me, Basil thought. Yet day after day, he sits here, grazing on my approval. If only he knew my gutlessness. "Well put, boy," he said, then finished reading Irving's quote directly to him:

> *They are the messengers of overwhelming grief, of deep contrition and of unspeakable love.*

Basil strolled to his desk, asked all the students to fetch an abacus from the front table, then strode to the window, hickory boards creaking under his weight. The wind whistled through the belfry and ushered in the balm of white clover and curing hay. Just beyond the schoolyard, the field of thistle slanted and furled in the breeze like a sheet on a clothesline, pink as a flock of band-tailed pigeons.

In his mind's eye, gamboling in the flushing blooms, Basil imagined his own children, a boy and a girl, about the same height, coal black hair like their mother's. He's kneeling next to the field, the blue-red weeds reaching just above his chest. They race toward him, arms spanned wide. But then they fall, just drop out of sight as if the earth had opened up, swallowed them whole. Basil scrambles to where they were playing, finding only more thistle, untrampled, brushing against his shins.

Chapter 11
At the Sea-stacks

Basil cut through the schoolyard and crossed over the meadow, then hesitated, looked east toward the hillside that stood between him and home, everything bathed in the yellow of the setting sun. Instead, he turned west, headed toward the chapel.

Arriving at the rectory, he cupped his hands around his mouth, calling out, "Reverend!" Hiram met him at the sanctuary door with a coyote grin. Being the only lettered men in Bellwether, the minister and teacher found solace in one another, respite from their public responsibilities. For fear of others thinking them lofty and exclusive, they kept their friendship discrete. Though they always began with surface talk and nuance, bigger discussions always came. And without fail, those bigger things eventually settled into Basil's needs, wants, and struggles.

Without an utterance, the men moved to the sea-stacks behind the church. They trekked over the sharp limestone then crossed the narrow slab that formed a bridge to what had become their meeting place, a lone sea-stack standing tall and awkward, like a thumb jutting out of Lake Superior. Its sides were rough and uneven, as if someone had tried to sculpt it with a hammer. There they sat in their usual spots—Hiram in a cranny amid the cover of two thin spruce trees; Basil near the edge, one foot dangling over—and began their dizzying banter of Psalms versus Emerson, Corinthians versus Poe,

Genesis versus Tennyson. They quipped and wheedled, relishing in one other's intellect, both at ease atop the precipice. The sea-stacks bent around them like a crooked spine, winding with the curves of Michigan's Upper Peninsula. Having washed over for decades, the minerals—copper and iron—shaded the stately pillars that were left in their wake, brilliant reds, pinks and blues.

"I'm a coveter," Basil uttered. The bluntness breached their routine, and the gravity of it was heavy. Hiram nodded, slow and methodical. That's all the invitation Basil needed. He pushed out the confession fast, as if he were to stop, he'd never start again. "Not only do I bear grudges against the fathers I see in town, sons and daughters at their hips, tiny hands swinging to keep stride, but I let Stella believe our childless marriage is her fault. I watch her suffer burdens that are not hers to bear. And though I see the toll it's taking on her, I'm not strong enough to end it." He paused, shifted toward the lake and spoke to the water. "There's a reckoning coming my way. I can feel it."

"Well, friend," Hiram lowered his head, "let's pray." Basil bowed his head, too, managing a contemplative expression. But he didn't hear the words. His mind was full of images, flashing like lightning. That boy and girl in the thistle field, dropping like rocks off a cliff. And Stella crying over the wash bucket, dark red spots on her white drawers. Then a glimpse of his own Pa, back to a time when Basil was going through a clumsy stage, spilling his milk at supper almost every night. How one night, as it was running off the table, dripping down into the spaces between the wood planks, Pa turned to Basil, flicked his own cup over and let out a whoop. He nodded for Ma to do the same. And she did. They all ate their milk-soaked corn and joked about how tasty it was, making hmmm sounds and patting their stomachs. Basil remembered right there how he promised that one day, his own son would look on his boyhood with fondness like he did. How he'd make him laugh every day.

Basil heard "Amen" and was hauled back to the present. He said it, too, then both of them looked out over Lake Superior, mostly flat but for a few ruffles near the shoreline. The sun was still high enough to strike the brightly hued stones on the lake floor, making them gleam from underneath, lighting up the clear, sleek surface with warm shades of blue and brown. The smell of northern sweetgrass lingered, floral and vanilla. And the loneliness killed him a little more this day.

Chapter 12
From Under a Porch

Where their property lines intersected, the Murray's and the Lovett's, there was a long, narrow patch of trees, then the Murray's outhouse, where Eva and Uriah first met. As far back as Uriah could remember, Pa spent Saturday mornings working on a tallboy for Ma. One time, he'd seen his Pa raze the dresser just when it looked to be done. A smooth wardrobe on top, double chest of drawers below. He'd even started tinkering with some cast iron mounts for it. But on a Saturday morning, Uriah watched him step back, look at the dresser with a cocked head like it was a question he couldn't answer. Then he inhaled—chest puffed out, shoulders pulled back—picked up the ax leaning against the workbench and said, "Stand back, son." He reared it overhead, took two quick steps forward and hacked downward, slashing and cleaving until there was no semblance of a tallboy left. Still panting, he rested the handle of the ax against the wall and began picking through the scraps of poplar, casual as could be.

Then he chose a wood slab from the pile, fetched his planer and sat down on the ground. He started taking long, full strokes atop the board. "There was a bow in your Ma's tallboy," he said. "Can't have that." Then he lifted the piece up to eye level, looked at it from all sides and down the middle. "A man knows if he's done his best." He threw the board back atop the hill of tinder. "He knows when he hasn't, too."

Pa stepped to the loft and reached behind a low wall. Then he pulled out a rolling hoop. A perfect ring, curved just so and smooth all around. "Thing is, son, it's hard for a man, 'cause he's got to know about most things, and be good at all of them. It's only when he ain't that folks notice." He gripped the hoop with both hands, showing every angle before offering it up. "I made a few of 'em before I found the right thickness," he said. "It's an inch and a half wide, a quarter fat. See?" Then he pulled a small dowel from the front pocket of his overalls and waved it like a magic wand. "Your rolling stick, sir."

Even at seven, Uriah understood that Pa would be uneasy if he prattled on about the toy. Instead, he ran outside and started trundling, knowing Pa would be peeking from the barn. He wanted him to see the hoop rolling down the bumpy field, see that he was good at rolling it, too, doing his best to push it through the coverts arching down on either side.

After Uriah crested the ridge, out of Pa's sight, he lost control of the hoop, chasing it as it spun toward the Murray's outhouse, just inside the thin copse. Finally, it hit a mound of earth, bounced against a tree and fell over.

Eva stepped from the outhouse, and Uriah froze. It felt wrong being that near someone—other than his Ma or Pa—using the privy, especially a girl. He figured she might start yelling. Instead, she ran to the hoop and held out her hand for the stick. "Can I try?" She wore a brown, heavy looking dress with a plaid pinafore—a smudge of dirt on her face. Her hair was ochre-colored, pulled back and tied with a sky-blue ribbon made of cloth. She pulled a strand of it from her mouth with her pointer finger. Her face was older, like a mom's or a teacher's, pulling down around the brow. But her eyes were kind and bright. He liked looking at them.

"Well, can I?"

Uriah handed her the dowel. They had seen one another at church and at school now and again when she came. Their families were cordial but not close. And sometimes at home, from across the way, the two of them saw one another's silhouettes amongst all the bigger shadows and waved like their parents did, but they had never spoken. They didn't talk much now either, just focused on the hoop and stick, racing it, and each other, until they were almost used up.

Then Pa Murray called for his daughter. His words barreled through the open space, yet Eva kept trundling, heading away from his voice. She looked back at Uriah, as if to say, keep playing, pretend you didn't hear it, please. Uriah started to chase her again, but her father's voice boomed a second time and neither could deny the beckoning any longer. They slowed to a halt.

"Can I keep it?" Eva asked, the hoop tight in her grip. "Just a few days?"

It was hard to say no. But he did. He told her it was special, from his Pa. He stepped next to her and spoke fast, earnestly. "I'll bring it next Saturday, same time."

She observed him again, even closer than before, the back of her hands on her hips like a scold. Her demeanor was that of a haggard woman, but her voice was high and soft. "Promise," she said. Then she held out her pinky. Uriah reached with his little finger, and they linked them together like brick work.

* * *

The Murray house smelled like smoked meat and molasses. Eva sniffed at the beans curing with ham hocks as she set down the plates and forks. Pa sat in his chair at the table, and besides the clink and slosh of Ma doling out the greens, it was quiet, as always. Eva cut open her sweet potato as she eyed the ceramic bowl, full of brown sugar and cinnamon. It wasn't often there was such a treat on the table. Pa Murray was a miser, pinching every penny, always talking of prudence and provision, even when there had been bumper crops, year after year. Never made sense. Just seemed like another excuse to be mean. After he nodded for them to eat, Eva heaped brown sugar and cinnamon high as a sand dune—she couldn't help herself. She rubbed her hands together, mouth watering some.

Though Ma smiled at her excitement, Eva could tell it was the anxious kind. With real smiles, Ma's upper teeth always showed, the tiny folds by her eyes were bigger. The nervous ones were in her lower jaw, neck muscles clenched tight like a bat's wing. And with the fake smiles, Pa was always nearby.

His eyes fixed on the speckled mound. And her stomach doubled up. She knew what she'd done wrong. Pa would see her indulgence as disrespect, a challenge to the thriftiness for which he always fought so hard. She wanted to quickly spoon it all back. But it was best to sit still, take what was coming. Ma filled their cups with water and said, "Sure nice of the Lee's. Hauling home so much sugar and rice, all the way from St. Ignace. Passing on the bargains to Bellwether." Pa didn't speak, just emptied his cup, letting out tiny grunts with every gulp then nodded at Ma to fill it again. The more Ma kept talking, the sicker Eva felt. "They said sugar was the cheapest they'd ever seen, just had to bring some home for the rest of us," she jabbered. "Prices will rise again soon, that's sure. Too much left over, on account of summer ending—"

Pa eyed her as he dished himself a jumble of ham and beans. "Bless this food, amen," he said, then stuffed the spoonful into his mouth and chewed greedily. Then he did it again. And again. Ma tested the waters, began to eat herself as Pa kept feasting, nary a word. Then she nodded, and Eva scooted forward, poised herself to eat, not because she felt at ease but out of fear not to. She swallowed a dollop of stew then tried pushing down the mound of sugar with the bowl of her spoon, flattening it down into the orange flesh of the potato. At one point, Pa told Eva he saw her pushing a hoop with the Lovett boy. And when Eva replied yes, he said, "Looked like fun," then picked at a string of gristle in his back teeth. And Ma ate like a bird, waiting.

* * *

Eva made her way to the breakfast table the next morning, saw Pa sipping his coffee, eyes peering over the ridge of his tin. Ma's distress was palpable, wearing one of her anxious smiles. Eva pulled out her chair, glanced down at her plate. A grainy, dark mound on top of her boiled eggs and hash. She saw the empty sugar bowl and her heart dropped. Pa slurped more coffee, and Ma started jabbering again, something about a loose heifer in town square. Eva stared at the clotted mess on her plate, her eyes starting to dampen.

"We got plenty of money, ain't we, Eva?" Pa said. "Hell, we could buy all the sugar in Michigan." He aimed his thick finger at the plate, pecked at the air. "Well, go on then. Waste not, want not, child."

Eva's muscles stiffened. But her anger shrunk the fear, then gave way to defiance, the quiet kind. She sliced the eggs into chunks and with each bite, dug to the bottom of the drift, scraping her spoon against the plate, metal on metal. The hard yolks and shredded potato were caked in clumps of sugar, but she shoved the mishmash into her mouth. When the sweetness overwhelmed her, she pushed the gritty mix into her cheeks, trying to dissolve it faster. After the urges to gag and spit had passed, she swallowed the syrupy mound then raked her spoon across the plate again. Pa got up from the table, narrowed his eyes at her then headed outside, cup in hand, coffee still steaming.

Later, Eva retched up the sickening sweet brew beside the privy. She looked out across the sloping field to the Lovett's farm, praying to catch a glimpse of Uriah, maybe running with the hoop or helping his Ma hang the blankets or tend the chickens—anything, anything at all.

* * *

That same night at Uriah's house, the dinner conversation was old hat. All about integrity and what it means to be a man. "A fella knows if he's red-blooded when he's in a crunch," Pa said. Uriah was creating two-fisted scenarios in his mind, taking note of where he might fall short. Things like, if a black bear wandered into the yard, would he run or stand firm, deadlock his eyes with the beast. Or what if someone was gibbing at Ma or stealing eggs from the hutch, would he take a sock at 'em? *Yes, for sure.* But then he thought about the barn roof, and what if the wind blew a hole in it. Couldn't fix it on his own. And he knew he couldn't re-shod a horse if need be, either. By the end of dinner, Uriah pledged to himself to watch Pa do both of those things, first chance.

He wondered if other boys had to try this hard. Or were they just born to do man things, never having to think about them. He asked to be excused, scooped the leftover goulash into the slop bucket and headed for the barn to pick out the stalls, something he always did in the mornings, never at night. He didn't look at Ma or Pa, didn't want to see the show-me expressions on their faces, the curiosity bending their necks as their eyes followed him out the door.

He went straight to the stall that held the newly geld-ed yearling, patted its haunches for a while. He moved to its right side and still stroking its rump, lifted a hind leg. He fingered the bare hoof and eyed the row of shoes hanging on the nails above the workbench. He tried to picture himself sit-ting on Pa's stool—the horse's bony leg gripped between his knees—hammering a nail through the iron and into its foot. Then he let the leg fall and picked up the tine-fork, started prying dry manure from the walls. *Well, at least if a coyote came stalking through, I'd take a jab at it. Damn sure.* He gripped the fork in both hands, raised it up to his chest and poked at an imaginary fiend. "Get!" he charged and took a hefty swing. "Hightail it!"

Then, at the Lovett breakfast table, Uriah said no thank you when Ma passed him the plate of venison. Pa said, "Go on, son. It'll put some hair on your chest," then bit halfway into the sausage in his fingers. Uriah stabbed into a piece of the soft, curvy meat, then wrenched it from his fork with his teeth and gnawed ravenously, lips smacking, jaw moving like a gear. With his mouth still full, Uriah announced, "If a coyote came prowling, you can bet I'd take care of him."

Pa stopped chewing, gave an attaboy nod. And Ma said, "I'm sure you would, dear," then told him it wasn't polite to talk with food in his mouth.

* * *

For Uriah and Eva, Saturdays were full of trundling and running and knowing one another, their likes and hates. Between bouts of play, they rested under the biggest sugar maple, the only tree still holding most of its leaves, the others having succumbed to autumn's early reach. There, they talked about things they wished for, things they couldn't have. For Eva, it was pretty dresses and a house all to herself. "Maybe even a castle," she said. "On a mountain top or on the shores of Lake Superior." For Uriah, it was about strength. "Have enough muscle to fell a tree, pull back Pa's bow, or stick a hog for butcher." They drifted into simple childhood things, too, like how cold it is in the outhouse, how they'd both seen their Pa's naked in the creek. "My Pa's holy-poker's hairy and kinda floppy," Uriah said. They complained about the hard pews at church and how they both had bad dreams about Ada Williams, always thought she was lurking outside their windows. How they tried to hold going to the outhouse till the sun came up, afraid she might jump out from behind a tree, hair all tousled and ratty, trying to bite them or scratch at their eyes. With that, their conversation shifted to more intimate matters:

"You like your Ma and Pa?" Eva asked.

"Sure I do," he said. "Don't you?"

Eva didn't answer right away, just fiddled with the hoop, running her fingers over the round top. After a while, she said, "Think my Ma means well."

* * *

One early Saturday, Eva spotted Uriah trekking up the field toward her house. She ran to meet him, took the hoop from his grip and set it on the ground. "Let's go exploring today, getting tired of chasing that thing all the time."

"Where to?"

"Dunno. Let's just start walking, see where we end up." Before Uriah could respond, Eva had already started trudging north toward the woods. The sky was the color of stone and the air was moist. Even after they could no longer see anything but the thickets—behind them and ahead of them— Eva hiked with abandon, stepping high, ducking low. Uriah's heartbeat hastened as he knew Ma and Pa would not approve. Yet there was pleasure in it, too. Not so much for himself, but for Eva. He didn't understand why she was so determined, always so quick and eager. But he was glad he was with her as they broke through the branches, steering themselves to no certain destination. And never slowing, not even when Uriah asked her to.

It was between fall and winter, and the ground was still a bit spongy from the autumn rain, with each step they sunk down a little. And after clamoring over a low knoll, a brown and grassless clearing came into view. In the middle stood a slanted shack. There were spaces above and below many of the two-by-fours with makeshift chinking of oakum, grass and manure that had hardened and chipped away in random spots. Both second story windows held twelve small panels, many of them cracked with wood pieces nailed over the gaps. On the bottom floor, a single window looked out over the porch. Its mullions were bent or broken, so the crisscross pattern was hit-or-miss. At one time, the house had been painted, but the only proof was near the gable where several dingy swaths of white still showed through the black mildew. There was a thick rope tied around a metal pole and fastened to the side of the house. A sheet was pinned to it, waving and snapping in the scant breezes which refuted Uriah's assumption that the house was abandoned.

Eva saw the boy first. He was under the porch, chained to a corner post with a ramshackle collar around his neck. When she stepped toward the house, Uriah knew he couldn't say anything to stop her. Their feet made sucking noises in the mud as they neared. Across the top of the porch, the wood planks were still in place but thinned and curled up at the ends. There were two or three feet between the bottom boards and the ground, clumps of dormant grass filling the dark place, except for a much trampled area.

The boy peeked out. His eyes were black, bulging and wide set. Though he didn't want to, Uriah stepped up next to Eva, knowing that if she wasn't there, he would have already run. They met the boy's glance and held it. Beside him was an empty plate, remnants of some kind of stew smeared across the white ceramic. A dirty fork lay in the dirt and next to that, on its side, a tin cup. Uriah felt lightheaded, unsteady. He thought his knees might buckle. But Eva stood still, poised. Just as she started to take another step forward, heavy footsteps thudded from inside. They looked in that direction. The little boy, too. Then the clack of boots grew closer, and Uriah began to back away. A second later, Eva did the same. Then they hurried back toward the grove.

Back in the thicket, they squatted behind two thin spruce trees and watched intently. Though they couldn't see anyone, they heard the screen door swing open, the rusty springs moaning as the door slapped against the frame. A thick, hoarse voice banged through the trees. But the words were a muffled din of snarls and stammering, just broken, discordant sounds, as if the man's mouth and throat weren't cooperating or there was too much saliva on his tongue. Even so, the anger was clear.

They waited for the tangled noise to cease and the screen door to squeak and thump again, then they started to move out. Uriah was still breathing through his nose, heart thrashing in his ears. They had only made it a few steps before Eva shouted over her shoulder, "Leave him be, you son of a whore!" Then they ran as if the earth was burning.

They didn't vow secrecy about the boy under the porch. They didn't need to. Both knew what their father's responses would be. Pa Murray would say, "That's a family matter, best to stay out of it." And Pa Lovett would load his rifle, crash through the trees and make more trouble for the boy, good intentions or not. But keeping the secret from his folks was eating at Uriah. If the boy got sick or froze to death, it was his fault for not telling.

Two days later, Eva came to the Lovett's door, just after dinner but before the light of day had come to an end. She was genteel in asking Uriah if his chores were done and if he could go trundling for a while. Ma asked her to step inside and offered her milk and a biscuit which she politely declined. Pa told Uriah "No," that he couldn't keep romping away all his spare time. "Too much fun turns a boy into a pigeon-heart," he said, then turned to Eva and asked her to come back and see them again soon. Uriah was a little relieved, as he knew why Eva was really there. Now, he could tell himself it was Pa's fault he didn't try to rescue the boy.

"Manners, boy. See your guest out," Pa said.

As soon as the two of them were outside, Eva spewed out her worries. "What if a black bear gets him? Or a cougar comes down from the Porkies? Or his funny talking Pa beats him bloody?" Her voice was strained, all treble. "We should've let him free."

"I know. Been feeling bad about it. But you can't go back there by yourself. We'll go on Saturday, you hear?"

"I can't wait till then. I'm going now." She turned and ran. Uriah knew it was pointless to call her back.

The clothesline had been taken down, and there were several boards nailed across the opening where the boy had been.

Eva knew they were gone, but she looked through the wood slats anyway, trying to convince herself that the boy really existed. She cupped her hands around her eyes and leaned in. She was alone, but still, fear of the boy or his queer sounding Pa jumping out made her shake. She pulled at the boards until one of them came loose then crawled into the stark space. There was a round indentation in the dirt where she settled in, the soiled plate beside her and next to it, the overturned cup.

Eva stayed under the porch a long while. She leaned her head back and stared out at the vast woodlands, the hilltops rising up behind them like giant loaves of bread. It's not the same, she told herself. You can climb back out whenever you want. Then she guessed at the boy's thoughts, his dreams and hopes as he studied the same landscape, day after day, far reaching meadows to the east and rows of fat firs to the west. Somewhere deep in her guts, she could feel the boy's approval, swore he knew she was there. It was big-as-life, in her teeth and bones. When the rain set in, she stuck her hands out, letting the mist gather on her fingers. She rubbed the cup and plate clean, hugged them against her chest. Then, she promised God, heart and soul, that one day, she'd love her own child fully, guard it like a soldier.

Chapter 13
Coming of Age

Come spring of '55, Eva Murray would turn fourteen. She was allowed to attend school for just one more year, a compromise Ma groveled for. The summer before, Pa began his badgering, reminding them about the deadline nearly every day. Aiming a finger at his wife, he'd say, "She's in the fields come May," then waggle the same finger at Eva. He'd scowl at them before returning to his bowl, sopping up the last of his stew with a torn bread piece.

Eva wanted to tell Mr. Brandt that her time at school would be short-lived, but she was embarrassed. She hoped he knew that she loved being there and that she mulled over his words most every night, letting herself dream big dreams. She crinkled her brow harder every time he looked her way, hoping he saw her thinking hard about the passages he read aloud, the ones unlocking worlds of wonder and exception, betrayal and pride—*The House of the Seven Gables, David Copperfield,* and *The Scarlet Letter.* She wished, too, that he could see the scenes that unfold at her house when school is over, especially the one when she sat by Ma at the table, recounting the day's lessons to her. "Listen to this," Eva said, clutching the case-bound book like someone might rip it away from her. "'The scarlet letter was her passport into regions where other women dared not tread.'" Then she pulled the book down from her face. "See, Ma? Hester was fearless, just like—"

"That'll do." Pa bolted up, his chair scudding then toppling over. He pounded toward the kitchen, his bare feet thumping against the floor. His outbursts weren't new, but the unpredictability was. Though they still hastened Eva's pulse, the thrill of Hester Prynne's determination was irresistible. She angled into Ma's ear, and read low—

"'Shame, despair, solitude,'" then snapped the page and continued, "'these had been her teachers, and they had made her strong,'" but not low enough—

"Enough!" Pa smashed his plate against the sink, and Eva quickly folded Hawthorne into the hem of her skirt, trying to look contrite. She dropped her head and pushed the mashed potatoes around her own plate. The vision of independence rollicked in her stomach and crept up her throat, frothing like cream. She held a hand across her mouth, afraid she might nicker—a cooped up pony set free.

It wasn't too long after that Pa started showing up in places he hadn't before. Like when Eva stepped out of the outhouse or when she was getting into her nightclothes. And the first time he followed her down to the creek. That's when she felt the pang of rebellion inside her, just being born, a hatchling squirming in the thick of a broken yolk sac and brittle shell pieces. Not yet ready to slither or hiss or strike.

There was a towel and bathing cap in her hand, so Pa knew she was going to wash. Besides, she had gone to the creek on Saturday mornings for as long as anyone could remember. Deep down, she understood why he was trailing her. Ever since her chest had stiffened some, Pa started standing closer to her, his eyes shiny and darting back and forth, like he could see the berry lumps forming under her dress. And when the dark hairs started sprouting between her legs, Eva swore he could sniff out the leaking that sometimes made her itch and fidget. The image of a stray sheepdog flashed in her mind, like the one she'd seen in Mackinaw City once, twitching its nose at a steaming mound of horse dung in the road.

On the wooded path to the water, Eva stopped walking and looked back to see what Pa would do. This was all new. She didn't know how to handle it. She could feel his careful movement, lingering by a big cedar then skittering across the dirt to a spread-out pine. She wanted to see what it looked like, him having to duck and amble for cover. So she paused. His clever timing was thrown off, and the crackle of his boot against the forest floor sounded out.

Eva felt nauseous. Yet she had to go through with it, couldn't skip out now. None of it made any sense. Pa was hunting her down like a hungry coyote, but she's thinking of how best not to anger him. It was a twisted game of hide and seek. Inside, Eva screamed so hard it rattled her bowels. Dear God, is this happening? she thought. I have to take my clothes off and pretend he's not watching? His bony face and patchy black whiskers peeking around a tree like a skunk, doing Lord knows what to himself.

When Eva approached the river's edge, she slowed down, thought about trying to slip on the agate stones, hopefully landing on a pointed shale piece. If she could open up her shin then maybe he'd leave her be. She sucked in deep through her nose, stared at the tangled mass of tree roots on the far bank while reaching back to where her collar and sleeves were gathered into a cuff, then unbuttoned the nightdress and let it fall. She didn't hurry or waiver, just picked up the slab of lye, pulled back her shoulders and stepped into the water, eyes fixed on the snarled roots. The autumn wind was chilly and the water cold, and her mind eased a little, knowing it was likely one of her last river baths of the season. She squatted down in the shallow bed of the stream and waded up to her waist, turned to the side then dropped down on her knees. That felt less vulnerable. She doused the cold water on her belly and against her chest, then her face and neck. Though she didn't dare look Pa's way, she stopped splashing for a moment to listen for him.

Snap, crack.

Out of fear and a warped sense of duty, she started sploshing around again. But the tinge of defiance within her had grown bigger now, and it rasped its scales together, seething like never before. It was on the move, sidewinding through her entrails. As she lathered the lye wedge in her hands, she heard a low moan from far off. She thought about Pa kneading himself like a lump of dough, the way Uriah told her he does it when he sees a girl bending over at the mercantile or a woman switching her skirt. The image made her stomach churn like ale.

For a few weeks afterward, Eva didn't bathe in the river. She used the washtub, blamed it on the weather turning colder. But she could feel Pa's anger growing every time she did. One morning, after Ma came inside, full buckets in each hand, Pa declared, "Washtub ain't good no more. One of you two put a leak in it." He stepped to the tub, drew his hand across the slats that he must have jimmied apart. "I'll fix it in a week or two," he said, eyes cast down as he lied.

"But I just used it for—" Ma stopped, stroked the side of her head with her pointer finger. "I could have sworn it was only yesterday."

Chapter 14
The Poetry Group

After the hard winters in northern Michigan, school ended early on days marked for spring planting, took many hands to get the peas, beets and spinach into the hard ground. On one of those shortened days, Uriah and Eva straggled after class, giddy and anxious:

"We like the stories you read, Mr. Brandt," Eva blurted. And for a fleeting moment, she forgot about the life growing inside her, didn't blush or wonder if Mr. Brandt could sense all the goings-on beneath her linen dress.

"And the poems," Uriah said, straining to look Basil in the face.

"Me too," Basil said. He had a feeling he knew what was coming and thought it best for them to work through the discomfort of their request. Eva traced a crevice in the floor with her toe. Beside her, Uriah gnawed on his thumbnail. "Well, I must be heading home," Basil said. Then he began gathering the papers on his desk and opened his satchel. "There's tilling to do."

"We're hoping to meet," Uriah uttered, head down. "After school sometimes. To read and talk more about—"

"Look at me, boy."

Uriah lifted his eyes, "—about Mr. Irving and Mr. Wordsworth." He paused. "Y'know, without any clodhoppers around?"

Basil couldn't help laughing. "Oh, I know alright." He

studied their ardent expressions, soaking up the modesty. "Certainly we can," he said. "I'd like that." Eva glanced at Uriah with wide eyes, her lips bunched to one side. What a sight to behold, Basil thought. Teaching all day, plowing all afternoon, the weekend harvests—it's all worth it for a moment like this one.

After they left, Basil thought to himself, it's a pretty good life. Then his thoughts shifted to Stella, and he pictured her pursed lips as he tells her about another commitment he's made, needing to spend even more time away from home, from her.

* * *

"You aren't happy." Stella's voice and face were resolute. It was her intuition and plainspoken manner that Basil fell in love with, but now, he resented it. Even more, he hated being dissected. And she knew that, yet here she sits, scrutinizing every word, every gesture. Basil swirled the spoon inside his mug, several coffee droplets spattered onto the table; he stared at the dark brown globules.

"Why, Stella?" he spoke uneasily, "because I'm reading poetry with some kids?" Basil knew the ruse was thin, but he persisted. "Little selfish, don't you think?" Even as he talked, he damned himself. He told himself, just concede, you wobbly milksop. In her reticence, Stella's despair was palpable, curdling the air between them. Still, Basil jutted out his chin. "That's what I thought," he said.

Stella took the spoon from him, set it down on the table then placed her hands over his. "As to why I've yet to bear your child, I am tormented," she said. "And the sadness you feel, Basil, it's mine too." He clenched the muscles in his hand, and her grip loosened. "If your idea of strength lies in avoidance, my love, you are sadly misled," she said, then shook her head.

Basil worked hard to remain expressionless, but it was getting harder to hide in the shrinking space between backbone and pretend courage. He could feel the infertility staking its claim, growing louder in their quiet house. It was everywhere—on the edge of every sentence, the flames flicking in the woodstove, the wax of the candlesticks, the picture frames, the daubing between the logs. Their lungs were filled with fruitlessness.

Basil rose from the table, announcing that he was headed to the stream. He veered to the bedroom to gather his towel and soap bar, feeling Stella's eyes on his back. Once alone, he rested his forehead against the armoire, placed his open palms against the smooth wood, pushing until its front legs lifted off the ground. I'll come clean soon, he tried to convince himself. I'll come in from the field early, beckon her to the table and blab it quick—"Stella, maybe it's me." But her despair was like skin now. He knew he'd waited too long. If he confessed, she'd hate him. How could she not after letting her bear the blame, year after year. For letting her fight not to cry whenever a child came near.

The clank of pots and dishes sounded through the house, and he knew Stella was busying herself with dinner like she always did, letting him make his way outside so he could steal away unscathed. He couldn't decide if he still admired her endurance or loathed it more than anything in the world.

He reached the bend in the shallow brook where he and Stella sometimes bathed. There was a light wind, the current slow moving. On either side of the bank, dozens of slim maple trees stood tall, their foliage newly blossomed, little clusters of buds everywhere and the earth soft, damp. He stripped off his boots and long-drawers then made his way to the middle of the stream where he lowered himself into the toothy silt, head and neck above the surface. Through the clear water, his pale genitals were prominent and his pubic hair thick and dark. For a long while, he stared at his pelvis, reliving the day he was cutting up that hardy oak and struck the impenetrable knot.

And now, as he squats in the placid water, listening to it ripple over the sediment in the shallow spots, he wonders how life would be if he had aimed the maul's head an inch to the left. Would he have a son? Or if he'd had the courage to tell Doctor Henley about lancing himself, how old would his daughter be now? As he lathers up, the smell of ash and lard drifts about, and he looks between his legs, wondering at the seemingly lifeless flesh hanging down, the power it holds to break his spirit, his marriage.

* * *

With much maneuvering, Pa finally yielded. Eva could go to her poetry group on Saturdays after her chores were done. Though Basil had petitioned for more participants, there were no other takers, so the club of literary inquisitors was only a trio. Every weekend, in the lane between the reedy schoolyard and the northern timberlands, the highbrows took flight, sans clodhoppers. At first, Eva and Uriah puttered through the readings. But with Basil's guidance, soon enough the verses smoothed out some and then they were reciting the likes of Longfellow like seasoned orators, the syllables rising and falling like mandolin chords.

By the time that Spring had fully sprung, Basil said to Stella, "The poetry group is really quite a joy," then he invited her to go with him. What he wanted to say is "Come see me at my best, in my ivory tower where I put aside my inadequacies for an hour, where the man you thought you married has been hiding." During those hours in the grove, there's no barrenness, no secrets, just rhyme and revelation. Basil knew those Saturday morning circles were more for him than Uriah or Eva. And from her soft "no thank you" and heavy, blank eyes, it seemed Stella knew, too.

* * *

*A child said, What is the grass? fetching it to me
with full hands; How could I answer the child?*

Uriah was reading aloud from Whitman when Pa Murray's carriage approached, clapping and jostling as it neared.

"L'il late, Brandt," Murray called out. "Don't you think?"

"Of course," Basil replied. "Just finishing."

Murray halted the horses, surveyed the scene. "Sittin' mighty close to the kids, too, wouldn't you say?" Basil watched Eva rise, quietly glide to the wagon and climb in. Murray said nothing else, just snapped the horsewhip with one hand and with the other, patted his daughter's knee. Eva stared straight ahead, the brittle cones crackling under the coach's wheels as it lurched forward.

"Good evening, Eva," Basil offered. But she sat like an effigy. Both Uriah and Basil looked on, watching until the Murrays disappeared behind a clump of pine trees. "That's all for today, boy," Basil said.

Uriah's breath flattened out, and he slumped down into a cluster of milkweeds, the hairy leaves brushing against his face.

"Sorry, son. Just not in the mood now." Basil stalked out of the covert, into the noonday. He glanced back to see that Uriah hadn't moved, that he was watching Basil walk away, the book of Whitman's poems balanced in his lap. For an instant, Basil let himself appreciate the boy's admiration. It made him feel noble.

Chapter 15
Eva in the Outhouse

Eva had little doubt that she was with child, two missed periods and heaving nearly every day. Always running behind the house, trying to stifle the retch sounds with her hands, vomit spewing through her fingers. It was an overcast morning, gray and damp, when a ravenous urge finally swamped her—she had to desecrate herself, just had to. Get even with God for letting Pa make her feel so dirty. She figured that a fallen girl should stink like hell, be filthy, talk vulgar. So instead of wiping away the sticky contents of her stomach, she let it trickle down her arms, settle on her skin. The chyme was milky and tepid, and the sour smell made her gag all over again.

As the vomit dried, Eva lifted her nightdress with one of her sullied hands and with the other, scooped up the damp soil at her feet and smeared it on her bare legs, caked it in her crotch. Then she gathered more, reached up and slathered it across her breasts, flinching as her skin was pulled taut, hurling vile words under her breath at no one—"Cussed cockchafer! Dratted lickfinger!"—as if Reverend Hiram was exorcising a demon out of her. And with her back teeth grinding like a pepper mill, she called herself a tramp and her Pa a randy son of a bitch.

There, God, happy now?

Chapter 16
Less Respect, More Fear

At first, no one gave it much thought, not even Mr. Lovett. He just figured all kids were a bit delicate, both girls and boys. It was back on Uriah's eleventh birthday that his gentle ways were made his own, loud and clear. Basil prompted the class to sing "Happy Birthday" then turned to Uriah. "It's your special day, you choose recess."

Anguished, Uriah thought, just say stickball, like you're supposed to. His heart loped, his skin turned clammy. He thought, no, then wrestled within. Tell the truth. Be a man. Before he could talk himself down, he uttered, "Can we read more? From Walden? Maybe Hawthorne?" Then he saw the surprise on Basil's face, like he was puzzled but wanted to look approving.

"Well, we could do that Saturday," Basil said. "Thought you might want to—"

Uriah put his head down and Basil quickly changed course. "Certainly," he said. "Let's read some." Uriah could see him quietly nudging the bag of balls and bats back under his desk. All the kids groaned, boys louder than girls, deriding Uriah under their breaths. But Basil shushed them, gave them his teacher look—narrow eyes, scrunched up face. That week after Sunday services, Basil tugged on Mr. Lovett's shirt, and Uriah picked up on the hint from his teacher's awkward glance. They needed privacy. He walked ahead of them but curiosity overshadowed prudence, and he ducked behind the archway, out of sight, not out of earshot.

"The boys are calling him an odd-stick," Basil said. "Really giving him a go."

"Any of 'em clean his plow yet?"

"Almost. I tell them to skedaddle, but the truth is, sir, if they ever set their minds to beating the boy, they'll do it when I'm not around."

"Thinking him soft, I s'pose?"

"That's the whole of it."

Uriah's heart pounded hard. He peeked around the doorway, saw his father rubbing his stubbly chin as Basil rocked on his heels. He heard all the "howdy-do's" as the God-fearing folks of Bellwether shuffled past him into the morning shine. Then, just the three of them were left alone in the chapel, except for Reverend Hiram still standing at the pulpit, gathering up the loose pages of his tattered bible.

In a dragging lull, Uriah's father spoke again, "Think I'll keep him home this harvest, Mr. Brandt, let things simmer down."

"But Mr. Lovett, he's a bright boy. I don't think—"

"Ain't your place to say. Mind yourself."

* * *

At supper—though Uriah knew why—he asked anyway. "Pa, I never stayed home for harvest before." His voice cracked. "How come now?" A glimmer of hope flashed through him, like maybe he'd misunderstood. Maybe there is word of an early winter, that's all. And Pa is pulling him from school because he truly needs his help.

"'Cause I said, boy."

And the glimmer died instantly.

* * *

Uriah's hiatus started the next day. His mother woke him early. "Get dressed. Your Pa's waiting in the barn." She kept her eyes fixed just above his head. "Hurry up now, child. Breakfast is getting cold. You know how he gets," she said, then stepped to the door and paused. After a deep breath, she turned to him, offered half a smile.

"What is it, Ma?"

"You make Pa proud out there." She stepped through the door, pulled it closed. For a long while, she stood on the other side. Uriah watched her silhouette through the thin gap between the floor and the bottom of the door. Then she slipped away quickly, like a mouse changing course, the shadow replaced by the yellow slant of dawn.

After dressing, Uriah scurried to the kitchen and sat at the table alone, a plate of bacon and eggs and steaming grits awaiting him. He scooped up a heap of grits, dabbed them into the orange yolk and raised it to his mouth—

"Boy! Bring my rifle, quick!" Pa's voice crashed through the house. Uriah dropped the spoon mid-air and ran to the corner of the loft where the rifle leaned against the wall. He was afraid of guns. When he was five, Grandpa Lovett had called him to the stables to watch a lame colt be put down. He said, "You need to know about these things." Uriah watched as his Grandpa traced an imaginary "X" with his finger, from the horse's left ear to right eye, then right ear to left eye, then placed the barrel just above the intersection. The bullet thumped into the colt's skull, but it didn't die, just fell to the ground, scouring its legs against the gravel, trying to stand up, trying to live. Then Grandpa reloaded and shot the colt again. It grunted several times, seizing hard and slow, like poured molasses.

Uriah grabbed the rifle—a Kentucky Flintlock slender as a finger and glossy from Pa's diligent polishing—and the small wood box next to it. He put the ammunition under his arm and held the gun away from his body in upturned palms like it was made of glass, then he stepped lightly but hasti-ly outside. Pa Lovett was standing in front of the henhouse, hands on his bulky hips, looking in, scratching the back of his head. The chickens bawked wildly, shuffling about the pen. Rumpled feathers wafted through the open wire fence up top. Without looking Uriah's way, Pa said, "That you, son?"

"Yes, sir."

Pa took a step back and glanced at him. "You're holding that gun like it'll bite you," he said. "We gotta coon in there. And it's out in daylight, so it's likely rabid."

Uriah's breaths quickened. *Don't make me do this.*

Pa took the rifle, set its stock on the ground, barrel point-ing skyward. He pulled a dented red tin from the wood box and dumped the black grainy powder into the muzzle. Uriah watched his deep concentration with mixed emotions—fear, respect and a bit of gall—his father's fat, pink tongue peeking from the corner of his mouth.

"I can't shoot," Uriah said. "Best if you do it."

Pa said nothing, just stuffed the metal ball into the cylin-der and reached for the ramrod. His face slackened. "Where's the start rod, boy?" Uriah played dumb and looked around, knowing he'd forgotten it. Mumbling under his breath, Pa picked up a stick and plunged the ammunition down the barrel. He set the flintlock and shoved the piece into Uriah's hands. The emotions tipped—less respect, more fear.

"Pa, I can't—"

"'Bout time you tried, son. Hear that rascal hissing? You want it killing the whole damn flock? Now, I'll roil it out of there, then you blast him." He shuffled backward to the side of the coop. "Set her at half cock," he coached, "and step back some." Uriah raised the gun, unwieldy in his grip. "That's it. Now push her against your shoulder. And focus." Pa lifted his arms above his head, angled them toward the henhouse. "Ready?" he yelled.

Uriah's hands shook wildly. And he lowered the gun.

"Take aim, boy!'"

He raised it again, thinking, I can't do this.

Pa Lovett slammed his fists against the shackly coop, beating it like a drum, and whooping a frenzied war cry. From the A-framed roof, twigs and leaves slid to the ground, several chickens flapped through the small, oblong entry. And the raccoon followed. Its beady eyes shone wet and wide amid its black mask. It scampered down the wood plank and darted after the slowest hen, lashing out with nimble claws, snarling like a mad dog.

"He's out, Pa!" Uriah tried to steady, but he shuddered hard, and the rifle's stock struck his cheekbone. The throbbing made his eyes blur. To wipe them, he lowered the gun a second time. When they cleared, he saw Pa looming over him, hairy arms across his thick chest. Uriah marked the crestfallen look in his eyes and knew that he'd never be able to shoot now. The frustration overtook him, and he began to cry, trying to hide his face in the crook of his elbow, knowing that his mettle had never really matched his hankerings, not yet, anyway.

Pa Lovett ripped the rifle from his grasp, dropped to one knee and tilted his head toward his shoulder, the rifle balanced between. He plucked back the hammer and fired. The blast echoed through the farmlands. Uriah lowered his arm from his eyes to see the creature wriggling, twitching. It clicked savagely then mewled like a newborn. The gray-brown fur darkened as the blood issued forth, then it stilled. Beside it, the mauled hen lay listless.

Pa Lovett picked up his fallen hat—the curling brim and dusty ribbon tight against the crown—plopped it atop his head. Uriah studied his father's face, watched the aspiration drain from him. Then Pa veered east toward the barn and over his shoulder said, "Bury 'em both. Put your gloves on first." His voice flat, wooden.

"Yes, sir."

Before Pa disappeared, Uriah called after him, "You walking the perimeter this morning?"

"Not today, boy."

"Alright, Pa." Uriah tried to sound stoic. He donned his own hat, much less worn, and lumbered to the house for his gloves. Then he thought he saw Ma duck from the window. His heart sank even further.

"What's all the commotion out there?" she called from the kitchen.

"Ain't nothing," he answered. "Just a coon. Pa took care of it."

"Pesky things," she said. "Wished they'd all jump into the big lake and drop like rocks." Uriah knew she wasn't speaking of him but couldn't help but wonder if maybe she sort of was, accidental like. He took his gloves off the highboy and crept past her.

Outside, he bent over the animals, the raccoon's eyes were sleek like marbles and its coat was slippery and matted. He picked up the wounded hen by its yolk-yellow feet, toes like rubber. The white plumage was spattered red and the feathers were coarse and tousled. Then it lurched once. And Uriah did, too. "She ain't dead yet," he said aloud and walked across the yard, down the slope that led to the cabbage patch just past the barn. "This is a private thing," he spoke as if the hen might understand. "No one needs to see." He laid the bleeding bird in a sedgy stretch, its thin head perked upward. Tears formed, but he would not let them fall. Not for pride's sake but rather the dignity of the bird.

He wanted to scream out to his father, to everyone, "My strength is big! You just don't see it!" He reared the shovel high, arms bent out in triangles. The hen peered into his eyes, light glinting off the shovel's metal tip. "God, just one fell swoop, please," he whispered. He sucked in through his nose, fast and hard, then thrust downward with all his might.

Uriah dug a shallow grave, set the lifeless foul in slow then stroked its crimped feathers a couple of times. He patted down the stirred-up earth and covered it with ryegrass and thistle. Resting on the handle of the shovel, he made a cross in the mound of dirt and weeds with his boot. In the distance, he spotted Pa, strolling the perimeter, after all. Several geese flew overhead in a perfect "V" and Uriah looked up, shielded his eyes from the sun, listening to those in back honking at the skein, urging them southward. And he wondered if things would ever be the same.

Chapter 17
Tending to Eva

The night Basil visited the Murrays, making a plea for Eva to stay in school, Mr. Murray was a mannequin. "Your daughter, she's bright as a whip," Basil said. Then he scooted his chair along the pine wood, facing Murray head on. "She needs to finish school, sir."

"No." Murray turned to the fire. "She's turnin' fourteen. We had a deal."

"If you please, sir—"

"No." Pa Murray's eyes glinted with furor. His coolness made Eva shrink down.

"I'm simply making a case for—"

"Coffee, Mr. Brandt?" Ma Murray twittered between them, pot in hand.

"No thank you," Basil said, angling around her. "She's a bright girl, and—"

"Go to your room, Eva," Pa Murray said, a colorless pitch.

Eva obeyed but before turning to go, she locked eyes with Basil and lipped, "Sorry." After she'd gone, Pa Murray vaulted to his feet as if to square off, but instead, started pacing wildly.

"Thank you, Mr. Brandt, for tending to Eva," Ma Murray said. Mr. Murray stopped abruptly. The silence bore down on his wife until she looked away. Then he resumed his rigid march, Ma Murray flinching with every clack of his heel.

"Good evening," Basil said. Though he showed himself out, for Ma Murray's sake, he hovered at the front window, peering in from the porch for a while, watching as she tapped her worn brogan against the table leg and tugged at her thin, yellow hair. Pa Murray continued his hasty cadence, eyes poring over his wife like a current. Then, just like that, he traipsed from the room.

Ma Murray sat still, head cocked to the side as if listening to a secret. In the periphery, Basil could see Pa Murray hesitate at Eva's door before stomping past it. Another door snapped shut, and Ma Murray dropped her shoulders, planted her hand on the table and muffled her sobs with her frock. After a minute or two, she straightened, tucked a tired curl behind her ear and began clearing the table.

Chapter 18
With Palms Up

Of all people, it was Ada who kept Hiram buoyed. He would have told her so if he thought she'd be moved by knowing. Her allegiance to Christ was honest. Not on display like many folks in Bellwether. She sought the light of God simply because she wanted to know Him. Every Sunday, Hiram greeted her on his way into the church where she sat on the steps just outside the doors, waiting for worship to begin—shaggy hair pulled back; big, black bible in her hands—and that's where she stayed. Time and again, he had pleaded for her to come inside. "The Lord ain't in those walls," she'd say. "But he's in you, Hiram. In your words. And I'm here to hear them. Plenty loud out here on the steps."

When the first winter season came that Ada began listening from outside, a late November chill had clamped down on all of northern Michigan. One bitter Sunday, Hiram stopped mid-sermon and with all eyes on him, descended the pulpit and walked down the aisle. He opened the big, wood doors, and an icy gust pushed through the congregation, making some of the women and children gasp. Ada stumbled some as she'd been leaning in, ear pressed to the door. Hiram extended his hand to her. She declined. Then he took off his greatcoat, pulled it across her shoulders.

After that, he never invited Ada in again, just made it part of his preparation ritual for Sunday services through the winter months—lay out the burlap piece, then the thick wool blanket; and on top, place the tin of hot coffee, which she always left empty.

She heard people calling her a witch, listened as they gathered near her house, shouting, "You're Satan's finger!" Still, she drew strength from the cooked-up judgment. Like when she stood at Hiram's doorstep with a three-foot muskie in her hands, holding it in both hands like an offering, her eyes cloudy, tired. Someone had thrown the fish through her only window. It was beautiful, silver with thin, green stripes on its flank. Hiram took it from her, stepped inside and set it on the table, hoping she would follow.

He turned back to see her standing in the same spot, still reaching out, palms up, as if the fish were still in them. He returned to the porch and sat on the edge, legs dangling down. It took a minute or two, but Ada joined him, keeping a sizable space between them. She asked if he'd help her fix the glass in her window. She started to cry but filled her lungs, held her breath until it passed. Hiram's instinct was to put his arm around her, tell her it would be okay. But he knew she'd coil at his touch. Instead, he promised to start on the window come morning, said he'd fry up the muskie and bring the filets with him.

"They shouted out, 'Pagan' as they ran away," she blurted. "Sounded like children." She sucked in and held it again. Then exhaled. "That means, they'll never stop. Next generation is learning to hate me, too. Seems like folks are always gonna cure their ills by chumping me. It's the town's habit. And telling the truth don't make a difference. They know darn well Reverend Williams deserted them, left the parish high and dry. Not to mention me and Elinor."

Hiram waited. Let her speak her mind, he thought. The buzz of cicadas swelled up, floated around them. And a tree frog let out a short trill.

Then, in an even pitch, Ada said, "Bible says the good

Lord won't give you more than you can handle. But sometimes, when the blows keep coming, I think He's getting mighty close."

"You're not a scapegoat, Ada." Hiram paused. "You're a memorial. You're here to remind Bellwether of what they did. It's a hard calling. And it's not fair. But you already know the reward isn't in this life." Hiram still remembers how his compassion made her fidget. How she thanked him for his kindness, bowed at the waist when she left, running a hand over her slick, snarled hair. She suffered more than anyone in Bellwether and lived with towering humility yet loved God in earnest while neighbors pulled their children closer whenever she walked by. But Ada never withered in their presence. Because of her, Hiram discovered that faith went deepest for those who bled most.

Chapter 19
Wasteland

Night after night, Basil made love to Stella. He still found pleasure in seeing her bow her back, writhing beneath his weight. With each fruitless gyre, she moaned softly, almost whimpering. The moon hung high, casting white light over their tangled bodies. In the fall and winter, the bitter frost clung to the windows, and in the spring and summer, the balmy air slid through the house, welcome and unseen. As always, when Basil eventually let himself go, Stella pushed into his thighs, clutching his hips in despair. And as he trembled in the sensation, he knew she would turn her head to dab away the tears, thinking herself unworthy. A wasteland.

* * *

Though Basil could shift the blame for their infertility, he could not hoodwink Stella as far as his self-doubts, uncertainties. She knew them all. And she told him so:

"You're not a buckle to be polished, Basil Brandt. The more you keep living like you're perfect, the sooner you're going to cave in. You don't have to keep carving out every damn word before you talk. For once, speak your mind! Tell a bootlicker, he's a bootlicker. And stop avoiding situations where you might fail. Isn't it tiring, Basil? Why didn't you go hunting with Oscar when he asked? Or play in the horseshoe tournament?"

Basil waited out the pause.

"You thought Oscar might outshoot you, that's why. He might find out you aren't a good aim. And what's more, you didn't want to lose at horseshoes. Heaven forbid that the marvelous Mr. Brandt, farmer and teacher extraordinaire, has flaws like the rest of us. That he might even be unremarkable—"

Basil reared up his fist, not high, but clenched tight. It felt oafish, like he had no fingers, just thumbs. "What's the matter, Basil?" Stella shouted. "You unsure now, too? The air was brittle, as if it might crack open. And their short-winded breaths bumped against the walls. Basil looked at her balled up hands, then his own fist shaking in the air like it had a fever. Stella's face was trembling.

Slowly, Basil brought down his arm, and Stella exhaled through tight lips. He looked out the window. "Sometimes I wish I could tear open my chest, just pull it apart, skin and bones. Let everyone see what a fraud I am."

Chapter 20
The Lecher

It was unseasonably humid the night several rocks crashed against the front of the Brandt's house. A caustic voice bellered, "Get out here, teacher man!" The words were sharp as blades. Basil scrambled from his slumber and dashed toward the noise, Stella at his heels. In their front yard stood Pa Murray, wobbling and sputtering. Basil opened the door and stepped onto the porch.

"Let me take you home, Mr. Murray," Basil called out.

"Fuck you." Mr. Murray gathered his balance then charged at them. Basil braced for the affront, planting his feet and pushing Stella all the way behind him. But as soon as Murray came upon him, he stopped. The two men were face to face, Basil looming large and Murray's dearth made clear. Basil smelled the rye and oak on Murray's breath, tasted the burn of spirits on his own tongue. They glared at one another until finally Murray thumped Basil's chest with his middle finger, took a step back and hissed, "You're a lecher." Stella loosened her grip on Basil's shirt and peered out from behind him.

"Well look there, even your wife knows."

"Let's get you home," Basil repeated, less amiably. Murray rasped then spat his gall in Basil's face. Calmly, Basil wiped the sputum from his beard, about-faced, and walked Stella back inside. Through the window, he watched until Murray stumbled away. When he turned to Stella, she tilted her head one way, then the other, and her gaze was pensive, deliberating. Basil stood solid, unblinking. Then she stepped to him, swabbed at his cheek.

* * *

Eva came to school a few times in April but come May, not at all. The rapture for poetry seemed to have melted away with the last of the snow. From then on, Basil only saw the Murrays at Sunday services, always seated in a pew on the other side of the drafty church and Pa Murray always wearing a sideways sneer.

For a couple of months, Pa Murray tried launching a campaign to raze Basil's honor but besides a few murmurs at church and a leer or two at the mercantile, the crusade never gained momentum. Sometimes, though, in the midst of a cordial chat, certain neighbors would hold Basil's gaze just a bit too long, like they were searching for signs, looking for contrition. But there was none. In those moments, he held Stella's hand a bit tighter, took in the lemon verbena that she drizzled on her nape. It smelled like assurance, like home.

Chapter 21
The Color of Earth

Not telling Ma hurt just as much as the growing baby did, pushing and kicking, making room for itself. Eva had always told Ma everything. Keeping this a secret made her feel even dirtier, though a part of her wondered if Ma knew. Did they simply not dare talk of such unholy things? Even so, Eva understood Pa's sin could only stay hidden a little while longer.

For three days, there was a glimmer of hope. Maybe she was wrong about being with child on account of the stains in her pantalettes. She was desperate to believe it, even told herself, if I'm bleeding, there's no baby. At first glance, though, she knew something was different about the blood—the texture, the amount. So, she simply stopped looking, let the delusion linger a few more days. She even let her daydreams flare again, the ones when she is wearing a bridal gown—ivory taffeta and buckram trimming, puffy shoulders and lacy sleeves—and the men whisper "Damnation" while the women lean into one another in the pews, saying things like, "Ain't she something." The same dreams that disappeared the night she felt Pa's seed taking purchase inside her.

Eva resisted looking for three days, that's when something solid slipped out, a stringy clump. Only then did she trek to the outhouse to see. She set the lantern on the ground, hoisted up her skirt and peeled down her linen drawers. Squatting on the bench, she bent down over the light, held the undergarment in the flood of yellow light. It was just like it was a couple days before, the blood hadn't soaked through but was speckled. When she angled in close, she saw that the color was off—bright red, not brown. Eva forced herself to look at the glob, long as a pinky finger. She began to pray, pushing out the words so hard that her body strained.

"Please take away the suffering, Lord," she begged. The honesty poured forth like a river undammed. And she confessed that she often hoped that the baby didn't come. The clear admission took her breath away. She tried covering up the guilt with good thoughts, rocking it to sleep in Ma's big sewing chair, stroking its cheeks with the back of her hand. She said aloud, "Coming clean isn't making things easier, God. Sure feels nice for a second, though. Can't remember when I last felt anything but bad."

The air was cool when Eva stepped outside. Her skin was clammy, and she was scared, like when it's dark and she has to pat the walls trying to get to the kerosene lamp, heart pounding, waiting to smack into a door, trip over a chair. Or for Ada Williams to jump at her.

Back in bed, when her pelvis clamped down angry, she pulled her knees to her chest, trying to squeeze through the twinges. She knew the baby was dying, nothing else could hurt that way. And she knew that this was bigger than her. The baby was scampering to Heaven as an angel, never needing to take a breath. The confusion thundered loud. Though she had wished it gone so many times, her heart was breaking that she wasn't dying, too. As she lay there writhing, letting God's will take hold, she thought about the baby never having to hurt, never being betrayed or losing hope. Those thoughts helped her endure the ache, even as her lower back was tearing open as if someone was wedging rocks in her spine. Then a fire flared in her womb. She started crawling.

When she had inched her way into plain view, Ma leapt from her chair, crochet needles tinking to the floor. She took two steps toward her then dropped to her hands and knees, got face to face. She lifted Eva's chin with a shaking finger. "You're losing the babe, ain't you?"

Eva stared through her—the parted lips, face pulling tight around the mouth as she spoke the unspeakable. A wash of mercy amidst all the throbbing. She managed to nod before slumping to the ground with a gangly thud, twisting like a hooked worm.

Seizing, hemorrhaging.

The lifeless mass was ropy, like oysters and jelly—the color of earth—so peculiar atop the wood planks. She wailed just once, but it hovered in the house. She felt the baby lifting up, making its way home, a big piece of her going with it.

Pa had found his way home from the Brandt place but passed out, sitting upright against the barn like he sometimes does. Surely it was Eva's shriek that brought him to. As he stumbled inside, Ma was guiding Eva back to her bed. She shut the door behind them, both of them knowing Pa would soon push his ear against it, listen hard, then begin his mad pacing. Ma wet a cloth in the basin and held it on Eva's forehead, humming the same three notes—two low, one high—over and over. Eva felt shredded, body and mind. And the emptiness was like a battle wound. "Never figured babies had to be pushed out if they're dead."

"All babies are worth the pains of labor," Ma replied. The fury of the cramps was abating some, and Eva could better see the craze in Ma's eyes. Whenever Pa's measured footsteps made the floor creak just outside the door, Ma's cheeks flushed hotter. Though there was rage in Eva, too, her exhaustion dulled it some. From Ma, the indignation poured out, clawing at her throat like a feral cat, as if there was no air left in the world.

Pa was in the kitchen now, jostling through the shelves. "Where's the Makers Mark, Goddammit?" Eva had seen Ma dump it just after he left that night. Her skin started burning, thinking of the hell to come. Ma jerked her head in the direction of the ruckus then slowly turned back to Eva. She gently placed the sopping cloth on the basin's edge and spread her fingers, laying them softly atop Eva's belly.

As she rose up, Ma reached down into the sagging pouch of her housedress, the top part of her arm flexing when she gripped the neck of the whiskey bottle. "Stay put," she said.

Ma didn't close the door all the way. And Eva knew why. This was her apology. This was Ma saying, we are strong. Watch this. Though she was sore and scared, Eva craned her head to see all she could from the bed—

With a straight back, Ma stepped willfully to the center of the room, called Pa to her. Eva knew she did it that way on purpose, making sure her daughter could witness a woman fighting for honor, see what a woman who'd had enough could do. "I've got your rotgut," she said, calm and smooth. "It's right here." Ma patted her pocket. Then, Pa stepped into view. They stood inches apart, and Eva held her breath as they stared one another down in silence.

Finally, Pa made a rowing motion with his hand, saying, "Give it to me."

"Not till you wipe your feet," Ma said.

Pa pulled back his head. "What the hell are you saying, woman?"

"You're tracking your baby across the floor." Pa lifted his boot, looked behind him, noticing the glistening vestiges of a failed birth underfoot. Ma lifted the bottle to her ear like she was pulling back a bow. Eva shut her eyes, but the muted tunk still made its way to her ears. When she opened her eyes again, Pa was still standing, as if he'd just come in for supper. But then, he crumpled to the floor, one leg bent underneath him, the other straight out. Ma came back to the bed, looked deep in Eva's eyes and with unflinching resolution said, "No telling how long he'll be out. Now's the time. Fly far away from Bellwether, child."

PART II

Deliverance from
Bellwether

1858 - 1872

Chapter 22
To Escanaba

Eva arrived first. She dismounted, hitched Uriah's horse then dashed for cover behind a dogwood, not far from the shipping dock. She and Uriah had gotten separated a couple miles back, but she knew the trail dead ended on the shoreline of Lake Michigan, and if worse came to worst, she knew Uriah's seafaring cousin was named Samuel. When the husky voices of the merchantmen fell into a lull, she peered around the tree to glimpse the steamer. It was dark, but the stars and kerosene lamps on board showed the ship's enormity. In the thin light, she could see her breath, dissipating into the night. She made a game of it, trying to pass the time until Uriah caught up, blowing through "O" shaped lips, watching how far the mist would carry. Finally, she heard hooves pounding the dirt.

"Eva," Uriah called out. "Where are you?" She stepped from behind the tree. He had dismounted—reins in one hand, the other stroking the horse's back. She ran to him, and after he hitched his horse next to hers, she took his hand. They scurried across the gravel toward the ship As they neared, Eva turned her head from bow to stern and back again. "It's bigger than Hogback Mountain. Don't you think?"

Uriah halted, grabbed her shoulders hard. "Listen to me. This ain't no joke. You go where Samuel tells you, no place else." Eva felt her smile fade. "He'll check on you for privy breaks, things like that. Otherwise, stay put. Got it?" Eva nodded. "He's waiting for you on the dock." He pointed to a hefty silhouette, and the two cousins exchanged salutes. "I gotta get back to Bellwether before first light. If Pa sees his horses missing—" He ran his hand down the back of her head, clumsy, toddler-like. "Just don't feel right putting you on a boat." He shook his head. "You in Chicago. Alone."

"It ain't right not to." She leaned into his awkward touch. "You know what my Pa does to me. And you know he won't ever stop, too." The ship's horn groaned, and Uriah pulled away, kicked at the dirt. Eva reached for him, placed both hands over his heart and held them there. She angled upward and quickly pressed her lips to his then bound to the pier, winding through the incoming cargo.

From the main deck, she turned back just in time to see Uriah traipsing back to the mares. He mounted one of them, the reins of both in his fist. Part of her wanted to burst back through the darkness with arms wide open and beg him to board with her. But she knew the devotion he had for his own Ma and Pa, and that it just couldn't be.

The full moon sat high and grand over the still water as Samuel greeted Eva with a slight nod. He was a thick man and judging from the heavy stubble on his face, a bit older than Uriah. He pulled her behind him and whispered out of the side of his mouth, "I only told one other fella about you. So you gotta stay hid. I can't lose this job." He ushered her past the cargo and other men like she was a grenade, pin pulled. And they seemed too busy babbling to care what Samuel was doing. Though she tried to sneak peeks at the ship's interior—the wide spaces and more iron, ladders and pulleys than she had ever seen—Samuel told her to keep her eyes straight ahead. "Head down," he said. "It's a big risk we're taking." And even with her mind swimming in fantastic anticipation, something about Samuel's high-handed tone felt amiss.

Chapter 23
A Sea of Nameless Faces

Eva sat rigid on Samuel's bunk, screwed up her eyes and took in the dimly lit surroundings. The white walls were muted by a lamp in the farthest nook. The overhead compartments were blank, casting square shadows. Most of the paint had peeled and cracked, pieces curling up at the bottoms so the steel showed from underneath. There was a bulky metal locker by the head of the bed frame and a shoddy rug piece the color of grass that lay in the center of the tiny room, not big enough to cover dents in the floor. The vessel creaked and howled as the big Great Lake rocked her, to-and-fro. Eva's spirit was swept up in the speed and mightiness. She felt powerful, playing a part of the preeminence, an unfamiliar strength that tickled her some.

"Doing okay?" Samuel's voice was robust, startling. The lamp in his hand was swaying and she had to adjust her eyes to its shine.

"I'm okay," she said, still squinting. "But I have to use the privy."

"All right, little lady." Samuel helped her to her feet. "Sorry I took so long. Trouble in the engine room." Then the boat leaned hard and in the shift, Eva's body pushed against his. With his free hand, Samuel balanced them both. But he held her too long, even after they were steadied. In the teetering lamplight, Eva saw his eyes flashing, full and carnal. She knew that glint well.

Samuel made an exaggerated sweep with his arm, broad and sluggish, an indication for her to pass. Neither spoke as he followed her down the narrow passageway to the head. He entered first, made sure it was vacant then beckoned her in. His gracious air had gone.

In the stall, Eva braced herself, pressed her hands against either wall as thoughts spun like a waterwheel. Run for help? Only folly in that. She considered hiding but had no idea where to go. Or how much longer the voyage would be. She couldn't dodge Samuel and all the other seamen all night and day. But just as quickly as the panic rose, a calm set in. You've endured it all before, she thought. At least in this pillage, there's a light at the end. She didn't get to weigh matters for long as Samuel had knocked on the door, come to take away her choices.

He escorted her back to the dorm, his hand on her lower back. Once inside, he set down the lamp, pulled the door shut. Then he clutched his quarry, the tiny room closing in. Eva squirmed and pushed at first, but quickly ceded. He was too big, too strong. She knew he could do what he wanted, when he wanted. Only mercy could intervene. She knew, too, that the shame would burn for a long time. Always did. When he shoved her down on the mattress, she searched for the crinkled paint strip she'd spotted earlier, the one that reminded her of Ma's feathery hair when she preened for Sunday services. As he stood over her like a behemouth, Eva fixated on that splintered paint, holding on to her Ma's durability, the hard life of a frontier woman showing in her face—the corners of her mouth pulling down, the creases in her forehead. She knew that the sound of Samuel grunting like a swine, his back arching into a board, was imminent, and she saw Ma standing in the open meadow behind the church, the brilliant sea-stacks rising behind her and Lake Superior rippling below—Then,

"Dad-blame it!" Samuel was looking down, his hand working inside his trousers. He cursed himself again and again as he buttoned back up, then said in a whisper, "This here special date's gonna happen," his breath reeking of salt pork and ale. "You can count on that, little lady."

The creature inside Eva reared up again, pivoting its tiny head, hissing and rattling. It was ready to lash out, but Eva bid it to stay poised. Always before, the slippery vermin would bridle in her chest then twist back down through her innards. Eventually, she would feel its buttery skin wrapping quietly around her heart. Not this time though. It reared up to strike—bulbous eyes, pink tongue madly flicking—as if to say, never again.

* * *

Over the next couple of hours, Eva sat inside the tiny coffer, heart thudding like a drum with every snap or whir beyond the door. The room grew more stifling by the minute. And when the suffocation proved too much, she'd pace— three steps left, three right—until her heart slowed again. Then she'd sit again, thinking through every possible scenario: Ambush him when he enters. Play dead. Beg and plead—

The doorknob rattled. Then the lock clicked and the door swung open. A tall man with broad shoulders and a round belly stepped inside. He planted his feet, filling the threshold like a giant. Low light made his thick, red beard glow. His pale eyes were almost see-through, like a looking glass. All was still for a moment. Then he reached behind his back and shut the door. "Samuel's right. You're damn pretty," he murmured. The tone was the same as her father's, throaty and hard. The likeness roused the hairs on her neck.

A split-second flash, Eva's mind shifted to a memory. She'd gone to Green Bay with her Grandpa to sell the winter's wheat harvest. Bartering barley and rye was more lucrative in Wisconsin where fewer freighters were willing to pass through the tricky waterways. At the edge of the bustling port town, Eva watched the painted women on the stoop of a brothel. "Stop looking at those ol' strumpets," her Grandpa said. But even at ten, she recognized the mischievousness in their manners and was fascinated by it. As Grandpa haggled at the exchange nearby, Eva studied the fallen women out of the corner of her eye. Their gestures and expressions amongst each other and then those when a constable approached. There was a line of gold buttons down the middle of his blue blazer, and he wore a boxy, stovepipe hat, centered on his head. Eva recalled fearing for them—and herself for watching. But the women didn't scatter like she thought. Instead, they nudged one another, elbowing their way to the front of the bowed porch, the warped posts and sun-bleached spindles bouncing as they jockeyed for position, wriggling and waving hard like flags in a windstorm. The constable pointed to a black haired, buxom woman with snow white skin and thick cleavage. She hollered out, "Got yourself the best cocksucker in the place," and reached out her chubby arm. To Eva's bewilderment, the man shook his head, looked down at his feet.

"A fella don't like that kinda talk from a lady."

"Well, damn, it ain't talkin' you want, honey. And I sure as hell ain't no lady." He stepped onto the porch, walked past the vulgar woman, offering his hand to a brown-haired lass next to her, sprawled against the railing like a magnolia tree. Eva turned away, certain that she didn't want to see anymore.

Pretty, Eva thought. So you think I'm pretty? She turned herself around on the bed, back to him. He straddled her, his thick legs on either side. He reached his arms around her, clasping his hands at her navel. She twisted in his grip but tried to play demure. From a distance, they might have looked like lovers in an honest embrace. Then she curled one hand around herself, hoping to seem delicate, but with the other, she crammed her middle most fingers down her throat until she gagged. Then she pushed him down more, and when she retched, his grip slackened. With little in her stomach, the first heave was nothing but bile, thin and watery.

"What the hell—" he boomed.

Fighting the instinct to wipe the mess from her chin, Eva let it drip down her face. That's it, make yourself unpretty. She forged on. When she felt the next surge coming, she turned into him, spit up what remained in her belly. The burly man leapt up and backed away. But she leaned forward, letting the vomit drip onto the floor between them. The smell was pickled, overpowering. Her heart thrashed like a fish in the forest, and her eyes wetted and burned from the force of purging. She looked at him, tears sliding down, mixing with the swill on her cheeks and lips. The man's eyes were blank, grim. Either he was dumbfounded or unfazed, Eva couldn't tell. He didn't move, just stared at her with a bunched-up forehead.

Eva took a big inhale and swallowed it. Then she met his glare and belched it out, making a loud gack that surprised even her. The man took another step back; his seeming wariness spurring her on. The bigger his disgust, the louder her courage roared. But she did not let the gull take over. It could all turn around in a tick, she thought. He's still wondering if I'm playing. She wiped the mire from her mouth with the back of her hand and flicked the teetering droplets from her nose.

The man reached out, grabbed her face, hand like a bear's paw. "I'm heading back down," he rasped. "Clean yourself up 'fore I get back." He released her with a push and stepped backwards to the door, waggling his pointer finger at her. "No more stunts." The door closed hard. The ensuing silence was dense as coal.

Eva breathed out, wiped her face on the pillow. The smell of her own stomach still engulfed the room. She checked the door. And it opened. She pushed it forward enough to thrust her mouth and nose out, breathe in some cleaner air. Then she opened it farther, stuck her head and shoulders into the hall. Nothing but the steam engine's low rumble.

Before she could sift through all the reasons not to, she snatched up her satchel and scurried back to the privy. *The whole ship is a prison now*, she thought. *But I don't have to sit in that putrid cell, waiting like a decoy. At least this way, they'll have to look harder for me.* She headed into the same stall and closed it tight. She sat the satchel in her lap, pulled her legs to her chest and bent her arms around her knees. The thought of those men inside her made her feel sick and she felt the need to clean herself, yet terrified of making any movements, any noise.

Besides the dirge of a steamship barreling full speed ahead, the night was still, the privy even more so. She laid her head against the wall and shut her eyes. Though the ship swayed some, she managed to calm her mind for a moment. Only to be startled by the hurried scratch of a rat's claws under the stall door—sniffing, then scuttling, then sniffing again. Its fleshy nose crinkled and pulsed as it paused, looked at her with beady eyes. Eva sat motionless as it perked its ears forward then turned and crept under the opposite wall, its thin, naked tail the last thing she saw.

Eva didn't rest her head again. Nor did she know how many hours passed. But a ruckus sounded out from far off. One man's voice rose above the rest, shouting, "Port, gentlemen!" *This is it. Stay calm.* She picked up her satchel, headed into the hallway, single-minded on getting to the cargo holds. Beyond the privy, there were more sleeping quarters for the crew, quiet and empty. Further still, she saw a hatch labeled "Deck." She rushed toward it, trying not to look left or right, fearful that even the sound of her head moving might give her away. It seemed the commotion had come from far behind her, but it was approaching, getting louder. She stood by some gridiron doors, praying they'd unlatch as soon as the ship docked. Then several seamen came into view, ambling her way.

She kept her eyes on the hatch as they drew near. Then their conversations slowed, and her heart pounded so hard she thought it might break her ribs. She peeked up. Amidst the half dozen was Samuel and the bulky, tufted man. Samuel mumbled something and they all laughed. After a few more steps, the red-headed man broke from the group and strode toward her, his boots clunking in time—one, then the other—the air in her chest felt sharp and hot, wringing her lungs like a rag. He came close enough that she could see the rusty whiskers on his face, like hundreds of tiny ferns, growing in different directions. Eva closed her eyes and held her breath, begging for the hatch to save her.

Then, a low rasp—metal on metal—and the bolts clanged open. The big metal doors whooshed upward. Eva sucked in, swung her leg over the edge and started scaling down the ladder as fast as she could. At the fourth and fifth rungs, one of the men let out a cat-call. Still clamoring down, Eva looked up. The wild-eyed, scraggly man was bent down near the top of the ladder, a cagey sneer across his face, curly hairs sticking out of his shirt at the neckline. He waggled his fat finger at her again but stayed put. When she reached the bottom, there was a small platform and another ladder. She pulled the satchel strap tight across her chest then descended that one, too. Her breaths came fast and clunky. She looked up again. There was no one there.

Every few seconds, she felt herself jerk, thinking a crewman might jump out from the side, cup a hand over her mouth and drag her back upstairs. She came to yet another ladder but at the bottom of that one, the glow of early dawn flooded the floor. Hope swelled like the sun, lighting her up on the inside. Still, she kept her head up, scanning for hunters.

The sting in her throat still lingered as she stepped toward the open space, a cool lake wind blowing in. Several men stood near the hull, but no one was coming for her. Dozens of grain bags sat on the main deck. She ducked behind several of them heaped next to a gangway that faced the city. She prayed that it would open onto the dock.

She was so close.

Another cat-call hooted down from atop the carrier. Samuel, the shaggy man and several others waved at her over the railing. Then the ship knocked once and steadied. The horn let out a long, resonant blast, like a million bees buzzing in unison. As soon as the ship locked into place, Eva threw her rucksack over the side then climbed over herself. Her feet hit the gangway, and she let out a sob—cheeks stretched, eyes narrowed. A crewman shouted after her, but she couldn't make out what he was saying, didn't want to. She tucked her belongings under her arm and started running.

High-reaching buildings and pointy spires pulled her forward like a magnet. The thrum of the city began to drown out the ship's clamor and the blathering men. She felt the horrors of the cargo ship fading as the masts and derricks grew smaller. Onward she trudged without a destination, just the buildings ahead, a curtain of mortar and windows and skinny smokestacks spitting out dirty clouds into the open sky. She stopped to check her ruck sack, make sure the bit of money she'd stolen from Pa was still there. He'd stashed it in the hutch where the family's only opulence was stored—Ma's heirloom crystal. *My childhood's worth,* Eva thought when she first stuffed the money away. *Tears and dignity, and a bit of blood, that's how all fifty-six of these dollars was earned.*

As she neared the looming towers, the city's tumult swept her up. Her spirit was a mine blast, ready to tear through the old and begin anew. The needling in her loins only spurred her more. She wanted to drown herself in the sea of nameless faces, none of them giving any notice to the dried vomit on her skirt or her snarled hair. The restoration folded over her like a purl-stitch shawl. She trudged across the tracks, turned onto Dearborn Street. The entire city appeared. She stood still, bent her neck trying to see the tops of the buildings. The people shuffled past, heedless and blank-eyed. Someone bumped into her and she nearly laughed, the anonymity exhilarating.

With no endpoint, Eva set her sights on a steeple not too far off, the wooden frame coming to a spear-like point, holding its own against the mighty banks and hotels. She made her way to the church and paused in the tiny patch of grass near the front doors, awkwardly green amidst all the dirt and gravel.

In the sanctuary, the altar was cloaked in linen. An image of Mary hung on the left wall. She was dressed in a pale blue frock and snow-white bonnet. Above the lectern, perfectly centered, a Christ figure stood on a large mantle, reaching out his scarred, bleeding hand; the other across his heart. He was draped in long robes of crimson and ivory, tucked into a coppery sash. His hair was parted in the middle, falling just above his nape. A full beard and wispy mustache weighed down his thin face to form a sad expression. Eva headed a few rows in, bent down on the closest kneeler. She rested her forehead against her knuckles and began to pray for courage.

Between her braided fingers, she peeked at the ceramic figure. Jesus was gazing out over the mostly empty nave, but she couldn't see his eyes. They were aimed just above her head. She moved back a row, knelt again. Still, his eyes remained unseen. Then she asked God why He saved her from Pa only to make her suffer Samuel's dirty hands. And she wondered what possible good could come from that. She called to mind the passage about the Lord's ways not being our ways, but it wasn't enough this time. There, on her knees, she demanded an answer, grappling with the notion that it wouldn't be given. Not now. Maybe not ever.

Eva shuffled forward again, past the only other person in the chapel, presumably absorbed in her own beseeching. Then she stepped onto the pulpit, traipsed past the lectern and stood facing the figure. Eyes still not meeting, she pulled up on her toes and with the tips of her fingers, touched Christ's foot. Then she confessed to understanding why some folks turn away. Sometimes, I doubt you, too, she thought. I wasn't sure I'd ever be free from Pa's wicked ways. And yes, I stole from him, but I don't feel bad about that. And the truth is, I hope Samuel dies. Or at least his privates don't work for the rest of his life. Not sure if I should be asking for mercy or not. Don't know what I'm supposed to be asking for at all, really. She held his foot a long while but thought no more.

There was a rustling behind her. From the corner of her eye, she saw that the praying woman had come forward to sit in the first pew. When she descended the stage, the tarrying woman said, "Pardon me." Her pitch was strangely deep. Eva regarded her fully but subtly. The woman was portly, her brow marked by heavy lines. When she stood to greet Eva, her gown flared out, purple as currants, with flounces of lace all about the skirt. She reached out her hands, covered by crocheted fingerless mitts, and nodded gently. Her neckline was high and a mauve-hued stone dangled at her chest by a strand of silver, falling forward just a little as she curtsied. Eva nodded back in kind.

"What ails you, child?" she asked.

There was something odd about the woman's eyes—one moved slower than the other. And it was darker, more rounded. Even so, they were soft, kind. They made Eva want to scream out all of her afflictions as fast as she could while the woman stroked her head and said things like, "There, there. I'm here now."

Eva stood mute and wasn't sure why. After several moments of silence, the woman pulled away. Palm turned up, she touched the side of Eva's chin with the back of her pointer finger.

"Well," she said, "people only take help if it's offered the right way." She took a quick breath, let it out through her nose. "Hope I get to try again." As she turned to go, her dress caught between a pew and the kneeler and she stopped, trying to tug it free.

"What happened to your eye, ma'am?" Eva called after her.

The woman looked back, mouth folding in the corners.

"Quite a tale to tell there," she said. "Let me tell you over breakfast?"

Eva followed her. It just felt right. Before exiting the church, she took one last glance at Christ, his eyes still eluding her.

* * *

The woman's name was Ruth, and her living quarters were like nothing Eva had ever seen. Though the space was not roomy, it was filled with more possessions than she thought possible for one person to own—furniture, dishes, paintings, and baubles, everywhere, collected over many years and experiences. She soon learned that Ruth was widowed at twenty by the Mexican-American War and moved to New England to work in the textile mills. "I made three dollars a week when I started. That was back in, let's see…" She counted her crooked fingers and lipped some numbers to herself. "54!" she declared. "And when the factory buckled a few years later, I was up to four and a quarter. Not bad for a single lady." Eva listened intently, scanning the dwelling, all the fancy relics. Then Ruth motioned to the florid carafe. "More?"

"Yes, ma'am."

Filling their slender glasses with cider—Ruth's hard, Eva's soft—she said, "You haven't told me why you're here, in Chicago."

"And you haven't told me about your eye." Eva took a quick sip and smirked.

"Lord have mercy. It seems I've found a lass as willful as myself," Ruth replied.

Before the night was over, Eva learned that for six years Ruth had worked in the Pemberton Mill in Lawrence, Massachusetts. And that she became a chieftain for several protests; one that succeeded in reducing labor hours per day; the other stopping mill owners from gouging workers at company-owned boarding houses.

All the while, Eva poured over a special box Ruth opened, letting her delve deeper into her history. When Eva came across several photographs—daguerreotypes in hinged, wooden cases, tarnishing around the edges. Ruth stopped talking and peered over her shoulder. They both looked at the heinous images of twisted ruins, burning rubble, and several charred bodies. Tapping Eva on the top of the head, Ruth pointed to her eye. "That's what happened, my dear." She pulled her lower eyelid down with her left pointer finger and with her right hand, lifted the prosthetic marble out of the cavity, holding it up to the light of the paraffin lamp. It was egg shaped with the ring in the middle painted a dull, dark green, almost like spinach. There were thin red lines branching out in every direction, in imitation of veins.

Eva knew the curiosity was strewn across her face like blood on snow, but she couldn't look away from the empty socket. And Ruth seemed to gather her intrigue because she began telling her how prosthetic eyes used to be made of glass but the cost of shipping them from Germany grew too high. "Now they're made of enamel, here in America," she explained. "An artist makes them using colored glass like a paintbrush. Then an eye doctor fits them so they don't hurt too much or get infected." She shook her head. "Strange when the oculist opens the drawer, all those different colored eyes, looking this way and that." She scooped water from the washbowl, filled a tin cup and dropped the eye in it. Then, after pulling a black patch from the wide pocket in her dress, she snapped it over her head, covering the hole. Without skipping a beat, she dove headlong into how the eyeless pit came to be.

"It was just before five p.m.," Ruth began. "The sun's rays were rich, softening the hard iron machines and brick walls." She looked out the picture window as if watching the scene unfold. "With the economy still fattening and production demands increasing, our managers cramped the upstairs with new equipment, so heavy it bowed the planks underneath. As you walked, the boards moaned and creaked. Under all that weight, the pillars holding up the floors began to totter. Workers joshed one another about the whole damn building caving in. But that's all we could do is joke because the truth was, we knew it would likely happen."

Eva watched Ruth telling the story, hearkening her every word. The woman's strength was a wonder. So was her forthright way. How different from Ma, so quiet and off-stage. Eva thought about which way she'd rather be herself. Or if she'd someday balance the two—plain spoken but careful.

"…like thunder at first," Ruth was saying, "but then, the snap of splintering wood, the bang of metal hitting metal and the shrieks of bloody murder." She stopped, took a swig of cider. Eva did the same, slow and quiet, anxious for more of the tale. "Bodies torn open, crushed by jagged wreckage. Then the ceiling above us cracked, branching out like a spider's web. My dear friend and I looked up, locking elbows just as the biggest girder broke in two." She turned from the window, back to Eva. "You sure you want to hear about this, dear?"

Eva nodded earnestly, and with another nip of the spirits, Ruth continued. "I don't recall everything that happened after, as the mill fell in upon us. But I know that I took the brunt of the blow when a steel beam dropped down, felt like someone cudgeled me with ten rocks. My head was ringing like a church bell and a flat ache started behind my nose. I remember trying to shut my eyes, but only one of them would close. And the air was thick with brick dust, like sitting in a storm cloud. I had covered my face with my hands and when I let them down again, everything was blurred. That's when my friend let out a yelp and pulled away from me. I knew right then my eye had come loose. Must have been a vile sight, one of my peepers sticking out like a half-laid egg."

Eva looked at the patch on Ruth's face, so crude against her mild skin. Out of sorts in her orderly, genteel space. Then she sneaked a glance at the tin cup that held the fake eye, imagined it quavering in the water like a fishing bobber.

The front door swung open, thumping the wall. A pretty girl, a few years Eva's senior, stood in the threshold. The glow of dusk lit up her contours. She looked like an apparition, a tinseled one. Blond hair lay in noodle-like ringlets upon her bare shoulders. Full, rouged lips, heavy as a clown's. She wobbled some, her head swaying back and forth. "Please meet Tina," Ruth said. "She stays with me sometimes." Then she shot the girl a hard glance. "But I thought I'd seen the last of her for a while." Eva stood to meet her, but the drunk girl tramped past her, bouncing into a bureau then stumbling into the stove before disappearing into the back. A door snapped shut.

"She lives here?" Eva asked.

"More of a visitor, really. Excuse her manners. She's quite a troubled soul. I've turned her out a dozen times, but my heart always takes her back." Shuffling and inaudible mumbles sounded out from where Tina had retreated. Ruth busied herself, scooping black pudding onto two plates.

Then, Tina reappeared, more thickly daubed than before. She looked Eva down and up and down again. "Your latest rescue, huh?" Her words spewed like vomit.

"That'll do," Ruth said.

The girl cackled, high and long, then spoke directly to Eva, "Once a whore, always a whore," she said. "May as well come with me to Levee now, you'll end up there soon enough."

"Tina!" Ruth slammed her fist on the table. Plates and forks clanked, and the tin cup fell over. The water spread, and Ruth's eye rolled out like someone flicking a shooter marble.

"Don't worry, Ruth. I'm leaving." She made a *tsk* sound with her tongue. "Ain't that a sight, the one-eyed hero and her newest little sprite." The door shut hard behind her, and an awkward lull ensued until Ruth broke it.

"If you're in need, you're welcome here, too." The kindness

was unexpected, and it sideswiped Eva. She fell quiet again. "Well, the offer stands," Ruth said, topping off their cups.

* * *

Eva woke to the clatter of Ruth bustling at the cookstove. "Seems as if you'll be staying on then," Ruth said. "Have to earn your keep, though. I like my eggs soft-boiled, dash of pepper and a pinch of thyme."

After many late night chats and gallons of cider, Eva learned that after the mill collapse, Ruth was offered an office job at Smith & Bailey lumberyard in Chicago's 2nd Ward, beside the train tracks. And Eva was determined to work there, too. Each morning, she made Ruth's eggs—seasoned just right—then after the lumberyard foreman, Edgar, picked her up for work, Eva went to work herself. She scrubbed the floors, laundered Ruth's clothes until she thought the washboard might wear flat, and even with limited provisions, prepared savory dinners of bacon, bread and potato pie. She was determined to prove her worth.

Just days after arriving, while moving sopping garb from the wash boiler, Eva slipped in the suds, her arm coming down hard on the dolly stick, prongs up. As she lay there in a tender heap, an air of defeat nearly swamped her. I deserve this new life, God, she thought. I'm done with Your tests. The boldness made the blood rush in her ears, curtailing the ache in her battered forearm and twisted ankle. But she pushed on, figuring that matters of faith hadn't been working the way she'd been handling them anyway. I need some joy in THIS life. And I can't lie, I'm not sorry for my sass.

At dinner, Eva set down the tin of potato pie with her good arm then tried to walk with a usual gait to her side of the table, but her foot dragged. After she sat and positioned her hands to pray, her sleeves dropped down, baring the bruise, already bluish red, like mulberries smeared across her wrist.

"You're quiet, Eva."

"Not meaning to be, a bit tired is all." Her words were flat. "How's the pie?"

"Wonderful." She paused for a moment. "Pass the cider, dear?" Eva looked at the pitcher on the right and cursed herself for setting it by her injured arm. She stretched her left arm across her body then passed it over with a grunt.

"Everything alright?"

She read Ruth's face and knew better than to continue with the charade. "I had a little accident today."

"I figured. Saw a mangled dolly stick behind the privy. How bad is it? And more importantly, why are you pretending you're not hurt?"

"It ain't too bad, my ankle swelled a bit. Arm's sore."

"Why the secrecy?"

"Didn't want you to think I'm soft." She rolled her tongue inside her cheek, trying to keep her mouth from trembling. "'Cause I want to work at the lumberyard."

"Good Lord, Eva. A young girl who ventures to Chicago alone, keeping the secret as to how and why. Well, she's anything but soft." Ruth shook her head. "Should've just asked me, girl. I'll see what I can do."

Chapter 24
All the Sacrifices

Stella Brandt was as pig-headed as she was stunning. She insisted on hand-making her own corsets—flannel and cane, and extra boning for heavier labors like firewood and sheaving. While stitching, she always praised thriftiness and chided vanity, talking about things like haste and idleness.

At the height of July, when the winter wheat was gilded and drooping, Basil looked behind his wife's curtain, hoping to see her trying on the corset she'd just finished making. But she was already dressed, standing with her back to him, a paisley sash in her hands. She said, "If you're going to gander like a hungry fox, may as well help me with this."

He went to her, lassoed the band around her waist where the bodice and overskirt came together then pushed himself against her backside. Through his long-drawers, he felt his shaft go rigid. She tilted back her head, and he could see that her eyes were closed. It always made him feel powerful, knowing his touch could make her do that.

"To the fields, Mr. Brandt," she bid. "Too much to be done," she said, her throat tittering in the neckline of her mantelet.

"Yes, my rib." He saluted, brusquely. As they headed out, he thought about the hidden fen just beyond Hillsdale's campus where he first said, "I love you." The cotton grass was purple and so much bird chatter—a flourishing scene, so rife with possibility.

* * *

The cool morning burned off, turning airless. As the yellow sun throbbed across the pasture, Stella heaved the bulky heaps of hay from the loft into the hopper below. The rumble of the horses sounded out as they powered the heavy tumbling rods. The rusty teeth of the thresher knocked like a cannonade, tearing each stalk with vengeance. Basil took a quick break, leaned against the barn and guzzled from the canteen, water spilling over the sides and across his jowls. He watched Stella trudging in the fodder, every now and again, wiping her forehead with the back of her wrist, the skin of her neck was slick and wet.

For a moment, however brief, Basil let himself take joy in her movements. But then, as it often did, his mind drifted to a nameless woman who didn't know his uncertainties, who didn't think she was the barren one, who offered no pressure to procreate. Flashes of a woman's body. Soft, smooth legs and small, round breasts. Never a face, though. He would stymie the images, try to deflect to more honest things, like tilling, or the horse to be shod, or Christ hanging from the cross, nails in his wrists, feet. But this time, he couldn't fight the trespass. Instead, he fantasized the tryst the whole way through—the supple flesh, the probing and moaning. Fearing the bulge in his britches might betray him, Basil turned his back, but the rot of infidelity had already taken hold. He'd gone too far, and just as the throb in his hips was starting to reach a crux, he peeked over his shoulder at Stella.

She was heaving another bale from up high, leaning too far out of the bay. Basil watched her tumble from the loft. No shrieks, no flails. She simply dropped like a sandbag. Her head struck the iron cast of the flesher's front end, and her body broke through the wood planks that he had set across the top to cover up the turning blades, just in case. The metal monster snagged her coif, brought her legs into its mouth. Basil scrambled for a pitchfork and rammed its tines into the circulating rods, screaming "Whoa" to the horses. But he knew Stella's feet and shins must be gnashed.

The thresher stood six feet tall, a rectangle, closed in front—except the opening where the straw was fed—and an open back end where the pelted straw pushed through, waiting to be hayed. Stella's head rested on the top of the machine but having crashed through the planks, most of her body was unseen, stuck inside, only the blades holding her up. She was a jack-in-the-box, blood spilling from her crown, thick in her hair.

Though he was looking right at his wounded wife, none of it felt real. He heard himself saying "No, no, no, no, no" as he met her stormy eyes and still, as he ran to gather two sawhorses up front and steady himself atop them. A fear like no other crashed through his veins like a fire-bolt. There were a million things to cry out, all of them starting with "I'm sorry," but the words stuck as if his cheeks were full of stones.

He bent down over her, put his arms under hers, and pulled with all he had. She came loose, letting out a whimper. He dragged her to the hay bales next to the barn and kicked at the topmost two until they fell to the ground. He laid her down on her right side, blood spilling from the left. Then he tore off his shirt, searching her head for the wound. With his fingers, he gently probed her hair for the source then crumpled the shirt in his hands, pressing it down. His breaths went shallow and his hands trembled. *How could there be any blood left in her?* He glanced at her feet, her legs. *Have to stop the hemorrhaging from her head first. Other gashes must wait. If I could just slow the—*

Stella twisted upward hard, held there, then wilted. Again, she jolted upward, then sagged. Basil whirred at the sight of his wife flopping like a snared trout. He knew she'd hate being seen this way. Through each convulsion, he kept a hand on her head, the other on her belly. When the flails finally let up, she opened her mouth to speak but couldn't. Instead, she reached for his face. Basil slipped his arms around her, lifted her just enough to slide under and lay her head in his lap. He took his shirt from the wound and cupped his hand there, blood still trickling through his fingers.

In the lingering grain dust, Basil rocked Stella for hours, swaying back and forth until her chest stopped rising and her arms turned cold and gray. He felt the resignation as it washed over her, taking every trace of suffering on the wing, far from this place, this time. And far from his failures as a man. He was plundered—stripped of spirit and purpose.

Overhead, the sky had shifted to black. It felt bigger than it had been just a few hours before. The cicadas scritched in the stillness. Their sounds were familiar, but seemed louder now, more intrusive. He thought of all the sacrifices that are made in doing God's work, and how in those sacrifices, a farmer's wife can be split open by a blunt, steel block.

Chapter 25
After Stella

Basil often thinks about the Lee family who lost their only daughter the same winter he and Stella arrived. Oscar was a mountain of a man, serving as an elder at church. He always greeted everyone with a toothy smile, his thick fingers burying yours in a hardy handshake.

It was early February just after a frigid northerly had blown through, bringing a foot of snow. The temperature was hovering at 20°. Though the boys stayed home, Oscar and Ethel, the youngest of five, donned their snowshoes and trudged the half mile to Trout Lake—fishing rods, chisels and creels in tow. Oscar always told listeners of his story how careful they'd been making their way to the middle of the lake, stepping lightly, keeping a safe distance. He in front; she ten feet back. The lake groaned underfoot. And the wind howled. Oscar never even heard the ice break open, didn't hear his baby girl gasp before sinking like an anchor.

At Ethel's funeral, Oscar fell to his knees next to the coffin, hid his face in the crook of his elbow and bawled like a hungry babe. All of Bellwether sat still, letting the man grieve with abandon. In the midst of his sobs, he lifted his head and cried out, "I don't know how to live now."

Years later, Basil still replays those words, hears the agony as loud as it was that day. He berates himself, asks why his own suffering wasn't instant like Oscar's. Why didn't he bawl uncontrollably as Stella went slack across his legs? It took him months to break. He remembers clearly when it finally struck him that his beloved was no more—quiet, unexpected, and crippling—

It was the first Christmas Eve service after her death and per Reverend Hiram's tradition, many in the congregation gathered by the wood stove at the back of the church to drink tea and eat stewed fruit, most men spiking theirs with shrubs. They shared memories from the past year and told new stories. Outside, by the dim light of kerosene lamps, the children slung snowballs at each other. The shared tales of the Yuletide spirit were playful, gay. It felt good for Basil to laugh, to hear others laugh. When someone said, "Your turn, teacher man," he knew right away that he'd tell them about the time Stella made him a pleated dress shirt for Christmas.

"White linen and plackets," he said. "A banded collar, too." In reverence, he brushed the fabric of his wool overcoat with a long, lengthwise stroke as he explained, "Down the front, there were three Mother of Pearl buttons given to her by her grandmother just before we moved north. It was a beautiful shirt." He began to chuckle, mild at first, but his laugh grew louder, less restrained. Though unheralded, it was welcomed by everyone.

Soon, he was cackling so hard that he struggled to tell the punch line, that Stella had stitched the right sleeve shut. He pulled his right arm up into his coat and shook it back and forth so that the sleeve wriggled. He knew the parishioners were laughing more out of courtesy than whimsy, but he didn't care. "She played it off like she was surprised, but I knew it had to be one of her tricks. 'Cause my Stella, she used to love to sew—"

And there on his tongue sat his reality, heavy as a barge. Speaking of Stella in the past tense made him choke. He stood motionless, his sentence suspended in the thick wood-heat like a spoon in custard. Though the men looked away, tipped back their spirited tea, the women watched him with loving regard. He supposed that some were truly troubled by his heartbreak, but others were more captivated to see a man unfolding.

* * *

That night, the tears finally came, flowing like the mighty rapids of the The Menominee River. No more Christmas Eve celebrations, Basil decided, nor any social affair for that matter. So it was that Basil's life split into two stages: before Stella, and after. In the years with her, under the surface, there was a semblance of calm because even when the storms were raging, someone knew his secret, that under the veneer, he was gutless. His wife had seen him cowering, tiptoeing and failing, yet she cherished him anyway. She hurt for him as he struggled to free himself from others' opinions, never being able to step down off the imaginary stage he had created in his head—thinking everyone was always watching. And post Stella, he was aimless. A blinded bird. A canoe without oars. Stella had been his compass, and now, he could not find his way.

* * *

Amongst Bellwether's four hundred or so residents, Basil lived out his life alone. He sold most of his land but kept the farmhouse. His hair turned gray and sparse as mockingbird feathers. To the world beyond the hinterlands of northern Michigan, he was indifferent.

As for the children of Bellwether, though, he continued to play the part. He was still the portal for them to live richer, fuller lives. He made good on the expectations of him as a teacher—setting busted bones with branches and string, hauling a mine's worth of coal to keep them warm, and tutoring them in their homes whenever they fell ill—yet the children came and went without much glee or sadness on his part. There were only the motions, nothing more. The only time he cried over a student, post Stella, was when the draft came through Bellwether and plucked away its boys like a ravenous falcon. It was a particularly sharp talon that seized Uriah.

Chapter 26
Rattletrap

It was years after the frenzy of several raids had subsided, that Sarah arrived in Cass County. She had found her way there after weeks of perilous travel on foot. But when she entered the village, she was greeted with open arms, the wonder and solace that she'd dreamt of ever since she could remember was coming true. She had never let herself think about a world without confines for too long, but she could taste the fruits of liberty in Michigan almost instantly.

The land felt wider, more vast, with red-orange leaves covering the trees and ground. The air was fresher, more pure, like it was cleansing her lungs as it slid through them. Within the day, Sarah was taken in by a fugitive family, the Browns, and soon became one of them, like she'd just always been there. She started working the very next morning, bending over the soybean plants like the rest—sweating, aching, pulling—side-by-side with new friends, ones she already knew would last a lifetime.

The Browns were a four-person family—mom, dad, and two young ones, Minnie and Florence, who came to think of Sarah as their oldest sister, even called her so. On that first night, she learned all about Cass County, where two routes of the underground railroad—one from the Ohio River, the other from the Mississippi—came together, an area marked by tiny villages and agricultural bounty. An unlikely place for a mighty abolitionist movement. Yet more than a thousand fugitives made their way there. For some, it was a safe stopover before heading to Canada; for others, it was far enough away from the iron fists of the South, so they chose to call it home.

Mr. Brown was still tingling about the raids, unstoppable in his telling. "The first one came when a group of Kentuckians trekked all the way up here, hoping to reclaim what was theirs." He chuckled. "It was a short-lived raid, by God. We met those blasted trespassers head on. Farmers with muskets and pitchforks, shoulder to shoulder, guarding our houses like mother bears. Bastards went on home licking their wounds. And I'll be damned if just a few months later, they didn't come back for more." He spoke of the thirteen angry slave owners who came on fine horses, broke into several houses and seized fugitives in their sleep. "They handcuffed men to their beds, held babies hostage, pinching at them till they whimpered, drawing their mothers out of hiding. They claimed newborns as their own. 'We own the women who bore them' they said. And one fugitive tried fending them off. He recognized his master's raspy voice and refused to let him in. Well, the raiders broke down his door. One of 'em dealt the man a blow to the head with the butt of his rifle, darn near tore his ear off—"

Sarah felt the anxiousness bristling inside, her sense of safety thinning out. And Mrs. Brown picked up on her jitters. "You're scaring her, dear. Get to the good part." Mr. Brown nodded, turned to the triumphant ending.

"Well, the second time an even bigger throng formed, keeping those blasted raiders at bay. A swelling crowd of farmers, freed slaves, and freedom fighters from nearby villages. It was something to behold. With all those knives and pistols in the hands of an angry mob, just waiting, why, those dirty scamps agreed to go to court instead." He told the tale of one staunch abolitionist, a king-size man, disarming a Kentuckian who had drawn his pistol then convinced another to dismount his horse and offer it to a sickly runaway as they all marched to the courthouse. "Just as the man got down, he slipped the fugitive's handcuffs over the raider's wrists, snapped them shut and threw the key in a murky bog." He almost sang the words. "Most beautiful thing I ever did see."

As Sarah would learn, the court case flared. There were claims of trespassing, kidnapping and assault. Still, after just three days, the Circuit Court Commissioner ruled against the raiders. And though the prosecution threatened to sue for the value of the slaves, there was no legal hold over them anymore. So, most of them left for Canada, including a runaway who had been jailed shortly before the raid began. When the jail was searched, he was gone. It seems a nameless citizen paid the slave's fine, making sure he went north, too.

* * *

The year after her arrival, Sarah was asked to serve as a sexton for the United Methodist Church. She maintained the chapel with a small team, kept the floors shiny, the garden weeded and the cemetery tended to. Often, she helped with the digging of graves, though that was her least favorite job. Her back always gnawed even more after helping with a dig and when someone died who could afford a burial vault, the bulky casing always bowed her back double.

Then there was the time that Mr. Thomas—oldest man in the colony—refused both a coffin and a vault, claimed he wanted to be closer to God when he left this world. "Just stick me in the earth," he said. And they did. Then, come spring, he pushed back up through the dirt, face and hands peeking through, teeth gone, nails gone. Nose and lips had disintegrated some but still frozen from the winter months, looked more like an early blooming tulip than a moldering man.

Sarah understood why so many never left for Canada as she, too, grew to love southern Michigan. She worked the tract of ground that a landowner offered the Browns, helping them pay off its value and possess it outright. Within months,

Sarah afforded a cabin of her own, still she spent most of her time at the Browns. Warm fruit tea, white fish on an open flame, and plenty of chewing the fat—no light jabber, but real jawing about blessings, and the constant fear of having them stripped away again. How even in the throes of singing hymns on Sunday, scrubbing dishes after supper or heading to the outhouse, there was trepidation, brooding over the stories of runaway slaves in Indiana and Ohio snatched from their homes before the morning light.

So, having the right to stroll to a neighbor's house just to visit or plucking some fresh basil from the garden simply because there was a hankering for it, that was all well and good. But there would always be that moment of panic whenever a strange buggy passed through town, or a creak from the barn made its way inside as it might mean, "My time is up."

Then another year would pass, and the colony lived in peace. No more raids. No fugitives gone missing. All except Celia, who ran off with Mr. Pratt, one of the widowed landowners. A fine fella, always greeting folks with a "how do?" and tipping his cap. He brought Christmas presents for the little ones each year and some hard candies on their birthdays. But he knew to stay his distance, let the runaway folks live their lives without interfering.

Celia was as nice as could be. Comely, too. Always polished and clean, even while she was wielding a hoe or on her knees in the thick of yellow-brown leaves, pulling soybeans from their pods and stems. It wasn't any wonder Mr. Pratt took a liking to her. They'd been meeting late at night, always sneaking peeks when he drove by. It wasn't much of a secret but being sly seemed to be part of the fun for them. So the colony kept quiet, let them think they were pulling wool over everyone's eyes. No one was surprised when one morning, they went missing. The word was that they went to live on the west side of the state, near the Black River, amongst the Dutch Calvinists and Ottawa people. Most likely, they figured religious freedom and smallpox—rampant in that region—were of bigger concerns than a white man and a black woman taking up with one another. Though Sarah prayed for their happiness, she couldn't help but be jealous. And that's what took her to Bellwether. If Mr. Pratt and Celia could be together, she at least deserved to visit Hiram.

Through letters Hiram had written to Leander, Sarah knew he lived in Bellwether. It had always been a small comfort that he was in the same state—just like Isaac in Virginia—but it was cruel, too, as he may as well have been in Massachusetts. Many years passed before she felt she'd earned the right to ask for time away to journey north. But before she could finish asking, Mr. Brown began nodding, waving his hand for her to stop. "We'll get on just fine," he said. "Don't you worry none. Go see this Mr. Hiram you're always talking of. Must be a helluva fella, the way you chatter on." Sarah grinned, trying to listen to whatever Mr. Brown said next. But she heard none of it. Her thoughts had already headed to Bellwether.

* * *

As Hiram made his way back to the rectory, the top of the sun lingered just above the horizon, casting a rose-colored tide over the village. The fading light softened the brownstone on the church wall, turning some of the rocks light blue. The tall, pointed windows facing westward ricocheted the glow of dusk into Hiram's eyes. He shielded them with his hand and veered to the front of the chapel as was his habit before heading to bed. Ever since talk of civil war began, he made sure to be available for any parishioner needing to grieve or confess or just ponder the question of the time: Is God really going to allow the carnage of combat? He understood that war sparks doubts and fears, but he hadn't anticipated such a wavering of faith—in God, and in one another. All the bloodshed that was sure to come, already wreaking more damage than he could have ever imagined. And he learned that during the darkest times, telling folks to trust and believe didn't always work. Listening was the only way. So he always checked around the building at sundown, just in case a weary layman was waiting on the steps.

As he cleared the side of the church, Hiram slowed. He thought he saw Sarah sitting on the stoop. But it couldn't be. He quickly dropped the notion, just kept walking. A few more steps and he slowed again. It was her. She was perched on the top stair, her head leaning against the wood railing. Hiram's chest felt like it was emptying out. His feet felt bulky, as if he was wading through a muddy bog. He was scared and gleeful at the same time. He wanted to dash to her, sweep her up and swing her around, then kiss her mouth, her cheeks, her neck. But he wanted to cut and run, too. Hide behind a roomy pine, wait her out, watch her leave.

He shuffled sideways behind a juniper shrub to steady himself, take her in. There was a bulging beige carpet bag at her feet, her dark, slender fingers stroking its leather handles. She was whistling quietly. Though he didn't recognize the tune, he knew it was Sarah's lips warbling that way. She shifted, angling more his way, head still pressed against the rails. Her hair was longer now, parted in the center and pulled back smooth toward the back, coiffed with fancy combs and ribbons.

The thought of her in his new world made Hiram lightheaded. Then thrill and nerves blended. He was giddy, like in his boyhood days at the market square whenever a pretty girl giggled at Leander and him. He wanted Sarah here, never knew just how badly until right then. He was waiting too long to show himself. It was starting to feel wrong. Before he could go to her, though, Sarah stood, looked west toward the blushing sky and then, directly at the juniper shrub.

Hiram stepped out from behind it. A thousand thoughts spun through him, but none of them stuck. The joy overtook him. He brought the crux of his elbow to his mouth, trying to reign in whatever was crawling up his throat—a laugh, a sob—he didn't know for sure. Sarah stepped down the stairs, slow at first, but when she reached the ground, he saw her take in a deep breath, thin shoulders lifting. She put both hands over her heart and closed her eyes and when she popped them open again, Sarah blew out and hurried to him. More than a walk, not quite a run.

Hiram opened his arms wide and she burrowed in. He tilted his head up so that hers could fit under his chin, against his chest. He breathed her in, lime flower and almonds. All the worrying halted. He didn't care how he looked—older, rounder or unkempt—the silence said it all. Nothing else existed. Just the two of them, no space between. They held one another as if one of them was dangling over a cliff, neither willing to let go first.

The church bells tolled to mark the hour, a peal of low bongs and high pings. Then Hiram pulled back, looked at her face, her round, dark eyes, glossy like crow feathers. Each of them reached for the other's hands at the same time. They held them out to the side so they formed a circle, like a stationary dance. She wore a wine-colored calico day-dress, long sleeves gathered into cuffs at her wrists. The wide, white collar made her skin burnish like onyx. She was soft and delicate, everything Bellwether wasn't, Hiram thought. In a world on fire, Sarah was a cool breeze. There was an overpowering urge to push his body against hers, feel the drumming of her heart, erase any life they had lived apart.

The clanking of an approaching carriage made them instantly let go. They turned to see how close it was and a shared sigh came when it veered north toward the copper mines. With their relief came the gritty truth, the fear that someone almost saw the Reverend holding a black woman's hand.

Again and again, Hiram glanced at her as they walked to the rectory. It was still inconceivable, Sarah being in Bellwether, traipsing next to him as if it was part of their nightly routine. He had longed for her to see his everyday, to be proud that he'd become a messenger of God. So often, it was her that he spoke to in his sermons—rearing up his hand just a little higher, lifting and dropping his voice—hoping somehow she could see him, hear him. And now, she was stepping through his door, breathing in the same air.

They looked at one another in silence, until Sarah said quietly, "So much to say, Hiram. Maybe too much."

"I haven't any plans," he replied. And then he fetched the whiskey from the shelf, filled two tin cups half full and pushed one in front of her. Though her taste for firewater was still tainted, Sarah took careful, tiny sips as she told Hiram all about her escape to the Shenandoah, apologizing for stealing his money. "But I promise to make good on my debt one day," she said, "if it's the last thing I do." But she mostly talked of Leander—his kindness, his fortitude, his devotion to Hiram— skipping over his lapses in judgment. She made a to-do over Cass County, all its peace and wonder. And when she spoke of the Brown family, she paused several times, verklempt at the thought of their friendship.

It delighted Hiram to hear her praises of his brother, but it delighted him more to know Sarah had found a safe place, a new family. Hearing her unfold the missing years was quenching a dog-hungry thirst. It was like he'd been emptied of blood when she ran from the mine, but now, with each new detail, he was filling up again, gorging. When he offered her more whiskey, she politely declined. "I'm holding out till I hear about you. The seminary? Bellwether?"

"I'll tell you everything," he said. "But you need to rest. You've traveled far." With a slight bow of the head, she agreed. Hiram folded the blankets down on his bed and left her to sleep. He poured himself another drink and sat at the table, thinking of all the things he would tell her come morning. He'd cut open his chest, pull back the skin and bone, bare everything. Every secret, every uncertainty, every tiny space in his soul. She made him want to do things like that, to be a better man. And when all was uncovered, they'd make plans. A job for her. A place to stay. Maybe Basil would lend her a *McGuffey Reader*, keep her reading, learning.

Later that night, when the thought of Bellwether's brick-wall judgment crept in, Hiram pushed it aside, trying to live in his pie in the sky as long as possible.

* * *

Before the sun had crested the horizon, a loud, ceaseless knock at Hiram's door jolted him awake. He pulled it open, and Mr. Turner pushed forward, attempting to step inside. Hiram blocked the way, asking the purpose for such an early morning visit.

"Several folks saw you bring a woman in here. Said she'd been waiting for you on the church steps. Rumor is she's a colored gal."

"They're right. I did. Why is it any—"

"Church board's already gathered. They're waiting in the chapel." With that, Mr. Turner stalked away, leaving Hiram with his mouth open, standing in the doorway. Sarah came to him, stood near, resting a hand on his mid-back.

He stepped to the wash basin, dipped his hands in and splashed the tepid water in his hair, patted down the sides. Having never undressed for bed, he simply straightened his trousers, pulled the suspenders back over his shoulders. "I'll return shortly," he said, tucking in his shirt at each hip. He slipped outside, fury and fear rising up, ready to swallow him whole. He'd have to bridle his temper and gather up some courage before facing the church's wicked storm.

First light was breaking and once outside the chapel, he stood still, watched the sun's rays sprawling out across the land. But even the restorative sight of dawn could not settle him down. He opened the door, ready for a fight. All four men turned toward him, stared him down as if Cain himself had just stepped in. Mr. Miller and Mr. Turner were in the last pew on the left. On the right were Oscar Lee and Deacon John. None of them spoke, just eyed him, their heads turned back over their shoulders. Wide eyes and somber faces, all except Oscar, the only one to give Hiram a nod. It was deathly quiet. The room narrowed into a tomb.

"Gentlemen," Hiram offered.

The deacon took in a breath, let it out with an audible push. "Let's not waste any time here. Fact is, Hiram, there's a colored gal in your room. Am I right?"

"You are."

"That kind of mingling ain't becoming of a reverend. Especially with a war on and all. You agree?"

"No."

Mr. Turner looked to Mr. Miller, who kept his eyes forward, then across the aisle, but Oscar and John stayed focused on Hiram. So he draped his arm over the back of the pew and started in again. "Care to explain, Reverend?"

"Sarah and me, we're friends. Share a long history together. And we haven't seen each other in years. Nothing wrong with us catching up, filling in some holes."

"Whole country is battling with itself about whites and blacks. You think our minister should be—"

"There's a war raging so that ambushes like this one don't happen anymore. So it won't be thought of a misdeed when folks like me have a visitor whose skin ain't the right—"

"Now wait a minute," Mr. Miller interrupted. "Don't go making this out like we don't approve of colored folks. I've never said either way what I think about this war. But I will say that charming a woman in the rectory ain't proper. And the fact she's colored, why, that's just another heap of rubbish, making things worse."

"And if she was white?" Oscar asked, not to anyone specific. The words hovered, thick as cream. "Would we still be sitting here?"

"Sure as hell!" Deacon John roared, slapping his hand on the pew.

"That's it. No more pussyfooting." Mr. Miller rose, stepped around the side of the pew, inches from Hiram. They were the same height, but Hiram was more brawny. And there was satisfaction in that. "You heard of Sheriff Thompson?"

Hiram recognized the name right away, the man Bellwether hanged for showing mercy to the Williams women. Ada had told him how Thompson tried protecting her. And how the man was sagging like a grapevine when she got to him. His flesh cold, already graying. But Hiram wanted to hear Mr. Miller tell the tale, make him confess to the sordid deed. "Can't say I have."

"He went against the town's grain, opposing things we felt strong about. We had a lesson to teach. Wasn't the place of an appointed man to fly in the face of our principles." Hiram glanced at Oscar, who turned his head away. "His loyalty was rattletrap," Miller continued, "so he had to be gone. Sometimes, the Lord needs us to take matters into our own hands. Of all men, you should understand that most." All the fury had shifted, only unease now. Hiram knew Sarah wasn't safe there, and that blood would boil if he pushed the matter further.

"What would you have me do?" Mr. Miller and Mr. Turner smiled at one another, as if they'd been here many times before, the outlier always buckling. Deacon John gave the orders:

"The girl leaves on the first train out. If not, we'll have to call the authorities. There are laws about fugitive—"

"Sakes alive, John!"

"Hush up, Oscar," Mr. Turner said out of the side of his mouth, his eyes never straying from Hiram. "And you won't be leaving Bellwether any time soon, Hiram. Not till we're sure of your devotion. You ain't no ten-cent minister. Folks here need to hear God's word the way you tell it. But we're not sure you understand the kind of allegiance we expect. Not yet anyway."

Hiram's throat went dry, and he was weak-kneed thinking about fending for Sarah. But he worked hard to keep a stoic expression, maintain their sleeted glares. *Should I stand my ground? Is that reckless? Imperiling Sarah's freedom, her life?* He tried to swallow but couldn't, felt like he took a bite out of the sand-dunes. He managed to say coolly, "Will that be all?" to which Mr. Miller replied, "Yes, Reverend, as you were."

Though he felt like a scolded schoolboy, Hiram buried everything deep and fast, in order to get Sarah out of Bellwether. As he was shutting the door, he heard Mr. Miller say, "Seems your loyalty needs to be checked too, Oscar."

In just one look, Hiram knew Sarah could sense the dread. In only one night, the bedeviled village dredged a crater between them, too wide to cross. He took her hand in his, the anguish prickly like thorns, poking from all sides. "Seems the board doesn't like me having a guest," he said. The wrongness swished in his stomach like swamp water. He knew Sarah didn't blame him for sending her home. But he knew, too, that if it were up to her, she'd stand against the villainy—no matter what—because she was stronger than him.

Chapter 27
Down on 22nd Street

Within the week, Ruth's foreman, Edgar, agreed to meet with Eva. She and Ruth stepped through the tall gates of Smith & Bailey together. Ruth was greeted by the men with what seemed to be the usual—a quick "Mornin' Ruth" or a tipped cap—but seeing Eva, the thickset workers slowed, watched the new, comely girl with utmost attention, the hankering made plain in their taut, sunburnt faces.

"There's work to be done, gentlemen," Ruth chided, without easing her pace. The workmen busied themselves again, but Eva felt their sneak peeks as she passed. She didn't feel scared, though, only a bit flushed. Don't look at them, she told herself. But then she did, catching the gander of Ephraim, a fresh-looking lad with sky-blue eyes, and the youngest of the crew, she'd later discover. They both looked away, quick as wild jacks.

Edgar met them at the door, nodded for Ruth to go, then led Eva to his desk. When they sat, Eva bounced her leg unwittingly. Seeing her wriggle, Edgar pushed aside a heap of paper to reveal a plate of cornbread. "That Ruth, she's a hoot, ain't she?"

"Sure is." Eva smiled, the tightness loosening some. He motioned to the bread with his hand.

"You know how she came to work here, don't ya?"

"Not fully, sir," Eva said, culling through the crumbling loaf.

"Well, you see," he leaned back in his chair, hands behind his head, elbows out, "there was a mill collapse out east—"

"Oh, I know all about that." Some morsels of bread fell from her mouth, and she dabbed them from the desk with her finger.

"Did you know the owners offered Ruth a fat sum of money?" Eva's mouth was full, so she raised her eyebrows to signal her interest. "That's right," he said, then leaned forward and widened his eyes. "But I'll be damned if the feisty ol' bird didn't turn it down. She says to those suits, 'I don't need your goodwill, men, I need a job.' And the scuttlebutt is that after the head boss offered her a job in Chicago, she put one hand on her hip and with the other, pulled her eyepatch way out then let it snap into place and said, 'That's the least you could do.'" Edgar belly laughed. He pulled the plate of cornbread back toward himself, pinched a chunk between his fingers— "Why work here, of all places?"—then shoveled the morsels into his mouth, chomping sideways like a mule munching hay.

Here we go, Eva thought. Be firm, look him in the eyes. She squared her shoulders. "I want to make my own way, sir, like Ruth." Edgar studied her a moment. But the silence was tormenting. "I don't want to be at the mercy of others," she said. "Not ever again."

"Slow down, there, Miss Eva." He stroked his chin. "I've only got work in the yard right now. Not the kind of grind for a—"

"I can't go home." Eva blinked her eyes hard but never turned from him, even when she felt them icing over.

Edgar leaned his face into his bent knuckles. "Well, lass, it's back-breaking work. Some of my toughest men get down and out. And I can't pay but $3 a week." It was all Eva could do to repress the howling in her throat. She imagined the new house she'd build her Ma soon enough, facing east so the sun shines through every morning. And something small for herself, maybe some of those new gathered skirts, the ones with four or five panels of fabric and the hem flared out like a bell.

"By hook or crook, we work," Edgar was still listing his admonishments. "So, unless you're halfway to the bone orchard, best find your way here." When he finished his spiel, Eva stood and as much as she wanted to hug him, she put out her hand instead.

"Thank you, sir. You won't regret it."

"Sure hope not." His paw devoured hers. As she made her way back to Ruth, Edgar brayed, "Eva!" She turned. "Never mind those boys out there, ain't used to a young gal out and about in the yard. Let alone a pretty one."

Eva started at the mill that Monday. Edgar called on Ephraim to show her around the yard. The young man greeted her at the gate, hair slicked back, thick and wet with Macassar oil. Eva could smell the castile soap he scrubbed himself with, but she didn't think much on it. She simply wanted to start working. And told him as much.

For months to follow, Eva hauled and stacked timber scraps against the far walls, alongside the burliest of men. Though they weren't overly friendly at first, they weren't rude either. Nonetheless, she held her own until finally, they began sporting with her as a show of acceptance. Though careful not to show it, she swelled with pride when they bragged of her tenacity—"Full chisel, lil' Eva" and "Biggest damn toad in the puddle"—as she passed by with arms full, trying to keep her back straight. She knew she was outworking the older men with their bald, shiny crowns and bushy gray hair on their sagging chests when they took off their shirts. She knew, too, that her wage was scant by comparison. But that wasn't a battle she wanted to fight just yet. It was enough to help Ruth with food and kerosene and to put a few cents away each week, hidden in the coin purse that was stuffed between the sofa cushions. Many afternoons, her hands were split and oozing, her back gnarly and barbed. But no matter. She was worlds away from Samuel, and from bathing in the river, the one Pa made dirty.

Nightly, the two women sipped their homemade cider—Eva drinking from the pitcher of fermented apples now—laughing about their aches. Eva's from the grind and Ruth's from growing old. They marinated their feet in Epsom salt and honey, trying to sooth their bloated muscles. Somehow, the twinging and panging only bolstered Eva more. Then, every few days, Tina reappeared, rumpled and insolent.

And one crisp night, mid-November, Tina was clamoring on the stoop. Eva jolted to her feet as Ruth bumbled to the door, still half sleeping, and her eye soaking in a cup on a side table. Tina's keys jangled from just outside.

"Is that you, Tina?" Ruth asked as she pulled open the door. Tina had leaned against it to steady herself, so the momentum of the hardwood struck Ruth off kilter and knocked her to the ground. The rings from Tina's knotted miser purse broke free, spinning on the floor like tops. All the coins and bills scattered wide.

Then, silence.

"Tina, you've lied to me," Ruth said, breaking the quietude. Her legs were folded underneath her, and she was leaning back on one arm, the other covering the hole where her eye should be. "It was for your own good that I asked for rent money. To teach you self-respect." Tina hiccupped once then held her hands over her ears like a child. "All the while, you were hoarding, telling me you were penniless."

Tina swooned. Lying face down, her hoop skirt butted against the floor, lifting the backside into the air. With an undone corset, her pale lanky legs splayed out like rabbit ears. She smelled of whiskey and cigars and when Eva dragged her by the arms and lay her on the sofa, the stink wafted through the room.

A bit of shuffling and the squeak of chiffonier drawers

sounded from the girl's bedchamber. Then Ruth emerged, carrying a sturdy satchel covered with glossy brown hide and decked with rows of slightly tarnished studs. From the dogged look on her face, Eva knew she shouldn't interfere. So she leaned against the arm of the sofa where Tina was gurgling in her slumber and watched Ruth haul all of the girl's belongings to the front door. Finally, Ruth skittered to the kitchen and back again, carrying a rag, baking soda and saddle soap. She positioned herself on the floor in front of the bag and began scrubbing. "Can't send her away in a ramshackle gripsack," she said aloud.

After Ruth had freshened the hide and polished the studs, she wriggled upon the floor, trying to gather all the girl's strewn money. She folded the bills carefully, opened the bag and gently placed them on top. With both hands, she scooped up all the coins and dropped them in, too. Then she reached into the pocket of her nightgown and pulled forth a wad of her own money. She tugged at the string that bound what must have been her life savings. She licked her finger, readying to pluck out some bills, but hesitated. After a moment, she tied the string again, stowed the whole bundle amongst the girl's wares and buckled up the glinting bag. She stood, looked through the front window and from farther back, Eva looked, too.

The lamplighter was making his rounds, blowing out the soft glow of the only nearby gas light. The lamp never produced more than a yellow-orange circle not much bigger than the post itself. But after being snuffed out that night, the darkness felt darker than usual. As if the unknown that lurked within it was close, touchable. Even in the dimness, Eva could see a few white strands of hair beetled out from Ruth's head, and she thought, she doesn't wear them well.

When the women returned from the lumberyard the following evening, the luggage was gone, as was the money in the sofa cushions. Eva's heart burned with spite, so hot that when Ruth started talking about mercy and how "it's more for the one who was cheated," Eva turned away. It wasn't until the following week, after Eva had moved into Tina's room, that the constant, quiet spurring from Ruth took hold, and she could swallow the notion of starting her little nest egg again.

That Christmas, Ruth surprised Eva with a cast-iron safe—black and heavy—with a silver bolt and latch. The delivery boys lugged it into the kitchen and slid it into place beside the highboy. Ruth fanned out a cream-colored table linen, draped it over the metal box like a veil and atop it, set an antiquated urn, the last vestige of her soldier husband.

* * *

The winter lasted well into April, frosting the hyacinth and crocus, bringing in a bleak springtide. One gray Sunday, the women listened with bent ears as the Reverend spoke of absolution and the purging of souls. "We weren't intended to bear a cross, too," he said almost pridefully, as if God just told him so at breakfast. "Wipe clean your conscience and live with the spirit of a child."

On this special day, the minister was offering communion and though Eva had never taken it before, that she could remember, the minister handed her a flat, stale wafer, whispering, "The body of Christ." She let the wafer break down in her mouth then held it there. Jesus's flesh. She'd heard the words before, but now, with the corporeal proof in her mouth, soft as porridge, she winced, strained to swallow it. Soon enough, she realized that as she was trying to find the nerve to gulp down the insipid gob, much of it had already dissolved, slid into her belly. She was digesting the Redeemer, just like black-eyed peas or bread pudding. Though she never expected the earth to shake or the sky to catch fire, she was hoping for a little something more, even if it was just feeling lighter. She angled her head toward the Christ figure—his scarred and trickling hand still reaching out—and searched for his eyes again, sat up tall, but to no avail. Guess it can't happen all at once, she thought. Christ's blood mixing with mine, that's going to take time, chewing those crackers week after week. I'm in it for the long run, she told God. You'll see.

After service, the women stopped in the patch of flaccid grass, gabbing with the other parishioners. The sun broke through the slated sky, thin rays of light slanting across peoples' faces. Then Eva clasped Ruth's hand in hers. "Today's the day I tell you why I'm here," she said.

Ruth crumpled her face, the dead eye slow to catch up to the good one. "Why today?"

"Why not?"

"Still spicy as ever." Ruth clapped her hand over their mingled fingers. "Sounds like I need to steep some cider."

That night was like their first. The women talked until their eyes closed with Eva filling in all the unknowns. She told Ruth about the toils of being a farmer's child and both the hardships and splendors of living that far north. From arduous harvests to unending blizzards. From harrowing deaths of ore miners to bloody clashes with immigrant laborers. Eventually, she came to the brief stint she had with schooling and couldn't hide her giddiness, lighting up like a firefly as she spoke of Basil Brandt.

"We read aloud *The Scarlet Letter* and sometimes, he took a turn. His voice was husky, sort of like he had a cold, but he really didn't. Sometimes, he'd pause to see if we were listening. His eyes were big, bluer than any I've seen." Eva knew why Ruth was grinning. And it was fine. Why wouldn't she have fancied Mr. Brandt? All the girls thought he was the rushing. Some moms, too. But she had to shift the tone, this wasn't about her little girl shine for Mr. Brandt, it was about sharing all her sadness so that one day, maybe she could start thinking less on it. She took a deep breath and let it out, the smile vanishing as she pictured Pa's face.

"Ma had to tend to Grandma over in Marquette, that was

the first time he did it." Eva didn't clam up like she expected. Instead, she spoke fast so she wouldn't stop. Just kept talking, spurring herself on, leaving nothing out. "He never said a word, just crept into my cot and shoved his chapped hands under the afghan." Eva looked at her own hands, ran her fingers over them. "I remember thinking they felt like tree bark. And they hurt, a stinging kind of hurt." A single, fat tear tumbled down Ruth's cheek and dangled on her chin—she did not wipe it away. "Then Pa pushed Ma to visit Grandma more. 'What if she kicks the bucket?' he'd say, then pause, raise his eyebrows, 'And you ain't there.' So, Ma went to live with Grandma for a spell. I thought about telling her, but it felt selfish. I swore someone was choking me as Ma waved goodbye. Hard fingers clamped down around my neck while Pa helped her into the buggy as if we were a happy little family. There was nothing I could do, sort of like watching the needle coming at you for that first stitch while you just sit there, waiting for the poke."

"Do you need to take a break, dear?" Ruth rubbed the skin beneath her dead eye with a knuckle then patted Eva's knee.

"No. I need to tell you these things, if you don't mind." She didn't wait for an answer, just kept purging. "Pa came to my room almost every night, climbed me like a tree, then left. Until—" Eva wavered. "One night, just before Grandma died, Pa was pressed hard against my front side, hands grabbing everywhere. He was hot and sticky, angry acting. And in all his shifting and such, our eyes met—"

She wavered again. "It was only a second, that's it. And he jerked his head away, held real still for a bit, then snatched off me, quick as a rat. I knew when I heard his door shut that he wouldn't be back that night. But a few nights later, by God, he came again. Told me to turn over on my belly." Eva's voice cracked as she bumped through the next few words. "His voice was dull, had no color to it. And before I could do as he asked, Reverend Hiram came rapping at our door, shouting for Pa. He'd come to tell us that Grandma passed and that

Ma was on her way home."

There was a brief bout of silence. Eva looked at the tears sliding down both of Ruth's cheeks now. And she felt silly wondering how eyes made of glass could cry.

Then she said, "That's when I knew that God was good," and scooted toward her, resting her head beneath Ruth's chin and between her breasts. "See, that very night, I had said to the Lord, 'I know you ain't in charge of others' sins, but I can't take much more of this.' And I told Him how I felt foul all the time. I said, 'Please, just make Pa stop, at least for a bit.' A day later, Ma came home for good."

Ruth pulled her in close and Eva pushed into her hold.

* * *

Ephraim didn't go to church. "Glad some folks find peace in it," he said. "Not me, though. It's not where I belong." Eva didn't judge, only told him she enjoyed their walks on Sunday afternoons and whenever he stopped by Ruth's and the three of them talked about worldly matters—the war effort, emancipation, and the Homestead Acts out west. And she liked it when Edgar assigned them an errand together, hauling lumber in the ox-drawn carriage, either across town or better yet, to the nearby settlement along Hubbard's Trail. That's when they talked the most and when Eva figured him for a truthful fellow.

"Gonna run my own mill one day soon. And have a slew of kids. They'll be running around the two-story house on the west end of the river, kicking and digging in the mud, fishing for bluegill." He said it with such vigor, as if it were already in the works, and Eva believed he would do all those things. She wanted the exact same life, one marked by hard, honest living and apt reward. While Ephraim was talking about the beets he'd be growing in the front yard and the buckets of morels the family would gather, she pictured herself by his side, young ones tugging at her skirt. It all seemed in fine-feather.

But out of reach, too, with a faithless man. She could not carry another when it came to spiritual things. Her own holy voyage was hard enough.

So the day that Edgar asked them to haul several hundred board feet of timber on a Saturday, out past the South Loop, Eva was delighted yet prudent with her thoughts. It was a breezy spring day, the sun directly overhead. The two of them were already give-out from loading all the boards into the carriage, so there was much relief to be traveling for a little while. They moved along Chicago's timber block roads, out of the industrial section of the city and over to Dearborn, the light wind blowing through their clothes, cooling their damp skin. They came to a free, open space between two clumps of buildings.

"Part of what they're calling a 'park movement,'" Ephraim said. "There's a lot of them. So now, forever and ever, nothing can ever be built there, no houses, no businesses. Nothing but trees and air for folks to enjoy." He veered the carriage to the side, brought the oxen to a halt under a silver maple with branches forking this way and that, spreading shade in every direction. She spun her head around to ask why they'd stopped and startled at the nearness of his face. Ephraim had gathered the reins in his lap, took in a heavy breath and was leaning in for a kiss. It wasn't happening in the maudlin way she'd always pictured—like in the woodlands of *The Scarlet Letter,* Hester Prynne's cheeks in Reverend Dimmesdale's hands, staring into one another's eyes, and the clear song of a warbler dripping in the distance. Nevertheless, she tried to adjust, match his unfamiliar motion.

At nineteen, she'd only been mauled, never kissed. The city's bustle was somewhat muted amidst the burgeoning maples, though beyond the trees, several passing wagons still clanked and a random voice called out inaudible words to another, on-again-off-again. The moment was imperfect, but still, Eva thought it might have been made for her and

Ephraim, a wink of time staged by God. Maybe Ephraim would try harder to find his faith, for her sake. She closed her eyes and sat still until his lips pressed against hers. They were wet and briny and he pushed too fast, too hard. Their front teeth tinked. Eva winced but tried to stay the course. Then he tried poking his tongue between her lips, but she held them closed. One of the oxen dropped several chips, and the smell of dung wafted over them. And in a trice, the sloppy rendez-vous was done.

When he let up, Eva could still feel the damp of his lips. She popped open her eyes, and Ephraim gave her a quick nod. She scurried for what to say, but he didn't seem to need any words. He snapped the reins, made a cluck out of the side of his mouth and shouted, "Giddup!" Neither of them said anything for a block or two. The silence wasn't bothersome, though. It was comfortable. For Eva, there was a strange ac-complishment in having been kissed—a sense of womanhood and courting, all new and good. Her tooth still hurt and the stink of oxen dung still hovered, but those were fond details of the story she hoped to tell one day.

Leaving their secluded pocket, the grindstone of the city switched on again like someone tugging a pull-chain. As they turned onto South Dearborn, the tone shifted. There was still much bustling, but not from toil and haste as much as loose-ness and carousal. An inebriated man swinging from a lamp-post, others prancing like toddlers, arm in arm, sputtering the words to "Camptown Races" and clinking their steins with each passer-by.

"What is this place?" Eva asked, her head turning slow like an owl's.

"Welcome to the Levee District."

She'd heard of it before. A place for sinners, Ruth had told her, where folks wander from the path. Even so, Eva couldn't stop pivoting her neck—saloons, dance halls and brothels. She heard Ephraim chuckle every time she pointed or let out a tiny gasp. They moved through the bulk of the South Loop that way, her gawking, him laughing. And on either side of them, the indulgent patrons made merriment. "All of them trying to forget about their hollow lots in life," Ephraim told her as he steered through the hullabaloo without incident, until they approached 22nd Street.

The doors of Kasey's Tavern swung open, the cacophony of swindlers and debauchery pouring forth. A buxom woman staggered out into the street sideways like a crab—half walking, half toppling. She wore a cherry red raiment, and the bodice had a wide, drooping neckline. No bertha, so her breasts were pushed up and flattened out. They were fleshy, looked like the ends of bread loaves. With only a few petticoats, the wiry corset could barely hold the woman's healthy rump and thick flanks. She steadied, regained her faculties and stalked toward the wagon, calling for them to stop.

"Whoa!" Ephraim yawped, heaving up the reins. That's when she hoisted up her ruddy skirt, just past her round knees, then scanned Ephraim with big, prowling eyes. She switched her hips with wide span and great strain, strutting like a peacock, unaffected by the tumult all around. Eva studied the hustler's gestures, bewitched by her gall, her lewdness. Then the woman grasped the horse's bridle and stepped around the side of the wagon. She touched Ephraim's arm and walked her fingers from his bicep to his chest. Although she understood this woman to be a harlot, her brazenness and command was fascinating. Even when Ephraim seized her hand sharply and chided, "You're a shame," the working girl maintained control.

"Let go." Her pitch was assertive, matter of fact. And familiar. Eva leaned forward, looked past Ephraim, directly at the woman's face. Tina squinted back at Eva, and a sneer broke across her face. She wrenched herself from Ephraim's grip and stood upright. Some of her hair that she had twisted over her ears came loose from the comb at the base of her neck. She tucked it back in and wrapped one of the fat ringlets around her pointer finger, looking both Eva and Ephraim over like goods on a store shelf. Then she moved the finger to her bright lips, forming a cross, either hinting to keep their chance meeting hushed or making another suggestive gesture. Eva couldn't tell.

Then Tina began to laugh, from a chuckle to an all out cackle. The tavern doors opened again and the sounds of free-for-all spilled out, someone tripped over the spittoon that sat at the threshold, the brown juice darkening the gravel. Tina's crowing was witch-like as she headed back toward the fracas. Ephraim scooted back in his seat and hoisted up the reins. When he caught Eva's eye, he quickly looked away, brushed his cheek with his knuckles a couple of times, the thin leather strap hanging down from his clutch. Eva felt strange, even vulnerable—a little curious but sad at the same time. Ephraim's behavior confused her, and so did her own reaction to it. Still, even after being thieved, she felt the need to linger, make sure Tina made it back inside. She reached for Ephraim's shoulder, patted it until he lowered the straps.

Tina halted, looked back at them and stopped laughing. Her eyes bulged but then quickly narrowed into slits. Through the din, she yelled, "Don't you do that!" then made her finger and thumb into a gun and aimed it at Eva, cocked and loaded. "Don't you look after me like a child, you hay-bag!" She weaved a little before traipsing toward the carriage again. She put her hand on a back rim for balance. Everything seemed to harden—her facial features, her body—as if she was spoiling. Then she reached for Ephraim a second time, touched the same shoulder that Eva had patted. "Not too late for a bit a'cuff." She stroked his arm with all her fingers, down to his elbow and back up again. Ephraim leaned away.

"Stop it, Tina." Eva's tone was ironclad and it surprised her. She was wondering why Ephraim didn't speak for himself.

"Strong fella like you, gotta get a little under-over, from time to time. But you already know that," Tina continued, reaching for the top button of his shirt. He covered her hand with his, lifted it from his chest, the linen pulling in her grip.

"Time to go," he said. As they began to pull away, Tina walked beside them then fell in behind. Her gaze held power; Eva couldn't look away. The girls maintained one another's stare—Eva in the carriage looking over her shoulder, and Tina sauntering not far back. Several others had stumbled from the saloon and were now between the carriage and Tina, whooping and yelping. Tina stopped, stuck her hand under her dress, rummaged around some, then pulled out several bills and fanned them over her head. "Missing something, sweetheart?" she hollered after them.

Eva flashed hot. In an instant, the intrigue of Tina's insolence and any semblance of pity vanished. She leapt over the side of the carriage, landed hard, but started running. "You're a crook and a whore," she shouted. Ephraim yelled for her, but it was too late. Even though she was still only a few feet from the carriage, it may as well have been in Bellwether.

Eva had been willing to let it go, told herself that Tina needed it more, but to be taunted with it was too much. She knew she wouldn't stop now, not until reclaiming what was hers, no matter what the consequence. Like the time she went back for the boy chained under the porch. Something in her could push away all thoughts, all ramifications when she was in pursuit of something bigger than the moment. She moved through the fray of drunkards and street girls just inside the tavern. The sounds of impropriety were striking—loud, banging piano and lustful laughter—and the air was thick with smoke. On all sides, men blew out long, gray wisps from their cigars, like little noxious ghosts, wheeling and shifting. But Eva kept Tina locked in her sights as they bumped and pushed their way through. Eva blinked the water from her stinging eyes, cupping a hand over her nose and mouth to ease the burn in her lungs.

As they neared the backside of Kasey's, the crowd thinned

out, opening a path to a narrow staircase. Eva approached the bottom stair just in time to see Tina disappear into the top floor. Dread roiled in her belly but she squinted into the shady stairwell, rolled her upper lip over her lower as she scaled the stairs, two at a time. The hallway was dim and though the harsh sounds of the tavern were still raucous, the emptiness of the corridor hollowed them out some. There was no one in sight. Three rooms in the hall, the middle room's door wide open.

Eva crept close to it, a wave of clamor from the street ushered through the only window at the end of the hall, Ephraim's voice tangled in the discord, calling her name. A torn, brown valence flapped in a passing breeze. Some of the folds had come undone, so it was hanging low and loose from the cornice like a flag.

There was a shaky kind of energy, and the sparks in her chest made her feel on the wing, but she pushed on, feeling a bit sinful, being a part of all the transgressions around her. A woman stepped out from the open door, leaned back against its frame. She was medium height and her hair hung free, falling over the sides of her narrow face and down her pointy shoulders. Eva stopped. It felt wrong to just traipse on by. She watched as the hustler drew her leg upward along the doorway, slow and easy, forming an A at the knee. She swiped her forehead with the back of her hand and asked Eva what brought her there. Eva answered that she was looking for someone, trying not to stare at the woman's features— broomstick limbs and long black hair, dangling over pale skin, almost translucent in the glow of muted light behind her—as well as her bone-colored corset squeezing her breasts into half globes.

"Never seen you here before." Her voice was flat, trawling, and she seemed tired, as if she'd been trounced upon. Yet she held her sheen, perfectly cool in her spoon-like pose.

"Never been." In the pause that followed, Eva wondered

for a split second if the woman had already lain with men that morning. "Do you know Tina?"

The woman leaned out, pointed to the last room on the same side of the hall.

"Check the balcony. She's always standing out there, looking at the city." A deep voice called to the harlot from within, told her to get back inside. "I've got another go in me," he shouted. The woman obeyed, took a step inward. Eva headed in the direction she had pointed but looked back in time to see the dark eyes still observing her. She hoped it was out of interest, not concern.

When she approached Tina's room, Eva gripped the glass knob, jerking it left then right. The door unlatched, moaning low as it opened. She stepped through. Straight ahead, through an open window.

Tina stood on the rickety balcony running along the outside of the building, her hands resting on the railing. With her back to Eva, she said, "Your money's on the bed."

Eva glanced at the bundle on the foot of the bed, then back at Tina. Eva could hear herself still panting from the run, from the fire of it all. She took the next couple of breaths through her nose and tried to let them out slow.

"Your boyfriend is down there. He keeps calling out your name, hoping you'll hear him in this big ol' rat's nest." Tina's voice was even. She raised her head, angled her body to the left. "He'll start searching for you any minute. Stubborn as a goat—" She stopped. "Well, seems like it anyway."

Eva took a step toward the bed, eyes fixed on Tina. Hearing an outsider call Ephraim her boyfriend stuck in her craw, roiling a strange sense of wrongness as Uriah flashed through her mind. She had learned to blink him away, fast as lightning, ever since landing in Chicago. Missing him was too damn hard.

"Go on. It's yours ain't it?" Tina climbed back inside. She stood near the window, the square toe of her boot behind her, upright, so the side laces were showing. "I put a few extra dollars with it. Thought it was only right."

Eva scooped up the money, flipped several bills back onto the bed, a couple of them drifting to the floor. "Don't want your help. Just want what's mine."

"Take it," she said, her tone harder now. The oaky stink of cigars was heavy in the walls. From the next room over, a bedstead thumped the wall—a series of knocks then a low, vomitous moan. Across the hall a peal of high-pitched laughter sounded out, too. The noises of carnal pleasure made Eva's cheeks burn hot. She looked at the money in her hand, kept her eyes cast down.

"You get used to it," Tina said. "The sounds of folks sozzling, that is." She picked up the stray bills from the bed and floor, straightened them into a perfect rectangle and pushed them at Eva. "Take it," she said again. "I've got plenty." To prove her point, she shook her head back and forth so that her droopy earrings swung and clicked against her face, the tiny diamonds sparkled in the lamp light. She stepped over to the lowboy and fingered the necklace hanging from the highest knob so that the polished silver shimmered some, too. "You and Ruth, you're fond of one another," she stated, though it felt like a question.

"Yes."

"You work at the mill with her. Go to church together?"

"Yes."

Eva felt herself going stiff but thought it best to stay mild. After all, she had her money back, and then some. She didn't know what Tina was capable of either. Maybe she had friends down the hall, just waiting for the signal to attack. "We do," Eva replied casually.

"You have a mama, don't you?" Tina was sifting through the top drawer of the lowboy.

"Of course." Eva crossed her arms and bent her neck. "Why are you asking?" Tina continued pillaging through her goods. She had moved onto her underclothes drawer, picking up several different pantalettes before lifting up what looked to be a linen pair. She put her fist through the open crotch then draped them over her arm, petting them like a cat.

"Ruth was all the time meddling where a mama should be. Telling me how a lady should act. Or shouldn't. Telling me what the Lord thinks." She shook her head again in disapproval. The earrings jangled. "How the hell does she know what the Lord's thinking?"

Eva waited, not sure if she was looking for an answer or just making an objection. After a moment, Eva said, "Guess I don't mind it much."

"Well, ain't that sweet."

Eva knew she should pause, gather her thoughts. But she couldn't. She just stomped forward, put her face inches from Tina's, then raised a finger to her chest. "Ruth and me, we aren't your concern. She lowered her finger to just above her stomach. "You quit on her. And that's your loss."

She looked down at Eva's finger. "That really got your goad, didn't it?" She hooted like a barn owl, her eyes big and glassy like one, too. "But don't it bother you none when she says things only your mama should be saying?"

Though her head was screaming for her to leave, Eva's heart kept her put. She couldn't quite pin it down, but there was a strange sense of curiosity, being surrounded by so much foulness, nobody feeling bad, or even caught off balance. She snatched up the bloomers, held them high. "Seems like you might need someone acting like a mama around. Maybe you'd be thinking more about family matters, less about things like this."

Tina grabbed onto the fancy pantaloons, hanging between the two of them, upside down like a sleeping bat. Eva's undeniable desire to stay a bit longer, to catch more glimpses of the mischief, made her grip them tighter. A quick tug-of-war, then the drawers ripped. Tina let go and said, "Don't matter none. I've got a drawer full. Besides, I'll make enough money this afternoon to buy two in their place." She stepped to the highboy, ran her fingers along the edges of a sullied daguerreotype sitting atop it—a military man, dark blue uniform and fat black mustache, and standing behind him, what looked to be his bride, sharply parted hair, an unadorned dress and white gloves, her hands resting on his wide shoulders. "Truth is, I don't have to be here. Got a Ma and Pa down in Indiana, write me to come home all the time. But I don't want to work on no farm. And I ain't waiting around till some peasant boy takes a fancy to me. Here, I call the shots. Stay up all night if I please. Spend my money how I want. Yeah, sure, I gotta let some of those drunkards downstairs do their business on me. But most times, they're all hell-fired, go at it like greased lightning. It's all over in a minute or two. Then they plank up quick as can be, still buttoning their sit-down-upons as they rush out of here."

Eva's heart was still beating faster than normal in defense of Ruth, but it was languishing some. And she was grappling with how captivating Tina's life seemed, the absolute freedom, to come and go as you pleased. Then she wondered if the men ever got mean? How much money each time? And what about being in a family way? When she spotted the pile of sparkling trinkets, she asked, "All that jewelry, you buy it yourself?"

"Damn right." Tina's painted lips hooked upward on the right side of her mouth. She bent down to the bottom drawer, pulled it open, then dipped her head, an invitation for Eva to look. A treasure chest of bauble and brass—more hooped earrings, several shiny necklaces, and a dozen rings or more. "Some I bought," she said, "but most were gifts."

Ephraim appeared in the doorway. He looked only at Eva. All the furor that surrounded the place seemed to flatten to a murmur. He was panting, but spat out, "Land sakes, didn't you hear me calling?" Then he looked around the room, hesitantly, almost sheep like. "Feeling disrespected, Eva," he said.

Eva thought to herself, so what, I'm not your wife. And then she brought to mind their lubberly kiss, wondered if that was where their future was headed? She took note of his expectant expression, as if he were somehow owed an explanation. The intrigue of Tina's grew stronger by the second.

A pudgy woman wearing only her corset—timeworn, dingy white, like an old man's teeth—and a stout, hairy customer, half-covered, tumbled out of the door from across the hall. Both of them were peeking around Ephraim, looking inside, curious and expectant. The man was bare up top, his lower half wrapped in a sheet that he gathered in his fist at the hip. Grinning like a child, he asked, "Who wants to join us?" Eva crinkled the money in her fist and stepped to Ephraim then guided him backwards into the hallway.

"Get back to all your praying and chiding," Tina called after them. "And keep bustin' your hump at the mill, wasting away with a blind ol' biddy trying to be your mama. I'll be here, high living."

As the wagon rocked along again Eva's mind cleared some, she remembered Ephraim's ill-ease, his skittish movements and bleary eyes, seeming more anxious than disgusted. Then she made a couple of attempts at diving beneath the surface talk—"Quite the vixen, that Tina" and "Good money in selling your soul, I guess"—but neither of them took.

* * *

It was after Eva's visit to the Levee District that all the friction crept in. It was slow to pass at first but quickly swelled like the belly of a rotting deer. Seeing Tina's freedom and grit was a knife to flesh, tearing the skins of Ruth's and Eva's bond. And even though Eva knew the angst was coming from her, she couldn't rein it in. Ever since she moved to Chicago, she'd been wiping black soot from the walls, beating the rugs, wiping the lamps' glass chimneys and trimming the wicks, pounding the sugar loaves, making trips to the well, rinsing the clothes in plain water then with bluing, pressing with a flat iron and stiffening with starch. But as of late, dumping Ruth's chamber pot had been added to the list as she had spells of the trots, couldn't make it to the latrine on time, her stomach too cramped to empty the pot herself. Resentment was starting to bubble up, move closer to the surface.

Then, Edgar the foreman traveled to Milwaukee to mourn his sister's death, petitioning the women to look after his three young sons while he was away. He didn't really give them a choice as the boys were standing by his side when he pitched the request, their packed haversacks slung over their shoulders. Ruth accepted without pause, tousling Herman's hair, the youngest of the brood. Edgar said, "Best behave, boys, or Ruth'll stripe you," as Eva ushered them inside, eager for the change of pace.

Before Edgar came, Ruth had already dipped into her not-so-secret stash of bourbon. The hoard was not as concealed as she believed (in her sleeping quarters, behind the folding screen). Probably one of the reasons her room was always off limits, Eva figured. When it came to the growing Temperance Movement, Ruth stood firm as iron, offered no apologies, always repeating the same adamant line, "Jesus Christ himself supped wine to rejoice in the Lord." And once she got started, she worked herself into a stir about it… "No way in blue blazes some lawmaking teetotaler is going to tell me I can't drink some spirits now and again."

After the boys said their goodbyes to their father, Horace, the eldest, sat at the table next to Ruth, asked if he could taste the hooch she'd just poured. "Not a snowball's chance in Hades," she said. And they both laughed. Not Eva, though.

"Why not?" she asked. Ruth stopped laughing, her smile fading. She tilted her head, as if doing so would make Eva's question sound differently, less insolent.

"Because he's just a boy," she replied. "That's why."

"But it's just a—"

"What's more, Eva, is your sassing me." She scowled. "Now look, you've gone and made my peeper dry up. Dip a washrag in the basin for me." She put her hand across the side of her face, shielding the air from her fake eye. "Seems like you've gone and lost all your manners." Eva did as she was told, but the malice was smoldering under her skin as she wrung the excess water from the rag. She could feel Ruth's overstep where it wasn't before. Or was it? Never felt like Ruth was meddling, until lately. Seemed Tina's words were building a wall, even if she wasn't there, bringing Ruth's tinkering to light. Eva did have a mama, a good one, albeit misled.

Eva didn't want to do what she did next. It just happened. One of those times when she plows ahead, any possible fallout obscured by the flurry of the moment.

Ruth took the wet rag and pushed it against her face, moistening her dead eye. Then she headed to her room for a patch, still mumbling through the cloth as she went, "Sassing and pooh-poohing." Eva turned to Horace, mouthed Ruth's words, rolled her eyes while opening and closing her hands like the mouth of a puppet. The flippancy felt good. Horace smiled, but she could tell it was out of nervousness, not amusement. Eva reached for the bourbon, grabbed it by the neck and took a hearty swig. Though she had to fight the burn, the grimace came easy. "Like drinking lightning with a taste of cornbread," she rasped and passed it to Horace. The boy eyed the bottle intently, stalling.

"Looks like a fat hammer, don't it?" he said.

"Go on. Take a nip." Eva dipped her head.

Horace snatched the bottle from her, tipped it and gulped. His Adam's apple bobbed once, twice, three times, then he bolted upright, knocking his chair into the wall. Puffing, wheezing. He grabbed at his throat, held both hands there like he was choking himself.

Ruth darted into view, sleuthed the scene with her good

eye. Everything moved slow, the air clotted all around them. It was an unexpected test—Eva the giver of it, Ruth the taker. From day one, there had never been any challenges, no jockeying for position. Ruth was the provider, the erudite, while Eva was happy to serve as the beneficiary. Now, she could feel the stone Tina wedged between them, knowingly or not, though instinct told her to apologize, to blame her salty behavior on something small like sore knees or all the mosquitos sneaking in through the window, it wouldn't come. She had seen the bigger Chicago now, the one beyond the four brick walls of their stagnant place. The city far beyond aching backs and calloused feet; far from all the dragging talks about righteousness and virtue, conversations that seemed like nothing more than lectures now, just piety and judgment. Eva remained silent. If she was honest, there was a strange empowerment in Ruth's discomfort. It was the first time she'd seen the woman dumbstruck.

"Not certain who the child is here," Ruth said, framing her words like a question, emphasizing the word child. "Thought I knew." Eva wanted to stop, to end her little rebellion that she didn't fully understand. But she was mad. And angry about being mad. Even as she was scolding herself, she raised the bottle high, smirked at Ruth then took another fiery swill.

"Cheers," she said.

* * *

In the morning, Ruth and Eva made a spare breakfast of griddle cakes and oatmeal for the boys. Though Ruth said good morning with a smile and Eva responded in kind, the space felt smaller than ever—the fuse was short. But there was common ground in feeding the young ones. It was still dark outside, and Ruth had lit two candles at the table. "To save the kerosene," she said. They were stocked up with plenty of cornmeal and sugar and beans, but the kerosene was low.

It wasn't until everyone had eaten that young Clyde said he didn't feel good. He said his belly hurt and that he was cold and hot at the same time. Ruth felt his forehead, "A bit of a fever," she announced. As she lay him on the squat, lumpy sofa, Eva gathered both kerosene lamps onto the table—a brass one, hand-painted black by Ruth, and a ruby one, with overlay glass, soda-lime, and cuts in the under layer—then carried the tinderbox to the cook-stove and opened the firebox. She pulled out some dry grass and dandelion clock, kneading the fineness in her hand a couple of times. Before she could ignite the springy mound, though, Ruth looked up from the sick child:

"No, Eva. We need to ration the fuel. I told you that."

"But he's not well. These will warm him."

"Keep the stove going. That'll do."

"My mama always set a lamp by me when I was ailing. It helped warm my bones and kept—"

"I'm not her," Ruth snapped. "Now do as I say. Fill a toilet can for me. Wet a cloth, too."

Eva glanced at Horace, caught his eye, then refocused on the tinder. She dropped it into the box, started picking at the strands and fluff, pretending there was something foreign that had to come out. Her face felt tight, her ears hot. She hated Ruth right then. "Damn right you ain't her," she spat. Then she remained tight-lipped as Ruth clamored up from the couch, pulled the patch back into place and ran a hand over the top of her head like she did when she was upset. Her scalp was glaring white where she always parted her dark hair down the middle and pulled it taut to either side. But Eva had never taken notice of the overplay before, the flair in her move-ments. Of course, she'd never been the reason for it either. Now, she felt the high-horse in all of her dramatic gestures, as if Ruth's hands were talking, saying, I'm too world-weary for this, too sophisticated for you. And she could feel the two of them unraveling.

"Not sure what's happening here, Eva. But this is still my house. You'll respect me in it," she said, crossing her arms over her middle section and raising her eyebrows so her whole face pulled with them. The lines around her mouth were deep, forming a prominent circle, starting at her nostrils and winding down to her pear chin. Eva saw all the flaws in Ruth at once, and there was a heavy jumble in her chest, a stew of guilt and woe. She wished guilt was the stronger of the two. Had Ruth always nettled at her like this? All the air was sucked from the room, taking any allegiance with it. Their affinity for one another seemed to vanish, just slide out. The gloom was unstoppable. And she knew that things had swerved forever.

Edgar came for the boys the following morning. Per usual, he brought a fresh supply of kerosene that he'd looted from the mill. Then he handed Ruth a Colt Walker, too, dull and nicked, with a small sack of lead balls that tinked as she took them from him. Eva saw them nod at one another.

With the boys still sleeping, Edgar talked of all the crime happening underneath the city. He must have been able to see the confusion on Eva's face because he started to explain how Chicago was built on marshland and how the muck often seeped up through the wooden streets. "Always held up traffic, toppling people over, even slipping their horses sometimes. Mud would cake everywhere, couldn't walk a block without being ankle deep. So, they put the city on stilts. And I'll be damned if it didn't work. No more sludge. But then—" Clyde stirred and all eyes turned to him, but he stayed put. "All these tunnels and passages below the ground, free from view, open to all man's misdeeds, that's when Roger Plant opened up. The big brothel over there by Monroe and Wells streets, an underworld whorehouse. There's a big ol' willow tree marking the spot—" Clyde stirred again, this time climbing down from the sofa and making his way to them. He stood between his dad's legs, nestling into his groin, rubbing the sleep from his eyes. Edgar stroked his head then called out for the other two. They roused, came to him with shuffling feet and matted hair, both wearing a bantam smile. "Wake up, boys. Fill all the buckets at the well. Show Ruth and Eva that you're grateful."

As the women readied for the day, Ruth stopped tinkering at the stove and spoke plainly and low. "Mind your manners, young lady. Or find a new place to live." She stared Eva down like a crouching cat having discovered a mouse. Eventually, Eva turned away, but only after she decided—it's time to go.

That night, when she heard the familiar gasp and stutter of Ruth's snore coming from her bedchamber, Eva packed her belongings into the same haversack she brought to Chicago years before. She buttoned down the canvas flap and stole away to the Levee District, trying not to think on it, just following the burn in her heart, the yearn for something more than a sore back and a thorny couch.

She made her way through the city without a hitch, just a few sideways glances from several working class men at different intersections, as well as an up-and-down glower from a steely woman as she turned onto 18th street, closing in on the seedy district. Eva regarded her face as they stepped past one another, so painted, as if her face were an easel. And then she came upon Kasey's Tavern, knowing that if she hesitated, even a moment, the brass tacks of being there would prick her, make her turn back. So she barged in, pushed past the patrons like she had just two weeks before, all of them looking the same—scraggly mustaches, high hairlines—then headed up the same narrow stairwell, down the hall to Tina's room. She knocked on the door and waited. After a minute, she rattled the knob and called out her name. Nothing.

Eva slumped to the floor, the strap of her haversack slackened and bowed out from her shoulder. She clutched the pack tight in her lap and closed her eyes, trying to shut out what she was doing, filth all around her. She searched her mind for yesteryear, the future, anything. The new home she'd build her Ma one day soon, overlooking Superior's sharp, blue waters, heavy waves cresting white up top. The fierceness of the big lake always brought her such comfort, even if she was only picturing its fury in her head, reminding her that there are so many bigger things than any given moment.

The door next to Tina's pulled open. Out stepped a lanky man with a silver, shaggy beard and a wide, toothy smirk. With his thumb and pointer finger, he clasped the rim of his hat and bent it toward her, the unbuttoned cuffs of his shirt fanning out and the bands of his overalls swinging at his sides. Eva felt her muscles tighten, her heart beat like footsteps. There was little air in the brothel, and she was straining for her share. Samuel's face flashed in her mind, his glinting eyes, big pools of black as he moved in on her. She could feel the uneven sway of the ship in her stomach and legs. Then she heard her Pa's gritty voice, too, scratching in her ear like a blade on glass, telling her to turn over. She forced herself to take deeper, longer breaths.

"'Evening, Miss," the man said. He turned toward the stairwell and before he walked on, he asked, "How do you do?"

"I do just fine," Eva said. Don't look down, she told herself. Look right at him. And then she flattened her voice, "And you?"

"Quite good. Thank you." He walked to the end of the hall and descended the stairs. She scolded herself for being too hard all the time, supposing everyone is bad. You're gonna need friends, she thought. And she questioned her own intentions, posed the question—if he's a wicked man just because he's here, then what does that make you? Then she muddied her thoughts even more, remembering that he just gave money to lay with a woman. That makes him a monster. Right? And she wondered if that made her a monster, too? For wanting more, wanting better?

Tina entered the hall just minutes after the smiling tomcat had dropped out of view. Eva wondered if they knew one another, if they had spoken as they passed in the stairwell. Had he ever paid Tina for love, too? She was wearing the same red dress from before. Her hair was pulled tight again, but several long ringlets hung down from the tight coil in back. There were waves of relief and dread in seeing her. A small version of the safety she felt with Ruth, or maybe it was just the familiar face.

Eva pulled herself up, watched the smile stretch across Tina's face as she came close. She was stumbling some but made it to the door. They looked at one another searchingly then Eva scooted aside. Neither of them spoke. The biggest panic of all rushed through Eva. *Oh Lord, she's gonna turn me out? What if Ruth won't take me back?*

Tina refocused on the lock, sighed a big sigh. She unbolted the door and stepped through, leaving it open. Still she was silent. Eva stood, stepped under the archway. Can't stop now. Fear and embarrassment mixed in her chest like flitting moths. From inside, Tina said, "Best get in here, 'fore some big, scary man touches you." She laughed that prairie-wolf cackle again, half shriek, half snicker. "I knew you'd be back."

Eva stepped in quick while the opportunity was still there. She had a semblance of that "gonna-get-you feeling" she got as a child whenever she was coming up from the ice cellar. In that below-ground, dark, dank chamber, Eva was convinced a cuckoo lurked, escaped from the asylum down in Kalamazoo. She could see his grotesque face in her nightmares. A misshapen head, eyes black as ink. He was always hiding behind the mounds of sawdust and straw, she just knew it, waiting to spring as soon as she turned her back to climb the stairs, her arms full of ice, defenseless for the taking.

Tina was at the lowboy, pulling off her earrings—gold ovals, wide at the bottom—and dropping them in with a tunk. "Had enough of Ruth's fiddling, did you?" Eva inhaled to form a reply, but Tina continued before she could speak. "You ain't gonna just stay here, sucking off me like a tick. You gotta work. I'll tell the boss you're staying awhile." She stopped, looked at Eva's hips, her chest. "Shapely gal like you, he won't mind. Hell, might kick me out, let you take my place."

The moths were really flapping inside her now. Eva's impulse was to cut and run, but she knew there was no going back. Something had changed. She thought about Ruth telling her another story, another gem about integrity and clean living. How making the bed each morning clears your mind, helps you start fresh. How leaving just a speck on the dishes speaks to your character. And she thought about the money. She wasn't saving enough at the mill, not enough to build Ma her new house. She couldn't stop this train now, even if it was headed for a cliff. It was like studying a hard autumn sky and knowing the clouds would never look exactly the same again. The white on blue. The shapes. Making more than a couple of dollars a day and living out here in the Levee District, living by her own rules, it was more than enough to make her drop the haversack on the floor and sit down on the edge of the bed.

But that old torment was there, too, like outside the privy, right before she miscarried, feeling as if she just had to foul her body, make herself dirty. Living at the tavern was her way of smearing more dirt on her skin, plugging it in her most private places, even swallowing it if she had to. After all, seems like she was made to suffer at the hands of men. Maybe this is what she was meant for.

Tina explained how things would work for the time being, very surely, as if she'd started mapping out the plan the second Eva left the first time. She jabbered on, answering the questions Eva had been thinking of, her thoughts as readable as the *Tribune*. "Some of 'em are foozlers. And some fat and grubby. Most of 'em is nice though. Just lonely is all. I'll be goddamned if sometimes they don't even stick their spindle in you. Just want you to rub it. Or they only put their fingers in your twat." The clunk of such a word made Eva flinch, but she tried to cover it up by clearing the smoke from her throat. Tina continued speaking the unmentionables without a shred of modesty, moving on to pregnancy. She showed Eva her porcelain irrigator, explaining how it all worked—the reservoir, the plunger and the nozzle. She talked of "womb veils" and "vinegar sponges" and other things Eva did not understand. Then she listed off the different douches girls had tried, laughing about one of them using olive oil and wine.

Chapter 28
In the Gloaming

Sarah had been gone for several years and though Hiram thought of her every day, she was closest at dusk. In Virginia, during their last reading session, Sarah talked about the gloaming, said she waited for it all day, every day. And when something kept her from seeing it, she pictured it in her mind. Hiram had always loved that time of day, too. How sometimes the colors splashed across the sky in blots, like an artist's painting. But sometimes, they melded into one solid mass, like a cut open watermelon, its pink meat stretching to the horizon. It was the last thing they shared, as the next day, he plummeted down the mine shaft.

Hiram was thinking of her this night. Nothing out of the ordinary, no jarring memory, just a cool, autumn evening. That's the burden of caring for someone you aren't good enough for, he thought. Everything calls her to mind. The sky had been starkly blue most of the day, the rich kind of blue that fills your soul. But it was fading to a smoky gray now. He grabbed his bottle of Mount Vernon by the neck and headed to the sea-stacks. The memories were going to sting tonight, he could tell.

As he neared the water, he saw Basil's hunched over profile atop their precipice. He knew it was selfish not to join him, to comfort him if he could. His friend was grappling with big things, like faith and loss, lamenting a good life gone awry.

But this night was for himself—not Basil, not anyone else. These fresh fall winds were Heaven speaking to him, softly and privately. And they were Sarah, sitting next to him, smelling woodsy and fresh, the way she always did. He prayed that he was right, believing certain moments are custom made by God—timely ones, beautiful ones—to comfort or calm or heal particular folks. It's not wrong to think the leaves have turned just enough to burnish in the dying sun, so one man can see them at the perfect time. Flawless reds and oranges and yellows, for one woman's sake, in one quick glance. Maybe not, though. The Lord has other fires to tend to. But it's nice to think that way for a little while.

He hunkered low in the tall grass, the sea-stacks sitting high to the north and west; to the east, the rectory. He looked behind him, glanced at the town square in the distance, the vanishing sun casting shadows on the few buildings, then lay back. The dewy verdure swaddled him like a baby, plush and cool against his head. The sky was a deep violet now with random swashes of pink. He closed his eyes, thoughts drifting to his brothers, his Ma, the Shenandoah.

Basil was making his way down, and Hiram watched quietly until his profile disappeared behind the slabs of limestone, then he resumed his position, hands behind his head. A few faint stars were shining through the purple and he focused on them, recalling Leander's final letter with a quiet sigh.

It was a coal dust explosion, buckled the whole damn pit, he wrote, followed by *No survivors, brother. Clint's in Heaven now, giving Ma and Pa plenty of crabbin', I'm sure.*

Hiram cried some as he recalled all the burdens he and his brothers bore, the fear he and Leander endured when Pa deserted them. He swatted at a bug that was humming near his face. Then he thought about the time Leander had a "girl dream" when he was twelve or so. Came to Hiram in tears, asking if he was going to Hell, showing him the hard, brittle crotch of his long underwear. Hiram put his arm around him and said, "If you're headed to the Devil's house for having girl dreams then I'm in a whole heap of trouble."

Hiram envisioned the last paragraph of the letter, the sentences still roll through his mind at all different times—during sermons he's giving, or in the washtub, shoveling snow from the church walkway, or even in the outhouse:

> *I won't be writing anymore. I miss the nights we'd have three sheets to the wind, talk about the things we knew nothing of. Girls, politics, aching bones. Boy, if we only knew. Please know that I'm proud of who you are, always knew you'd do something great, Mr. Preacher.*

> *Love,*

> *Leander*

Hiram laid his hands in the grass by his sides, palms down. It was more wet now, and his shirt had soaked through, his backside chilled, damp. He could see himself and his brothers, wading in the river's current, their britches pulled up over their shins as they stuffed shiny stones into their pockets. Then they took a break to tackle one another in the deeper waters, dunking and splashing and yelping. Hiram felt that same sadness he always felt when he thought about Leander—his averageness, his lack of grit. As they grew older, the whole family knew that he'd never tarry far. Thinking of his middle brother still roosting on the banks of the Shenandoah, alone, never seeing past Bluefield, that made Hiram's heart even heavier. There were too many memories on that river for his brother to wallow in, even the good ones can turn bad if that's all he has to hold on to.

The church was a mile from the stacks, but there was only a vast field between, so the sound of someone thumping the rectory's knocker echoed through the open space, shaking

Hiram from his reverie. Must be bad, he figured. Someone triggered Ada into a fit, creeping around her house, goading her with devil names. **Or maybe Basil has finally gone cat-skinning crazy.** With all that could go wrong running through his mind, Hiram still said a quick prayer, asking God to watch over his brothers—Clint in the next life and Leander spinning in the old—and to ease his own heart, help him understand why it's more important that he shepherd the families of Bellwether through the pains of war rather than serve in battle himself, helping to emancipate the only woman he's ever loved. And for the strength to lead his parishioners from their harsh judgment of others, to reconcile their unpardonable sin of having hanged innocent women, to drop to their knees whenever Ada passes by, think of Elinor's feet dangling above the earth, then beg for forgiveness.

The knock sounded out again and Hiram whispered "Amen" aloud, then headed home. As he neared, he could make out the mid-size silhouette on his porch. For a fleeting moment, the air caught in his mouth, and he couldn't push it forward or backward. *Could it be Sarah? A second chance at honor, hers and his?* But after a couple more steps, he saw that the frame was too wide to be Sarah's, taller than her, too.

Ruby Lee turned toward the noise of his feet swishing in the grass. She whispered his name, more of a question than a greeting. "Hiram?"

"It's me," he said. She didn't respond, just stood still and began to cry. Without any words, he put his arms around her shoulders, pulled her into his chest. He could feel her heaving intensify, so he kept her close with one hand, opened the door with the other. Then he let her go and they made their way inside. Hiram lit a lamp and dragged a chair in front of hers so that their knees were lined up together. The mood was vaguely familiar, a hint of the same warmth beneath the gray blanket when Sarah and he would brush against one another. That same drifting sensation, but milder. When he felt a tug in his groin and his bits pulling in tight, he pushed his chair back some.

"I've been having bad thoughts," Ruby Lee said. Her voice was high-pitched, like a child on a tire-swing. "I married Oscar on my fifteenth birthday. Had our first child by my sixteenth. He's a good man. God knows I love him. But he—"

That's when their eyes met. Hiram looked away, covered his lap with his hands. Ruby Lee leaned forward, lifted his chin with both hands, perused his face, then gently lifted up his hands. And something let go in his thighs, like his whole lower half had been constricted all his life, an unsprung coil.

His instinct was to fight it, contain it. But it was too far gone. Hiram let his erection show, let the bulge in his pants take full flight. He wanted the flare to dwindle. But he wanted to push past the control this time, too. He'd been good for so long. He wanted to go against his head, follow the lust. Have a dirty little secret like everyone else.

Oscar and all the Lee boys flashed through his mind; he blinked them away. Not this time. He flipped his hands so they covered hers, guided them back to the swell in his loins, moved them up and down the hard ridges, slow at first, until she started to do it on her own. He knew not to look at her face, that would surely make them stop. He closed his eyes, tilted back his head, heard himself groaning. Another flicker of resistance in the back of his brain tried to bump its way to the forefront, but the storm was raging. Thinking of the consequences now was like spitting on a forest fire. His shaft was pushed against the front buttons of his trousers. He tried to loosen the buttons, but they were too stretched. So he tugged until the top two popped off. His hardness sprung free and Ruby Lee took hold as if grasping a broom handle, her hands coarse as an orange-peel, but the undersides felt smooth. Though the dryness made the deed somewhat painful, the thrill of skin on skin was triggering. Hiram told her to go faster. And she did. Seconds later, he let go.

As he was still shuddering, the guilt already began to sur-face—like when the high winds churn up the lake floor, and the waves empty the muck onto the sand—especially after looking down at his seed spattered across his shirt. And when he saw Ruby Lee trying not to look at it, he pulled back his hips, tried to make his erection go slack. For a fleeting second, Hiram wondered if all men felt the same gratification when brought to the brink. Did their brains stop whirring for that moment, too? Did pleasure flood their whole body, making everything else go away? Like you've spilled part of your soul, all the trepidation leaking out with it. Didn't matter though. Already, the shame swamped him like the lake's dark sedi-ment, its foul-smelling algae.

Hiram spoke first. He said simply, "This is my burden to bear," then told her that more harm than good would come from telling Oscar. Or anyone. "You were only following my lead. The sin is all mine."

"I could've stopped," she replied. "You weren't holding a rifle to my head. And if I'm honest, I ain't sure my coming here was on the up and up."

Hiram unbuttoned his shirt while she spoke, folded the placket side over on itself. His back was still damp from the dew where he lay outside. Though baring his chest felt wrong, too, it was less disgraceful than the wet spots on the fabric. "I took advantage of my position. I knew you would do as I asked. There's no misdeed in answering a minister's—"

"My bigger fear is that you're gonna tell me to leave." Her voice cracked on the last word. "Don't try to tell me there ain't no shame in that, Reverend." Hiram stopped fumbling with his shirt, leaned forward, but not too much.

"The virtue comes from walking away, even when you don't want to," he said. Then he reached for her chin, lifted it up with his knuckles. "This is my sin. All mine. You hear me?" Ruby Lee forced her head back down, and Hiram pulled his hand back. After a moment of stillness, she nodded—slow, tiny bobs. "Go home, Ruby Lee. Go home to Oscar and the boys. If they are awake and ask you where you've been, tell them you went for a walk. Tell them you were ailing, but the cool air made you well."

Ruby Lee nodded again, faster this time. Then she stood, stepped lightly to the door and opened it a little. A fresh breeze rolled in and she faced the outside, moving her head back and forth as if the air held cleansing power. "Will God forgive us?"

"He's already forgiven you, Ruby Lee." Hiram's heart started to race at releasing her as he did not want to be alone with his thoughts. She was sweeping her head from side to side again, like listening to music that only her ears could hear. "Go home. Lay next to your husband. Don't come this way again."

Hiram took his shirt off, draped it over the wash bucket and thought about how disappointing it was to have given in. Not an inkling of the to-do he hoped for, only a heavy transgression to carry. He knew Ruby Lee would never tell, but for the rest of his life, he'd have to watch her sitting in the nave amongst the others as he preached, she thinking "what a fraud" and picturing his speckled shirt.

As Hiram mired in his dirty deed, he called to mind Reverend Harvey and their last night together. Hiram had been in Columbus for nearly a year, just days from being ordained, and decided to return to the wilds of Ohio to see his mentor one last time. He was greeted with a handshake and an offer from the hip flask. They picked up right where they left off, no awkward reacquaintance, just the Reverend's good counsel, always in the form of biblical passages and the trials and comforts on the path to salvation. They would talk until the sun came up, like they often did, arguing about the book of Matthew in particular—Would Jesus really come wielding a sword? Should anyone ever really hate their mother and father? Pluck out their eyes?—then, with smirks and sips of bourbon, they would eventually agree to disagree.

There was a mournful air from the moment Hiram sat down. They knew this was adieu. Hiram had made this final trek because the weight of becoming a minister was top-heavy. And only Harvey would understand. The self-doubt had bubbled up in Hiram's chest, acting as the bridge between the Almighty and every soul in his path was smothering. It was mere minutes after he arrived that he blurted out his uncertainty, "I'm harried, Harvey. What if my influence isn't enough. Nor my know-how. Can I really deliver others from—"

Harvey stood, stepped past him, then through the open door. Though he knew that was his way, Hiram always took a second to swallow the embarrassment of being left mid-sentence. This time, Hiram actually found comfort in the Reverend's lack of manners, enjoyed the familiarity. When he stepped outside to join him, Harvey was relieving himself next to a tall buckeye tree.

"There are other callings besides God's," he said. Hiram laughed. The crickets chirred in unison, and the fair glow of the stars had blued the vast, open space. The earthy scents of fall—subtle decay, wood smoke, the faint smell of lanolin, and the harvest pie inside—scented the air. Harvey let out a robust sigh, tucked himself back in place, then moved into Hiram's line of sight. He was a thickset man with broad shoulders and a stout belly. His age showed in the whiteness of his beard and eyebrows, almost luminous in the half-light, and his eyes were the color of oats and hickory.

"Doubt is not the opposite of faith," he said. "It's only part of it." He lay his brawny hand on Hiram's shoulder, let it set there. Both men took in deep breaths and exhaled, the splendor of the autumn backwoods in front of them. Still, Hiram fretted, waiting for Harvey's next line. He'd have to offer more than that hackneyed reply, he'd just have to.

"I'm no stranger to uncertainty," Harvey interrupted the quiet. "This life is flecked by hesitation. And those called to serve are no exception." He started to head back inside, his movements slow, a bear emerging from hibernation. And without provocation, he turned back, stated plainly, "'My God, my God, why have you left me?' Ring a bell?" Another step toward the house, then he turned back a second time. "When uncertainty creeps in, remember that the seeds of faith can only grow after they burst free from their shells. When they're vulnerable to the elements, that's when the roots take hold." He gave me a wink. "Don't look so stumped, son. Doubt and fear are the wind and rain, and you are the sapling." He stepped back inside, calling out, "Let's cut this pie, shall we?"

After polishing off Mrs. Wheeler's dessert, they scraped the gooey filling from the bottom of the tin, remnants of strawberries, raspberries and blackberries, and laughed at one another's violet colored teeth. Harvey offered a final pull from the flask then tilted it upward himself, gulped till it was gone. He did not say goodnight, just stretched his arms to the side, let out a big yawn and headed to the loft.

The next day, the parish gathered all around the church's sagging porch to bid Hiram farewell. On his way out, he took a few steps toward the woods to be able to see everyone. He looked them over a moment, painting a picture of all their faces in his mind, knowing he'd need to summon it from time to time. Harvey stood taller than the rest. He pointed to a burgeoning hickory tree then back to Hiram, and mouthed, "that's you." Then he saluted from his bushy brow, quick snap with his fat hand. By his side, little David Wheeler waved, his scarred lips curling into a roguish grin.

* * *

In the throes of imperfection, there was some lopsided satisfaction, too, a kind of pure humanness. Other than the few bumbling encounters with a mischievous lass from Blueville—lying next to Rock Lake, and once behind Shipley's tilted cabin—and the one visit to Bentley with all the other miners, trying to prove himself one of them, Hiram had been chaste. He headed back to his place in the grass, goosebumps on his bare chest, shivering in the night air, contemplating faith and impropriety, stepping down from up high, remembering that he's just a man, not even a special one at that.

Chapter 29
Teeth

He stuffed the pliers deep into his mouth, trying to clasp them down on the back most molar. But the handles were too wide for his jaw, stretching and thinning his lips. Then the hard, rigid metal glanced a front tooth and Basil winced, let out a low grunt. With the pliers resting against his tongue, he paused, looked out the window of the loft. Hundreds of winking stars dotted the sky. The expanse made him feel less alone, connected him to the other deserters, hiding in thickets or cellars or icehouses, pondering ways to mutilate themselves, too, all of them desperate to side-step Mr. Lincoln's God-forsaken war.

When the vice finally gripped, he clamped down fast. A low click. Bone on metal. But he couldn't pull. Not yet. "Work through pain, boy," his Pa once said, "That's how true men are made." Then his mind slipped back to his boyhood, the day he walked into the barn as the cow was being prepped for butcher. Grandpa was hooking the steel gambrel into the severed tendons of its hind legs while Pa had begun to crank the winch, the hulking carcass raising up like a great spirit. The veins along its neck had been opened and blood soaked the straw beneath, staining it a rich purple. The salty smell flooded his nostrils and he stared at the thick, matted coat, the hemorrhaging frame, its severed head atop a hay bale—sitting upright, normal as could be, as if cows were simply made that way—then he met the dead eyes. Big and blank and wet. His heart thrashed against his eight-year-old chest and he dizzied, emptying his stomach on the ground. Pa stared him down, shook his head, making several *tsk* sounds with his tongue before turning away. That same floating feeling was upon him, teetering on a tightrope, nothing but air. He felt like an unimaginable coward with a pair of rusty pliers in his fist.

Basil pushed his back against the wood planks, dug his feet into the floor. *Now. Do it now, you daisy.* He squeezed his fingers around the handles. His whole body clenched. Then he held steady, drank in the details of his backdrop, the stage he'd still be sitting on after wrenching out his teeth, not as a man, but an even bigger mouse than Stella knew. An unpatriotic yellow-belly.

To the left was the open space where Stella had tumbled to her death the year before. And the shame was a wildfire. Perched on a nearby rafter, an owl stared at him with big, glassy eyes then turned its ring-shaped head away. Basil glanced at the hoe resting against the wall behind him, remembered hearing about a father over in Escanaba who'd lanced his own man parts with the middle tine of a pitchfork, trying to keep from dying in a war that folks in the U.P. know little about. He wondered what the man thought about in the seconds before bringing down the sharp point through his family jewels. Did he think of the warmth of his wife's body pushed against him on a frigid February morning, the wind hollering outside, slapping at the windowpane? Or did he see his little boys, arms slung over one another's shoulders, the sun's rays slanted across their silhouettes, lighting them up as if God was wielding a lantern behind them.

"Enough," Basil said aloud, then sucked in hard, held it, and yanked out the first tooth. He dropped his head and wept. For pain, for truth, and for his wife, his dead, pretty wife. Then he managed to pluck out two more teeth before fainting, the last sound he heard was the owl squealing, human-like and shrill.

When he woke, Basil found himself coiled on the barn floor, the space drenched in the faint blue of night. There was a violent ache in his face that made his whole upper half undulate like a Lake Superior tidal flow, bulging then shrinking his eyes as the riptide took hold. His jaw had ballooned the bottom half of his face, rounding out his chin. With a thumb and two fore-fingers, he tried to stroke his jowls, but flinched. Then he gently slid his tongue over the curious new gaps and a loose clot broke open. The taste flooded his mouth—pennies, plums and salt—and he glanced at the three shiny molars gathered at his side like tiny white stalactites.

* * *

Basil knew he wouldn't be able to chew for a while, no meat or hardtack. Or anything, for that matter. And he knew his speech might be impeded some. But he was more concerned about the accusing looks and muffled whispers, the ones that would happen behind fanned out fingers and roving eyes—"Why ain't he off fighting?" they'd ask one another. Then with great curiosity and anticipation, they'd guess at the invisible affliction that was granting the town teacher an exemption. "Bet it's his pee slinger, don't work like it's supposed to. Never did have no kids, did they?"

It was in the early hours on a Saturday that Basil had extracted several of his back teeth and by Sunday morning, he still couldn't talk without forming the words from the front of his mouth, slow and rigid. When the throbbing flared inside the dried sockets, he thought of calling off school for the first time ever. Then he called himself a milksop and with his balled-up knuckles, struck the sorest part of his cheek. Again and again.

He rolled over and lay still, too weary to stand. He looked up at the ceiling, counted the rafters, eight in all, and recalled hauling them up, one by one, and how that night, Stella rubbed her soft palms against his spine until the ache subsided. He asked God to let him go back to that day, to let him live out an eternity with his wife's hands on his body, smoothing out the pain, not thinking about a filthy war and still hopeful for children. All of his teeth still in his mouth.

Chapter 30
Pull Foot, Boys!

On a sticky July day in '63, Uriah's father had come home later than he ever had before. Uriah couldn't recall a time when supper had to wait this long. From the hard expression, he knew it was time to be silent, stay still until Pa was ready to share whatever was burdening him. He took off his boots slowly then washed his hands in the basin before pulling a folded paper from his pocket and slapping it down on the table. Empty dishes jounced and the stew inside the Dutch oven sloshed. "Read," he said, then stepped back so both Uriah and Ma could see it. Uriah read the bold, black letters aloud:

Notice of Drafting! Avoid Conscription!

The undersigned, Commissioner for Keweenaw County, State of Michigan, will be at the town hall in the town of Bellwether on Tuesday and Wednesday, the 3d and 4th days of July next, between the hours of 10 o'clock a.m. and 4 o'clock p.m. each day, to hear and determine all claims of exemption from military service, when and where candidates for exemption should appear for examination.

Drafting will commence on Thursday, the 5th day of July, between the hours of 10 o'clock a.m. and 5 o'clock p.m. and continue each day, between the same hours, until the quota for Keweenaw County is met.

Before Uriah could grasp that war had found its way into Bellwether, Pa recounted the scene in town to them. How the county commissioner nailed the manifesto to a wood post in front of town hall and folks within earshot headed that way. "We all knew it was coming," Pa said. "Hell, some folks were passing through town even if they didn't need to, pretending it was part of their comings and goings to ride past the big brick building, glancing that way for a sign, any sign. I don't understand that. If folks were waiting for it, why do they sob and curse when it comes?"

Though Pa paused, Uriah knew he wasn't looking for an answer. Ma understood that, too. But they didn't wait in silence long as he fired up again a moment later. "A group gathered around the announcement, all of 'em shouting about the President, and Jefferson Davis, too. Then they turned on the commissioner, but he just stood there on the ladder, stack of handbills in his hand, like he was used to being blamed, used to suffering anger from folks that ain't got no one else to scream at."

Uriah's belly rumbled with nerves and exhilaration. But not fear. He knew that Pa had been leaving the fields midday like everyone else, making passes through Main Street, stealing a peek at the town hall. For Pa to take time away from the farm was rattling but lying to Ma about where he was going was all out frightening. He'd announce, "Have an errand at the post master's," or "Need to check our credit at the mercantile." Uriah followed him once, watched him loitering in town, riding through town several times before heading back home. Pa's worry about the war made Uriah feel strange about the thrill of being a soldier. It was his patriotic duty, a source of pride. But Pa was confusing that, turning it into something menacing.

"I can't think about this no more," Pa said. "Still some good daylight, boy, let's get to the field. Thought I saw a bollworm or two. Could've been beetles." Pa's slow gait and slumped shoulders made Uriah feel a bit guilty.

Ma's eyebrows slanted downward, pointing to the wrinkles that had formed above her nose. She pushed her lips together tight, lifting the pot from the table and setting it on the hearth to warm. Takes a lot of strength to have that much self-control, Uriah thought. She has an opinion on the war, the draft. Where does all that restraint go? Can't just disappear.

The long days of summer meant the sun was still high when Pa and Uriah headed back in for supper. On the fireplace, the heavy pot was warming and even with its cast iron lid, the smell of salted pork wafted through the house and beyond. Ma stood next to the flat hearthstone, stoking the fire with a maple stick. She added more corn, beans and flour to thicken the concoction, make it last the rest of the week. Pa splashed his face at the basin then wiped the back of his neck with the washrag. Uriah could feel the iron curtain that had draped over their house, casting shade over their tiny space. He picked up the mortar and pestle on the table and began grinding the coarse lumps of salt into dust, his gaze drifting from Pa to Ma, then to the window, then back again.

"Draft is here, boy," Pa said, matter-of-fact. Uriah watched them both closely, all of their movements were sedated, like somehow if they slowed down, the inevitable wouldn't come. Ma tapped the ladle on the top of the kettle then bent at the knees to sweep some corn husks from the floor into her apron. Putting his hands on either side of the tub, Pa leaned into it, like it was holding him up. "We don't have the money, son. And they're saying it won't matter none that we only got one boy," he said. "Seems that law is changing soon enough." Then he shook his head wide like he was trying to erase the moment. After a bout of stillness, he sat across from Uriah, angled his head down and a little sideways so their eyes were at the same level. "Think it's best you volunteer," he said. "May as well get the bounty."

Ma stopped moving and faced them, then just as quickly, turned back around. She emptied the husks into a basket, arched her back and stood tall. She dry-washed her hands, freeing several wisps of corn silk that flitted down like slender dragon flies, then doled out the stew without a word.

"You'll take my rifle," Pa said. "We need to work on shooting. We'll start this Sunday, after church." He tore a piece of bread from the loaf and set it on Uriah's plate, tore off another and stuck it in his mouth, gnawing hard as a heifer.

"Can we start tomorrow? Before sunup?" Uriah said. "Won't interfere with nothing that way." He continued to eat while he spoke, kept his voice even, trying to appear calm, blithe. Pa stopped chewing and looked to Ma, who held his eyes a moment, pottage and bits of pork dripping from the scoop in her hand. Uriah felt a gratification like none other when Pa gave a slow nod and began chomping again. The force behind Ma's smile was palpable, that familiar dimple forming a tiny hollow in her cheek. Uriah thought, that's the mark of a steady woman.

The next morning, Pa and Uriah rogued the potato field together then headed out past the cabbage patch, not far from where he had buried the wounded hen just a few years before. The first few times, Pa loaded the rifle for him and pointed out different targets on the crown of a hackberry tree—a conspicuous leaf, a fat knot, some misshapen limbs. Like it always had, the gun's jolt consistently knocked Uriah off kilter and time after time, he missed.

"Lead and powder ain't cheap," Pa said. He handed over the ramrod and the dented red tin and said, "Try loading it yourself. And keep your eyes on the target." Uriah poured in the black powder and packed it down, careful not to spill a fleck. He dropped in the round metal ball and crammed it in the barrel. Once again, he raised the gun and held real still.

"Where to, Pa?"

"Hit that broken twig, the one hanging down," Pa said. "Aim small, son." Uriah narrowed his open eye, splitting the middle of the brass sight. Then he fired. Missed again. The buck and ball swept over the tree without a sound. He set the butt on the ground, rested it against his leg. He put one hand on his waist and the other over his forehead, pushing on his eyelids with his thumb and middle finger until he saw dark streaks.

"Can't give up this time," Pa said. "This ain't no coon we're dealing with. This is about war. Your life."

"You misunderstand me. I'm not giving up. Just thinking, that's all." Then he took his hand from his face and looked at Pa head on. "I'm gonna be a soldier now. It's about time you know that I ain't chinless. Never have been." There was an unfamiliar surge in his blood, a fresh energy that made him draw back his shoulders. "And I ain't scared of war. I wanna go. Wouldn't pay no commutation even if we had it."

Uriah could see Pa stiffen, his stance wholly square. He drew back his head, looked him up and down. The sides of his mouth curled some—not quite a smile, but not a frown either—"Time to head in, boy," he said.

"Not till I hit my mark, sir. Didn't you hear what I said?"

"Oh, I heard you, boy, loud and clear." Pa took the rifle from against Uriah's leg and set it on his own shoulder, the stock resting in his palm. "You're gonna hold your own out there. Got no doubt now."

"But I keep missing."

"Don't matter. You're showin' guts. The gunfire, why, that'll come. We'll keep trying till it does. But You're talking stern now, boy. Ain't between the grass and hay no more. That's cause to celebrate with some hooch."

The sun was hovering just above the horizon, casting brick

and honey-colored stripes across the plain. Uriah stepped to Pa's side, kept stride with him back to the house.

* * *

Three days later, Uriah headed for the downbound side of the St. Marys River. Pa gave him the family's Quarter Horse—mild disposition, mushroom coat, dusty-brown mane—and told him to sell it when he got to Sault Ste. Marie. There were three other volunteers headed that way, too. Clarence was from Bellwether, and the other two, Mawkwa and Joseph, were from the far side of the county. Clarence was a bit older, mid-twenties, Uriah guessed. He'd seen him in town and every so often at church. Mawkwa seemed ageless, his skin was pure brown, even a dark wine color when he stood a certain way. His eyes were unexpectedly blue, so sharp it was hard not to stare. And last, was Joseph, closest to Uriah's age, around eighteen, and a bit nervous, hands always fidgeting, never looking at you when he talked.

They met at Uriah's farmstead as it was closest to the new township road. There, they topped their canteens and took sips of coffee that Ma offered. But they were eager to ride. It was a day's journey to the State Locks then a week's journey down Lake Huron before they could reach Detroit's waterways.

* * *

Not until the upper gates of the lock began to close and the emptying valve slowly opened could Uriah stop replaying Pa's goodbye. "I'd ride the river with you, boy," he had said then sucked in hard, his chest bowing with air and manhood. And after collecting himself, looked at all of the young men, deadpan: "Bed a man down when you have to," he said. "No time for hesitating." Then he swatted the rump of Uriah's mare and shouted after them, "Pull foot, boys!" Uriah looked back once, saw that Ma was left standing alone, and Pa with his arms clasped behind his crooked back was already strolling toward the perimeter.

Uriah was brought back to the present when he was pushed onto the deck of the ship and millions of gallons of water drained from the canal, whooshing and splashing against the hold. What were only treetops moments before came into full view. And the steel gate behind them grew bigger and bigger the farther they were lowered into Lake Huron.

After arriving in Sault Ste. Marie and selling the horses, Joseph stayed by Uriah's side. Clarence and Mawkwa remained on the periphery, yet never fully out of sight. It had been like that on their travels to the St. Marys River, too. Just beyond the east end of Trout Lake, they had come to an unforeseen mire and in the thick sludge, the horses sunk underfoot. All of the men made it out except Joseph who brought up the rear. The mud suck was too much for his old horse, but Clarence and Mawkwa were shin deep in a matter of seconds, tying a rope behind the mare's front legs, using their own horses to pull her out. They had commandeered the journey there—breaking trail, navigating and sharing provisions—more paternal than brotherly.

* * *

Fort Wayne was on the Detroit River, just a mile from the Canadian shore. It was a star-shaped fortification, newly reconditioned with brick and concrete, and the earthen ramparts were faced with cedar. The barracks were inside the fort; Uriah and Joseph on the ground floor, near the mess and washroom, and Clarence and Mawkwa assigned to an adjacent section, second floor. On the first day of infantry training, the regiment was issued all new gear and made to wear it every day leading up to their departure, conditioning them to the heat and heft.

Every morning Uriah pulled on the excess weight, forty-five pounds in all. He wore a fatigue blouse, wool coat and trousers; thick, leather bootees with iron horseshoes nailed to the heels for traction; a belt with a big brass buckle; and dangling at one hip, a cartridge box filled with ammunition and gun tools; on the other hip, a scabbard for the bayonet. He carried a knapsack which held the "dog tent" and rubber gum blanket; and a haversack, too, which held rations of salt pork and coffee. He rolled up a blanket and tied one end into a "horse collar" which it came to be called, then stuffed the less urgent things inside—paper, pen, toothbrush, soap, comb. With the leaden canteen, tin cup and silverware, he felt like a walking cabin, all of its guts hanging from him in some place or another.

The morning of their entry into war, the journey from Michigan to Tennessee, Uriah's company was assigned top of the line weaponry. Pa's smoothbore musket was replaced with a '61 Springfield rifle that used percussion caps instead of flint locks, shooting the new minié bullet that he heard could shatter bones. When they donned him with a corps badge made of red flannel cloth in the shape of a star, he poured over with pride, more so than he knew possible. He thanked God for his family and the chance to serve his country. And before saying amen, he petitioned for Eva's wellbeing, too.

* * *

The men had heard all about the luxury at the front of the train—private sleeper cars with mattresses, dining cars, and an extravagant parlor car—though such lavish conditions seemed impossible as they clambered onto the ledges of the 3rd class cars, stumbling over the feet and satchels of sprawling cadets and dozens of Asian immigrants. The wood slats smelled like rodent dung and the benches were all full, only piles of gathered straw left to lie in.

Uriah found an empty space, burrowed in some, then leaned back against the damp panel behind him. The cramped car began teeming with empty chatter—complaints about the meager food portions, the unusually hot autumn, and different bits of gossip from the men's hometowns.

Soon enough, the locomotive jolted into place and the passengers lurched then righted. As the train pulled away, the certainty of heading toward battle suffused the space, quick and potent, like a bucket of fish guts newly turned over. The anxiety was palpable as the sticky, wet breeze coming from a narrow vent near the ceiling.

After what Uriah guessed was several miles, one of the cadet's voices began to sound out above the rest, until eventually it eclipsed all the other conversations. He knew details about their mission in Tennessee, including the commanders on both sides and their triumphs and blunders. No one questioned the legitimacy of the man's claims or asked him about his sources. Uriah figured that, like himself, they were just relieved that someone stopped all the meaningless jabber, started talking about the warfare that was silently gripping them, all the anticipation wreaking havoc in their bellies, standing at attention on the edge of every brain.

Uriah listened hard as the man talked about Major General Joseph Hooker, or "Fighting Joe," and how he led the principal union army, Army of the Potomac, to secure the rail line in Chattanooga—the "cracker line" as the man called it—so food and supplies could be delivered. "'Cause to the west on Raccoon Mountain, the Commander of the Army of Tennessee, that son of a bitch Braxton Bragg, blocked it." The cadet was nearly shouting, but Uriah had stopped listening for the moment, found himself lost in thought, imagining what it would look like, marching straight into all the chaos.

One of the immigrants loosened the chain that held the door closed and slid it open. For a moment, all was still as the unexpected beauty poured forth. The train cut through Indiana's weald, meadow upon meadow of flaky browns and myrtle green. Some of the men shifted and nudged one another to catch a glimpse of the wide open prairies, already worlds away from their childhoods.

Seconds later, the man started up again, talking over the heightened sound of the train's chuffing and the gusts pushing through the opened door. "George H. Thomas is commanding the Army of the Cumberland. He headed west along the railroad while a corps under "Fighting Joe" went east. And when General Grant began forcing his way out of Chattanooga, he sent Sherman, some up-and-comer, to attack the northern flank on Missionary Ridge while General Joseph Hooker captured Lookout Mountain, the southern flank." The man paused to catch his breath, let the wind cool his face for a moment. His voice deepened as he finished speaking: "Word is that Sherman's assault was stumped by the ridgeline halting in a steep drop, a deep ravine sitting between his men and the target. And I suppose that's where we come in, fellas."

When the train came to its final stop, the commands from outside were loud, clear, and urgent. "Exit, boys! And look alive! There's a war going on, and we've got a mountain to climb!" Uriah looked at the man who had shared the intel, and it seemed all the others were looking at him, too, questioning how he knew, because he nodded and said without prompting, "Got a letter from my brother just before we left, he's been here for weeks."

To the south, Uriah could see Lookout Mountain rising through the fog, and he could hear more orders being shouted, but everything melded together. His lips twitched, and he couldn't stop blinking. Time was elusive, yet it felt like mere minutes before he began marching to battle. General John Geary took the lead, told them they were part of the Twelfth Corps and that there was no rest for the weary. "You best scale these slopes like your lives depend on it." And they did, going unchallenged for a long while, but encountering some resistance soon enough. "It's confederate major, Carter Stevenson," Geary told them. "Bet we outnumber him ten-to-one."

Chapter 31
The Oldest Profession

Tina spoke of ribbons on the doorknob and "all that's mine is mine," while Eva thought of a simple system of endurance to help her through the acts of harlotry. With a lead pencil, she sketched a picture of Ma's new cabin. On the white paper, she shaded the crevices where the logs came together and darkened the spaces where the windows would be. She drew a burgeoning maple to the right of the front door, made dozens of tiny circles for leaves and etched in heavy vertical lines to show the markings on the tree's skin. Then, she balanced the picture between two slender perfume bottles so it stood tall and plain, facing the bed. She would focus on the contours of the timber with every man that mounted her. Just as the peeling paint got her through the threats aboard the steamer—the sweaty hands, the putrid breath—so too would the penciled cabin.

The first trick wasn't the hardest like she figured. She and Tina were standing next to the upright piano when the big chested man waved her over to the table, folded down his cards and asked her if she'd like to head upstairs. Eva looked to Tina, still perched against the shoddy upright Baldwin. She gave Eva a nod and as they passed by, she pulled the ribbon from her pocket and shoved it into Eva's palm. Upstairs, the man spoke very little, told her that he wouldn't pay more than two dollars as he dropped his trousers to the floor. After that, it all happened so quick. He joined her on the bed then spat on his hand, rubbed himself some and pushed inside her. Eva gasped. He asked if it was hurting. She said, no, then angled more to the side, as his head was blocking the cabin picture.

It only lasted a couple of minutes. In less time than that, he had his britches back on and his money clip in hand. Placing some bills on the highboy, he said, "There's a little extra here for you." As he turned to go, he said he'd be back that way in a week or two. Eva sat upright, covered her breasts with her arms and responded with a smile. After he'd gone, she leapt to the highboy, snatched up the money and counted the four dollars several times, unbelieving that he left her double. Her privates burned as she picked up a washrag and readied to head for the privy, wondering how much timber four dollars could buy. She pushed aside all the wonders of calf-love, knowing that every move in this world was another deep, sucking step into the swamplands. With every prick and sting in her inner thighs, the likelihood of any more toothy kisses faded faster, and the picture of Uriah's face in her mind was gone.

But before she could lace up her corset, Tina pulled open the door, just enough to poke her head inside and scour the room. She reprimanded her for not taking down the ribbon sooner as she led in a fat man with shiny porcelain teeth, chortling like a little boy. Eva didn't have time to peek at herself in the mirror as Tina was already working at the buttons of the stubby man's breeches. Eva could still hear him giggling as she headed downstairs. In the stairwell, she started to figure how many tricks it would take to put a window in Ma's bedchamber. Or to buy a cast iron stove. Three tricks if she wanted one shaped like a beehive, separate from the hearth. Maybe another trick or two for one with a warming oven below.

* * *

Eva came to call the quiet spaces between tricks, the soft hours. They were the toughest, an opening for the guilt to seep in, for mulling over the disgrace of opening her legs to strangers. Remembrances of little things Ruth did for her always rose up, too, like the sips of fermented cider and the extra Epsom salts in her wash basin. And there were the glimpses of Ma's sad eyes watching as her daughter washes out her privates with a dirty towel.

Then one night, an ornery fellow with rye-colored skin was bucking on her hard, as if she were a broken-down mare. It hurt something awful. She was chaffed and wringing, felt the bruises forming. A minute later, the musty old cuss let loose, spurting like a firehose, in her and on her. She fought the urge to gag, laying there soused in his gravy, as Tina called it. Though she knew it was unfair to keep saddling God for the free-will mess she had made, it was her only defense, the only way to stop feeling like a hookworm slithering in the pit of an outhouse. She knew, deep down, that when all the lying to herself finally stopped, and there were no more flashes of true love, there'd be a treacherous journey to salvation, maybe even impassable at times. But she never doubted that she'd be forgiven, eventually, because she was already sorry.

* * *

The journey to redemption came quicker than Eva had imagined, just six months after coming to the Levee. It was Christmas time and the air was bone-chilling. Even so, the tavern was lively as ever.

Too cold to trek to the outhouses, Eva had come upstairs to use the chamber pot, the sounds of lust seeping through the rooms on either side. That was still one of the most trying parts of living there, the *oohs* and *aahs* of others pawing at one another. At least when a man was on top of her, she could float outside of herself, pretend to be someplace else, anyplace else. But those sounds, they were right there, as real as the air filling her lungs.

Eva heard a knock. She pulled open the door and a blustery draft pushed through, carrying the sketched cabin on the air before it landed on the foot of the bed. Ephraim stood tall, still as a sculpture. Even with a new mustache, thick and wiry, and the rounded crown of his derby pulled down over his brow, Eva knew him—the robin's egg eyes, the hard jawline. For a moment, they were silent, staring long at one another, trying to discern what the other was doing there. Another hard wind blew against the building, rattling the windows and whistling through the spindles of the balcony before it whirred over the roof.

Her brain swam with thoughts. Emotions flickered in every direction. His presence made everything lopsided again. She had worked hard to strip away all hope of any time-honored courtship. Now, there was such an immediate sense of relief with him there. And he looked so handsome. But just as hair-triggering, something felt strange, too. A familiar kind of danger blew heavy as the air, the kind that made her scalp tingle.

"This is where you've been? You're a whore?" His voice was deeper than she remembered, and his words were slow. The gin on his breath smelled like a pine tree.

Eva felt her eyes widen as the realization took hold. "Dear God, Ephraim—" She stopped. "You didn't know I was here, did you?" Her knees felt weak, like she was teetering on the crest of a hillside, that single instant between losing balance but not yet falling. She tried to push the door shut, but he stuck his leg inside. She kept pushing, then he thrust his shoulder in, and his hip. Finally, he pivoted his body and gave a big heave. Eva lost the fight.

With eyes forward, he let out a thin sigh and kicked the door shut with the bottom of his boot. Eva crept backward until she was against the wall, panting as Ephraim began to chuckle. She steadied herself, tried to rein in the panic. She searched for any kind of weapon. No pulling punches. Not this time.

"Me and Tina been going hard-to-soft since I was a boy. Thought you figured that out once upon a time," he seethed.

"You and Tina?" She looked at the bed and back to him, stalling, trying to look dumbfounded as she bent down for the chamber pot. She jerked it out from under the bed, and the lid toppled to the floor, wobbling back and forth before coming to a halt. With both hands, she held the pot at her chest. Then Ephraim laughed again, not quite as loud.

"Nothing's funny," Eva said. And she warned him not to take another step. When he did, she lifted the pot to her chin and hurled it at him, full bore. Ephraim turned, and the pot struck the side of his mouth with a low tunk then crashed to the floor. The earthenware shattered in every direction.

Both of them snatched up one of the bigger shards, the smell of stale piss filling the cramped space. Time stopped. Eva's heart thumped in her chest and ears, felt like it might push right through the skin and bone.

"Put it down, Eva."

"You first."

"Fair enough." Ephraim crouched down, slow and deliberate. "You gotta do it, too," he said. His words were even slower and his mouth was already red and swelling where the pot had hit him. "Didn't mean no harm to you. A misunderstanding, that's all."

Eva bent down. Once she was at his level, their eyes locked. He brought up his arm, and the floor felt like it had turned to mud. She was sinking in it, watching the shard come at her. She dodged the sloppy blow then sucked in a breath, closed her eyes and started scratching and flailing like a feral cat, scrambling to sink her fingernails into him, smash her fists against his head, his eyes, his groin. She squealed like a pig being butchered. In the broil, she could hear Tina caterwauling from the hall. Or even closer, she couldn't tell. A surge of hope swept over, and she thrashed even harder. So frantic and aimless that she didn't realize Tina had yanked Ephraim off her.

"You best be hightailing it, Ephraim," Tina snarled. "I'm

telling Charley you tried cuttin' one of his girls. And he's gonna get you." Eva had stilled some, enough to hear Tina's warning, to see that she had the collar of his shirt pulled tight, the pointed bit of their room key at his throat.

He was on his rump, hands in the air in resignation. Then, he pushed himself back into sitting position, still under Tina's restraint. "I'll be going now. You won't see me no more."

Tina tried to shift her weight so he could stand, but the pressure of the key bit loosened. In a wink, Ephraim leapt like a jack, snatched up a stray piece, and took another swipe. He scored Eva's upper cheek, lengthwise, below the eye to the temple. It seemed almost casual, like he was just waving goodbye. And just like that, he vanished.

The pain was too great for crying. Eva focused on Tina's ranting, calling men cocksuckers as she lay a cloth against the gash. "I've heard of men doing this—" she shook her head. "Maiming girls, making them unpretty." There was a small comfort in Tina's fingers, and Eva clung to it, the motherly touch allaying what she knew must happen next. "Have to fetch Charley," she said. And the dread set in. Eva's belly flopped, thinking of the alcohol he'd pour on her face, all the stitching he'd do.

* * *

The scar was in the shape of a checkmark, a small downward cut, stretching vertically at least an inch. The skin was raised up like someone wove it into tiny braids, just far enough in that her hair couldn't cover. Though Tina tried to tell her otherwise, she knew her time at the tavern was done. Eva forgave her for keeping Ephraim a secret. Betrayal was a part of her life, always had been. "Besides, it ain't you that split open my face," she said. "You're just trying to make your way, too. I tried keeping him out of my head when I came here. Took a bit of doing, but sure glad I did. It's plain to me that there's no such thing as that kind of happiness anyway."

Chapter 32
In Thin Air

The fog had created some dew and even though horseshoes had been nailed to the bottoms of their boots, the soldiers still slipped as they crept up Lookout Mountain. They kicked into the earth, pushing upward, the visibility shrouded. The sporadic gunfire was untraceable, blasts materializing from thin air. As Uriah's company climbed, wincing and jolting at every invisible crack from enemy rifles, the confederate soldiers' first line of defense came into view—a few makeshift emplacements on the mountain side made of tree limbs, rocks and dirt. Though flimsy, the structures proved dangerous. The murky air obscured their tiny walls, and the bullets remained ghostly, sporadically pecking off federal troops. The terror of not knowing where the rounds came from made Uriah's stomach clench and his temples throb. A soldier knelt by a tree, retching and crying between heaves. Uriah said to himself, it's a gauntlet, for God's sake, and we're running it with blindfolds on.

Because he was flanked right, Uriah did not see any comrades die, but he heard the pops of the muskets, the cries of sacrifice, the reverberating groans. As they pushed upward, the gunfire intensified from both sides, and the volume cleaved his ears like a hatchet, giving way to a flat echo after a while. He was close enough to see the gun barrels perched atop the rival mounds of sticks and branches, like each partition had long slender fingers reaching out, feeling their way through the haze. The blood pulled away from his skin, thrumming through his head then pooling in strange places.

There was a tavern just south of Bellwether's town square that Uriah thought of in trying times. It was a two-story, balloon framed building, the rafters extending from the sill to the roof. Being so close to the damp earth, the sill beam had deteriorated, and the exterior at the floor joists had turned a dank green in the most rotted places. There was scrap wood nailed over the windows, sturdier than most of the buckled siding. Several thin ash trees had grown in front of and beside it, like someone had carefully plopped the building amidst them. You could still see *The Lumberjack* painted on the side in big fat letters, mostly faded from the harsh seasons. There were several places to peek through the widened gaps in the walls, see the tin-punched ceiling still intact, holding its sheen. Rumor was that most of the miners spent their Saturday nights there before Reverend Williams came to town and told the owner to close it or he'd run him out of Bellwether with the Devil on his tail. On its final night in business, yet another scuffle broke out, more brief and contained than the others, but indelible—a village story nearly as eternal as the botched hangings of the Williams women.

There was a stately billiards table which you could still see through one of the gaps if you turned your head just so. That's what Uriah and Eva used to look at when they took turns pushing their faces against the building, scanning for signs of the epic tussle. Apparently, two Finnish immigrants finally broke after being heckled most of the night by a man from Keweenaw. The more inebriated he became, the worse the baiting, calling them "silver-tips" and "goddamn ice monkeys," poking at them for coming to America, taking good jobs from others.

The way Uriah heard the story was that the two big Finns set down their beers, quiet and calm, then stepped to the man in just two strides. They lifted him from his chair and carried him to the billiards table. The taller of the two bent the drunk man over the side and held him there. The other—not as tall, but hardy and wide—ripped open the seat of the man's pants in one effortless motion then coolly picked up a pool cue and broke it over his knee. The man twisted like a pinched grub, but the meaty hands pinning him down were immovable. With half a pool stick in each hand and the drunk man's round, white backside bared for all to see, the stockier Finn said in an even keel, "Against your head or up your arse?" The little man with the big mouth screamed like an adolescent girl, wriggling and pleading. But the Finn simply asked again, "Head? Or arse?" The man's yelping got more shrill. After the third time asking with no audible reply, the Finn decided for him. By then, all the patrons in the tavern were quiet, looking on with excitement and anxiety.

The stout Finn placed the cue stick between his palms and spun it back and forth like he was lighting a fire by twig and sunlight. He aimed it right into the drunkard's rear-end and according to hearsay, hit the target spot on, drilling it in a good few inches. The other held him down a minute or two longer so all the other men were sure to see, making sure they'd not suffer such mocking again. The man stopped resisting after a while, just lay there, soundless and bleeding. Neither the Finns nor the other miners laughed. Everyone understood that they had to, it was a desperate gesture to establish some semblance of status, to defend their honor and in a way, pay homage to the homeland they escaped from, oppressive and impoverished or not.

Uriah considered those men now: choosing grit and willpower or riding the coattails of those with true courage, like the do-nothing patrons at the tavern. He thought about who he wanted to be if he survived. Would he walk through Bellwether with pride, knowing that in battle, he forged ahead as a chieftain? Or would he cower, never looking folks straight on because when it counted, he merely trekked alongside his fellow soldiers, spineless, hoping those on either side were just a little farther ahead so they got hit first. And if one day when he tells his own son to be brave, would he be speaking the truth or acting a fraud?

Just as quickly as the shooting flared, it ceased. The absence of gun report was almost unbearable, more rattling than the firing itself. No more guessing about what being in battle will be like. In retreat, the Confederate men crashed through the trees, moving higher up the mountain. Uriah tried to control his breathing, uncertain if one of them may have lagged behind, waiting to leap from the tree line, pounce on him from out of the mist, or rear up his bayonet and plunge it into his skull. He knew there were a couple in his company further out to his right, still he felt like the end man, vulnerable from the front, the side, behind. Even in his own trepidation, he wondered at the horror the retreating men must feel, waiting for a bullet to tear through their vertebrae, or open up their heads.

In heavy woods on a mountain side, all the linear formations the company had practiced proved futile. The officers could not see from flank to flank as some of the men were swallowed into the tucks and furrows of land or blocked from view by the trees. Uriah knew the enemy had probably gone through drills like they had, drafted a clear-cut strategy for pulling back from a skirmish, but he did not blame them for thundering through the thicket with abandon now. There was an honest-to-God connection from every soldier's heart to the next, ally or foe. An allegiance to every fighter because they were all afraid of dying. He prayed all of them were grappling with the same intersection as him, choosing between coward or hero.

"Count Two's!" Uriah's heart began to thrash again. His breaths grew even more staccato, but he scurried with the rest of his company, focusing on the commands. "In two ranks, form company! Left, face!" He tried to stay close enough to his comrades on either side, making sure their elbows brushed, but the ground was too slanted, the natural impediments broke the rank and file. When his company leader shouted "Front!" he sucked in, held it.

"Center, Dress!" Uriah looked to his left, aligned himself as best he could, but there was at least five feet between each soldier now. The space made him feel like a lightning rod in a thunderstorm. Every muscle in his body contracting at the same time, fighting the instinct to run, to scream out. And he knew some had already lost that struggle. His brain floated, the ground beneath him undulated. And he hoped like hell that he wasn't more afraid than anyone else.

Still, he pressed forward. The bare twigs scraped his face as he climbed, faltering in formation as he tripped on the dead underbrush and slid in the loose soil. Though the bugle boy was hidden by the fog, the lilt of his metallic notes sounded from his horn to bring the soldiers to attention. They scrambled further upward, many of them dropping items from their gear to ease the burden. Sack coats and blankets were strewn about the mountain floor. And several pieces of paper had loosed when someone tried to lighten his haversack; they blew every which way, completely out of place, like random sweeps of snow in summer.

Geary's brigade made its way to level ground. The elevation, exertion and dampness made Uriah more conscious of his breathing. He tried siphoning through his nose then letting the air leak through his lips, that worked for a time. Then, a break in the low-hanging clouds. All the company spotted the colossal house at the same moment—a shared astonishment. No one dared slow their pace or let out a gasp. But a collective awe swept over. They would later learn it was known as the Cravens House, a lavish home built on a level plateau. Such a remarkable mansion atop a mountain seemed so bizarre, didn't look real. It was an expansive structure, like four or five houses from Bellwether set side by side. Uriah couldn't help but keep glancing up at the windows, more glass than he'd ever seen at once. There was a grand porch that wrapped around two sides, covered by a sturdy canopy slanting downward and held up by a dozen or more perfectly spaced posts. A balcony ran the entire length of the front, solid stones in the shape of rectangular pillars. They marched toward it, straight on. As they neared, there was an order to halt.

And they did. Uriah glanced at the other men to see if they were staring at the house, too. They all eyed one another, seeking permission to peek at the unexpected homestead. Then a shot rang out from one of the top windows.

The men dropped to their knees in unison, clambered to load their rifles. Another shot from a different window. Like an impromptu fireworks show, rapid gunfire blasted from the second story. Captain's voice thundered through the cracks and pops, but the words were muffled. The hue-and-cry was all around—echoing shouts and brisk, jerky movements. Uriah bent over his rifle, fingers trembling like a witching rod. Once loaded, he inhaled through his nose, rested the butt of the gun against his shoulder, then exhaled slow. The fighting had escalated into all out battle. This is it, he thought, I'm smack dab in the middle of war. He steadied his hands, and the rifle sat still, like it was simply part of his arm. Though it felt like he was wading in a dream, he persisted, focused on the blue-gray shirt cuff peeking out from the corner of the farthest east window and what looked to be a hand. Still a hundred yards out, he knew the target might not be what he figured. Better to take a shot than not, though. As his eyes centered on what was possibly the man's fingers, the hunch was confirmed. The soldier's hand lurched and a wisp of smoke rose up from his rifle's barrel that came into focus.

Before Uriah could fire back, a wail pealed through the trees—*the Captain's son*. He recognized the voice immediately. They had come to know one another at camp. Talks with the Captain's son were different than most. Their night-time conversations went beneath the surface, addressing the bigger things in life—public affairs, Heaven and Hell, and women. You hesitate out here, and people die, he thought. Good people. Uriah gathered himself. There was nothing he could do to help the boy now. Just keep fighting, vindicate his honor. He emptied his lungs again and without thinking too much, pulled the trigger. The blast was like the strike of a drum against his brain, enough to silence any shame for having wavered, for the moment.

The hand in the window went limp. A musket fell, end over end. He may have just killed a man. No time for shame or regret, though. Uriah was already reloading his musket. He'd grieve for the soldier he shot, that was certain. But he knew that he'd be mourning the loss of the Captain's son more. He took aim again, shot toward the same window, just in case he could hit a second time, kill him for sure.

Another whirlwind of bullets and smoke erupted. Shouts of command and agony cut through the fog. He didn't hear the order to storm the house, just followed the others as they bounded up the hill. In seconds, they were upon it, swarming like wet hornets. First the yard, then the porch. They kicked in the doors and traipsed across the wood planks, their boots scudding and clacking. Even though the dwellers had certainly cleared out as soon as the war began, it still felt wrong, ravaging someone's house, knocking over tables and the few personal things that remained—a framed picture of the Tennessee Valley lay cracked like an egg; some wood bowls wobbled on the floor like tops; and a trampled afghan sat rumpled in the corner, grass and mud from the hillside smearing the knitted waves of blue and what used to be white. Still, they barreled up the strangers' stairs, into their private spaces where they slept, talked about personal matters, made love.

With a dozen others, Uriah came to the second floor. The line of men paraded down the hall, syphoning off into the open doors. When they reached the final bedroom, there were only three of them left. They stepped inside, rifles perched atop their shoulders. Uriah entered last. The soldiers took a quick look around, kicked at the bed, glanced behind the door at the hardy trunk against the wall. Then the other two pushed back into the hall, Uriah still lagging behind. One of them shouted "Clear!" but it was lost amidst the other calls announcing the security of the different rooms. Just as there had been a collective feeling of fright moments before, there came a shared sense of calm, one big exhale. There was even some laughter from downstairs. Uriah took note of how unfamiliar that sound had become, how out of tune. Before joining the others heading back to the bottom floor, he stepped further inward, toward the room's only window in order to peek at the valley below. The city of Chattanooga sat like a portrait in the far distance. The wilds of Tennessee were browning with the season but an abundance of evergreens freshened the landscape some.

Something shuffled. A slow drag of leather on wood. Uriah swiveled his head toward the trunk as the top began to lift. He could see the man beneath it, unfurling like a freshly birthed calf, raising its head from the slick caul. The red collar of his shell jacket was clear as day. Their eyes met. And the rebel soldier halted, arm in mid-air, propping open the lid. Uriah aimed his rifle at the man's head, glanced at the confederate's shoulder. *No insignia. He's a private, too.* There was instant relief in knowing that he wasn't about to shoot a lieutenant or major.

"Put up both hands," Uriah ordered, trying to keep a level voice.

The soldier raised his other arm. A blood-soaked stump at the end of it. He had pulled his coat sleeve over his wrist, knotted his belt around it. Looked like the hemorrhaging had slowed, but the man's face was unearthly white. Uriah's chest tightened, breathing was a battle itself. He took a moment to concentrate on the in-and-out. The realization of which room he was in struck hard, the same room he'd taken aim at just minutes before. *I shot this man's hand off.*

Another bout of laughter rang out from downstairs. The two men held still. Uriah wasn't thinking about any tests of manhood now. Nor was he thinking about his Pa. Or Eva. Or anyone. He only wondered about doing the right thing.

"Can't keep my arms up no more." There was defeat in his voice, so hushed and drowsy.

Uriah kept his vision centered in the rifle's sight. The soldier's eyes were gray and his nose was skinny. Lips were thin, too, and the color had drained from them. His slouch hat was gone, revealing a dense, unkempt mop of black hair with a narrow part down the left side and slight creases on his forehead. Uriah guessed mid-twenties. He had an unflinching way about him, a coolness that could only come with wider experiences than his own—fistfights, sex, and war-time scars.

The man brought down his arms, resting the elbow of his good one inside the trunk to keep the lid open. "I'd be obliged if you'd just plug me in the head. Get it done quick. I'm plum bled out." He paused. "It's my mind that's really hurtin'. My thoughts are all balled up. I keep thinking 'bout my Ma. Keep seeing her face when they tell her I'm dead." He trailed off again, his cheeks slack. Then he whispered, "But then she rears herself up, and I'll be damned if her hand ain't blown off, too, just like mine."

Uriah stayed silent, kept his rifle fixed on the man's brow. The soldier tried letting out a chuckle, but it was more of a strained bleat, ballooning into a wet gurgle. "Thought I might make it out of here by the skin of my teeth," he said. "When I heard all you Billy Yanks leaving the room, figured God might've changed His mind 'bout me. Thought maybe I was s'pposed to be around a bit longer. Some pretty little gal waiting to meet me back home, waiting to bear me a boy of my own—" The man broke off, dropped his head like a ragdoll.

Uriah couldn't tell if he was overcome with sorrow or had simply lost consciousness. He waited as the man stayed motionless. Another peal of sniggering rose up, from outside now, not too far from the window. He wanted to call out to someone, look to others for what to do. A woozy feeling pushed through him, but he fought it, slid forward a step or two. "Not sure what I'm gonna do here," he said. "Think I have to shoot you." As he stepped even closer, the smell of blood flooded his nose, strong and brackish. It had soaked through the man's frock coat, darkening the gray fabric. He heard some raspy breathing, didn't know if it was his own or not, so he held the air in his chest to see. The wheezing continued as the man's shoulders lifted and fell. Uriah nudged him with the tip of his rifle, and the man grunted then started gasping again, even more shallow.

With the rifle still aimed, Uriah squeezed it hard between his shoulder and neck so he could bend down, reach out with his trigger finger and tap the man's bristly chin. There was a wrenching in his stomach, and he probed the inside of his cheek with his tongue, hoping to squelch the twitching in his eyes and legs.

And the man clamped his fingers around Uriah's wrist. The sudden movement knocked them both off balance. In the flail to free himself, the butt of Uriah's rifle slipped from his shoulder, dropped to his knee. But he held the barrel tight, the rifle dangling like a broken tree limb. It didn't take much to break from the dying man's restraint. In the tumult, the man lunged forward with a final glint of life. Uriah turned, held his left elbow in front of his face just as the man sunk his bowie knife deep into his forearm, through the tendons, down between the ulna and radius bones. Then the rifle fell from his hand, clunked to the floor. Both men clenching at the likely discharge.

But it didn't fire. Uriah looked at the knife in his arm, the man's fingers still wrapped around the handle. The splintered bone poked at his skin from the inside. When the man jerked it out, Uriah schlepped forward with the motion. He watched the soldier try to rise to his feet, rearing back a second time. But he faltered, slipped on the blood inside the trunk. He teetered some then fell backward. The man's head cracked against the wall and he crashed to the floor, one leg in the trunk, the other out.

Downstairs, the stirring stopped. Then, a flurry of boots thudded hard against the stairs. The man rolled onto his side and lay his stumpy hand across his chest. Uriah scrambled for the rifle, lowering himself to the floor. He pushed the butt of the gun into his stomach, his limp arm dangling on the left side, the pointer finger on his good hand poised to shoot. He tried quieting his thoughts, taking air in slow, letting it out evenly. There was a bright afternoon in October, at the height of corn season when he had run out into the full rows. He wanted to show his Pa that even at seven, he could be a frontiersman, a bold harvester. Almost instantly, he became disoriented. All the stalks looked the same, big and drooping. He spun all around, finally stumbling upon several tall shocks. He squatted down, set his sickle on the ground. He was too afraid to shout for help, too confused to remember which way the sun moves across the sky. His innards twisted like twine. He felt disconnected from the earth, drifting with the wind that whistled through the leaves, susurrating some secret message that he couldn't decipher. Wiping the wetness from his forehead, he wondered if his Pa would find him before nightfall.

The man began murmuring a Hail Mary. Before he could ask the Mother of God to pray for sinners at the hour of death, Uriah pulled the trigger. The bullet made a hollow thump as it entered his head, like a pumpkin hit by a hammer. The soldier didn't cry out, only jarred then lilted. Between the gun being fired and his fellow footmen bursting in, Uriah was overcome. His arm throbbed and he stared at the opened skull in front of him. Surrounded by men yet such profound loneliness. He was back in the hot, autumn sun, waiting for his Pa to break through the corn stalks, call out his name.

Uriah's ears had deadened from the blast. He could only see his comrades' mouths moving, read the astonishment on their faces. Their eyes darted from the fallen soldier to the open trunk, to the wound in his arm that had soused his sleeve. He watched the medic charge past the others, making his way over. He guided Uriah into a flat position and waved a hand over his face. Uriah read the questions on his lips, "What's your name? What year is it? Who's the president?" as he tore open his coat, inspected his arm from different angles before tying a cloth above the torn flesh. Though he couldn't hear his own replies, Uriah knew from the medic's nod that he'd given sufficient answers.

Joseph knelt beside him, swooped him onto his shoulder then hauled him downstairs like a grain sack. He was laid up in one of the bedrooms, all of which had become make-shift infirmaries. The medic dipped the blade of his knife into a vial of white powder then sprinkled it into Uriah's wound before bandaging it with gauze. He told him to open his mouth, then put a pill on his tongue, saying, "Swallow that and rest while I make the rounds outside."

Uriah counted four others in the room, managed to nod at the man next to him before getting woozy. He was losing consciousness then coming to, unsure as to how long that went on. A couple more wounded had been brought in, and the same man still lay in the cot beside him. Turns out, he was a father of three, a chimney sweep from Milwaukee. He'd been shot below the knee.

"Hate to tell you, son," he said, "but I'm figuring this room is for men who need a limb lopped off." He nodded toward the window. "You can bet there's a heap of legs and feet not too far off. Company medics always make piles under a weeping tree or a low hanging pine, helps hide it some. None too inspiring to see fellow soldier parts lying out in the hot sun or being pelted by the rain." He sucked in through closed teeth, twisted and yellow, then let out a short, husky groan. Like a cornered cat, he arched his back and fought through the wave of pain. Uriah looked away. Behind them was a legless soldier, a photo clenched in his fist, tears rolling down his dirty face. So he turned back around—the lesser of two evils.

By then, the man was tilting up a shapely bottle of bourbon. Some of the spirits spilled down his chin and he lapped at the brown dribble, making a wide half circle with his tongue. He held out the fifth and read the label: "Elijah Craig," he announced, his tone reverent, as if paying homage to the mash of corn and grain. "Says here it's the father of bourbon." He turned the bottle, front to back. "Lord almighty, says it's been aging in a barrel since 1789. Damn near twice as old as me. They brought along the good moonshine for the lame," he said. "Guess I should be sharing." Then he looked around the room. "Hm. Most fellas are blacked out, slobbering on themselves like rabid coons." His eyes stopped sweeping over the injured men. "And that one there's already taken the big jump."

Uriah turned back to see the legless soldier—eyes closed, mouth open, arms flopped out on either side of the cot. The picture he'd been holding was on the floor, face down. "I'll take his share," the man said, taking another swig. "Heard there might be a hundred of us killed up here already. And maybe four times that are wounded. That's not even counting the ones they can't find. Or the ones the Rebs might've took. Seems Stevenson's men withdrew, headed toward the mountain's crest to wait for reinforcement."

"What about the Captain's son? Heard anything about him?" Then the pulse in Uriah's arm and head reared up. He bridged his back, too, trying to disperse the ache. He took in a breath, held it, motioning for the bottle. The alcohol scorched his throat and he coughed hard. "It's the itching I can hardly stand," he said, "I want to scratch my skin straight through to the other side."

"Drink more of that tincture, son. Opium and liquor. Gotta get some in you, dull the hurt. Like this here." The man took back the bourbon and poured it in his mouth like a watering can. He let out a sigh of fatigue and relief. "Captain's boy was taken out from up high, single shot to the head. I only know 'cause Captain was standing just outside the door here when they told him." He pointed into the hall. "Ol' Captain let out a sound I ain't never heard before. A sob and howl all at once. Kinda like when you shoot a deer up close, that same, sharp squeal. I heard them try to comfort him, telling him it was a quick death. 'Bullet to the head' they said. 'No pain.' That didn't ease him though, 'cause he made that same damn sound again, even louder."

Uriah's arm began to tremble. Though he couldn't feel it shaking, both of them could see it plain as day. "Damnation," the man said. "It's floppin' like a bluegill cast ashore." Uriah felt like he was watching someone else's body, had to be another man's arm seizing that way. It was then that the medic returned with two others, pointing at the chimney sweep. The men went to him. Each of them wrapped one of the man's arms around their shoulders then hoisted him up. He let out a crow-like squawk, and they fell into a clumsy piston-like motion as they bounced out the door. "I'll be a hop-along soon enough, boy," he shouted. "Save me some of that fancy fire water. I'm gonna need it."

"Yes, sir." Uriah watched until all three men disappeared. Then the medic stopped, pressed his hand atop his forehead, inspecting the bandages on his forearm, asking if he felt hot. Uriah said no. Then the medic picked up the nearly empty bourbon bottle and shook it, what little remained sloshed inside. He set it in Uriah's lap, told him to finish it as he hurried back out the door. Uriah started to call after him, to ask how Captain was doing but he already knew the answer. And he understood that the medic had lives to save, limbs to sever. No time to comfort men for anything other than broken pieces and bleeding wounds.

Uriah drank the rest of the tincture in one swallow, felt the smolder in his mouth and chest. The contents of the bottle and needle took over and another slumber set in. He started thinking about home, folks passing through Bellwether's town-square—on foot, in buggies. He could see the brownstone of the church walls, the sunlight reflecting off the tall, pointy windows. Reverend Hiram and Mr. Brandt standing in the schoolyard, sea-stacks tall behind them. And Ada stomping her way to the post, frizzy hair sticking out from the sides of her loose bonnet, sadness gnawing at her heart. He saw the fields around his house, the corn stalks thick, leafy like cabbage. His Pa strolling the perimeter, whistling a tune that Uriah's muse couldn't quite register. And Ma beating a rug that she'd hung on the rope between the house and the limb of a wide-reaching walnut tree.

In the same scene was Eva's house. Her Pa at the kitchen table, head hanging down. Her Ma outside pruning a lilac bush with a handsaw, a bunch of purple and pink blossoms beside her. Try as he might, though, his vision didn't include Eva. He yearned to see her running through the yard like when they were kids, cool grass brushing against her bare feet. He needed to picture her face, her body. Anything. But she would not appear. Only the rounded tops of the Porcupine Mountains floating in the distance like smooth, green waves.

When he woke, Uriah wasn't startled to see Joseph sitting on the chimney sweep's cot. It felt natural, though he did second guess if he was really awake or not. Joseph was gripping a wood pencil in his hand and balanced on his knees was a piece of paper atop a bible. "You clear-headed?" he asked. "We're gonna draw up a letter. A couple of 'em if you'd like." He positioned the pencil on the paper, ready to scrawl whatever spilled from Uriah's mouth. "You talk, I'll write."

The air was thick with death. Until that moment, Uriah had not counted himself vulnerable to it. As they were trekking up the mountain side, he feared dying but hadn't actually thought about not living, seemed like two different things now. His mortality was palpable. No different than a grandfather clock or a butter churn. He knew he was half stewed as the tickling inside persisted. He could see the blood-soaked bandages on his arm, but the sting had numbed, spread evenly in every direction. Can't feel nothing, he thought. Yet there was a keen alertness to all the sights, sounds and smells around him. Everything was rich, distinct. All the voices crisp, almost thunderous—exaltation from victory and the suffering that came with it. The smell of blood mixed into the clean, cool mountain air while mist from the Tennessee River drifted upward, into his nose and throat, clinging to his hair, his uniform. He glanced at Joseph, still poised to take his dictation, eyes on the paper, not Uriah. "You think I'm heading to the marble orchard. Don't you?"

"No. Just trying to keep your mind on other things. Doc says if that son of a bitch cut the bone, he's gonna resection you, friend. You're about to feel a world of hurt. Best to think about your Ma or Pa. Or that girl you talk about all the damn time. What's her name?"

"Eva." And finally, her face came into view. Round, milky white. Yellow-brown hair falling down on either side. Her hazel eyes glassy and light. Just a flash in his mind, but a sweet diversion. "Yes. Write to her for me. Tell her she's beautiful. And that I've loved her since she first tried taking my trundling hoop. Tell her that I think about her. All the time. How her hair is curly in some places and not in others. Tell her that being a soldier isn't what I thought. That it makes you think about different things. And write this down, that I shouldn't have been looking but sometimes when we were sitting in the grove, I could see her bloomers. Her skirt would pull up her leg some and—" Uriah paused, looked at Joseph who was looking back at him now. "Your hand ain't moving," he said. "You getting all this?"

"'Course I am. He started shimmying the pencil back and forth like he was drafting a novel. "Why did you stop?"

"Tell her I should've done something about her Pa. That I'm sorry about that. And when I see her again, I'll make it right. I'll make him bite the ground. Any man that hurts her ever again, I'll put him under—" He stopped. "Where you gonna send this, Joseph? I don't know if she's still in Chicago." He paused. "Or if she even wants to hear from me."

The medic interrupted them. His shirt was sodden and he wiped the sweat from his forehead with his palm, pushing it into his damp, black hair, matted where the blood of other men had stiffened. He looked pale and tired as he bent down and unraveled the sopping bandages. Uriah stared at his coat, guessing at the different stains—blood, pus and whatever else came out of gashed open soldiers. Then the medic probed his arm with a finger, feeling for bits of bone and when he found them, he shook his head, told Joseph in a weary voice to get him to the tent outside.

Joseph put the paper and pencil down, stood and offered his shoulder. Uriah put his arm around it and pulled himself up. Once on his feet, he glanced down at the paper—blank. On instinct, he was mad. As if he'd been tricked. But even groggy, in his heart of hearts, he recalled Mr. Brandt explaining what it meant to be illiterate, telling the class how lucky they were to be learning how to read and write as many folks in their neck of woods could not.

Just beyond the tent, Uriah spotted the pile of limbs he'd been told about and wished like hell someone had taken better care to hide it. A mound of lower legs mostly, but there were a couple of feet and a single arm sticking out from the top. His brain didn't seem to accept it, the amalgamation of body parts, stockpiled like firewood. Most of them still holding the color of living, as if at any moment, they might stand erect, head out in search of their owners.

Inside, most of the men had already been severed in one way or another. Uriah spotted the chimney sweep right away. His skin was gray and he lay quiet, a threadbare blanket over his lower half. The medic saw Uriah looking at him and offered up that the man was still in shock. "Now we wait, see if he catches Surgical Fever. Or Gangrene."

Two men carried another soldier through the entrance on a stretcher. One of them shouted, "He's hit in the guts!" to which the medic pointed to the back corner and said nothing, never looking up from the chloroform tin in his hand.

The sweet elixir was wearing off and Uriah was sobering to the aftermath of being a soldier—the mangled thew, the consternation, the hardening to human suffering. Already, he was less bothered by the jumble of limbs that reappeared every time a breeze blew open the front flap of the tent. The medic began mumbling to himself. Or maybe he was talking to Uriah. Either way, it seemed to be an effort to stay sane. "I've got to work on the ones that still have a chance," he said, a dripping rag in hand. "Picking and choosing who gets to live. I never asked to play God. Two years of medical school and I'm carving up men like cattle, hacking off their arms, the ones they should be hugging their sons with, loving their wives with. I'm a damn butcher. 'Sawbones'. That's what they call us battlefield doctors." He held the rag over Uriah's nose and mouth, continuing his soliloquy, talking about other soldiers he'd operated on. "Why? Why did that minié ball split that poor boy's bone damn near three inches up? If he doesn't get some God-forsaken infection, he still has to bounce around like a frog. Life's not worth a plugged nickel, I tell you."

Joseph delivered the wash basin and extra rags the medic called for. The water was dirty and dark like beetroot and oil, and the pieces of cloth were frayed. "Keep this rag over his face till he goes out. That blasted Reb cut into the radius bone," he announced. "Have to resection his forearm." Uriah could feel himself becoming light again, but not yet weightless. For the most part, he was still lucid, able to hear the conversation yet too sluggish to move. He watched the doctor open his medical bag, all of the sharp, hooked implements laid bare.

"Looks more like a carpenter's toolbox," Joseph said. Then he asked why there were two saws.

"Smaller one's for severing skin and muscle. Bigger one's for cutting through bone." He lifted up a scythe-like piece, the size of his middle finger. "This one's for pulling out the arteries so they can be tied off," he said. "Now, no more questions. I gotta concentrate." Uriah tried to speak but his tongue was clumsy, didn't know what to say anyway.

A commotion rose up from the corner of the tent. All eyes migrated that way. The man shot in the belly had perished, rolled off his cot and crashed into a table holding all the porcelain cups for feeding the invalids—most of them broke. One of the soldiers began picking up the pieces and putting them in a wood crate. He sliced open a finger, stuck it in his mouth to suck the blood, then cursed the man for dying.

Uriah turned back to the doctor who was wringing another tattered rag into the murky water. "Take a swig of this," he said and handed him another brown bottle. After a hearty swallow, the relief was almost instant but far from absolute. It was a strange release, like the freeing that comes with a hard sneeze but five times stronger. Uriah watched the men's preparations as if the medic was an actor on stage, and he was a mere spectator. He handed Joseph the smaller saw and shouted above the tumult still boiling behind them, "Cut off his sleeve at the shoulder then stuff this in his mouth." He handed him a stick, round as a wrist. "Lodge it in his teeth nice and tight. When I give the word, stand behind him, hold his head still." Then he waved over the soldier with the wooden crate, told him to help keep Uriah down. "Can't have him jerking any."

Uriah's thoughts felt slow and watery, yet everyone was moving fast. Their actions weren't comprehendible, but the soldier's knees were real, digging into the thin flesh of his hip and thigh, hands pressing hard against his chest. The light of day shone through the tent and just before the medic pierced Uriah's skin, there was a brief lull. A second of stillness. Everything and everyone seemed to halt, even the air was motionless. He thought he heard the high-pitched chirring of a robin, rising in sonority until it sounded like a child laughing. He tried to commit the rise and fall of its song to memory, so he could replay the *yeep* and *chirr* in his mind—

The medic folded his brow in concentration, the smaller saw in his fist. And as he leaned in close, placed the cold blade above the open wound, Uriah squeezed his eyes shut, listening hard for the bird's trill. "I hope you're a right-handed man," the medic said. Then, the bite through tissue was overpowering, a blinding surge that spared not a cell in Uriah's body. With a mouthful of birch, he heard himself garble, "Oh, dear God."

Uriah came to when the medic started rasping the ends of the bone. He was even more hazy, felt buried to his neck in the coarse sands of Superior. The throb was not as full as before, though. That pang had charged outward, struck every part of his body then tempered. This ache was deeper but dull. Everything was blurry, but Uriah could feel Joseph's fingers gripping his head. And he could hear the medic talking, recounting how he'd once recruited a soldier to hold a patient down, but the bastard vomited when the blade struck bone.

The first thing that came into focus was the medic's face. His narrow eyes and patchy skin. There was a small red blotch across his forehead, smeared in what looked like a weak attempt to wipe the blood away. He looked down at the divet where the bone used to be and at the stretch of skin that had been pulled over and sewn shut. *My own flesh, mended like a pair of torn pants. Eva's gonna think my arm queer. She'll doubt me as a protector, a provider. What if she's right?* He blinked his eyes, trying to stop the spin of thoughts. It was childish to be pondering a life with Eva, especially right now.

"It's lame, but it'll fill a sleeve for now," the medic said. Then he dipped his hand in the foul water and pressed a piece of gauze against his highest knuckles—the saw's teeth marks were scratched across all of them but only the bigger two were bleeding. "Government is giving $75 commutations for fake limbs. Not to Confederates though, on account of rebelling. There's a new arm just came out of Massachusetts, patented by a man named Marvin Lincoln. Made of hardwood. Maple, I think. It's got an elbow that locks," he said. Then he bent his arm like a hinge to demonstrate. "And I know they'll put one on you in no time, right here in Chattanooga. Might not help you when you're bailing hay, but it'll be sturdy enough for most things. You won't feel like folks are looking at you all the time, either." With closed lips and a straight face, he moved to the side of the cot, patted Uriah's shoulder with his uncut hand and stepped further into the tent, fading into the dread and mayhem.

Joseph appeared where the medic had been. "You're going home," he said. "And I'm glad of it. All that quiet. Nothing but the lake breezes." He sat at Uriah's feet and looked out through the front of the tent. Someone had pulled open the flaps and tied them to stakes in the ground. He was emotionless when he told him that the Captain was found in the mountain stream on the other side of the ridge, belly up. They said he'd stripped himself down, folded his uniform nice and neat, set it on the bank. Both his and his son's kepis sitting on top. "The gravel and rocks had already washed over his naked body. Seems war kills men in all kinds of ways."

Uriah watched Joseph walk out the opening. He knew that if they both survived and saw one another again at home, it could never be the way it is now. He tried picturing the Captain's body, not covered in soil, but floating in crisp, clear water instead. He hoped that robin had flown the Captain's way, warbling its tune just for him.

Chapter 33
He's Your God, Too

Tina and Eva walked side by side, huddled together against the winter, their noses running, fingers prickling. Though there was little snow, the arctic winds dipped down over the buildings, pushing through the streets. They tried to laugh about the cold, calling it a three-dog-day but from Clark Street onward, the sharp currents silenced them. When they arrived at Ruth's place, Eva slowed some—Tina didn't. They plodded up the familiar sidewalk single file. How strange that what was once a safe haven now felt forbidden and intimidating. Like when she and Uriah snuck between the sugar maples by the bathing tubs at the ore mine and watched the naked diggers, listening to their dirty talk, hoping for a fist-fight. Eva felt like an insect as they approached the door, each step heavier than the one before. She held her head up straight, letting the wind whip her cheeks as a kind of contrition. As soon as Tina knocked, though, she dropped it down. They waited, listening for Ruth's heavy gait, clumping against the floor. But there were no sounds from within. After another knock and more waiting, Tina pulled out the key.

"That ain't right," Eva said. "We're not tenants anymore, not even friends. We're trespassers."

Tina didn't hesitate, just slipped the key in and twisted it back and forth. Nothing clicked. "Oh, hell," she said, "the old bag changed the bloody lock."

Eva felt a tinge of relief. But Ruth's absence made her vagrancy more real, more imminent. Just as Eva turned to go, Tina reared back her foot and fired it against the big, wood door. Amidst the stillness, the thump was loud and awkward. Again, she kicked. Eva reached for her shoulder but thought better of it, the stitching still fresh in her cheek. She backed away, covered her face with both hands, making a "V" over her left eye with her pointer and middle fingers, so she could peek. Even through the fabric of her gloves, the sutures felt coarse and strange, like her face wasn't her own. Tina kicked again and again. The girl's fury made Eva's heart race. The rage was frightening, but she understood it. She'd been there. Nothing could stop Tina from bashing in that door. And then, like a wild mare, she charged with her whole body. And the restraints gave way. From behind, Eva could see inside. The furniture and knick-knacks were positioned in the exact same manner, orderly and tasteful. The only sound was Tina's gasping and a single rush of wind that whistled through. She took a step forward.

But not another. Ruth rose from behind the sofa, slowly, stealthily. Then, a resounding click. She raised her Colt Walker, chest level, and aimed the barrel at Tina's head. "60 grains of black powder per chamber, girls," she said, calmly, factually. "Built for close range—" She pointed to herself with her free hand, then to Tina, then to Eva. "—about this distance, I'd say." Neither girl moved. Eva felt a pulse in her bladder and clenched her lower half, trying not to leak. Ruth told Eva to come inside, too. And she did, shuffling like a spooked hen. When she opened her mouth to speak, Ruth shook her head.

"Where's all that goodwill shit now?" Tina spouted. "Ain't you supposed to turn the other cheek?"

Ruth said nothing, kept the gun aimed at her. The girls exchanged a quick glance before Tina tried to speak again. "Ruth, we—"

"Luke, Chapter Six, verse twenty-nine," Ruth interjected. "To one who strikes you on the cheek, offer the other also." Tina stood firm as Ruth stepped forward, pushed the gun's barrel into her forehead. Eva couldn't see her face, but she knew Tina would be staring straight ahead without a blink. "I ain't offering another cheek today, you floozy. Only the lead in this here six-shooter. I'll ask for mercy later."

Tina swatted at the gun. In the space between, both women stumbled, and after the pop of its discharge, there was a sluggish lull. A flash of bitter air blew through the open door, slamming it against the wall, upheaving the women's hair. Several whatnots fell off shelves with tinks and tunks. The girls surveyed the room for the metal ball that was fired, where it might have struck. Nowhere to be found. Must have flown straight out the open door, Eva hoped.

Ruth had squatted down on all fours, her skirt fanned out, searching the floor with both hands, frantic, like a skittering chipmunk. Then Tina's laugh exploded, primitive and shrill. Eva stepped from out behind her and saw the empty socket in Ruth's head, pink and bare. Ruth stopped patting for her eye, lowered herself into a sitting position with her back against the sofa, and let out a breath.

Tina stopped cackling and moved to her, hovering like a proud lioness. Ruth angled her gaze through Tina's legs, locked onto Eva's scar and inhaled with a gasp, placed a hand over her mouth and nose like they might fall out, too. Eva turned away.

"You been living the wicked life," Ruth said. I just knew it. Oh, Eva, your pretty face—"

"Stop judging folks, goddammit! Ain't that your God's job?" Tina spliced in.

"He's your God, too," Ruth said matter-of-fact, but there was defeat, too.

"Horse shit," Tina said, then spat at Ruth, more contempt than actual spittle. "Not here to talk about your fairytale

Maker. We're here 'cause Eva ain't got no place to go." Eva felt as small as an ant. Smaller than the first time she looked into Ma's eyes after Pa had befouled her. Smaller than when the trick made her privates bleed and called her a whore while he was still inside her. She wanted to speak out, tell Tina she could fend for herself. But the smallness held her tongue.

That's when Tina held out her palm. In the center, Ruth's eye shone like a new coin. She stood still for a moment then clinched it tight, headed for the door. On her way, she picked up the Colt Walker in her other hand, let out another chortle. "Ought to kill the old biddy," she said, turning the gun over and back. "See if her precious God saves her then."

Eva couldn't tell if she was serious. But the thought of her hurting Ruth jostled her enough to find her voice again. "Let's just go."

"Go where, Eva? Tina faced her directly. This is your last hope, missy. You ain't coming back with me. I told you that. You can't turn no more tricks with that cut up face." She flicked one of her earrings. "Now you know the truth. A working girl gets lots of showy things, but it don't always pay the rent." She set down the gun and stepped under the doorway. Then she held her hand high and turned toward the outside, poised to cast Ruth's eye into the snow. With her back to them, she said, "It was nice being with you for a while, Eva. But a girl's gotta look out for herself." Tina cocked her arm back even more, took a big step with her right foot.

"Tina! Don't!"

She stopped mid stride, let down her arm. After turning back to them, she set Ruth's eye on the floor, nudged it with her foot. The look on her face was vacant as if she'd just had her turn at kick-the-can. She left without saying goodbye.

And the silence after the door closed behind her was the loudest thing Eva had ever heard.

"How could you do it? Just up and leave that way?" Ruth was still sitting on the floor. Her eye sat where it had stopped rolling, graceless on the floor, like a raisin in the milk jar. Her voice gave way when she asked, "For what, Eva?"

Eva knew it wasn't her turn to talk, not yet. All her filth rose up, so much bigger than she'd imagined. The waves of Superior in an April windstorm, soaring twenty feet into the sky. Bigger than the fear she had running from the ship into the mouth of the city. It was God talking to her in the outhouse when her baby came loose. It was rolling her first trick's money between her fingers, knowing it was all so wrong.

"You gave yourself to the Devil. I can smell Him on you." Her voice wasn't cracking anymore. It was clear and stable. "What do you have to say for yourself, child? Seems like you should be the one down here on the floor, pushing your hands against that marked up face in prayer, begging for forgiveness."

"I want to earn my way back to Michigan, Ruth." Her voice sounded ragged, unfamiliar to her own ears. "I miss my Ma. I miss the woods, the open spaces, the quiet." She swallowed, wetted her cold lips. "I have no right to ask if I can stay, but I'm asking. And you have no reason to believe that I'll be true to you. I'll just have to prove myself all over again, day by day. As for praying, I know repenting needs to be done. I ain't a fool. But I've been feeling mighty dirty, Ruth, too unclean for God. Sometimes, before the sun came up and while Tina was still downstairs, I felt the Lord trying to come back into my heart. I could feel His anger. His sadness, too. The fact that I could feel Him at all, why, that comforted me. 'Cause I figured, why would He even bother with the likes of me, letting men disgrace—" Intuition made her stop. And Ruth looking away confirmed it. A clear boundary was set. Time at the brothel wasn't to be shared.

"I can't make you right with the Lord, Eva. That's between you and Him." A big wind whipped the broken door and it thwacked against the wall again.

Eva picked up one of the wooden chairs, propped the door shut, then sat down on it. She undid the top button of her duster coat. "I've been thinking about a poem that Mr. Brandt read us. It was by William Wordsworth. I remember because I always thought it was funny, a poet whose name has the word "word" in it. It's like it was meant to be. Anyway, I can't remember all the lines, it was really long. But at the end, he wrote about a flower being mean. How sometimes, when it blows, our thoughts are so deep that we can't even cry. I always liked that verse but never truly understood it. Not until now."

"Eva, I can't make this better for you, don't even want to. You dishonored me. Left without a word. I kept asking God to mend my heart, and to keep you safe. I asked Him to forgive you. And to give me the strength to do the same. I'll be damned if your leaving didn't make me shilly-shally some, make me wonder why He'd let you treat me that way. But then I realized, it wasn't about me. Never was."

"You're telling me I can stay?"

"My head says no. But my heart—"Then Ruth crawled over to her eye, picked it up and blew off the dust. She clamped her upper teeth over her lower lip then let it slide through. "Such a hateful girl. I can still feel the barrel of that gun pushed against her skull. Felt so bad, metal on skin. And I blame you. That'll always remind me of what you did." She nodded her head, as if she had been given some kind of affirmation—from God, or herself. Or both. "Blankets are in the trunk by my bed." She bent her legs, braced her back against the sofa. With both hands at her rump, she hoisted herself upward but plopped back down with a thud. "Seems I turned my ankle pretty good." After a moment, she readied herself for a second try. Eva stood to help her, but Ruth said, "Don't you dare," then pulled herself up with a single heave. Her bulky exhale whirled like cigar smoke in the cold air.

That night, Eva propped up Ruth's pillows but when she tried to put one under her swollen ankle, Ruth swatted her hand away. "Stop it," she barked. "Just 'cause I'm aging some and my eye was almost tossed away like rubbish, doesn't mean I'm frail." Then Ruth told her to go back to the mill the next day, beg Edgar for her job back. "Take a pay cut if you have to, redeem yourself," she said.

The thought of seeing Ephraim hardened her insides, like her blood turned to molasses. She saw his narrowed eyes again, that flicker, right before he took the last swipe. But she couldn't tell Ruth. No brothel talk. All part of the shrift, she thought. *Working next to that monster is just some of the price to pay. When he laughs at my face, crows to the men about what he did, I'll work harder. But if he puts his hands on me, I'll whack him with the nearest timber piece, push it down on his tallywags until they rip right open. That ain't a bad thing. That'll be me doing the Lord's work.*

Eva thanked Ruth for giving her another chance, told her that saying sorry didn't feel right, that she'd just have to show her. She asks if she needs anything and lays her eyepatch on her lap. Ruth tells her to stoke the fire in the stove then motions her closer. Nearly face to face, she says, "I don't trust you, child. But I've got faith, and that's the stronger of the two." She touches Eva's scar, studies it for a moment. Her finger feels consoling, even healing. "You hurt me," Ruth said. "Don't do it again."

* * *

When Eva arrived at the mill, she paused just inside the front gate. The same men were bustling around the yard, many of them too busy to take notice. Then she strode toward the office, and a couple of men walked by, staring directly at her scar like she was fresh from a P.T. Barnum show. One gave a friendly nod, but Eva couldn't return the greeting or look for too long as she was scanning for Ephraim like a jackal.

She barged into Edgar's office before losing her nerve. He looked up from his desk, glanced at her face then back down at the fanned-out papers. She didn't offer a "hello," just spoke what came to mind. She told him Ruth's eye was scratched and dented and that she needed a new one. Then, blunt and plain, she said, "I'm here to make amends." She couldn't decipher Edgar's look, so she stopped talking, stared at his lunch pail. The round top of a pear was showing, its stem standing at attention; a rumpled cloth hung over the side. Outside, the head-saws began to *brum* and *whir*, and the brawny laborers barked orders to one another.

"I aim to give you a stern talking to," he said. "Mull over things like dignity and duty." Eva raised her chin. "But today's not that day. Right now, you need to get busy working. Got to buy Miss Ruth a new peeper."

Eva's instinct was to hug him, but she stood still, holding his gaze. Soon enough, though, she realized it was best to break the connection, for his sake. It was hard for people to look at her—the knotty mark on her cheek, raised-up skin still pink, grisly like a chicken liver.

Edgar told her she'd be taking Ruth's place until she could see straight again. "I'll show you as much as I can," he said. "Gotta tell you, though, Ruth's got a hell of a way with figuring supplies and shipments and such. Things run like clockwork around here." He laughed heartily. "But only she knows the system, by God. Too damn stubborn to show anybody how she does it."

Watching Edgar's eyes light up as he bragged about Ruth made Eva feel even more like a rat for all her double-dealing. She thanked him then turned to go. But Edgar told her to wait.

"You wondering about Ephraim?"

Eva's heart sputtered. She figured Edgar knew the two of them had been keeping company before she left, but the thought of him knowing of her harlotry made her nauseous. "Maybe a bit," she said.

"He ain't here no more. Cussed stupe was in the yard one morning, going on about you working in a—" Edgar stopped mid-sentence. He clasped his hands together in front of his chest. "Anyway, the bastard was boasting that he cut your face."

Eva pivoted, hiding her damaged cheek. She looked out the window, studying several early morning stars in the faint light of dawn. She held her breath as Edgar rushed through the rest. "Turns out the fellas didn't think him none too funny. They cornered the rotten masher, took turns clobbering him with wood scraps. I ran to the ruckus, thinking I'd stop it, but when they told me why they was whoopin' him, well, I grabbed me a board, too."

With each word, came release, a morsel of pardon. Not from hearing the details of Ephraim's reckoning, there was no satisfaction in picturing his bloody and battered, hollering out in agony. That made things worse, as she counted herself the cause of it. But realizing that he wasn't coming back, that was an unexpected blessing. She let herself believe it was a harbinger, a divine one. Edgar was explaining how one of the men thwacked Ephraim between the legs, "Swore you could hear the boy's nutmegs pop," and Eva shifted from one foot to the other, drew her head back. Edgar must have read her discomfort as he hurried to a conclusion. "Bottom line, that old crank got the boot, won't be bothering you no more."

With the underside of her thumb, Eva brushed the new skin that had formed over her wound. Felt dead to the touch, bringing her back to reality from the joy of Edgar's kindness. She asked if she could start tomorrow and he said yes. As he walked her out, Edgar spoke of commitment, telling her that "Pride and competence go hand-in-hand." Eva listened earnestly, offered what she hoped was a beholden smile.

When Eva arrived home, Ruth was lying on the sofa, legs stretched out, feet dangling over the far end. Eva sat on the floor next to her, thinking how strange it was to see Ruth in such a devil-may-care position. "I'm gonna buy you a new eye," she said.

"Damn right you are." Eva thought she meant to upbraid

her but then Ruth let out a little titter and snapped the black patch against her face. She added, "Hells bells, let's have a nip of cider."

"But it ain't even noontime."

"Well, it is somewhere, right? China maybe? Let's have a swill for them folks."

Something in the way she spoke reminded Eva of Ma, and she wondered what she might be doing right then. Cleaning up the breakfast dishes? Melting snow for her tea? Or maybe she was sitting at the table, reading her bible, and thinking of her. In that moment, the loud flush of her scar felt a little softer.

Chapter 34
Abide With Me

Uriah was home before Christmas and in the few short months he'd been away, something had changed. It wasn't his wider frame of reference. Nor the inanimate limb hanging down like an unbuckled stirrup. And it wasn't Bellwether itself. Not the houses or the church or the post. Certainly not the sea-stacks. They still took his breath away, the way they changed color with each season—red and orange and yellow in the summer, then gray, brown and blue in the winter. Behind them, the hills were just as tall and rounded. The fields were empty of crops as they always were that time of year. Wide, vast and covered in white. A layer of wet snow had fallen, and the brisk winds formed drifts of varying slopes, wave after wave, rising and falling. It's how Uriah pictured the surface of the moon as a child, used to imagine himself bounding across it, a floor made of clouds.

And that's what was different now. It wasn't the things, but the way Uriah saw them. Scenes weren't as fanciful. They weren't to be dreamt about or embellished, but respected as they were and lived within. The trees were bowed, laden with snow. From the window, he could see a group of whitetail deer creeping near the corn stover, grazing for overlooked kernels inside the brittle stalks. He didn't turn to his mind's eye, didn't think how it would be to live as one of the browsing animals like he would have as a boy but to tread toward them as himself. He was still a stargazer, and he knew he always would be. But a more sensible one now. He knew his heart would still beat faster whenever he read Whitman, but plowing and poetry didn't have to be separate things anymore. Within the toil of furrowing the fields, there was beauty to be had, if he looked for it. There was pleasure in the aching bones that followed a hard day of planting or reaping or threshing, if he chose to see it that way. *What more does Whitman do than find wonder in the quotidian? Isn't that what all poets do?* Then Uriah thought, the only thing that distinguishes a poet from the rest of us is the decision to find sweetness in the day-to-day, to see things as they are and be satisfied. War taught me that, he concluded.

A towering urge swept through him, the need to be outside, to inhale the sharp, wintry air. He traipsed past Ma and Pa, both sitting at the supper table sipping hot tea in silence and pulled open the door. A rush of cold wind pricked his skin. As he stepped into the dusk, he heard Ma ask what in God's name he was doing and it made him grin. And Pa's reply, "Just leave him be," made him laugh out loud.

He thumped through the shin-high snow to where the deer had been, plopped down atop their hoof prints, his good arm out to the side and his slinged arm resting on his chest. He stretched out on his back and began to move his legs in and out like scissors, pushing down into the snow, making a perfect one-winged angel. He wished folks could see him lying there, not caring about what others thought. He'd never brood over such things again.

War taught him that, too. Under the northern lights, Uriah unfurled. Fear would no longer rule. All of his doubts felt like they were melting into the frozen ground. He resolved to sow the family's fields again. And to treasure every moment of it. No harboring hatred for a dead arm, only giving thanks for a working hand that he can put into the earth and squeeze the soil through his limber fingers. He vowed to the Captain and his son and the rebel soldier he killed that he would breathe deeper than ever before, let the fresh smells of every season—the brittle leaves, the buds, the grass, the rain—fill him up, restore him every day.

At Sunday services the next morning, the Lovett family sat in their same seats: Uriah farthest in, then Ma, then by the aisle, Pa. The pews were tall and straight and blemished, and their familiarity brought both comfort and anxiousness. He made a sweeping glance of the parish. All the folks of Bellwether sitting in the same spots and still arriving early to claim them. Everyone greeted him with gladness—a hand-shake, a pat on the back—a genuine, welcome-home spirit. He could feel the relief in seeing one of their own return from war not wasting away in a casket.

There was a grimness in their faces, though, a lived-in look that he'd never noticed before. Rough, rigid lines in their jowls. Their eyes were brimming with torment, but there was staying power, too. They lit up in a way that could only happen from enduring Michigan's brutal winters then seeing glimpses of God each spring.

As the congregation settled, he thought of all the suffer-ing these people had known, both inflicted and that which they brought upon themselves. How they hung the Williams women because they refused to see that their lionhearted minister was a son of a bitch, and how every time they pass by Ada without a word, they sin a little more. He pitied them for that, figuring that the fakery must be heavy. It didn't have to be that way. He thought about the rebuke they cast upon one another, how it isn't holy, just shackling the happiness God intends.

Uriah glanced at the Murrays. Mr. Murray was flipping through the hymnal, too quickly to actually be reading the lyrics. And though it was hard not wanting vengeance on such a warped man, he knew the man's burdens were the big-gest of all. What a ghastly life, he thought. To know the day is coming when you'll answer for the trespasses against your daughter, bearing down like a carriage full of bricks.

Hiram made his way to the pulpit, his robes snowy white and bulky, brushing the floor as he walked. It seemed he'd grown a bit of a paunch in the few months Uriah was away—robe tighter around the middle—and his hair thinner.

Uriah knew it wasn't that Hiram had aged quickly but that he saw things more clearly, free from gilding and pies in the sky. Before starting the liturgy, he stepped down from the pulpit and into the nave. He stood silent, his fingers woven together at his chin. His lips began to tremble. The congregation kept still, gave him the space to lament or rejoice, whichever was being wrought. The passion of Hiram's grappling showed in the creases of his face, his puckered lips and labored breath. Then he swiped at a drip in his nose, looking directly at Uriah. His eyes still glinted like precious stone and he smiled that same hearty smile, full of dimples and teeth. "Welcome home, son," he said, tone still brassy as a foghorn. Then his eyes iced over. He took in a couple more hard breaths and let them out. "You sacrificed selflessly as Christ did. For that, I thank you. And I must confess, I envy you for it, too." Then he approached the pulpit again, opened his bible and ran his knuckles down the middle. He took in another deep breath and asked his flock to join him in singing the opening hymn, "Abide with Me."

Uriah felt everyone's eyes on him. The pride helped shrink away some of the shyness. He kept his head high, watching Hiram with an admiration that he hadn't felt since Basil Brandt was his teacher. That strength that lets a man be vulnerable in front of others. Uriah swelled to know that it was inside him, too. But right now, in this time and place, something even bigger was shifting. He could almost feel his insides sliding over, making room for the new man emerging. He could feel every drop of blood pushing through each vein. His chest was chock-full, about to spill over, and it was getting harder to contain by the second.

Glimpses of Ada and Basil flashed in his brain, their faces clear and large and coming fast. He had another hurry-up urge. To jump from his seat, to right all the wrongs in the world. To run into the town square and call out to Ada. To put his arms around her and shout to the heavens, "Bellwether wronged you!" Tell her to hold on just a little while longer, that change is coming soon. To scream to Mr. Brandt for all to hear, "You changed my life. You changed many lives." Like a vision, Eva appeared, and he wanted to pull her close, tell her that he thought about her every day. That all these feelings and revelations were because of her, for her—eyes on the stars, feet on the ground—it was all for her. Wanting to strip down to nothing at midday and stand waist deep in Lake Superior, dip his face and both his good and bad arms in her cool waters. For Eva. To be the kind of man that others look to for courage. To let himself make mistakes. To drown all things that made him linger outside the remarkable. All for her, too.

He couldn't stop his legs from bouncing as he panned the parishioners again, hoping Mr. Brandt might have snuck in late. He looked at every pew, craning his neck to see. Then another wave of vitality washed over. He was not in charge anymore. His movements were not his own. Uriah leapt from his seat. And the singing stopped.

"I must go," he announced. "Something's pulling me—" All heads turned. He rubbed the back of his neck, kept his eyes on Hiram. "Thoughts are coming from someplace else. And I can't stop 'em." The words sounded foolish to his own ears, especially after interrupting the Reverend and now standing amidst the fellowship like some kind of diviner. "Mr. Brandt should be here. And he's not. And Ada Williams? Remind me why she's not welcome?" There was a shuffling throughout the parish. He turned to Mr. Murray and said, "We all know why Eva's not here? Right?" Mr. Murray stared straight at him like his life hung in the balance. Mrs. Murray's eyes searched the hymnal, for answers or reprieve or a hole to jump in. "I'm so filled up right now, Reverend Bell. Feels like I might bust open. All this rightness wanting to gush out of me like water over a cliff."

"Go on, boy. The Holy Spirit's working through you. Do what it's telling you to. Ada and Mr. Brandt, they've been waiting for you for quite some time, it seems." Uriah had never seen his Pa cry, didn't think it was possible. The tears looked strange on his face. Ma had brought her hand to her face, eyes peeking over, full of worry and gladness. Uriah climbed over them and into the aisle, then walked fast toward the door, looking back one last time before stepping out into the cold. Hiram said nothing, just opened his hands like he was holding the moon.

Uriah scrambled toward Ada Williams' house, punching through the snow with every step. The air burned his lungs, but he pushed on, not knowing what he was going to say, if anything at all. He called her name over and over before she finally opened the door, just enough to see his face. Her woolly black hair was undone and her big, black eyes were slick with inquiry. Her skin was as white as the snow that whirled between them, hiding his feet and ankles. She wore an oyster-colored shawl—the yarn stretched from wear—wrapped around one shoulder and draped down to her elbow on the other side. The expression on her face was middle-of-the-road, unreadable. But she looked old, that was certain. His heart was heavy to know that Bellwether had wearied her more than Mother Nature could have.

"We've done you wrong, Ada Williams," he said. She tried to close the door, but he held it open with his good hand. Each of them pushing equally so it moved an inch this way, then that way. He'd never seen her this close, never knew that her features weren't as hard-lined as he imagined. Something radiated from her, just as the starlight casts upon the water and pulls up the soft blues from underneath.

"I'm here with a promise, though you have no cause to believe it. Or anything one of us tells you. But know this, Ada: Never again will you pass by me without a smile or a bow or a kind word. And maybe, in due time, you'll even invite me in for tea. We'll discuss your day, your wellbeing. Maybe you'll share memories of Elinor. Or you'll teach me to be half the marksman you are. Rumor is that Sheriff Thompson passed along all his secrets to you. And now you're the best hunter in Bellwether." He formed a modest smirk. "Hell, maybe one fine day, we'll hug one another and say, 'See you at church.'" Uriah felt her pushing the door harder, but he could see that the sharpness in her eyes had melted some. He kept talking, kept pushing. "You'll never spend another Christmas alone. Not as long as I'm here."

Her face folded, lips tightened.

"And I'll pray that your heart will be full for the rest of days." A final push from inside and the door slammed shut. Then the bolt clanged hard. "That's okay, Ada. Bellwether has closed its doors on you since I can remember. We brought down judgment that wasn't ours to bring." Uriah leaned against the heavy wood. "You're still there. I can feel you on the other side. I'll come again. And again. However long it takes for you to see that I'm here to make things right. Let the healing begin, Ada Williams."

Then, Uriah leapt from the porch, stomped two miles west through the mounting snow. The cold bit at his toes and hand and nose, his breaths puffs of liquid droplets floating upward then spreading out thinner and thinner. As he neared Basil's house, Uriah saw him standing by the barn. There was an unlit pipe in his mouth and in one hand, a bloody paring knife; in the other, a gutted pheasant, pink and smooth and meaty. Basil's coat was undone and his beard was coarse and uneven, like he hadn't let it grow to fight the cold but simply forgot to shave.

Basil stopped moving when he spotted Uriah. Then he

shifted the pipe to the other side of his mouth with his tongue and held up the ravaged pheasant. "Hang them for a week before all the stripping. That's the trick for keeping game from tasting ratty and stinking." Uriah watched Basil's eyes as they scanned his face then landed on his hand dangling from under the sleeve.

"I had to see you, Mr. Brandt," Uriah said, still panting from the trek.

"Why, boy?"

"Not sure yet," he said. "I was hoping you'd help me with that."

Basil nodded toward the house and they headed that way. The sides of his coat flapping in the wind. He made no effort to button it against the chill. Once inside, Basil slapped the carcass down on the chopping block, threw the knife in a full basin. He pulled off his mittens and settled down at the table. "Glad to see you home," he said.

"Good to be here, sir."

The snow was falling faster, big flakes flurrying outside the window which Basil watched over Uriah's shoulder. Silence crept in. Then Basil folded his arms across his chest and gave a skulking frown.

"Why aren't you at church, Mr. Brandt?"

Basil looked long and hard at Uriah as if sifting through the possible responses, picking and choosing his words like apples from a tree. "I have an apology to make," he finally said. "Can you stay awhile?"

As the sun stayed hidden behind the clouds and the snow piled up past the porch steps, Basil confessed his cowardice. He pulled back his lips with his pinky fingers and showed Uriah the empty spaces where his molars had been. Told him how the infection hurt so bad that he would stab the flesh of his thigh with a steel point pen for a welcome distraction. "I'm not telling you my private sufferings for pity sake. Only showing what a man without honor will come to." And he thanked Uriah for his valor and sacrifice as a soldier. "You're more of a man than I could ever be."

When he asked about his arm, Uriah told him it wasn't worth rehashing the incident. But he did share that his biggest sorrow as a cadet was losing a friend. "His death came because I didn't act fast enough." But what was harder to swallow than losing a limb and the Captain's son or shooting a man point-blank was seeing Mr. Brandt as a faint-heart. His weakness lay loud between them, bare as the raw bird on the hearth. Never would Uriah have thought he could be ashamed of his teacher. But then again, the day was full of firsts. Even more dispiriting was learning that Mr. Brandt's time at the school was coming to an end.

"I'm no longer the man to guide the children of Bellwether," he said. "But just as I've lost my way, you've found yours."

"What's that mean, Mr. Brandt?"

"Believe it or not, I still pray, even though it seems useless most of the time. And what I've prayed hardest for is the Lord to let me disappear quietly. Slip away without any let-up. The boys and girls aren't to blame for my coming undone. It's time to pass the torch to someone who can talk to them about integrity without feeling like a liar. There's but a shred of dignity left in me which can only be salvaged if I accept my disgrace, put you at the helm. You must show them what unbending principle looks like, as I cannot."

"Me, a teacher? Never crossed my mind. That's a life's work for highbrows, not the likes of me. And it's a pursuit that costs money, the kind my family doesn't have." Though he was saying the words out loud, Uriah couldn't help but picture himself behind a desk, a *McGuffey's Reader* in hand, and the air thick with curiosity.

And just like that, the two men hatched a plan. A plan where having a dead arm was a smaller matter than it would be taking over Pa's farm. A plan where Basil could retreat from the public eye without having to offer any explanation other than Uriah had come home to roost, and a flag-waving veteran has more to offer the children.

Uriah's path unfolded like a second parting of the Red Sea. Come spring semester, he would enroll at the Michigan State Normal School. Basil would pay the tuition. "It hasn't been much, but over the years, my earnings have stored up. There hasn't been anything I've wanted to buy since Stella died." Though Uriah agreed to the offer, he insisted on helping Basil with his chickens and the gardens, or in whatever way he could until the money was paid back in full. He didn't think his heart could pound faster than it had that morning, but it was beating wildly again. He was eager to get home, share his new journey with Ma and Pa. But Basil said, "There's more to tell," and Uriah knew his obligation was to sit a while longer, that this visit was about his wayward teacher, not himself.

Uriah listened while Basil talked about Stella, all her modesty and charm and spunk. How she was always playing with words and could make him laugh, even when he didn't want to. How she waved her hands all around when she was talking but held still when she was listening to someone, squinting her eyes, soaking in every sentence before responding. And though he hesitated, Basil finally shared that he and Stella couldn't have children. "It burst our spirits like balloons," he said. And with his head hung low, Basil confessed that he was the sterile one. Uriah scratched his prosthetic out of habit, leaned away. Hearing Mr. Brandt talk about private things, his neck turned instantly hot. But this wasn't a teacher, student conversation. It was man-to-man. All the lines redrawn.

"How can you know for sure that your maypole doesn't work?" Uriah asked.

Basil hesitated again then picked up his head, looked Uriah straight on. "When I was just a couple of years younger than you, I hurt myself." He looked down at his groin, "Down there," he said. "Something fierce, too. Swelled up, turned all different colors. Couldn't walk right for weeks."

Uriah felt the urge to cross his legs, stroke his chin. But he held still.

Basil breathed in and out once, put his hands on his knees like he was preparing to shove off. "I won't tell you any more about that, just needed you to hear that it was probably my fault we never had little ones. And though I can't be certain, what I'm sure about is that I never told my wife." The wind had picked up and the snow was turning to sleet, striking the sides of the house with tiny little pings.

"Why are you telling me this, Mr. Brandt?" Uriah asked. Then he thumped his wooden arm on the table in a show of focus, seriousness. "If we're having a straight-shooting chin-wag, then I'll be plain. It feels wrong to talk about a couple's marriage bed."

"I'd never talk ill of my bride," Basil injected. "Careful with that. Stella would want me to share what I've come to know about being weak. I'm only saying things that will make you the best version of yourself. Things that will help you be truthful and brave." He shook his head, made an *umph* sound. "I used to be those things, once upon a time. Not sure when it all changed."

"I think it's wrong to talk so hopeless. Making your living with the best interests of children at the center, why, that's not the measure of a fallen man. Going astray doesn't make you Godless, only makes you a man."

"Thank you, Uriah. I'll hold on to those words."

"Do you believe them?"

"They're proof that you're the one to take my place," Basil answered.

* * *

Uriah knocked on Ada's door every couple of days, to no avail. Until one time, as he was about to leave, the latch clicked. "Well then, if you're gonna keep being a pain in the ass, just come on in," she said from inside. Though the seeds of affinity were planted, the cultivation took time. A few clumsy moments in the first weeks, like when Ada showed him a likeness of her daughter, ran her finger along Elinor's chin, then wrenched into a ball and burst into sobs. Uriah reached for her but pulled back. Or the time Ada said, "There ain't one holy soul in that whole damn church," then sniffed in hard, and backpedaled some. "Except you and Hiram." Soon enough, they bumbled their way into a friendship, met every weekend, sipped licorice tea and talked about everything under the sun—Mrs. Caldwell being pregnant, though her husband went to war a year ago, and Mr. Brimley sneaking into the watermelon patch every afternoon, sometimes coming out with his drawers undone—and true to Uriah's word, Ada did not spend Christmas alone. Pa took more convincing than Ma, but eventually they agreed to open their hearts and home to Ada. "So that others might, too," Uriah had petitioned.

The Lovetts understood when Ada declined the invitation. A lifetime of loneliness and betrayal could not be remedied with some cranberry sauce and plum pudding. However, when Uriah showed up at her place with butter mints he bought in St. Ignace, Ada motioned him in. They chewed the treats with abandon, laughing at their gluttony. And when the night grew to a close, they drank eggnog by the stove, and Uriah told her that he was heading downstate to become a teacher.

The letdown was heavy—in her face, in the room. "Won't be but a few months, Ada. Besides, Bellwether is changing. It'll take more time, sure. But soon, you'll be sitting beside us at church. Not because we've allowed it but because you'll have chosen to forgive all of us." With that, he said goodbye and leaned in to hug her. She stilled and her face cringed. Uriah patted her knee instead. "Merry Christmas, Ada."

Chapter 35
As It Should Be

When an outbreak of syphilis spread amidst Chicago's brothels in 1870, word made its way to the mill. The men spoke freely in front of Eva, though respectful enough to leave out some of the gruesome details. When one man started talking about infections and blisters and leaking sores, several workers hushed him. She just shook her head and said, "Talk like that don't bother me much," already thinking of how she was going to check on Tina without drawing much attention. After all, Tina helped her when she could have turned her out. Eva thought herself in circles about getting back to the Levee District but finally decided just to ask Edgar if she could borrow his horse and buggy on a Saturday morning. To which he simply nodded, told her to be careful and not be gone long. Eva was much obliged and even more relieved when Ruth did not ask her where she was going when she left the house earlier than normal. Maybe she thinks the mill is overburdened with orders, Eva figured. She knows how busy they are, seeing it first-hand all week long. It wasn't lying not to mention otherwise.

The trip was quick and the horse compliant. The tavern was nearly empty, only two pickled old men in the far corner, still soaked from the night before. One with his head bobbing, the other with an empty shot glass in his fist. The smell of rancid ale swamped Eva's nose and a wave of heartache crested through her body, feet to lungs to head, where it culminated into a dull pricking. The truth was stinging—her life as a harlot wasn't worlds away, but mere blocks.

Tina was sitting on the floor, her elbows wrapped around her legs which were pulled in, crossed at the ankles. Her back was against the bed, and she was looking forward, eyes twitching, hands shaking. Her hair was tangled and slick. Eva had seen her undone most mornings but this was different. Tina's face was sunken. Her frame thin now, even her once ample breasts looked meager. "Inspector came," she said. Her voice was haggard, and she just launched into conversation as if they had been talking all night. "Didn't look like no doctor. Just a plain fella. No fancy clothes or mirror on his head. A bit on the chubby side, bunch of table muscle pushing out his shirt as he poked between our legs. Charley made us pay the fifty cents ourselves, and they used the farthest room, empty on account of that girl being kicked out for good. Word is, she slapped a John across the face when he called her a harlot. When she was leaving, all her clothes crammed into a basket, I said to her, 'We're all whores. Ought not be getting angry when someone calls you one.'" She stopped talking, turned to Eva sluggishly, like bread rising, and said, "I forgot what I was telling you. Seems I do that a lot now." Her face was fraught with despair. "You look fuzzy, Eva. Everything does."

Though it was midday, the room felt dark. The somberness seemed to pull everything earthward, their faces and hearts. Eva became heavily conscious of their friendship. Even if their history was brief, it was potent. There was something hugely binding in having shared such a close space, one stained by dishonor and sin. A deeper caring came with such measures, the kind that brought you running when someone was sick. Eva had heard about the symptoms of syphilis from the millworkers. How it shakes your brain, makes you ham-fisted and forgetful. She sat down next to Tina, crossed her legs, too.

"You were talking about the doctor, about how——"

"That's right." She paused again, the quiet was almost viscous. "He called us in one at a time, made us sit in a chair, lift our dresses and open our legs. Moved us through like cattle. He found the red sores. I knew there were some near my hips but didn't know they'd gone and spread down my backside. Turns out, I got the sickness a lot of working girls are catching."

Though she tried not to, Eva glanced down at Tina's legs. She knew there was nothing to see atop her clothes, but it was a reflex she couldn't fight. "They kept me at the hospital over on Rush Street," Tina said. "Not much bigger than here. It's called Mercy, which is kind of funny, I think." Then she explained how the mercury the Sisters rubbed into her skin was turning it gray, even purple in some spots. "And it's thinning out, too. I can't even bump into a table without bruising. I lost track of how long they kept me there. Couple weeks, I suppose. Don't remember things like I used to." Tina shifted, pulled her legs in tighter. "You don't want to hear none of this, do you?"

"That's why I'm here. There was talk at the mill of women being sealed off. I was worried that——"

"The mill? You went back to work there? You best have trounced that dirty son-of-a-bitch when you seen him." Tina's words were harsh but her voice was still drained. Eva told her that the men took care of Ephraim but didn't say much more. Tina clenched her neck and swallowed hard, her teeth bared. There was blood leaking from the gums, forming thin red lines between tissue and bone. Eva didn't have to ask as Tina shared that the ointment had loosened her front teeth. "Doctor comes every week, rubs me and another girl down with more mercury, head to toe. Then he makes us dress in long dresses and petticoats and sit by the hearth downstairs when there ain't many folks around, usually late mornings. We have to stay there till the sweat drips down our necks and arms. Always feels like I'm a step away from falling down. Every day it's worse. I'm shivering all the time, running to the outhouse damn near every hour." She scratched her arm, and the sleeve of her dress came up some. Where the doctor had kneaded the poison into her, the skin was light red and galled, like freshly cut deer loin. Eva reached for her arm and to her surprise, Tina held still, let her see all the bumps and welts. "Looks like a damn toad, don't it?"

Eva didn't answer, just gently pulled her sleeve back down and asked how she could help. "We're friends, Tina, whether you want to be or not."

"Charley said if I don't clear up soon, I gotta go. He tells fellas they can't put their corks in me. 'You gotta do other things,' he says to 'em. Well, they ain't dumb. Most of 'em know that means I got the—" She hesitated, then whispered, "You know, the French Pox. Truth is, Eva, I'm so damn whooped, I don't know if I could be in a bread-and-butter way no more." She shook her head, nodded toward the chifforobe and told her that most of the trinkets were gone. "Sold 'em all but a few," she said. "Had to."

A few loud thumps sounded against the side wall, followed by a series of grunts and a long, drawn-out sigh. "The noise of others having a brush is getting to me now. Never did before. I feel like I gotta wash up every time, even though I ain't dirty. Feels like there's a man still on me. His skin and breath. Or maybe when he triggered, it left a stain that I can't see. Used to be able to think about the money, then I wouldn't care so much. But the grotty feeling ain't going away."

"God's calling you from this place, Tina. Maybe an honest cowpuncher from Indiana is what you need after all. Seems all the cavorting, all the clodhoppers, that wasn't the path you were meant for." Eva reached beneath her petticoat, pulled several coins from the pocket. She counted them out—four and one-half dollars—set them in Tina's lap. "I'll be back with more when I can," she said. "Until there's enough to get you home." Tina scooped up the money with cupped hands. The shaking began again, and the money made low clinking sounds. Eva lay her hands over Tina's, and they sat wordlessly for a minute, fingers atop fingers, waiting for the tremors to pass.

"I'm pretty sick," Tina said.

"I know."

"Not many people been kind to me. Just you and Ruth. And look what I done to her." Tina tried to pull her hands away, but Eva gripped them. After a quiet struggle, the muscles in Tina's hands went slack again. "Not sure why I did her that way." She paused. "Like I said, my memory ain't too good now, but there's one thing I recall clear as bells. It's been showing up in my mind, more and more. Not that special of a thing really."

Another round of hubbub flared in the hallway. Eva wiggled in even closer, then nodded for Tina to continue. "What was I sayin'?" Tina's eyelids started flitting and she squeezed them shut, her whole face wrinkling. Eva drew one hand from their hold and lay it lengthwise across her forehead, her fingers calming the quiver. "There was a little girl, Charlotte, lived by the farm. Same age as me, or pretty close. She was an ugly ol' thing. Lopsided nose. Shaggy hair. And one of her eyes floated, so you never knew if she was looking at you. Kinda like Ruth's but worse. We used to make dolls together, mostly corn husk ones, but a few penny ones, too. Pa would carve the pieces—the arms, the legs, the heads—and we'd tie 'em together with string. He always made the heads too big though, looked more like biscuits with bodies than people. We'd sit for hours, stuffing in the yarn, sewing new dresses from scraps of fabric Ma saved. But it's not the dolls I think of—" She trailed off again.

"What is it then?"

"Well, I didn't think of it until just now. But I'll be damned if it wasn't the quiet. See, she wasn't much of a talker. Me neither. Didn't matter, though. We just sat there working on our dolls. With most folks, if someone ain't jabbering on about something, they get all antsy. Have to fill up the space with noise. Not Charlotte and me. Ain't sure I've had that kinda swap with anybody since I left home. Sort of funny how this mercury makes most stuff foggy but leaves some things well enough alone."

There were a few moments of stillness, and Eva wondered if somehow even the revelers next door had paused for their sake. Then, Tina broke the peace. "I can taste the blood in my gullet," she said. "It's sour and salty at the same time."

"Go home," Eva replied. "No shame in the fields of Indiana. Just rows of corn and earnest men whittling their way through 'em. A whole lot more goodness than here."

* * *

It was the following Saturday when Eva made her way back to Kasey's Tavern. She borrowed the horse and buggy again. Still, no questions from Edgar or Ruth, just "be careful" send-offs. The saloon was a bit more lively. The same two drunkards sat in their corner, plus a couple younger men at the bar and between them, a new girl, working hard for an early morning patron. Eva watched her prancing and teasing, listened to her blood-and-thunder laugh. When they caught one another's eyes, Eva motioned her over. The girl strutted like a peacock, looking back at the men, swishing her hair and swaying her fanny. Her efforts were paying off, as one of them pulled a wad of bills from his pocket, licked his thumb, and began flicking through them. She was pretty, and Eva told her she was. And young. Eva told her that, too. But when she did, the girl turned up her nose, looked Eva up and down and started heading back to the hungry men she'd baited.

"Wait," Eva said. Then she grabbed her by the wrist. "I'm not judging. I was living here not too long ago myself." She squeezed the girl's fingers so her palm opened, then dropped in several coins. "This is honest money. Made it at the mill down by the water's edge. No dirty men pawing at me for it, neither." The girl glanced at the money then over her shoulder again.

"Don't need handouts. I'm doing just fine," she said, her fist still out, poised to return the coins. Her voice was squeaky but her words were clear. Eva closed the girl's fingers, told her to keep it. The girl said, "No more," then cavorted to the men and plopped into the lap of the closest one, who welcomed her with open arms.

Charley had come from the back and Eva approached him. Her heart quickened some, not from trepidation but timidness about her scar. The last time they saw one another, he was sewing sutures in her face. But she swore off the diffidence, greeted him quick and sharp. He responded in kind with a hearty nod, one hand wiping the counter with a thick cloth, the other pressed against the bar for support. "Face healed up some, I see," he said.

"Mighty kind of you to lie," Eva said.

"Hope you ain't asking to come back." He stopped swabbing. "Don't mean to be nasty, but with all the sickness going on, I need girls without scars."

"My living is plain again, Charley. I've only come to—"

"Tina's gone, headed back to Indiana. She was hacking and wheezing and roaming around like she was lost. I couldn't have her taking up space no more. Things are bad off as it is. Bought her train fare just yesterday."

"Well, it's as it should be," Eva said. Charley hollered at the gray-haired drunkards, telling them to order more drinks or get out, and Eva thanked him then headed for the door. As she did, the pretty young girl stepped past her, steering one of the young men toward the stairs. They stopped at the bar, and she bent over it to grab a box of Three Stars, presumably for the unlit cigar that rested arrow-straight in the man's teeth. That's when he reached down by her knees, put his hand between her legs and slid it up to her backside, lifting the skirt with it.

From across the room, his sidekick laughed and shouted, "She ain't no biddy," then cupped his crotch like an apple, jostled his privies up and down. "I got her next, ol' boy." The girl tittered, too. But Eva recognized the phony ilk, the nervous, toying pitch. Her stomach flopped and she turned away, stepped outside into a light wind, not quite strong enough to sweep off the musty smell from inside.

Chapter 36
Pa is Dead

My dear Eva,

Thanks for sending postcards. I'd only heard of them, never dreamed of getting any myself. They are all pinned on the wall. Chicago looks to be quite the city.

I write to tell you that Pa is dead. Doctor says his heart was bad. Not sure if you want or need the brass tacks, so I'll only tell a few. It was two Sabbath eves ago. He stumbled from his chair, holding his arm real tight. It was hard to hear him whimpering like a child. Then he cursed the Lord and fell against the hutch. Your grandmother's crystal is broken, the plates and flutes are gone. It's all I had to leave you.

I watched him kneeling in the shards of glass, elbows and hands bleeding out. When he finally fell face down in the wreckage, I finished the dishes in the basin then sipped from the special Canadian Club bottle, thinking about you, wondering what you were doing right then. I know you'll understand why I waited to call on Reverend Hiram until the next morning. And may the Lord forgive me for letting Pa hurt you for so long and for not feeling as sad as I should be that he's gone.

Uriah is home from the war. He's penning this very letter for me. (Now your Ma is flattering me and telling me to write the flowery words down. I'd like to start writing to you myself, Eva, but I won't unless you say it is okay). Please don't let your spirit go cold, daughter. There should be no joy in Pa's passing. True strength comes from pity and compassion. I believe your Miss Hester Prynne would agree.

Love, Ma

Eva held the letter tight. She thought, yes Ma, you should have stood up sooner. *I shouldn't know the sadness of a baby dying inside me, always wondering whether or not I'm grateful that it did. I shouldn't have memories of Pa slipping into my room. Or always be thinking someone's watching me—in the privy, at the mercantile, when I'm changing into my nightclothes.*

When she first arrived in Chicago, Eva felt like Pa's wickedness would always follow her, like it might split her wide open, right down the middle. But now, she was starting to fill up again, a little at a time. She knew Ma didn't forsake her to be mean. Only warm things come to mind when she thinks about Ma. Combing the tangles out of her hair with that big wood brush until her head turned pink. And sneaking an extra pasty in her lunch pail the year Pa let her go to school, throwing in some wild berries because spring had come early. Most of all, she thinks about reading Mr. Brandt's books to her. How she pretended to be listening close, even though her head dipped from time to time, tired from working hard all day, but never saying so. And she thinks about how the trees in Chicago aren't as big as the one's back home, and the sky is never as blue.

She reread the passage that Uriah wrote directly to her. Then again. And as she folded up the letter, Eva tried to slow her breathing, her fluttering heart. She tried pushing his face out of her mind so that she could no longer see his down-hearted expression when he finds out where she's been.

Chapter 37
The Great Chicago Fire

Early Monday morning, October 9th, 1871, Ruth and Eva woke to the smell of smoke. They huddled on the front doorstep, searching for the source. Then Eva pointed south toward the low clouds stretched over the building tops. "Looks like a bunch of cotton bolls."

"Oh dear one, those aren't clouds. They're smoke plumes," Ruth said. "And they've settled. Something big is burning down." Ruth traced them in the air with her finger. "See how they're dark? Dwindling out on either side?"

A flash of pale-yellow shot high through the haze and lit the sky like a kiln. A thunderous boom sounded out. Several muted shrieks echoed up from the lower wards. Then a second blast. A third. Each one higher, more potent. All out screams from every side now—sharp, shrill, and close. A fourth squall of fire flickered white and wild, spinning upward until the hot air met the cooler winds and they whirled together into a funnel, carrying the city's debris far and wide. Firemen bayed orders through their speaking trumpets, vibrating in the metal tubes then resonating into the streets. The discord of a big city fire and the panic of hundreds sent Eva into an ethereal state, as if her dream-self. She felt cornered, paralyzed. Above all the havoc, their church bell tolled.

"Time to go," Ruth pressed. "It's too close." When Eva didn't budge, Ruth gently pinched her chin between her knuckle and thumb, turned Eva's face toward hers. She repeated herself calmly, as if talking to a child, "Let's go, Eva. We'll burn up if we stay."

Something clicked. Eva nodded slowly. "Will our lockbox burn?"

"Perhaps," Ruth replied. "Come. Let's get it outside, quickly." As they tried to haul it out, Ruth complained of the pressure behind her dead eye. Still, Eva tried pushing without her, the unwieldy safe scraping the floor as she inched it along. The shouts were just beyond the window now. Then Ruth joined her again for a final push. The bulky safe thumped down the stairs, into the street.

And the bedlam overtook them.

Clamoring buggies. Scampering footsteps. Frantic cries of children. And the unstifled wails from a mother and daughter, each of them taking turns to shout for a lost wee one between sobs. A series of blazes wisped overhead, raining down in broken strands of flame, hitting the rooftops of neighbors. "Dear Lord, Eva, the world is burning." Frightened by the flatness in Ruth's tone, Eva focused on the safe, knelt behind it and kept pushing. Where to, she didn't know.

"Leave it, child!"

"I won't!"

"You will!" Ruth shouted over the mayhem. Then, Edgar came into view, wagon and all, lashing his horse their way. The two younger boys were in the back, Horace in front. "Pull 'em up!" Edgar roared. Clyde scooted to the side so his older brother Reuben could help Ruth onto the wagon floor. "Eva, you sit on the foot iron," Edgar ordered. "Hold on tight. We ain't gonna go too fast, but I've seen a lot of mean ol' rips reaching in, trying to chisel folks' possessions."

"Can we get the safe in?" As soon as Eva asked, she wished she hadn't. Ruth turned away, and Edgar narrowed his eyes in disapproval. That was that.

"Where we headed?" Ruth asked. She held a hand over her bad eye, trying to keep the ashes from sticking to it.

"Lightin' a shuck for the lakeshore," Edgar answered over his shoulder. "With the winds blowing like this, the river ain't gonna stop this fire. Too much rubbish burning. And it's all drifting north. Whole damn city will be up the spout soon." As he spoke, Edgar lurched the wagon forward. The bunch of them fell back some but gripped one another for stability. When they came to the end of Clark Street and turned onto Dearborn, the chaos was tenfold. The innards of homes had spilled onto the streets. Piles of furniture and clothing lined the thoroughfare, and scores of wagons jerked along, their hitches jangling and clanking, trying to dodge the fire's devilish reach. The people were scurrying about. None of them seeming to know where to go. The prairie? The waterfront? Above them, the city blazed, flames hissing and spitting like an angry nest of copperheads. Eva and the boys twisted their necks as if they were on hinges, watching the frenzy with big eyes. A gust of wind blew downward, and a wall of smoke swept through—

All the movement halted. No one could see through the gray murk. For an instant, there was only stillness. Clumsy, suffocating stillness. "Ruth?" Eva choked, her voice dry, hoarse.

"Don't talk," Ruth said. She felt for Eva's knee, then patted it. And Clyde called out to his dad.

"Hold on to the girls," Edgar boomed. When the soot cloud passed, everyone rubbed their eyes like they were just waking, adjusting to the morning light. Eva was the first to see the blazing church. She gasped, pointing at the flames fulgurating from the steeple. Ruth's eye cleared, too, and she followed Eva's finger. Both women cupped their mouths as if their tongues would topple out. Just then, the spire collapsed inward. Then, the building just vanished, swallowed whole by a churning black blur.

Eva came undone. An overpowering loneliness pushed through her, a disconnection from herself, from Ruth, from everyone. The crumbling church frightened her more than anything else. Before she could think better of it, she leapt from the wagon, bumbling her way through the raucous and rubble to get to the chapel's ruins. Ruth and the boys howled after her, but it all faded into the pandemonium.

When she came to it, there were no walls left to speak of. Still, she climbed onto the open floor, skirted around several flaming pews, searching for the Christ figure. Amidst a charred heap, she found it, face up and cracked open, crossways, through the midsection. All the noise slipped into the background as she knelt by his head, picked up his left arm and tried to place it back into the craggy socket where it used to be. Inky grit was smeared across his ivory robes. Eva positioned the figure so that his face met hers, then she stared deep and hard into Christ's eyes. The thick, torrid air rendered her dumb.

Standing among the church's remains, Eva looked out into the timber street. Most of the prairie folk had freed their cattle and opened up their chicken pens. Dozens of barnyard fowl were strutting aimlessly, cock-a-doodle-doing and pecking at random debris. Some rumpled bantam chickens formed a cluster nearby, and she listened to them clack and quibble as she sat next to her mangled redeemer. The shouts from Ruth and Edgar heightened in volume and panic. So, Eva bid Christ adieu and clutched her chest, a millstone where her heart should be. Then, she stepped through the wall, back into the havoc.

The chickens frenzied as she traipsed through their circle, trying to follow Ruth's beckoning, loud even amidst all the roiling. She spotted the caravan as she stepped through the clutter and soupy air. When they saw her, the bellows stopped. No words were exchanged at first, only another condemning glance from Edgar. Then Ruth climbed down from the foot iron and stood in front of her. She grabbed Eva's cheeks with both hands, poring over her greasy face, snatching it left, then right. "You're not hurt?" There was no intonation in her question, rigid as a tabletop.

"No."

"You've disregarded me again, Eva. Thought we were past that." Eva nodded three quick nods and Ruth let go of her face. After the girls had settled back into the convoy, Edgar clicked his tongue against his teeth, and the horses carried them to the end of Dearborn then down 18th Street, the southern tip of the Levee District. Eva already felt like everyone was staring at her, and now, being in the same place where she sold herself to strangers, she felt even more red-faced. She never thought about her two worlds merging like this. There was a blood rush in her ears. She was naked, meek. A consequence of having lived so wickedly, she thought, knowing it was a feeling she would grapple with forever.

As they advanced, the temperament of the crowd did an about-face. From terror and dismay to pure merriment. Though they were on the periphery and passed by rather quickly, the all out shindy in the streets was ubiquitous. Drunk men swinging from lampposts like primates, others prancing arm in arm, sputtering "Camptown Races" and clinking their steins with each passer-by. Though many folks had taken a straightaway for the shoreline, it seemed just as many had journeyed to the Levee District, indulging in their vices as the world came to an end. Eva could only imagine what was going on a few streets deeper in.

"What is this place, Ruth?" Reuben asked with unblinking eyes.

"A place sinners wander from the path," she answered. Then she gently guided his head into her chest, covering his face with her hands. Heading out on 18th, they approached the first upper ward. The smog was still thick, and the city appeared to be at eventide. The sound of scamps and swindlers was behind them and the flocks of people had thinned out, though the distant sounds of hoopla were still in the background.

There was great relief in their exit as it felt like more than just a departure for the sake of safety, there were nagging memories for Eva, and great guilt yet to be reckoned.

They made it to the northern shores where all of the displaced sat in camps, huddled together, watching the city burn. Their belongings were strewn about the beach—clothes, cookery, picture books—and when she spotted several iron safes in the sand, Eva's stomach turned over. Shameful to still be thinking about money when homes and lives were being lost, she thought. The people mingled with one another, an instant camaraderie rooted in a common disaster. Come nightfall, they shared what they had to eat—beans from cans and freshly gutted chicken meat, feathers still fluttering in the air. All of them waiting for the city to cool, praying they had a home to return to.

On the second night, firemen brought news of churches opening to take people in. Still, most remained. Edgar said, "Best to be hungry with a good clan of folks"—he nodded toward the flaming city—"then being in there with all the pillaging and do-or-dying." Dusk fell across the water like a slow curtain, and Eva found a private place on the water's edge, hunkered down in the dank sand. She listened to the waves rippling and breaking over the pebbles, sounding out like a thousand tiny hands applauding a job well done. She had heard the constant bark of a dog since they arrived, but now the pup came to her. Though its long coat was matted some, the mahogany sheen held in the glow of sundown. It stopped less than a foot away, cocked its head as if it could better discern Eva's demeanor that way. Then it sat, brought a hind-leg to its ear and scratched hard and fast. Eva saw he was a boy and beckoned him with her fingers. There had been a stray Irish Setter that scrounged behind the brothel some-times, and she remembered how even cold and hungry, it was always spirited. Good humor must be a trait of the breed, she thought, as the dog trotted forward, stretched its torso, then circled several times before dropping down next to her. A soft, droopy ear splayed out across her lap. As she pet his side, Eva tried smoothing out the knots in his fur.

Down the beach a ways, two boys chased one another, giggling and screeching, but the dog lay still, too tired to play. Someone began playing a guitar, the notes clear and crisp. Eva recognized the song right away, "I've Left the Snow-Clad Hills," the same song one of the mill workers played during their lunch breaks every so often. The chords felt good, familiar. She closed her eyes, let the airy tones soften the troubles for a moment as she stroked the dog's neck and tried thinking of nothing.

A woman's voice called out for everyone's attention. Eva popped open her eyes, and the dog raised its weary head. Even from a distance, she could see the hefty woman who had climbed atop a mound of things in her buggy. In the oncoming twilight, her silhouette was stout and ghostly. She bid silence from the people a second time and all went quiet. Then the dog scurried from Eva to its owner, climbing onto the pile next to her, tail wagging. She patted its head then pointed to the smoldering city and shouted, "God's not in there, folks. He's here on the lakeshore with us. All His mercy and warmth, it's in the blankets and food we're sharing. And the hugs between strangers." Eva heard Ruth call out, "Amen." Then the man with the guitar began to play "Onward Christian Soldiers," imploring everyone to sing along. It all seemed a bit theatrical to Eva, and she wasn't moved to participate, but she admitted that all the voices in unison was consoling. And the Irish Setter began to bark again.

Later that night, a rumor swirled through the camp that the remains of that woman's brother were found in a pile of rubble near the Union Depot. Her wails thundered, then bounced across the water. There was a mad scrambling near her carriage, followed by several shouts and a series of splashes. Some folks plunged into the cold, black water to save her, but word spread that she swam far out and dropped below the surface.

On October 11th, those on the beach learned that the powers-that-be had declared martial law to end the looting and anarchy. Soon after, a company of soldiers arrived to lead them back home—to see if they still had one. And there was even more shared relief amongst the straggling bunch because the pooled heaps of oats and crab apples had diminished and the animals were feeling the ache of hunger. It was in their dullness, their inaction. After everyone had boarded Edgar's carriage and they began to pull away, the Irish Setter jumped into Eva's lap. She looked around for another owner, a relative of the drowned woman. There were none. Edgar said, "I think he's yours," and Ruth nodded. Eva and the boys took turns petting him as they wound their way home, the toppled city on all sides.

There was a collective inhale in the carriage as they neared Clark Street and when Ruth's building came into view, a group sigh. In all the fire's jumping and twisting, their place had been spared. The safe was tipped on its side and there were deep, discernible dents in the door that looked to have been made with an ax blade; the pull-handle had been cut in half. After Edgar helped her pry it open and the money spilled forth, Eva wasn't as relieved as she thought she'd be. Instead, there was a strange sense of emptiness, one that money couldn't satisfy. In that instant, she knew it was time to go home. *Bellwether is calling.* She savored the lightness in her chest, northern Michigan flashing through her mind—the sea-stacks, the fresh water, and Ma's corn-colored hair pulled behind her ears as she kneaded, chopped and stirred—amidst all the gloom and wreckage.

Edgar was not as fortunate. The boys would stay at Ruth's until he could fix up a room for them in the back of the mill. One morning, just days after moving in, Horace went out to explore the city's rubble before anyone else had awoken. He slipped on a mess of bricks, his hand coming to rest on the smoldering embers underneath, his kneecap broken. And that became Eva's impetus for heading home. She created a timeline based on his injury. Care for Horace until the burn heals—wash it out with cool water, smooth butter atop the blisters, change the soiled dressings—and he can walk without crutches. Then, when the boy is mended, say goodbye to Chicago.

It was mid-winter when Eva determined Horace to be rosy-cheeked again. She held his wrist in both hands. "No swelling. Nothing but hardy scabs." Then she felt his forehead and declared his fever gone, too. "And I saw you chasing your brother around the lumber yard just yesterday." Still, she waited until April to leave. Edgar told her that there was no sense trekking that far north with a foot of snow on the ground.

The sky was cloudless on the day Eva chose to go. No more smokey haze hanging over the city. And the smell of burnt wood was replaced with a tincture of earth—wafts of soil, lichen and chickweed. Ruth was fumbling at the bureau when Eva stepped into her room, a jumble of feelings climbing up her throat. "I'm going home," she blurted. It felt sharp coming out, and she raised her hand in front of her face as if trying to pull the words back in. But they floated there. Ruth straightened her back, breathed in deep, fingered whatever was atop the chest of drawers.

"I know," Ruth said. "I could feel it." Her voice was less sonorous than usual. When she turned around, her eye was patched, and the good one was wet, red. She reached for Eva's hand that still hovered. "There's nothing for you here. I thought there might be once upon a time. I was wrong. And don't you worry about me. I'll survive. Always do." Then she brushed the patch with her knuckles. "As long as I never lose this eye you got me." She forged a chuckle. "Life can't get any better." She fetched a cameo brooch from the top-most drawer of the bureau and lay it across Eva's palm. "It's 18k yellow gold. The carving of the hardstone is perfect." She rubbed her thumb across the pristine figure of a Roman woman in the center as if trying to solidify the story inside it. "My husband bought it for me, just before he left for Mexico. He was one of the first twelve killed when the Mexican army attacked an outpost. Hard to believe, men dying over which river a country's borders come to. The more I've thought on it over the years, though, I'm thankful. That lousy war lasted almost two more years, and my husband didn't have to see any more of it. He died a valiant death." She stroked the brooch again then held it out for the taking.

Eva wanted to reject the gift, so much sentiment still held within it. But she knew it would ease the burdens of getting to Bellwether. She knew, too, that trying to freeze a celery stalk was easier than steering Ruth in a different direction after she'd made up her mind. So, she took it from her, studied it a moment, respecting the history.

"We're not going to make a big to-do about this," Ruth said, motioning Eva to her. "I'm going to say my goodbyes right here, right now. That will be the last of it. When you go, there'll be no train station for me. No tears. I don't do well with those things." Eva stepped into the embrace, wrapped her arms around Ruth's waist. Warmth passed between them, but there was a shedding of something, too. Eva understood that God gave her Ruth to serve as a guide through the bad things. No one else could've done it better. But things shift as they're supposed to. Their reasons for knowing one another had passed. Holding on to anything beyond shared memories would only dam up the future. The best way to thank Ruth was to offer the better version of herself—the one Ruth helped mold—to those on the wing, those she hadn't even met yet, awaiting her influence, her humility.

Though the rail house had suffered damage, the passenger depot for Great Central Station was located on Water Street and had remained unharmed. The trains never stopped operating. Before boarding, with nothing but her haversack and the money from the pawn shop down on South Clark Street, Eva kissed the top of the Irish Setter's head, rumpled both its ears and told Edgar to call him "Titus." She watched as he stood between the boys on the platform of the depot; they took turns stroking his silky, auburn fur. She said, "He's where he should be."

"Why Titus?" Edgar asked.

Eva bent down, kissed Horace on the cheek then pulled Reuben and Clyde to either of her hips and squeezed them close. "Because it's a title of honor. A worthy name for anything akin to you and your fine young sons."

PART III

Bellwether Rising

1872- 1874

Chapter 38
Say What You Need to Say

Basil had to have heard the crunch of loose slate underfoot, but he didn't look up. Even after Hiram came into sight and said, "Fancy seeing you here," Basil kept his head down. He knew Basil wanted him there, wanted him to intrude. Knowing how to read between the lines had become the bane of his job as minister. And it weighed him down sometimes, being the scapegoat when things went awry. Folks blaming God and the church in bad times, especially during war. Didn't make sense.

Basil did not offer a greeting, just started talking, mid thought. "I've been thinking about 'The Prodigal Son' lately. Not about the boy who did all the squandering, though. I've been wondering about the older brother. The devoted one who toiled away, reaping and sowing while his younger brother cut through their Pa's savings." Basil quieted for a moment, but Hiram read his scrunched-up face and knew he wasn't ready for questions. "You've got a boy who's been working by his father's side. Day after day. Year after year. No complaints. And then, he has to watch from the fields—back throbbing from seeding and hoeing, feels like a nail's been shoved up his tailbone and his skin might blister right off—as his Pa kills the fattest calf for his nincompoop brother. Sees him showered with fancy robes and a ring and sandals, rewarded for all his gallivanting. The boy wasted a life's worth of work on wine and women, then he simply says 'sorry' and *poof* he's a prince."

Hiram had grown accustomed to Basil's tired tone. It grew flatter with each passing year. He couldn't recall what he sounded like before Stella died. The days when they could banter about world affairs, argue heatedly, then shake hands and laugh; they were long gone. Hiram wanted to discuss the deadly fires all along the Lake Michigan shore, debate his assertion that all men are created equal. Or how about Major League Baseball? Or the Staten Island Ferry explosion? He remembered how the year before Stella died, they fought over the *Origin of Species*, Basil always trying to provoke him—"Well, not to offend you, Hiram, but I can kind of see Darwin's argument. I mean, natural selection is practiced by every other species, right?" Hiram relished in their badgering, took comfort in it, loved him for it. He wished his old friend would bait him now, tell him that evolution is a fact, then grin like a feral cat.

"Feeling bad again, Basil?" There was a bite in his words, but Hiram couldn't soften them. Seeing Basil sit in the same damn spot with the same woe-is-me face had become a bore; he'd worn it for too long now. It was an instant riling. He recalled the first time Basil started accusing God of dirty dealing, his voice cracking like a child's. It had stunned him then, sparked great pity. He couldn't truly know Basil's pain, the love of your life bleeding out in your lap, knowing she's leaving this earth in a matter of seconds. When Basil described how Stella's eyes went blank then just started floating, half mast, Hiram couldn't help but see himself and Sarah. It was the only way he could make it real, the only way he could truly put himself there. He saw himself rocking her through the rain, too, smoothing down her bloody hair and talking of the life they could have shared. Her round, dark eyes fading out. Only then could he relate. Only then did his heart come loose, drift in his chest like an ice floe.

Basil let out a sigh, bumping Hiram back to the present. And he was glad. It wasn't the time to meander through his own remorse, even if Basil's self-pity was becoming harder to bear, to the point that Hiram bemoans their friendship, wonders if it ever really was.

"Why has God deserted me?" Basil murmured. He kept his eyes straight ahead, looking out over the water, shaking his head wide as if in the chorus of a Greek tragedy.

Something jolted in Hiram's chest. Instead of searching for compassion, the righteous words to say, he thought about the holes in the back of Basil's mouth where he'd plucked out his teeth. *Low down lily liver.* He couldn't push aside the judgment this time. The resentment shot like a bullet when Basil spoke, hearing the slight drawl where the sides of his tongue must slip over into the gaps, watching him wipe at the spittle that gathers in the corners of his mouth now. "You know, friend, I've had some trying times lately, too." He waited for a response, knowing that it wasn't coming. Deep down, he didn't want Basil to reply. He wanted to be galled.

Everyone knew that Basil had shirked his duty, but no one would confront it. The folks of Bellwether were masters at looking away when they needed to. They held the pedestal high for some but sacrificed others without a second thought. Basil was a pillar of the village, so they couldn't let him backslide. Just as they maneuvered the sins of Reverend Williams, so too would they finagle Basil's villainy. But Hiram had tired of the put-on. The ire was too strong today. He felt hot all over, afraid of his own angst. Resentment bubbled up large, fueling the constant burn he felt for the town's abandonment of Ada. He saw glimpses of her walking alone, people stepping past her with nary a word, looking over their shoulders with disdain. Talking of her as a witch in their tiny circles outside the town hall. The blight of the village they called her. And he thought about the hours he spent crafting sermon after sermon that chided hypocrisy and scolded piety: "Who amongst us is pure enough to pass judgment?" he had asked one Sunday morning. The congregation sat stone but for a couple of women waving their bamboo hand fans. And Basil sat at home, thinking himself the duped one, chewing bread with his foremost teeth.

Basil didn't ask about Hiram's trials, but he did stop talking for a moment. Sounds from the village wafted up through the sea-stacks. High pings from someone's hammer and a couple of intermittent shouts—one more angry, the other motherly, like calling a child home—both too distant for the words to be audible.

The silence between them made Hiram's heart start to pulse. And for the first time, in a long time, his temper flared. "You really don't give a damn about others, do you?"

Basil looked at his face, but still, he didn't speak. The wide open space felt cramped, and the blood in Hiram's veins felt thick as dirt. He crossed his arms over his chest and looked out at the lake. There was a distinct line where the depth dropped, the shallow place from the shoreline to the shelf was grayish-white but beyond that, the water was cornflower blue, almost piercing to behold.

"The oldest Butler boy was killed, you know. Battle of Spottsylvania. We buried him yesterday, up in the canyon, near the top of Shallow Spring. In case you might ever want to pay your respects." Hiram sat next to Basil, in the same groove as always, pulled his knees in then wrapped his arms around them and spoke close to his ear: "Let me tell you what happened after we put that boy in the ground. How about I do that, Basil. You see, at the break of day, Mr. Butler put a shotgun in his mouth. Yes, sir. Hunkered right down on the barn floor and planted his feet nice and solid. Then he wedged the butt of the gun against the wall. He was fumbling for the trigger when his wife came in, carrying water for the cattle. She was startled, as you can imagine. Or maybe you can't. And so, she dropped the bucket on her foot, broke her toes to hell. Still, she hobbled to her husband, tried wrenching away the gun. But he overpowered her. So she fell to her knees, begged God for mercy, pleading and wailing for the sake of their living son. Hearing all that, Mr. Butler changed his mind. When he realized what he'd almost done, he pushed away from the wall, scooting back like a worm on a hook. In the frenzy, the gun went off. The ball glanced his right ear, took the top half with it."

Basil offered a quick *oomph* and a slight head shake. His dullness was expected but it needled Hiram more than he anticipated. "Of course, Mrs. Butler was choking on her tears as she recounted the story to me, so I might not have all of it straight. I could've asked little Jonathon, Basil, but you see, he'd crept to the barn beforehand, saw his Pa with a shotgun pushed against his face and ran back to the house without a sound. He hid under his bed and wouldn't come out till his Pa crawled under there with him, promising he'd never turn a rifle on himself again. Seems Mrs. Butler was listening, said she couldn't tell which of them was crying harder."

"That's terrible, really it is. And I get what you're doing. Looking for me to get upset, to feel something outside myself. Maybe head on over to the Butler place to lend a hand. Truth is, though, I'm not rattled."

Hiram's body clenched tight. He felt as if he had to defend the Butlers, guard the honor of their patriot son. But he drew a deep breath, reminded himself that Basil was a friend, a lost one. And a son of God.

"Go on, then."

Basil waited, his face was turned up as if the next words spoken were calculable. "See, I feel a bit of sorrow for those folks. And I'm sorry for you, that you have to see such things, but I swear, it's like I'm frozen, have been for a long time. So long that I'm certain nothing can thaw me. Just now, I kept saying to myself, 'Comfort him, damn it. Tell him that everything will be alright,' but I couldn't do it. The worst part is that I don't care too much about that either. I used to feel guilty for losing heart, figuring, well at least that's a feeling, so I must still have a conscience. But that's gone now, too."

Hiram couldn't loosen. It was too late. Basil's self-pity was like sap in his stomach. He could feel gravity's heft pulling on him, anchoring him to the sediment. With an even keel, he said, "If we're sharing truths, friend, then I'd be remiss if I didn't tell you that I'm sad you're still mourning Stella. It's been years."

"Fifteen."

"Well then. It's time to let go of—"

"Don't finish that sentence, Hiram. For your sake. You're wiser than any man I've known, but you're out of line." He pointed at Hiram's chest. "You don't understand the love a husband has for his wife."

"Don't I? And why is that? Because I'm a minister?" Hiram leaned in. "Guess what, friend. I'm a man, too. Same pains, same frustrations. Believe it or not, the same desires as everyone else, too. Hell, maybe more so. Difference is, I swallow mine. Fight against them so I can listen fully when selfish folks like you are feeling sorry for themselves." Hiram leaned back, stretched his legs in front of him and crossed them at the ankles. "There was a woman in my life, but you wouldn't know that. You never asked. And let me tell you, she was the berries. Lit up the night with her smile. And so damn strong. She could climb the tallest mountain with the world strapped to her back." He leaned back even farther, laid his head on the rocky surface. "I've yet to meet another when I don't see her face." He hesitated, then said, "Actually, you've met her."

"Is that right?" Basil pushed himself up on an elbow. "A Bellwether beauty, heh? Good for you," he said, rubbing the dust off his hands. A shade came over the sea-stack, starting at Basil's feet then dimming his body, his face, as if someone had thrown a blanket over him. They both looked toward the source, a single cumulus cloud, flat base and cauliflower head, just big enough to blot out the sun for a moment before moving on. Then Basil stood and said, "Give my best to the Butlers," before he began heading back down the worn path.

"Well, well, Mr. Brandt. Cutting and running again?" Basil stopped. For an instant, Hiram thought he might keep walking, but he turned around, took two steps forward and rested his hands on his hips. They were several feet apart, yet Hiram could see the flare in his eyes.

"Say what you need to say," Basil said, turning a palm upward as a prodding gesture. There was a ubiquitous fury. One that brought Hiram back to his boyhood days when Leander would jeer him too much and he was ready to bound across the cabin like a mountain lion. And he thought of Ox again, too, saw his fat, pocked face, just before plummeting into the darkness of the mine. How since then, his back didn't bend like everyone else's. How his spine felt like a metal rod had been lodged there forever. How his guts still churned every time he thought about sitting at the bottom of that cavern, wet and contorted, wondering if he were dead.

He couldn't cool the embers, not even long enough to pray for more patience. He'd already done that and it wasn't granted. Maybe it was best that his wrath be released. He was boiling over, felt his skin turning hot. "Well, isn't that your way though, Basil? Let's look at the past, friend. Shall we?" The deriding was hectic but purging, too. Like a sneeze still at hand, tickling the back of his throat. Hiram watched Basil cock his head, push his lips together tight, waiting. The sun was high overhead. To the east, a Cooper's hawk circled the sea-stack once, belting out a sequence of yawps that sounded more like cackling. Then it swooped toward the greenery below, searching for an unsuspecting songbird, Hiram supposed. The stillness between the men had solidified, ready to be chipped away with a pickaxe which Hiram was happy to yield. "You couldn't have children. So, instead of comforting your wife, you turned from her. Isn't that right?"

Basil took a step forward then halted, as if a wall was spontaneously erected in front of him, made entirely of sensibility and pride. The struggle was strange to witness, Basil's neck muscles raising up as he wrestled between walking around it or kicking it down. But Hiram was having an internal battle, too. *Pull back? Or forge ahead?* He was already the victor in this quarrel. It's clear as bells that I think him a phony, Hiram thought. But then a dubious part of himself, the non-minister part that rears up now and again, didn't want to stop the browbeating. Even with a spleen full of muck, Hiram still knew he'd have to repent for any more words he spoke. It would be another moment he'd look back on with regret, that time he wanted to see Basil squirm. That time he let resentment overshadow his duty to God.

Still, he stood, wiped his hands on his trousers, then let loose all his grudges in a series of gibes: "Everyone knows why you garble your words, even if they won't say it to your face. Behind closed doors, many have confessed to me. A paper tiger, they call you. But staying true to the Bellwether way, just as quickly as they talk of your cowardice, they turn to your triumphs as a teacher, hail your wisdom and influence. It's easier for them to bear your yellow-belly that way, I suppose. Even Oscar Lee says, 'That Basil, he has the light of God in him,' knowing damn well you tore out your own teeth to snake out of duty to your country. It's a damnable place, Bellwether. Seems that here, certain men are held on high, even if folks know they're chicken-hearts. And all the while, one of their own makes her way through town each morning watching parents steer their children away as she approaches. Then, come Sunday, she sits on the church steps instead of listening from a pew. A shadow amidst the living." Hiram could see Basil's resignation coming, shoulders slumped, cheeks slack. Surrender was close, and the air thickened like a clot.

"You know, after I prayed over the Lee boy, when they

were lowering him into the ground, I actually thought of you, Basil. Imagined you shoving pliers in your mouth, twisting and pulling at your teeth. That's how you did it, right? When I came to check on you, saw your jaw, round as a cantaloupe and black as soil, I knew in an instant what you'd done. I remember thinking, was it worth all this? Can he even eat? I used to daydream, picture some of our young men walking in on you as you were doing it, witnessing your treachery. Would their hearts break? Would they lynch you? But then I'd remember, this town sees you as one of its disciples. They need you to play that part. Not me, though. I can't keep seeing heroes where there are none. Your shirking made me sick, still does."

"If we were ever friends, Hiram, you'll stop." Basil spoke even and clear.

But there were still some ashes in Hiram's airways, one last sneeze in the sequence: "I can hear the words pulling from the back of your mouth, that wretched little slur that gives you away. Maybe others don't hear it, or moreover, they refuse to hear it. But to me, it's as loud as a cannon blast."

Basil got down on his knees, one at a time. His movements were slow and rigid, a hickory tree in spring's heavy wind. "Of course I'm a coward, Hiram," he said, his voice still flat. "And we both know Bellwether's an island floating on falsehoods. Though you weren't here to see it, you feel the aftermath of Reverend Williams' desertion. It's like he started digging a ditch around this place the day he left it, thrust his shovel in the ground as he pilfered all these pious villagers. And the day they hung poor Elinor, why, that's when the moat was complete. Now, with each passing year, folks just keep scooping the dirt, maintaining the gully. Lord knows, if good sense ever broke through, this place would flood over, drown every last one of us." Basil looked up at Hiram now. "You're right about the role I have to play. None of us could handle it any other way. But what would you have me do?"

"That's between you and God," Hiram replied. The Cooper's hawk returned, belting out caw after caw, a black squirrel wriggling in its talons. Hiram watched the bird glide overhead then disappear between two lean spruces atop their rocky ridge.

"An empty answer, Hiram." Basil stood, brought his hand to his brow and snapped a half-salute. "Seems we're both a little weak-kneed, old friend."

Hiram watched him climb off the sea-stack and only after he couldn't see him any longer did he lay his head back down. His big brother popped into his mind. He wondered if Clint ever doubted himself, too. Or if Leander had ever learned not to. Maybe that was the true reason Leander stayed near the Shenandoah. He was simply afraid to leave, scared that others might see into his heart, discover he was weak. Hiram closed his eyes, longed for the shiny, rapid river again—its silver fish, and his mischievous brothers splashing in the flow.

Chapter 39
Casted Shadows

In 1872, Eva stepped off the train in Marquette and onto the station platform. It was a new railway system, hadn't existed in her youth. Immediately, she recognized the lighthouse to the east, though a bit different now. It still sat atop the same rocky peninsula, but the lantern room was higher in the air now, wider. Made her think of a bird nesting in a tall tree. And the catwalk wrapped all the way around. These things could have been the same, but maybe as an adult, she noticed the details more. She guessed the rubble tower reached forty feet or higher. She stared at the rounded cupola roof peeking over the maples, remembering the first time she ever saw Marquette.

They had traveled there to see if the meager cherry crop from a few trees in their backyard would sell at market. Though they did manage to peddle their fruit to a local merchant, Pa was bartered down too low to ever try it again. Seems a couple of Presbyterian missionaries had taken to harvesting cherries on Old Mission Peninsula near Grand Traverse City, and they had made the trip northward across Lake Michigan, bringing their bounty with them. Eva still remembers seeing their wide baskets sitting in the booth, brimming with ruby-red cherries, shiny and vivid, stems poking every which way. She was lagging a few steps behind her folks, so they didn't know that one of the men offered her a handful as she passed. Mr.

Murray had forbidden her and Ma to eat any of their own, so she gladly accepted the stranger's kindness, her teeth breaking open the tangy goodness like popping bubbles.

Eva inhaled the foliage of home—heady, sweet lilacs and citrusy trilliums—made more potent by the absence of Chicago's bustle. Starting the day-long hike to Bellwether, she thought about how as a child she swore the stars had a certain smell. She had forgotten about that. There was never a specific fragrance to liken it to, nothing she could name. But it was soft, something she wanted to bite into. Even though they weren't flickering and winking in the daytime, she always knew they were there, their mellow scent on the wings of each breeze. Then, come nightfall, the smell always grew more salient, more rich.

Rucksack over her shoulder, head high, Eva walked. Though she only passed a handful of people on the way out of town, they all wished her a good day, none of them staring at the pretzeled scar on her face. With every step toward Bellwether, she felt as if a wooly scarf was wrapping around her, letting loose the thick, muddy scraps that she didn't even know had roosted inside during her time away, clogging her impulses and blocking any path to joy. Though sleeping behind the sunlight, the stars of the north sky filled her lungs and slowed down time, letting it roll on by, nice and easy.

She knew her feet would ache for days, the callouses already forming on her heels. The skin on her toes had chaffed; she could feel them splitting open in places. But none of that mattered when several hours later, the shape of Bellwether came into focus, the vast hemlocks and the few buildings in town—the church, the post and what looked to be a new mercantile of some sort. Bellwether went ahead and changed some while I was away, she thought. Doesn't seem right. Though a sense of peace had cooled her spirit, a certain grief wove through, too, a woe that had been eclipsed by other kinds of sorrow for the past few years. But here it was rising up again, familiar and unsparing. What if Pa's memory lurks in every corner? she thought. Or maybe in death, he'll finally let me be.

She wound her way through town, past the closed-up saloon where she and Uriah used to spy, past places that had never stood out as special before but did now. She breathed in the stars that weren't quite visible in the coming dusk, glimpsed the smooth surface of the millpond just a bit north. Though she was reeling to see Ma, something made her head toward the water and sit on the same grassy slope where she'd caught batches of panfish, barely big enough to hold the pole by herself.

It wasn't often, but Pa took her fishing there sometimes. Though he never said much, he always handed over his bamboo rod while he untangled her line from an overhead branch. And it seemed he knew Eva got queasy about cutting the nightcrawlers with her fingernails because he pinched them for her, quietly setting the twitching parts back into the bucket. He always let her hand over the string full of perch and bluegill to Ma, too, like it was only hers to give. She could see his tapered face again—high forehead, sooty eyes and that thick, bushy mustache, always holding random crumbs. She let the scene play out for a few seconds but then, like scissors to paper, she cut it off. There'll be no harboring of fondness for you just because you're dead, she promised herself. I won't soften like some folks do when a loved one passes, trying only to remember the good things. If one of these meddling memories creeps back in, I'll just swap it with one of you crawling in my bed or peeking at me from behind a tree, making me feel dirtier coming out of the river than going in. And as time passes, I'll push you from my mind altogether, until I can't even remember what you looked like. And as for praying for your soul, Ma and me will be too busy feasting on roasted venison and boysenberry pie, she declared. We'll be making plans to build our new home, the one with walls that never knew the likes of you.

Eva approached the door but paused. Fourteen years had passed. Barging in felt strange, but so did knocking. She glanced up at the sky—a few stars just beginning to emerge—and garnered strength from their thin light before opening the door slow and slipping inside. Ma was bent over near the woodstove, pulling a tray of corn cobs from the heat. Eva smiled, knowing Ma was thinking ahead like always, making more than needed, canning for the next winter store. She cleared her throat and Ma bolted upright, turned to face the trespasser, tongs like a sword in her grip. Eva held her breath and waited for Ma's brain to catch up to her heart. She knew right when it did, too. Whenever Ma was trying not to cry, she always pushed her tongue around the inside of her mouth, moved it up and down so her cheeks bulged out. It was best to stay put, Eva decided, let her take her time. She looked smaller somehow. Her hair had thinned, grayed around the ears.

Ma tilted back her head like she was studying the ceiling and when she brought it back down, the tears, big as beads, loosed from her eyes, rolled down her face like dice. She lay the tongs atop the steaming corn husks and drew a sharp, stuttering breath. Then she made her way to Eva, almost leery or ghostlike, as if she were dreaming and afraid to wake up. A foot or so away, she stopped, reached for Eva's scar, scanning it with the tip of her pointer finger, the bead-like tears still falling. The other hand was atop her heart, the fabric of her pinafore gathering in her fist. Eva could see her swallow hard, her throat bobbing.

"Pretty as ever," Ma said. Her voice was holy. It made Eva feel lighter. Her arms dropped and the haversack fell to the floor. She leaned into Ma, rested her head against her chest. The burdens were still hanging on, but melting some, too, making room for new ones. The two of them stood in the doorway, looped together tight, Ma stroking Eva's hair, head to shoulder. So much to say, too much not to say. And there, like a blemish, sat Pa's chair. The hutch gone, though, the one he knocked over when his heart gave out.

The savory smell of cooked corn was heavy in the air, mixing with the purple aster on the table. Eva stayed in Ma's arms, shifted her focus to the flowers, carefully arranged in a clear vase, teeming over the sides. Ma pulled back some, enough so that their faces were close. There was great warmth in searching one another's eyes, pouring over their expressions, their tender miens. But it was too much, too soon. Eva looked away. And after she did, they both spoke at once. Ma started to ask, "Think you'll ever tell me how your face—" while Eva said, "The flowers are—"

Each of them waited for the other.

"Maybe one day," Eva finally said. Ma took a step back, held out Eva's arms. "Now, let me see that smile of yours."

* * *

Their days consisted of harvesting vegetables—turnips, radishes and winter squash—canning tomatoes, pickling Brussel sprouts, and cellaring the cabbage plants, green beans, and potatoes. They dried out basil leaves and celery root, made jams and pies from blackberries and rhubarb. Outside, in the greenery, Eva always found herself hovering, pretending to still be weeding while trying to catch a glimpse of Uriah across the field. And inside, sipping hot tea at the window, she'd look for him, too. Each time a shadow moved in the distance, her breath caught in her throat. Usually, it was nothing—a coon or tree limb bending in a breeze—but once, early dawn, she glimpsed him heading to the outhouse. He was in his long johns, naked up top, his back broad and white. His steps were slow and awry as he hadn't laced his boots. Like broomsticks, his arms swept him forward, one seemingly a bit more rigid than the other. Look away, she told herself. It isn't proper. But she couldn't, not even for a second. She waited, praying Ma wouldn't wake before he came back out. Then, when he did reappear, Uriah looked toward the Murray house. Though she knew he wasn't looking at her, she dared not move. He stretched an arm to the sky, arched out his hips and yawned loudly. A muted version of it traveled up the field, through the windowpane. She felt her cheeks blush when he put his hand in his underwear and scratched. He made his way back inside and she felt full, hopeful she'd see him again, if only from afar.

* * *

As they worked, Eva would answer all Ma's questions in great detail. She told her about Ruth and Edgar and the boys, a surge of joy pushing through her veins. But when she mentioned Tina by accident and Ma asked more about her, Eva dropped several berries on purpose and spent too long picking them up off the floor. What good would ever come from telling her that I sold my soul? she thought. Her heart would shatter. And she'd refuse to live in a house built with the fruits of a whore's labor, even if it never saw the likes of Pa. Eva managed to change the subject to the sway of the ship and how sometimes she can still hear the waves crashing into the cargo holds. For a second, she thought about telling her what Samuel and that red-headed sea-dog tried doing to her. But the lines in Ma's forehead, and her thin shoulders and bony hips made Eva change her mind. She thought to herself, Ma's life has been weary enough.

She didn't talk about the great fire much either, not until she'd been home for a couple of weeks. She started out with the truth, describing the whirling black clouds that floated over the city and the drunkards whooping in the streets while most folks were fleeing to the water's edge. "I remember Reverend Hiram asking for prayers for the people of Chicago," Ma said. "He told us many folks had died. And I didn't know if you was one of them." She shook her head a little then asked if Eva knew anyone lost or hurt by the flames. The question struck hard; Eva hadn't seen it coming. She flashed back to the beach when the woman walked into the water, all the splashing and screaming from folks trying to find her in the dark. And she saw Titus, too, when he first came to her, circling then plopping his tired body next to hers. She told Ma what a soft, loyal dog he was, even tried imitating his thunderous bark for her. Then, she told an outright lie—

"Me."

"Pardon?" Ma's brow was angled downward.

"I suffered in that wicked fire." Eva took a deep breath, readying herself for the unexpected performance. *This tall tale must be told to perfection as it's going to last a lifetime. Told just right, it will stave off a million questions and keep Ma's spirit from breaking.* Eva pulled from the anguish of all the bad things to make the lie believable, called up Ephraim's face just before he took that final swipe—lips tight with fury, eyes flashing, the ceramic shard poking out from his fist. She thought of Tina's raw skin, bruised from all the mercury and rubbing. Then she forced herself to see the naked body of her first trick again—shaft still pointing upward, poking into the fat of his belly—climbing out of her soiled bed, plopping down dollars on the dresser like he'd just bought a sack of grain. And she envisioned Ruth's eye, too, saw the flying beam at the mill in Massachusetts as it tore her sight from the socket.

She turned slightly, pretending to tell the story to someone sitting next to Ma, watching it play out so she could believe it herself. "We were making our way down Dearborn. People pushing and hollering and thieving one another. Smoke was floating through the city, thick as pasty filling, squeezing and burning our lungs. I looked out at all those scared folks, running wild as Edgar wove us through all the fuss. And the blasts, they just kept coming from all sides. All that wreckage flying through the air as if all at once, everything grew wings. That's when the wood scrap hurled at my face." Eva ran her thumb up the scar. "It dug at my skin like a spade in gravel." She shuffled from one foot to the next, then back to the first. Ma said nothing, her eyes big, expectant. "Hurt something awful," Eva said. Then she picked up the spoon inside the pot on the woodstove and started softly stirring. She could feel Ma's eyes roving over her, so she stared hard at the stew, drawing the spoon back and forth through the brown, bubbling medley.

"My strong girl," Ma said. "I just know you took on all that pain with grace. I can see it." Then, she began to scamper amidst the canning goods again, and Eva let out a long sigh. The lie didn't feel that bad as it wasn't for her own sake, though she feared that fibbing came too easy. After a few moments of wordlessness—only the sound of glass jars clinking at the table—Ma mentioned Uriah's return from the war, mild as could be. She talked about his sacrifice. "Even with a dead arm, Mr. Brandt is grooming him to take over as teacher." She didn't prod Eva to respond, never asked if she wanted to see Uriah or if she missed him. But Eva noticed her peeking sideways every time she said his name. "Matter of fact," Ma said, "it's time for you to get out and about. You haven't even been to church."

That night, Ma insisted Eva soak in the wash basin. She filled it with lukewarm water and poured in some ammonia. After Eva immersed herself, Ma massaged the pungent broth into her scalp and hair. There were a few scrapes on her legs and arms from harvesting and still a few sores on her feet from the trek to Bellwether weeks before. The water felt brackish as it seeped into the cuts, but the sting felt good, healing and cleansing at the same time. The following morning, as Eva dressed for Sunday service, Ma brought out her special houndstooth cloak, such a rare sight that Eva forgot it existed. She shaped two cotton pieces into half-moons and told Eva, "It's all I have for dress shields. Now, put them in your underarms and hold still in the pew so they don't fall out." From the hearth, she brought over a basket filled with dried lavender, rubbed a few of the pale whorls on the back of Eva's neck, under her chin. Everything felt so imperative, far beyond hearing the word of the Lord. And just as they were heading outside, Ma shook her head in disapproval. She tugged on the hem of Eva's blue and brown flecked dress, ran a hand across the pintucking, then fluffed up the gathered sleeves. She made an *humph* sound in good favor. "Lovely," she said.

In that moment, Eva believed her. She didn't instantly reach to cover her cheek but let herself feel pretty, like she used to. It wasn't until she saw the folks of Bellwether assembling on the church's front steps that her scar started to loom large again—a limestone slab atop a fresh, white sheet. The Lee family was the first to say hello, though Eva barely recognized the boys. All grown men now, the eldest with a wife and child of his own. Oscar gave Eva a quick hug and an off-center smile. But Ruby Lee wrapped her hefty arms around her, held on awhile. She said welcome home several times into her ear, each with a softer tone, drawing out the words as if Eva's return was mending something inside of her, too. Most of the others offered a greeting of sorts, some more enthusiastic than others, but all of them genuine. Even the men Eva remembered as crotchety, like Mr. Wilkinson and Mr. Turner, seemed pleased to see her.

As the parishioners began to file in, Eva caught a glimpse of a bedraggled woman making her way toward the church. It took a moment for her to recall that Ada Williams always wore her hair in a sloppy bun, donned that same blue-gray dress—the flounces more frayed, more undone. Her gait was still teetering and crabwise. She approached the Lord's house with a hell-bent expression and fixed lips. Amidst all the shuffling and salutations, Eva stayed behind, watching Ada totter to the stairs then halt like a blown-out candle, her head held high. The last few believers slipped inside, none of them acknowledging her.

For a few seconds, it was only the two of them. Eva standing at the door; Ada on the bottom stair. Though awkward at first, as they continued to eye one another, their faces loos-ened. Eva could feel Ada straining to remember her, as if she might know her but couldn't believe it was the same girl. Ada took in a quick breath, her eyes growing into big rings as she pressed her fist to her mouth. Eva felt flattered that Ada rec-ognized her at all. And in that short-lived exchange, there was a world of revelation.

Those eyes aren't wild, Eva thought. They're gleaming. Maybe her life of humility, of always standing on the out-side, made her push through all the sadness and fury, past all the muck, until she found light, a light that most in Bell-wether do not know. Seems there were two choices the village gave her—quit or be fearless. Eva remembers passing Ada on those very same steps, Ma always offering a quick nod to her, even whispering "pardon us" sometimes, but only after Pa was out of earshot. Eva once asked why everyone treated her so mean and Ma's reply came back to her now, "We're all cowards, that's why."

Ma called her from inside the church, but Eva hesitated to let go of the door, to let it close between them. The two women held one another's eyes until Ma called a second time. Then, she pulled the door closed slowly, until it shut with a low click.

Inside, Eva didn't look up as she headed to her seat. But unwrapping the cape from her shoulders, she took a curious sweep of the cramped parish, the same folks from her youth, perched like birds on a branch. Though a sincere but cautious sense of home was in her chest, Eva had never realized how tight eight rows of pews could feel, especially after living in Chicago, endless benches and hordes of churchgoers. Still rapt by the shared moment with Ada Williams, she spotted Uriah. Her mind went dumb. His nearness made her tingle. And Ma's intentions for scrubbing her with ammonia and lavender were made sure.

Uriah was sitting between his Ma and Pa, same place as

always—front row, on the right side. Eva could see the top of his dark blonde hair, still thick and bushy, yet others' shoulders and heads were in the way. After Reverend Hiram made his way to the pulpit, the congregation quieted and Mr. Turner sat up straight, his shoulders pulled back. That's when Eva's eyes met Uriah's. She sucked in sharp. A soft shuddering in her chest and head and everyplace else. There was a strange ache inside her and she flushed, feeling like people could see her longing.

The church doors flung open. A crisp wind caught them, and the hinges groaned. The parish about-faced. And there Ada stood, just inside the threshold. A couple of folks let out a gasp but most just shifted in their pews, mouths wide open. There were murmurs and sibilant whispers as she took several steps forward, eyes roaming, neck pushed out. The sound of her worn out brogans was loud, the wood of her soles clicking against the floor. She stayed focused on Hiram as though she might actually be heading to the pulpit, stepping up next to him. But when she reached Eva she stopped, nodded toward the bench. Without hesitation, Ma and Eva scooted in. Though a bit shaken, Eva patted the space beside her, and Ada lowered herself down. She tried to appear at ease, but her movements were stiff and slow as if her muscles were freezing, one by one. Eva looked at Ma, gave her a subtle "I don't know" shoulder shrug. Ma smiled, and they both turned toward the pulpit, natural as could be. Then Ada did, too.

Hiram poured over his flock but remained quiet. Eventually, he turned his gaze to Uriah. Then, to Eva. And finally, to Ada. "God is good," he said, before letting out a hearty chortle. Miss Moore up and walked out of the church, followed by Mr. Turner. But Eva refused to give either her attention. She just flipped through the hymnal to the opening song of praise and held it out for Ada to see. Ma leaned behind Eva, put her hand on Ada's shoulder. "They don't belong here anyhow," she said.

"Anyone else want to leave?" Hiram asked, crossing his arms over his chest. "We'll wait."

Uriah stood. Several more gasps sounded out, and Eva looked up, her heart dropping. *No. No. No.* Every eye followed him as he made his way around the front pews then up the aisle. He stopped midway, Eva holding her breath. "Room for me?" he asked. All three women shuffled further in. Uriah mouthed "Welcome home" to Eva as he sat down calmly and faced frontward with a poker face, ready for the day's scripture. Eva felt skittish, wanting to throw her arms around his neck and shout out, I miss you. And I love you. And I'm sorry that your arm is dead. And you're such a belvedere, more handsome than ever. She pressed her knuckles against her scar and kept them there.

"Yes, indeed," Hiram said, "Seems God's called three people home now." Then he repeated, "God is good," and declared that change was coming to Bellwether. Throughout the sermon, he stopped several times and looked at the three newest arrivals. Eva figured he was trying to be sure they were really there.

* * *

After that, Uriah called on Eva every chance he could. He spent his days at the school learning tricks of the trade from Basil then headed home to help with the chores that one arm would allow. And last, he'd trek through the field and knock on Eva's door before the sun went down. Ma always answered with a smirk and offered him some of whatever was cooking on the stove. She would announce his arrival as if Ulysses S. Grant had come. Eva would position her bonnet just so before coming to greet him. Even on balmy evenings, she tied it tight under her chin, pulling the brims down hard so they covered her cheeks, only the bottom most part of the scar peeking out.

They walked each night. Sometimes through town, and sometimes to the sea-stacks. The conversations were heavy and intimate, centered around the postwar state of affairs—Reconstruction, Susan B. Anthony, and the diamond frenzy in Wyoming—but when the dialogue lent itself to Uriah's brief tour as a soldier, he became reticent, changing the subject altogether. Eva sensed the uneasiness and always obliged, pointing out a vibrant red vein running through the limestone or mentioning the fierce blue sky that day. She loved that he did the same for her should their talk veer too deep into her years in Chicago. Their respect for one another made it hard for Eva to pull away when one night, Uriah reached for her hand.

They were standing behind the abandoned saloon, reminiscing about their childhood fears of the place. And how good it felt each Sunday when Ada showed up at church. That's when he slipped his hand over hers and started swinging them back and forth. Eva knew it was only a gesture of unity, but it proved too much. "I fear you might be trying to court me. And I want to save you the trouble." She pulled her hand away. There were so many words to say, but they were lodged somewhere between her brain and mouth. They walked in silence for a few steps. Then Uriah filled the void with idle chatter, the lame foot of his Pa's lead horse and the season's staggering number of mayflies.

"Slender little things," he said. "And those delicate wings, you can see right through them. How can such a—"

"I can't be with you," Eva spouted. "And Lord help me, I'm not strong enough to tell you why." She couldn't look at his face, couldn't bear to see the hurt. But she forged on. "Find another, Uriah. For your sake and mine."

"But why?"

"Oh please, no questions. I'm begging you. Not now." Silence ensued a second time, until Eva could not take the torment any longer—head full of doubts and indecision, squeaking like a swarm of beetles. "I'm gonna go on ahead," she said. "I'd be obliged if you stayed behind."

* * *

For a few days, Uriah stayed away. Eva had denied him on a Tuesday and by Saturday afternoon, he came knocking on the Murray door again. She heard Ma say, "Land sakes, Uriah, thought you'd gone and forgot about us."

"Never, Miss Murray," he said. Upon hearing his voice, a magnificent relief washed over Eva, from her ears to the tips of her fingers. She reached for her bonnet, pulled it over her head, then loosed a lock of hair, tugging it toward her cheek, trying to sweep it forward a couple of times. She knew it couldn't cover the awful track mark completely, but maybe it wouldn't be the first thing he noticed after being gone a few days. When she stepped into view, Eva saw the book of poems in his hand. He held it up. "A collection of the early Romantics," he said. "Join me? Only reading poems, that's all."

Eva smiled, then checked her modesty and said flatly, "Okay." They trekked past the grassy schoolyard and into the same space they had met as children, amidst the swollen trees of early summer. The nostalgia was warm but with an edge, too. Like if they relished in it too long, thoughts of Pa Murray's wagon drawing near might ambush the memories. Uriah read several poems—"Annabel Lee" and "The Tyger"—but when he began to read "How Do I Love Thee," his voice strong but watery, Eva's tears fell without warning, spilling out from all the dashed hopes. The craving was harder than she thought it would be. She tried thinking of something cruel to say, any-thing to sever their ties, prevent any more tangled moments like this one. But nothing came to mind, no matter how hard she tried. Eva hoisted herself off the ground and said, "Thank you for the surprise."

Uriah stood, too. "I'm not sure what happened to you down there, Eva. Or maybe you're still suffering from your Pa's wicked ways. But it doesn't matter. I'll still be waiting when you're ready. I'm never leaving Bellwether again, and if you allow it, I won't be leaving you either." Eva fought the tears this time and when she was sure they had sunk far enough back, she said, "I love all that you've been doing. I sure do." And then suddenly, the pitiless words she'd been looking for hurled out like vomit, "But I don't love you."

Uriah's smile drooped. "Well, those words hurt worse than losing my hand." He forced out a hollow chuckle. "Not sure I believe you though, seems like something else." Before turning to go, he handed her the book of poems. "Love me or not," he said, "I aim for you to have this."

* * *

Come Sunday morning when Ma brought out the basket of lavender, Eva said, "No putting on airs today. I just want to hear the word of God." But she couldn't say too much for fear of faltering, not being able to keep quiet once she started talking. It was too early to disappoint her with the truth—that she could never be with Uriah. Nor any man. "No need to worry, Ma. I'm fine." Eva could tell from her tapering eyes that Ma wasn't satisfied. It was enough for the moment, though, because she headed to her room to put away the houndstooth cloak. As soon as she'd gone, Eva stepped to the window and looked down over the field, even though she knew Uriah wasn't coming.

At church, Uriah greeted Ma and Eva with kindness and told Eva that she looked as bonny as ever. He told Ada that the light in her eyes was brighter every time he saw her, and that now, she need only smile more often. When the women took their seats, Uriah headed to the other side. That's when Ada turned to Eva, looked at her long and hard. Eva felt all the weight of her glare. After the opening hymn, Ada said, not in a hushed church voice, "All these years I spent being shunned, why, it makes keeping to myself easy." Then, from the pulpit, Hiram began to speak. But that didn't stop Ada from saying her piece, loud and clear: "But when two young ones love each other and one of them is pretending otherwise, that's when I'm willing to meddle. God grants us but one life, young lady. No room for pretense. My sweet Elinore used to say whatever was on her mind, didn't matter when or who she was talking to. My baby girl didn't know how to pretend. Wish to goodness none of us did. We'd all be better off."

As the parishioners began to sing "Rock of Ages," Ma whispered "Amen" to Ada. Then Ruby Lee leaned back from the pew in front of them and whispered the same out of the side of her mouth.

* * *

Come fall, Eva had yet to visit the rickety house where the boy had been chained beneath the porch. But ever since she'd been home, there was an urge to go there, to pay her respects, just sit there and be near where he used to be. She told Ma that she was going for a walk, to which Ma asked, "Alone?" Eva acted as if she hadn't heard the question and quickly shut the door behind her.

She remembered the way to the shack without a hitch. It felt closer as an adult. Looked smaller, too. The place was still abandoned, nearly the same as Eva could recall. The biggest difference was that it leaned now, to the left. One too many winter winds, she thought. In the trampled space where the boy once peeked out, there were wide bramble bushes and thin stalks of pigweed. Though her curiosity was piqued, Eva felt it wrong to go inside. Nor did she want to encounter any critters that might have snuck in. Besides, there was no need. The boy's presence was almost touchable.

She found a smooth spot on the porch and lay down, hands under her head. With each passing breeze, the leaves tumbled, and in the light of the sun, they looked like they were burning, red and orange flames falling from the sky. She listened to them rolling over one another on the ground, like a thousand feet running to escape the approaching winter. The woodland smells felt clean in her lungs and she called Hester Prynne to mind, wondering if the two of them could have been friends had Hester ever stepped beyond Hawthorne's imagination, been able to breathe in this heavy autumn air. She closed her eyes, imagined the two of them sitting on one of the fluttering leaves, riding it together as it swirled, not thinking about their places in the world, just floating in silence, emboldened by the sisterhood.

The crunch of trampling leaves snapped Eva from her reverie. She recognized Uriah right away—big shoulders, straight back, and lifeless arm dangling—as he marched toward the porch. There was no time to think. She couldn't tell if she was sad or anxious. Maybe both. Maybe neither. Uriah came near, sat down close. Her belly began to toss. She made sure the rim of her bonnet was in place, then pulled herself upright, fighting the urge to lean into him. Neither of them spoke right away, just hung their feet over the edge and synchronized their swinging.

"I've been coming here every few days since I got back," Uriah said. "Wasn't sure if I was coming for the boy or because it reminded me of you." He took in a big breath, let it out. Eva kept quiet a bit longer, knowing her heart was still ruling her head. "It's no secret that I'm sweet on you, Eva. Always have been. And I aim to tell you that a lot of folks know your Pa was a bad man. Not sure how, I just get the feeling they do. Not even sure why I'm bringing that up right now. Maybe there's lots of things all stirred together and I can't split them apart. You can't sift the venison out of the stew and still call it stew." Uriah screwed up his face, like someone just gave him an impossible riddle, and laughed large, no inhibition. Then he sputtered out, "Some teacher I'm gonna be. The best I can do is liken my affections to deer meat."

Eva let herself laugh. "Yes," she said, "even I could've done better than that."

The chuckling worked its way through to quiet again. Then Uriah's face turned serious and straight. "I've been trying to find a poem that would tell you how I'm feeling, one that would say things just right. But none of them fit. Not Wordsworth. Not Whitman. And unless it was an ode to venison, I'm clearly not the man for the task." He made a *tsk* sound with his lips. "Truth is, you're the reason I'm alive. No poem can tell you how when I was eye-to-eye with a Johnny Reb, him waving a knife at me, your face gave me strength. Or that after he plunged the blade in my arm, I fought the pain, for you. And that when they were sawing away at my bone, I pictured your hair, your skin, your spunk. I haven't told anyone about the war, Eva. I'm only telling you now because I know it's what you'd do if you found something worth fighting for." He reclined some so he could see her whole face. "Sometimes, I forget that I don't have an arm. I reach for things, try to grab 'em. It's the dry sound of wood thumping wood that brings me back. Then I always look around, praying no one saw." She looked down, and he lifted her chin with his wooden hand. "I'm not a poet, Eva Murray. I'm nothing special at all really. And Lord knows that I'll be lugging around this useless arm for the rest of my days. But I know that—"

"Look at my face," Eva spat. "You act like you're not a pretender. But you are." She yanked the strings of her bonnet, snatched it from her head. Then she pushed her fingers into her cheek as if she could rip the scar from her life. "Stop acting like I ain't ugly, Uriah." She pulled the bonnet back down on her head. "If you knew where I'd been, you wouldn't be sitting here."

"Is that right? And who are you to be doing all my thinking for me? That's not fair. Not very Christ-like, either."

"Oh, believe me, I'm not aiming to be like Christ. Not anymore. I'm just hoping for a little mercy come judgment day."

"So now you're doing the Lord's thinking, too? What about all you've done for Ada Williams? Your Ma? Don't you think there's—"

"I gave myself to men." The words rolled out fast, like they were on a wheel. The truth bubbled up from some deep place that she had to dig into her own earth for, dig until she struck a pool of pure water. But she didn't feel free. There was no cleansing, no exultation. One look at Uriah and the freshwater turned to muck, thick in her veins, killing her slowly.

Though he kept his face forward, Eva could see all she needed from the side view—cheek raised up, eyebrow downcast, pulling his eye with it—the disgust was plain. In the lull, Eva's confession flitted with the leaves. When the parley started up again, no words were pretty enough to cut through the milky air, to crush the pulsing letdown. Uriah only mentioned what he could see in front of him. "Fields look more slanted in autumn. Clouds are whiter, more hefty."

"Please stop trying, Uriah. Empty talk only tears at the seams."

"Not trying to do any mending here, Eva. Just not sure what to say."

"Say nothing. I'm sparing you." She waved him on with her hand. "Just go."

Uriah took in a sharp breath, slapped his thigh with his good hand. "Well, that's rich. Tell me you aren't maidenly no more, then shoo me away like I'm the vermin."

She hadn't counted on such a hard-boiled parting. Whether he meant to or not, Uriah had just made it clear that he'd never see her as anything but foul. So she made it even easier for him. It's the least I can do, she thought. "You've wanted to skedaddle from the second I told you. I felt it. Anything else is just more bluffing."

"Feel better, Eva? Blaming me lighten the burden, does it?" He slapped his thigh again, then stood. "I'm thinking I'll oblige you, then. I'll head on back home, maybe try to figure out a name for what I'm feeling. Can't imagine Mr. Webster took care of this one just yet." He shook his head. "Well, life's just gone and made itself real hard."

Inside her head, the screams were insufferable. She wanted to rip her chest wide open, let him see her heart. Then he'd know it was taking all she had not to chase after him, not to shout out, I'm doing this for you! Instead, she called after him, "You think this ain't tough for me? Well, it is. Damn tough."

Without a beat, he turned and said, "You sure make it look easy." Eva watched him walking away, his bad arm swaying, the other bent upward at the elbow as he stroked the back of his neck. Before he vanished into the tree line, a rush of leaves whirred up from the ground, some landed on his shoulder and head, then each fell away. The crackle underfoot faded, as did he.

* * *

It was in the dawn's earliest light the very next day that Ma and Eva woke to the sound of yelping in the field. They both made their way to the window. Ma mumbled, "What in tarnation," as Eva rubbed the sleep from her eyes. They gathered in the tiny wood frame, both of them quiet as Uriah came into focus. He was trotting forward, the hoop bouncing just in front of him. Once Eva and Ma had made it outside, Uriah nudged the ring toward them, still trying to keep pace with it. He waved the dowel in the air like a sword. Then he tripped hard, sinking like a boulder.

Eva ran to him, worried what a fall could do to his prosthetic arm. When she heard him sniggering, saw him splayed out on the dewy ground, her heart swelled up and she let out a peal of laughter that she didn't know she was capable of. Instead of taking her hand, Uriah offered his and pulled her to the ground. Down there, too, she felt his grip tighten. She didn't pull away. The two of them lay in the wet grass, the boxelder bugs starting to skitter over them. "With all my talk about the Lord, seems I forgot that I shouldn't be doing any judging myself," he said. "And I know there must be a reason for you doing what you did." He sat upright, pulled his legs in. "I'm not the walk away kind." Eva shifted some then lay still again. "You know, you sure look better without that bonnet," he said. "Always covering up that pretty face of yours."

Eva reached for her cheek, tried smoothing down her unbrushed hair, but Uriah took her hand, held it tight. The vulnerability was rankling and raw. She wanted to hide the scar with her free hand, but she understood that if she ever wanted to begin anew, the time was now. Still, knowing so didn't make things less brutal. The urge to cover her face was stupendous, like watching the wick of a dynamite stick burning down. She let out a low groan and soon enough, held still, stopped fighting Uriah's grip.

"Can't make any promises," she said. "Feels like I'm buried down deep inside myself. Someone's gonna have to pull me out. I'm not even sure if I want to—" she cut off. "You weren't teasing," she said. "Life did go and make itself hard." Uriah tilted in, pressed his lips gently against her scar. And though it was hard-won, Eva resisted the instinct to resist.

Chapter 40
Wedding Day

Not a day passed that northern Michigan didn't flash through Sarah's mind, how after the people of Bellwether denied her, all its beauty dulled, the clear blue water turned oyster and the extraordinary sea-stacks became nothing more than tall piles of rocks. And she couldn't help but wonder if Hiram was a little relieved that the village forced him to send her away. If maybe he wasn't ready for her either. Didn't think her worthy of the risk to find out. She was tormented by how close they had come. She was right there, in his arms, heart against heart. It was bringing a fresh picked apple to your mouth, maybe even sinking your teeth through the skin, a touch of its sweetness on your tongue, then having it torn from your hand, leaving you standing there, mouth still open. That's all she had to hold on to—one shared night, full of warmth, recounting and hope, and the quiet uncertainty of Hiram's affections for her.

* * *

Eva felt a bit deceptive when it came to the wedding. She had the money to offer her guests more than she was planning, but her savings was earmarked. She couldn't bring herself to part with any of it for trivial things like fancy food, or clothes, or anything that wasn't about building Ma's new home. So she kept her stash a secret. Just like the other mistruth of how her scar came to be. Only she would know about the money stuffed in a sock, still buried at the bottom of her haversack.

In the months between Uriah's proposal and the wedding, Eva and Hiram became fast friends. Just after the engagement, Hiram visited Eva to congratulate her and from that day forward, Sunday visits to the Murray house became a habit. The three of them—Ma, Eva and Hiram—ate pie and bread with different fruit jams, each of them taking turns at the woodstove, refilling the coffee tin from the kettle, never letting the conversation slow: Ulysses S. Grant as president; Ada Williams' return to church; and of course, Uriah's new role as teacher. They talked about the weather, God's mercy, and eventually, Sarah. Though it took some time for Hiram to mention her, once the trust was there, he never failed to include her—sometimes subtly and sometimes bluntly—but there would be no Sunday parleys without Sarah. Ma and Eva were happy to oblige, sneaking smiles at one another as Hiram prattled on, his voice higher and words quicker whenever he mentioned her name. And with time, their conversations seem to embolden him during sermons, too, as he talked about tolerance and acceptance, not just amongst the congregation but with all mankind, and "... with every shade of skin that the good Lord made."

* * *

Ma stitched Eva's wedding dress by hand. It was a fair brown, like the color of potato skins or a perfect pie crust, and the silk taffeta was patterned with tiny, checkered boxes. It had a round neck and long sleeves, and the trim at the cuffs was even darker brown. The front hook-and-eye closure was hidden behind a row of fabric-covered buttons. The waist was high, the skirt full. Ma worked for weeks—taking it in, then letting it out again—until Eva had to tell the truth, that it fit the same as it did four alterations before.

The wedding was in mid-spring, just after the snow had

gone, but the air still had a nip. The nuptials took place in the morning. Ma brushed Eva's freshly clean hair until it was smooth then pinned it into a chignon at the back of her head. Looking into Ma's Jenny Lind mirror, Eva turned her head one way, then the next, pretending she was happy with what she saw, pretending that she wasn't solely focused on the scar. As casually as she could, Eva suggested a few barley curls, "to lay on the sides of my face." Ma told her how beautiful her hair looked the way it was. But Eva persisted.

"It's your day," Ma conceded. She tore one of her wash rags into strips and wound Eva's hair in spirals around each cloth piece. "Uriah loves you for who you are. He don't give a hoot about any marks on your face." She talked about pride and vanity and blessings and faith, how they are a tricky maze that everyone must find their way through. "We're all like ship captains in a way." Then Ma's voice lowered, and the conversation flipped to intimate things, her manner becoming more muffled and rushed. She asked if Eva had any questions about a man's affections, then she hesitated a moment before saying, "If you're afraid or curious about anything, why, I'll listen."

Eva wormed in her chair. She knew her unease was barefaced. And that Ma assumed it was because of unfamiliarity, not the opposite. In that instant, Eva felt a push to confess everything, a flicker moving up her spine. Before she could speak out, Ma said, "You know, dear one, matrimony is the holiest union, one that lets a man and wife spend a lifetime learning about each other. Themselves, too, if it's done right. I went about it all wrong, though. I lost myself in marriage. At least I can tell you what you shouldn't do. There are duties that come with being a wife, that's for sure. But there's things a husband must do, too." Then, in a quieter voice, she said, "And not do." She pulled at a lock of Eva's damp hair, twisted it around a piece of cloth and tugged it tight. Eva stayed still, not wanting Ma to stop talking. This was a rare offering.

"You're to submit to your groom, says that outright in

Ephesians, Chapter Five, I believe. It says, 'the husband is the head of the wife, just like Christ is the head of the church.' But if folks kept reading, just a bit further, they'd get to Colossians. Then they could put two and two together. Yes, the bible says wives must fold to their men, but it says husbands must love their wives, too, and not be harsh with them. So the way I see it, if a husband is supposed to be the chief but he ain't doing his part, then a wife can't do hers either."

Eva marveled at Ma's openness, loved her for it.

"Your grandma, God bless her soul, used to say that if a husband is the head, then a wife is the neck, put there to hold him up. But I don't think that works sometimes." Ma pulled another cloth piece tight, kept still a moment.

Eva knew she was looking to be spurred on, needed a shot in the arm that what she was saying mattered. "Well?" Eva said, curving her voice high, loud. "Why not?"

Ma held the silence a second longer. When Eva was a child, she would do the same thing, just stop talking in the middle of a story, fishing for validation. The key to opening her up again was a question, some petitioning to continue. Eva was always willing to play along. And she was even more gladdened to now as Ma's stubbornness proved she was still full of steam, had plenty of life left to live without Pa. "Go on, will you?"

"Sorry, didn't think you were listening. If your grandma was still alive, I'd say to her that sometimes, a man ain't a man. He ain't doing what the bible says. Then, the marriage head is just dead weight. But instead of bouncing all around, it's held strong from underneath. No one sees the neck straining behind the collar, though. The only thing folks see is an upright noggin, looking natural as can be. And that ain't fair." Ma paused again, and Eva turned around to see her. She could tell from her pulled eyebrows and the way her mouth was snapped shut that she wasn't needing confirmation this time, just searching for the best words. Then her lips parted, eyes softened. A final strip of cloth dangled in her hand. "There's no such thing as a head breaking, see? The head always stays whole. It's only the neck that breaks. And that's what I'd tell my mother."

* * *

It was in 1873, nearly twelve years after Sarah was put out of Bellwether, that a battered letter made its way to Cass County. When she saw Virginia in the address, her heart leapt. Since moving to southern Michigan, she would hear from Leander but once or twice a year. She always tightened with joy at the sight of his swirly longhand. Though the greater anticipation came with the hope of news about Hiram—his holy endeavors, his wellbeing. Anything. Sarah tore open the envelope only to find another inside. She pulled that one out and flipped it over, on the front—Bellwether. Her breath caught in her throat. After nudging her finger into the corner where the flaps came together, she dragged it across the seam, pulled out the cream-colored paper and unfolded it carefully, as if it might crack. With the flat of her hand, she pressed it out against the table, smoothed it in every direction. The writing was unfamiliar; the ink sloe and clean:

> *Dear Sarah,*
>
> *Though you do not know me, I wish it were otherwise. My name is Eva, and we share a common friend. I live in Bellwether where Hiram serves as our beloved minister. He's become so special to many. And I'm honored to know him.*
>
> *First, you should know of Hiram's high regard for you. Every Sunday after services, he visits my mother and me. Though our discussions always begin with world concerns, they quickly turn to affairs of the heart. And it is certain that he will bend the conversation to you. I realize this letter may be bold, even*

foolhardy, but as Hiram has told us so much about you, I feel like we are sisters. If it were me, I would want someone to tell me how his eyes grow wide and shiny whenever he says my name. That they light up, fill with hope and faith, as if the Holy Spirit was perched inside them.

I know that you were treated badly here. For that, I am sorry. We have many more sins to count, but Bellwether is changing. What I wish to say, Sarah, is that we would like you to visit again. Though my asking might seem odd, even coarse, there's a reason for it. Soon, I will marry the love of my life and Hiram will preside over the joyful day. I understand that even if you're half the lady I've heard about, you're sure to have wed yourself by now, but that's not the matter at hand. It would do Hiram well to see you, if nothing more than to see an old friend.

I know you've suffered. I will not pretend to understand the wounds of your trials, but I have prayed for your healing. I do not know if you will even receive this letter as I've placed all my trust in Hiram's brother, whom I've never even met, to deliver it to you. If you are reading this, please come again to Bellwether. God does not promise a tomorrow, and our days are numbered. Yours, mine, and Hiram's, too.

With love,

Eva

Sarah reread the last two lines, over and over. Each time trying to finagle the words so they didn't sound like Hiram was in danger or unwell. But she couldn't. Her stomach hardened and a familiar floating sensation overtook her. The same lightness she felt whenever she wasn't in charge of her own will or body—being pulled away from Isaac back in Charleston; or Master Hardy taking what wasn't his to take; or leaving baby Aaron in the middle of a dark road, watching from the bushes like a mole as he was swept up in someone else's arms.

Though she felt panic and sadness, there was a little gall, too. Her face felt hot as she remembered the shame when Hiram told her that she had to leave Bellwether. She could have handled the townsfolk just fine, though Mr. Turner's words stung, calling her a coon and nodding toward the gallows as she made her way back to the train station. But Hiram staring at her blank-eyed, keeping still as she gathered up her things, that was a boot to the shins. He should have tried to make it better, could have said, "I'll fight if you want me to," or "We'll see each other again soon," but he didn't. And the pain was real, like a toothache or a fishing hook in your thumb. She felt like a fool.

None of that mattered now. She couldn't blame him for being scared; he was a new minister then. If he hadn't knuckled under to the town's edict, she would have missed out on all the blessed years in Cass County. And the sweet independence, though thoughts of baby Aaron always lay just beneath the surface, ready to burst through her skin at any moment. She knew that no matter where life took her, that heartache would never soften. And she already knew that she'd leave for Bellwether the first chance she could. If Hiram was in peril, she'd go, no matter what ghosts the past held.

* * *

Up north, the wedding had arrived. The sky was fiercely blue and though it was a cool, April day, the sun was high and a brilliant yellow. Most of the pews were full for services that day, Eva figured about thirty people. When she scanned the parish, her nerves got the better of her and she felt a bit sick. She had never seen Uriah in a tie and thought him more dashing than ever. Hiram's sermon evaded her as she was only thinking of the vows she'd be taking afterward. She tried to focus, hear his words about patience and learning to support one another, but her thoughts kept turning back to the wedding. And to their first night as husband and wife. Whenever the consummation of their love had pushed to the forefront of her thoughts, she started spinning. So, she avoided it. Until now, of all times and places.

They were going north to Houghton for two nights, some of the parishioners donated to pay for their stay at the Douglass House as a wedding gift, the bulk coming from the Lovetts and Hiram, Eva learned. The hotel was the gem of that town, folks knew of it all the way down in Bellwether—fifty rooms, a dance hall and dining room—the social center of the county. But even in the midst of such luxury, she feared that as they lay together, he might be thinking about her being with other men. She wondered, too, if maybe she would be his first lover? Then her thoughts turned to children. *Was twenty-seven too old to bear them?* Ever since Uriah asked her to be his bride, she couldn't stop picturing the merging of the two of them—eyes and hair and skin—

"Please turn your hymnals to the closing hymn," Hiram said. Eva snapped to, tried joining the parishioners in singing "Come, Ye Thankful People, Come," but she merely mouthed the words, her thoughts too heavy. Looking past Ma and Ada, she caught Uriah's eyes across the way. She smiled, and he lipped, "I love you." He had asked to sit next to his parents that morning as Ma Lovett was feeling a bit sad, said she was "losing her baby boy today."

"Now, I do believe that we have another little service to tend to," Hiram said, a smirk forming. "Miss Eva? Uriah? Might you know what that's all about?" Only after Hiram called them forward did Eva instinctively press her hand against her cheek. She was disappointed in herself for trying to cover the scar again, but she couldn't pull her hand away. Then, as she and Uriah met in front of the nave, he reached for her hands, and she had no choice. Hiram beckoned them near, whispered the plans to them—when to say what, when to kiss, and not to look at the guests on their way out—"That's bad manners," he told them.

Then Hiram spoke loudly, told the parishioners how much he loved the young couple. "They've helped kindle beautiful changes in Bellwether," he said. "And this day is about their lives becoming one. About growing and compassion. And tolerance. And truly living in the light of God." With those words, he looked over their heads, smiled at Ada, and she said, "Amen." Then Ma Murray reached for Ada's hand, and the two women held up their ball of unity, fingers wrapped around palms for all to see.

Hiram called Uriah's parents forward, then Ma and Ada, nodding for them to move to the front pew. Eva couldn't help glancing toward the doors, willing Sarah to walk right through them, take a seat amongst everyone and give Hiram a wink. But as well as the grain of hope that her would-be sister might arrive, there was guilt biting at her, too. She wished she had confessed her harlotry openly, subjected herself to a wider, more ruthless shaming, other than her own conscience whenever she flashes back to the brothel, feels a stranger bucking on her like a wild stallion and has to turn away from Uriah. The disgrace rising in her cheeks, sure to seep into their marriage at some point, spilling into different places as they live their lives. Maybe the time for telling was still to come, and it will be made plain.

Like the sermon, the nuptials were a bit of a blur. Eva's mind still wandered to visions of what lay ahead, all that she dreamt of as a younger woman, as a stow away on the steamer and in the shady edges of Chicago. A life with a cooing newborn in a bassinet, its tiny, pink arm waving over the side; bowls of fresh sliced apples, sugar, and salt on a warm July day, and that same baby as a toddler, pulling on her apron, pleading for the applesauce to be ready; and a husband treading toward her from the fields, shirtless, muscles flexing then letting go in the hot sun. And now, Eva can put Uriah's face on that body, picture a rainy night, the window open wide so the cool air drifts over their bed, her handsome partner holding her at the waist, smelling her hair as he draws her in close.

"Marriage is about husbands loving their wives, as Christ so loved the church. It's about one heart. It's about faith, hope and love. And as the bible tells us, the greatest of these is love." Hiram looked out over the crowd and said, "But we already know these things, don't we?" Eva jolted from her fancying, focused again for fear that Hiram might ask her something directly. He continued, "We are gathered today to witness the union of this fine couple. Sometimes, though, the Lord gives us opportunities for guidance at unlikely times and unexpected places. Like now." He whispered to them, "Didn't plan on this, but I have to go with it. God's telling me to talk of something even more today."

Uriah gave a slight bow from the waist and Eva offered a head nod and a loose-lipped smile.

"For all of us assembled here, this is more than a wedding. More than a new beginning for only these two. It's a new dawn for all of Bellwether. It's a time to reflect, forgive and begin again. God tells us in Psalms that He doesn't treat us as our sins deserve, 'For as high as the heavens are above the earth, so great is His love.' The time for change is upon us. From this day forward, the doors to this church are open to everyone. And so, too, shall our hearts be."

Eva glanced toward the doors again. She understood that the mercy Hiram spoke of was about folks treating Ada more kindly, or at the least, not treating her like a leper. But she figured maybe, whether he was aware of it or not, Hiram was thinking of Sarah, too. All the trials she'd endured, her treatment when she came years before. Or maybe hoping that one day she would come again and be accepted. No matter what, this was his chance to plant more seeds about goodwill, and she was happy that her wedding was a time to beckon for softer hearts. If he only knew that there was a chance, however slight, that the letter found its way to Sarah and at any moment, she could appear. Eva looked at the doors one last time then gave up on the pie-in-the-sky wishes. It wasn't the right way to start her marriage, thinking about other things when she should be listening to Hiram more than ever, hearing his counsel for being a good wife.

Then, several things happened at once. Eva accepted that Sarah wasn't coming. She let it go, told herself it wasn't meant to be. At the same time, she understood that Hiram's message of renewal held meaning for her, too. It was like he was giving her permission to let go of her own bygones. And though it wasn't a splendid lifting of heavy weight, there was an unblocking of sorts, instantly more space in her heart for her groom. Then Uriah fetched the gold band from his pocket, showed her the engraving on the inside—her new initials, E. L., and the year, 1873—and slipped it on her finger. She melted like snow held to fire.

Hiram told Uriah to kiss his new bride. So he rested his prosthetic hand in the hollow between Eva's shoulder and neck and with his good one, guided her face to his and brought his chapped, leathery lips to hers, soothing her bustling mind. To Eva, they were the only two people in the church, in the world.

Then Hiram introduced the new Mr. and Mrs. Lovett, and led them up the aisle. Eva tried not to look at anyone as she was told not to, but she never understood what was so boorish about looking folks in the eyes on your wedding day. *Why not see friends smiling, making merry the new union?* So she sneaked several peeks, soaking up the warmth and approval. Pride bulged in her chest as Uriah squeezed her hand tight. She wasn't thinking of herself as the new bride with the scarred face or of her husband with the lifeless arm, only how blessed they were.

* * *

Sarah borrowed Mrs. Brown's carpet bag, asked Minnie and Florence to help her pack. She pretended that folding her four dresses was an overwhelming task so the girls could feel like they were taking part. Even though she promised it was only for a little while, their drawn faces and slew of questions avowed the sadness—"Why do you have to go?" and "Why can't we go, too?" and then "Are slave hunters there?" She told them she had to tend to an old friend who might be sick then handed one of them some castile soap and the other her big bristle brush and made a big flap about packing them for her. Minnie giggled and said, "I think the friend is a man." Sarah didn't say anything, just handed them more sundries.

Mr. Brown took her to the depot in Battle Creek, told the girls they had to stay home and keep an eye on their mother, then winked at Mrs. Brown. The trip felt short as Sarah talked about Hiram the entire way. She knew Mr. Brown was only asking questions to be polite and that he already knew most of the answers, but she loved him for bobbing his head with vigor like he was hearing it all for the first time.

He didn't walk her into the depot but sat in the carriage and waited for the train to pull away. Her second time on a train, and she was just as scared as the first. The whole idea was terrifying, people moving faster than the wind on thin metal tracks. She kept peeking at Mr. Brown; there was safety in knowing he was still there. When the train knocked into place and all the steam and racket from the boiler burst into the air, she mouthed "thank you" from the window and waved goodbye. He tipped his cap and she turned forward, focusing her full attention on Hiram.

She was afraid, returning to the place that cast her out and likely tending to the man who didn't stand against the iron hands of Bellwether for her, not even a little. But then she thought—it's Hiram. And if he's not well, nothing else matters. He's the reason she escaped Virginia, the reason she isn't cooking for men who don't know her name, isn't still being pawed by a pot-bellied, dirty old man. Before her thoughts slipped into Master Hardy's world, she turned them to Hiram's eyes, gray-blue, like a blue jay's tail feathers. Then she tried to imagine him now, years older—hair weeded out, maybe even white in some places; teeth longer and neck thicker. But he'd still be a dash-fire, his husky voice making her feel even more alive, more free.

Then the last lines of Eva's letter ran through her head again: "God does not promise a tomorrow," and "all our days are numbered—yours, and mine, and Hiram's, too." *Why was his name at the end?* She'd mulled over the words for two days, contemplated until her stomach clenched, all the doubt and worry flaring up again. *Why would Eva write? What was in it for her?* She tried picturing her, too. She saw her as winsome and delicate with soft, pale skin, fair hair flowing down her back.

There were a lot of folks who had shown Sarah kindness over the years and some of them were white, but the ones who had wounded her deepest were always, always white. She'd be leery of all mankind for the rest of her days. *What if it was all a trick?* They might use Hiram to get her back to that sour little village then snare her like a pheasant, ship her south to be whipped and scourged for deserting her owner all those years ago. Slavery had ended but Master Hardy's ruthlessness and pride would never die. Sarah knew that. If it is a swindle, it's sure working, she thought. *Here I am on a swift moving train, already halfway to Bellwether.* The bleak thoughts were taking over, so hefty that she couldn't reel them in, cast them somewhere else like usual.

She thought about cholera, knew it was mostly a southern disease, but remembered hearing that bouts of it were still breaking out far north of the Mississippi. Maybe Hiram was cramped from head to foot with the sickness, heaving up his supper and suffering those awful spasms like the one she saw a farmer's boys have in Cassopolis, shuddering and jerking in the dirt like someone turned his bones to marmalade, his bowels letting loose. Or maybe one of those ornery villagers took out their frustration on him, snuck into the rectory in the middle of the night, hit him with a crowbar while he was sleeping. She'd only seen a couple of those folks in passing, but they looked pretty rotten, like they might leap at you any second, claw your face open.

She tried to sleep but the locomotion's chug and rumble forbade it. So did the buzzing in her brain. The scenarios in her head went from bad to worse—pneumonia, horse bite, tumble from a sea-stack—nothing dreadful went unimagined when it came to Hiram's fate. What began as scattered thoughts that she could shift to other things had swelled to an uncontainable blaze by the time the conductor announced they were nearing Mackinaw City. The last two hours of the trip were almost unbearable as her chest boomed and her nerves jangled. She had to get to Hiram.

The train had left in the early morning hours, arriving in Mackinaw just after sunrise. Though the boat ride across the straits was uneventful, the fear heightened. An endless expanse of water opened up more possibilities. *Did Hiram fall into the big lake? Is his brain all flubbed after being revived? And what if he's fine? This Eva girl might have only been speaking the truth—God does only give us one day at a time.* She could see Hiram in her mind, the round, glistening eyes and squared chin. She could hear his voice, too. Smooth and sturdy. No matter what circumstances unfold, she'd have to steel herself against his charm. Once Sarah sat down in the boat, watched the shoreline of the lower peninsula getting smaller, there was a fleeting pang of regret. She wished for a second that she was back at the Browns, dipping rhubarb stalks in honey and nibbling away, the girls on either side of her. Once the boat docked, there'd be no turning back.

In minutes, signs of life on the other side of the bay came into view. The homes and people of St. Ignace were in sight. She swallowed the notion of turning back, left it to die in the swirling freshwater, and forged on, boarding the next train headed for Marquette. She arrived on shore within the hour, full of worry and carrying her colorful carpet bag. She tried not to push past the other passengers but when some did not heed to her "pardon me," she nudged through them.

The anguish of being so close was harrowing, her chest felt like it had shrunk but her heart had ballooned, pounding with abandon. She scurried into the railway station and scrambled to the counter. There, a wide shouldered man sat upright, thumbing through a stack of tickets. All the features of his face pointed downward, like the burdens of work were strings, pulling him toward the floor. He wore a John Bull top hat—black wool and high crown—and his skin was pasty. Sarah blurted "Hello" then launched into her desperate need for a ride to Bellwether.

But before she could finish her plea, the man said, "Just a minute, ma'am," quick and sharp. The bite in his voice pushed Sarah too far. She let out a hideous sob, unrecognizable even to herself. The man stopped shuffling, studying her with glinting eyes. Sarah put her hand over her mouth to keep the sniveling at bay. The man took off his hat, revealing slick, black hair parted into a high wave atop his forehead. He gave her a loose smile, told her the last train of his shift had departed. Sarah started to cry, but he held up his hand.

"Don't do that. I'll take you there myself, if you like." Sarah kept her hand on her face, squeezed her lips between her fingers and nodded with fast up-and-down motions. Though she still couldn't ease the lather in her heart, she silenced any more wails. She pulled two-dollar coins from the front pocket of her calico dress and set them on the counter, the gold liberty heads facing up. The ticket man had busied himself again but stopped when the coins clicked against the wood. He shook his head.

"No, ma'am," he said. But Sarah was already searching for more, thinking it wasn't enough. She couldn't take the chance of him changing his mind. She dug out two more dollars, set those atop the others. "Not taking any money, ma'am. Just doing a kindness." He patted the tickets in his hand until they formed a perfect rectangle. Then, he tied a string around them, crisscross, and tossed the bundle under the counter before heading toward the door, beckoning Sarah with a jerk of his head.

Sarah picked up the coins and followed him to his carriage in silence. After they had climbed in, the man announced, "Bellwether, here we come," and Sarah let out a long, low sigh. "You sound like steam in the blastpipe of a train, when it starts chuffing." The man laughed, and Sarah knew from his heady smile that she'd get to Hiram safe and sound.

* * *

Though Eva held back the bulk of her money, there was nothing short of a feast at the Murray home, cooked by Ma Murray, Ma Lovett, and a few other ladies from the congregation. Ada made the bridal pie—apples from the cellar, peaches canned from last year's crops, and a flaky, nut colored crust—all the guests fussing over the rich smell of cooked fruit.

"Not sure if folks still do it," she said, "but I baked the glass ring right in. Over the years, folks started leaving me things, always at night when I was sleeping. I'd wake up to a box by the door. Most of the time it was filled with rubbish that I'd never use. One time, I even got an old dress, tattered and stained, big rip in the underarm. And I understood they were only doing it to make themselves feel better 'cause they knew damn well that when the sun came up, they'd be treating me like a trash heap again. Turns out one of the hand-outs had some nice things in it after all—a kingly looking bottle of perfume, nearly full, a couple of quarter eagle coins, and a gold ring." She started cutting the pie into slices, peeking at the women to make sure they were listening. "Never spent those coins, even when times got tough. Always felt like dirty money to me. Not sure why, now that I think on it. But the ring. Now I know why the good Lord sent it my way. I sure hope folks still put a ring in the wedding pie like they used to, giving a poor spinster something to wish for. Even when unwed gals would say, 'that custom is for the birds,' deep down there was a little voice whispering, maybe it'll be me, but it could have all changed. As you know, I haven't been to a wedding for a few decades." With that, Ada laughed. "Guess everyone figured my social calendar was full."

Eva didn't know if she should laugh, too. But then Ruby Lee and Ma did, so she joined in. Their laughter grew from little har-har-hars to unrestrained bellows. Others began to laugh just hearing the four grown women lose their inhibitions. As the celebration ensued, the sound of idle chatter and playful chortling made Eva wonder if it was possible that in that moment, she could be the happiest woman alive. If no one else on God's green earth was filled with as much love and gratefulness, so much that they might crack open. When the time came to eat dessert, the women gathered around Eva, doling out slivers of pie to one another.

The three amongst them who were unwed were told to eat first. In just a bite or two, Margaret, the oldest daughter of William and Edna Scott—a mill family that had mostly kept to themselves—found the ring. She held it up for all to see. Everyone clapped, and Mr. Scott shook his finger at the single boys in the room. "Don't be getting any thoughts." Everyone laughed, especially Edna. Then each of the women took turns holding the loaf of bread over Eva's head as they tore pieces from it. Eva knew it was coming. Another tradition she thought silly, but nonetheless, she obliged. The crumbs scattered down over her, and Eva smiled at Uriah, both of them shaking their heads at the foolishness. Though she was still anxious about the intimacy ahead, she wanted to snap a finger so the guests would just offer their blessings and be gone. Then she and Uriah would whisk away to Houghton, nothing between them but their words and the night air.

* * *

Sarah and the ticket taker made their way northwest. The conversation was full but one-sided, mostly returning to Sarah's fears about Hiram's welfare and her being too late. They never spoke of her trials in Virginia, the horrors before finding refuge in Michigan. She knew white folks this far north had to wonder about such things, so she admired the man's gentility in not asking those questions. She felt impolite for not steering the conversation his way, but she couldn't help it. Nothing felt natural. Not her manners, not the letter, not the trip, and most certainly not all the panicking—cold sweats, lungs rattling like they were full of bones. Sarah did learn the man's name, Charlie, and that his wife died in childbirth, his baby boy not long after. For that, her heart felt even heavier and she told him so. But then, too much time passed without worrying about Hiram or mentioning his name, and the consternation set in again.

Charlie raised his brow. "I'm just like you, wondering why someone would write things that way. Wording's all queer, making you guess at the point of it." Then he made an *humph* sound and shook his head. "Can't make heads nor tails of it. But I do know a shortcut that'll get you there faster, get you the answers quicker. It's just a little ways from here," he said. "It can get a bit rocky between Michigamme and Keweenaw Bay, though. Lots of woods. But we could save at least an hour or—"

"Oh, please," Sarah said. Then she caught herself, took in a deep breath and spoke again, more calmly. "If you're willing, I'd be much obliged."

"Wouldn't have told you of it if I wasn't willing," he said. "It'll be bumpy, but the trail cuts straight through, ends just outside the town of L'Anse. It'll put us there in no time flat." Sarah didn't know if she said "hallelujah" out loud or only thought it, so she asked him. Charlie laughed. So did she. A few minutes passed, and she found herself repeating the end of the letter to him again, the jitters flaring anew.

"It is fishy, ain't it?" she asked. "You think Hiram's sick, too. Don't you?"

* * *

Eva felt the cramp of the small house and gently ushered the wedding guests outside, feeling pretty and deserving in her wedding gown. The men folk gathered near the edge of the field with one of the wives stepping near, now and again, then reporting back to the women. "Talking about some big circus that opened out in New York. And a couple of them are jabbering about a railway system that'll soon connect Traverse City to Petoskey. Same old prattle about bigger things than Bellwether, things that'll never touch us." Eva sat on a blanket on the ground, watching the children play, dashing every which way with such urgency. To them, their play was so real, so important. She envied their earnestness to romp and frolic with carefree devotion, wished she could have done more of that as a child.

Ma and Ada soon joined her, a plate full of salted asparagus and a jar of canned cherries. Eva eyed the mix of colors and nosed the fresh, light scents before trying both. The three women did not say much, just chuckled intermittently and pointed a finger when one of the children took a tumble or sprinted past them like the world depended on it. Eva savored the greens and fruit, as well as the deep camaraderie that comes from comfortable silence. The other women seemed to understand that in that moment, the blanket was only big enough for three.

* * *

Several spokes broke right through, and the wheel itself split apart, as if someone took a swipe at it with an ax. Though there had been some uneven ground and a few rocky patches, for a long while, it was smooth enough that Sarah managed to close her eyes, imagine that things might be okay. Neither of them saw the crevice that the wedges of bedrock had formed. The wagon lurched hard, jolting them forward. They climbed out of the angled carriage, eyed the broken wheel. And Sarah began to cry again.

"No need for tears," Charlie said. "We're at the far end of the trail, only a couple miles to L'Anse. You can hoof it there faster than it'll take me to fix this blasted thing."

Those words were a match, lighting a wick inside her, a bright yellow flame burning bright and large. "We're that close?"

"Just keep on the trail and once you hit L'Anse, take the main road, shouldn't be no more than four or five more miles after that, dead ends in Bellwether." Charlie was assessing the damage as he spoke. He stepped to the back of the wagon and brought out an assortment of tools—mallet, chisel, hammer— and cursed a pair of missing tongs. "I'll have this wheel fixed by high-noon, be back in Marquette at sunset. And you, Miss Sarah, could be sitting with Hiram by supper."

"But I can't just leave you here. I won't—"

"You will. You ain't got any say in that. Besides, I won't take you any further no how." Charlie held his elbow in one hand, rubbing his temple with the index finger of the other. "Ah, yes," he said, making his way to the driver's side. He reached beneath the seat and pulled out the tongs. "Knew I'd find 'em," he said, holding them high like a trophy. "Now go, I've got to light a fire to bend the iron rim. And I don't need you standing there hearing me cuss if I mess things up."

The horses whinnied and stamped their feet, and Charlie

told them they were good boys, repeating the word "easy" until they calmed. Sarah mooned about being so close to Bellwether, an hour, maybe two. Her heart sped up again. Charlie had already started carving out a fire-plow, sharpening the stick to a dull point. Sarah knelt next to him and said, "I kinda want to kiss you on the cheek, then walk on out of here."

"Get on with it then." Charlie stuck out his cheek but kept whittling away, eyes on his work. Sarah put a hand on his shoulder and gave him a peck.

"You're a godly man," she said. "And your wife was a lucky woman." With that, she stood, shifted the carpet bag on her shoulders and headed down the trail. She heard Charlie call after her, repeating the directions to Bellwether, but they were already etched in her brain. The trail angled away, out of sight of the crippled wagon. Sarah looked back, saw the fire and Charlie holding the jagged iron rim over the flames.

Once she was lost from view, Sarah ran like lightning. Her dress was starting to feel heavy, even in the coolness, sweat was forming on her back and arms. She unbuttoned the sleeves and pulled them up as she trekked on. The ground was hard but flat for the most part, and she could hear the soles of her shoes thumping against it. When the earth rose up or the gravel was loose, she would slow, but only until it evened out or her footing steadied. Then she'd tug on her dress and underclothes, unstick them from her skin and start running again. And if she was winded, she'd walk for a while, then soon enough the race against time would overtake her weariness and she'd pick up the pace, a brisk walk to a jog, to an all out, mad dash.

In one particular bout of walking, Sarah had lost herself in many-sided thoughts, musings that reached past Hiram—Cass County, brother Isaac, and Charlie's safe return to Marquette—then a mosquito stung her neck and halted the reverie. She couldn't tell how long she'd been strolling. The sun was overhead and she shuddered to think that she'd lost precious time or somehow veered off path and was going the wrong way. Her nerves began knocking together. Then she remembered a game she sometimes played as a child, pretending the Devil was chasing her. It always made her run fast as a red fox. So she pictured Lucifer on her heels, coming hard. That helped her hotfoot down the path for a mile or more, but just when she decided it was too blasphemous to be feigning with the Devil as a grown woman, the woods opened up.

The wide, bustling sawmills of L'Anse were in the distance but plain as day. And she guessed that the long, two-story building straight ahead was the township hall, bigger than anything in Cass County. She trekked toward town, walked behind the first couple of buildings to avoid being seen, but thought it silly not to veer onto the main road. Nothing to fear this far above the Mason-Dixon line, almost to Canada for goodness sake. So, she traipsed out of the shadows and entered the street, staying close to the storefronts. She didn't feel in danger but didn't want to poke at fate either, bringing attention to herself.

Some folks nodded and some just stared, but it felt more like discomfort with a newcomer than cold shoulders. Most just minded their own business. While most people on the street were white, after she had made her way north of the village, a black man and his young son approached in a horse and buggy. But when they slowed, Sarah merely nodded and picked up her pace. She didn't have the spirit to explain why she was journeying this way. To tell strangers how she and Hiram met in a hopeless place and that he risked his life to teach her how to read. How he saved her from the nightmares of Virginia and led her to a life of self-reliance. Though she had to admit, there was relief in seeing skin as dark as her own.

There was a boiling in her stomach. It had been there awhile, but it was growing, as if her belly was mad about all the burdens and growing hunger. She couldn't do anything about the first, but she pulled some venison jerky from her bag, unfolded the greasy cloth and bit into the chewy ribbon of meat, all without missing a stride. When she reached for another piece, she saw the two rolls of hub wafers that Minnie and Florence had insisted she take. When she had told them no, to save their candy for a special time, they looked as if she'd just pulled their hearts right out of their chests. So she took them, stuffed them in the bag and kissed each girl on the forehead. She tore open one of the rolls of candy now, took out the first three pieces—black, purple and green—put them on her tongue. Hints of licorice, clove and lime, a comforting taste of Cass County.

Sarah walked and ran and walked again for what she guessed was two miles or so, chewing more jerky, more candy. She snuck water from two different wells along the way, filling her canteen to the brim. When she realized that she'd eaten an entire roll of wafers, she stuffed the wrapper away, then spotted Eva's letter, folded up where she had placed it after reading it to Charlie. She swallowed the last sugary mound as the familiar dread started to prickle. She stopped for a moment, hoping to curtail the onslaught, but as she focused on sucking in through her nose, letting it out through her mouth, she glanced far down the trail. The horizon appeared, an open space just beyond the dark of the trees, and what she knew to be the open blue of Lake Superior. Her heart was pounding hard in her mouth now. She took a big inhale, said a quick prayer, asking God for the calmness and courage to get to Bellwether in time. Her shoulders dropped as she moved forward, eyes set on the open stretch in front of her, getting wider, more vast.

She remembered how the splendor of the village had overwhelmed her before the townsfolk showed their spleens—the rejection, the dominance, the scorn—a landscape like she'd never known. She strode on, and though her heart was still throbbing, she felt it sliding back into place. She ran harder than ever. Time sped up and stood still all at once. There was no sense of space. As she drew near Bellwether, the unspoiled beauty overtook the bad memories. She was still wrecked by Hiram letting the village turn her out, but the wave of allegiance kept cresting over, making her swallow the gall. She knew she'd have to throat it up again, some time, some day, chew on it like a dog does cow hide, whether Hiram was alive or not.

Everything was just as she remembered. Mighty sea-stacks reaching toward Heaven, and fat, full evergreens everywhere you turn. The blur of sky and water, more blues and greens than an eye can bear. There were a few more houses on the edge of town and a mercantile that she didn't recall, but the brownstone on the church was exactly how she saw it in her dreams. The tapered windows still reflecting the sunlight, and the chapel standing proud and vigilant.

But there was a strange stillness in the village, as if it had been deserted. Not another soul in sight. The only sound was the wind blowing through the trees and far off, a strange rumbling that Sarah couldn't decipher. She headed out back to the rectory and knocked on the door. No answer. She called out Hiram's name and hit the door hard, then harder. She ran to the front of the church and pulled open those doors with a heft. The emptiness was infinite. It felt staggering and wrong. She spoke aloud, as if the echo of her plea inside the church walls might carry more weight. "Dear Lord, help me. Tell me I'm not misled?" Her knees grew weak and she grabbed hold of the door frame on either side. "Tell me that You didn't bring me this far just to—"

The distant clangor sounded out again, louder, more clear. There were voices, boisterous talking. Sarah turned toward the noise. A high-pitched peal made its way to her ears, but she wasn't sure if it was glee or suffering. She followed the din, having to slow when it quieted, spinning around like a carousel in the middle of Bellwether, looking every which way until it reared up again, then she'd scurry further toward it. It was in a matter of minutes that Sarah came to the Murray house, unbeknownst to her.

Though the forms were coming into focus—men, women and children—the tones were shapeless. Were they blithe or somber? Merrymaking? Grieving? Sarah kept walking toward the people, too numb to be afraid. Hiram could be amongst them. Someone in that crowd will know where he is. If he's okay. Or even alive. As Sarah approached, the wedding guests began to turn toward her, one by one, the bustle lagging. Soon enough, all eyes were on her as she stood on the edge of Ma Murray's yard. When she caught sight of Hiram, she dropped the bag from her shoulder, brought her hands to her chest. And the tears burst forth.

Eva was the first to move, rising from the blanket and bringing her hands to her heart, too. Hiram was standing behind her, still eating pie, slow to recognize the quietude. He began to look around. "What is it?" he asked, still chewing.

Eva pointed to Sarah, then her tears came, soft and quiet. The fork and plate fell from Hiram's hands. Though he knew it was Sarah, he still squinted at her, felt like he had to, like doubt or disbelief was sure to come. But it didn't. He stepped over the plate and blanket then glanced back at Eva, for approval or affirmation, he did not know.

"Go to her," she said with a nod. He traipsed past the gawking eyes, made his way to where she was standing. Her deep-set eyes were slick, glazed by sunlight. She tried shifting her dress some then patted at her hair, clumps of it having loosed from the comb. He was reminded of the first time they met, standing outside his shack at the coalmine, her trying to primp herself as best she could while he spied through the window. He thought of her dignity, too. How badly it must have hurt being turned out.

But then he thought about how much has happened since then. How much Bellwether was fixing itself. When he was just a couple of steps away, he became clumsy. Like a newborn doe, he ambled, desperate to keep going, yet his heart and feet were divided. He had to regain his composure before they were face to face. He'd been here before—same circumstance, same stakes—and botched it all to hell. He gave others too much power, let them determine what should and should not be. Not this time. Bellwether is rising, he told himself. And so am I.

He let go—a laugh and cry and whoop all at once—then bounded forward, his nose almost touching hers. With a swipe of his thumbs, he wiped Sarah's cheeks then held her face. He knew his words couldn't possibly tell her what was in his heart, so he delved into her eyes. The two of them locked into one another, and Hiram leaned her way, trying to make himself see-through, trying to convince her with his expression—never again.

"You're okay? You're not sick?"

"No."

"But I got a letter?" Sarah said.

"A letter? From who?"

"A gal named Eva, said she was a friend of yours. Made it seem like you was ailing." Hiram instantly knew what Eva had done. He looked back over his shoulder and shook his head at her. He marked the anxiousness on her face but simpered at her to let her know it was good. He faced Sarah again, told her that Eva meant well.

"You let them turn me away, Hiram," Sarah spliced the airy tone.

"I know."

"It left a bruise."

"I know that, too."

"Not sure my teeth could bear a kick like that again."

"Look at me," Hiram said. "And keep on looking till you see me, fully." He bent at the knees so they were at the same level, then he took her hand and put it on his chest.

"Can you see me?" Sarah nodded, more tears spilling out.

"Never again," he said.

After a moment, Hiram spun toward the gathered on-lookers. "What's everyone gaping at us for? There are newly-weds here!" Slowly, the chatter rose again and Uriah and Eva made their way to Hiram and Sarah. "You ready for Houghton?" he asked them.

"Bags are in the buggy," Uriah replied.

"You hoodwinked me," Hiram said to Eva.

"I did," she said. "There were two letters, Hiram. One for Sarah and one for Leander. I asked him to come see you, too. But of that, despair."

Hiram sighed, as if he was giving his brother a moment of silence. But then his face hardened, and he abruptly started up again, "Anyhow, Miss Eva, I'm pleased to introduce you. This is Sarah."

Sarah reached out her hand, but Eva threw her arms around Sarah's neck. The two women embraced without words. Hiram looked at Uriah and asked him if he had known about this. "Not a thing," he said. "Still don't. But you can bet I'll be posing plenty of questions soon."

Though muffled, Hiram heard Sarah when she whispered to Eva, "Don't like being tricked, young lady. Finding it hard to be sore about it though."

"Come on folks!" Hiram beckoned. "Let's give these two a Bellwether send off!" He reached down and unbuckled his shoe, slipped it off his foot and held it overhead, waiting for everyone to do the same. Each of the gathered guests took off a shoe, too. Most of the children took off both. Sarah looked to Hiram and raised her shoulders. "Go on," he said, nodding toward her feet. She took off her brogan and held it up like everyone else. When Eva and Uriah approached the wagon, Hiram shouted, "Toss 'em, folks! But keep 'em low. You don't want to hit the married couple!" All the guests lobbed their shoes at the wagon, two and three at a time, hoping to pull a bit more luck from the new twosome before they left. Laughter rang loud through the village.

"Now I know for sure you folks are loopy," Sarah said. Then she gently pitched her shoe, too. The space between the crowd and the wagon was riddled with boots and shoes of all sizes, some dirty, some clean. By the time Uriah and Eva were seated, ready to go, Ada had limped her way to the front. As all the others waved and shouted their well wishes, Ada blew them kisses, over and over, making sure that if Eva turned back, she'd see. Hiram's heart swelled when he finally saw Eva turn around and blow one back.

* * *

Hiram, Sarah, Ada and Ma Murray were the last of the wedding guests. Ruby Lee had left with the others, which was a bit of a relief to Hiram. Though their indiscretion had happened years before, there was still a strain whenever they were in close proximity, one that pestered his duties as minister. So the foursome sat at the table, sipping coffee and talking about the good times awaiting the newlyweds. And the trials they would have, too.

Sarah was slow to participate at first, but soon enough, she was an equal contributor. Though it was not the time or place to talk about her history, when they asked how far she'd traveled to Bellwether, she did tell them about the wonders of Cass County. Ma Murray noticed Sarah itching and offered soap and water to clean the scrapes on her forearms and above her ankles. "I've never walked that trail from Michigamme, but just riding through, why, that underbrush is what a jungle must look like. And these wicked boxelder bugs this time of year, they're little villains."

Ada yawned and quickly said her goodbyes. Then, Ma Murray offered Eva's bed to Sarah. Hiram knew she would try to stay awake as long as he was there, so he bid them farewell, too. "Would you walk me to the door?" he asked. Once there, he told her to step outside, away from the sets of eyes he knew were on them. Then, he bent down so they were level again. "Look at me," he said. Sarah looked into his eyes and though he felt his starting to water, he kept them wide, fighting the hankering to blink. "Do you truly see me?"

"I do," she said. "But I saw you back then, too. Years and years, Hiram. That's how much time you let pass. I can't just forgive that in a day. I can't heal that quick. Don't want to. And it ain't fair of you to ask me to."

"But you wouldn't be here if you—"

"Stop." Sarah held up her hand. "Don't be a fool. Of course I care for you. I've loved you since day one. And I know you love me, too. I don't doubt that. But don't be acting like you're the one with all the strength. When the going got tough, you quit. Not me. I'm the one with my arms all cut up, bites the size of dollars 'cause I hiked all these miles after Miss Eva fibbed about you being sick. I ain't a faint-heart, Hiram. And in these past few years, I've gotten even stronger. So it's you who needs to be looking at me." She stepped closer to him. "You see me? You see my courage? Cause this is who I am. This is the Sarah you've been missing out on."

Hiram knelt on both knees, dropped his head.

"Don't do that," Sarah spat. "Don't bow down like I'm wounding you. We're just telling truths here. Are you always that quick to break?"

"You've got it wrong," Hiram said. "I'm not bowing. I'm trying to pledge something to you. If you'd stop talking long enough to let me."

"Well then?"

"However long it takes, I'll prove myself. I'm the same man you sat with under that scratchy gray blanket, the man who picked up dirty oysters when that peckerwood knocked them from your hands. That was me." He was carried all the way back to the Shenandoah, waters whispering to him, sweet laurel in the air. And when Sarah said, "I believe you will," a warm thrill moved through him, outward from his heart. He vowed to himself that Sarah would never want again.

* * *

As the newlyweds made their way north, Eva fielded all of Uriah's questions. And when he nudged her some about the crafty letter to Sarah, she said, "All I wrote was that none of us are going to live forever. And that's true isn't it? So I didn't really tell that big a thumper."

"You're a wily one, Miss Lovett," Uriah said.

"I love hearing my new name."

"Well, I love saying it. I'll call you Miss Lovett every day, for the rest of our lives." Evening had fallen by the time they arrived in Houghton, but the sun had yet to clear the horizon. The Douglass House was majestic and after they had both stepped from the wagon, Eva stood still, staring at the towers atop the grandiose entry. Uriah tied the horse to a hitching post, gathered their bags then came back around to the passenger side. He put his arm around her, looked up at the towers, too. "What are you thinking?" he asked.

"I'm remembering Wordsworth, the piece where he's thinking about childhood. There's only one line that I can ever recall—

'The innocent brightness of a new-born day is lovely yet.'"

"Seems like a good one to remember."

That night, Eva's fears of lying together for the first time melted away the moment Uriah skimmed her face with the fingers of his good hand. Their consummation was clumsy, but Eva knew the intimate part of their lives would keep them close, both laughing at the bumbling, unexpected sounds as they came together. And the hotel porter's knock at the door just when their passion was at its peak.

Later, after Eva awoke to Uriah snuffling and grunting in his sleep, she pulled herself up, rested on an elbow and watched him for a while. Though the snoring kept her from any rest, she was not bothered. She made her way to the window, the moonlight felt more rich this far north, more blue than silver. She looked out over Sheldon Avenue, the street and buildings all bathed in the nighttime as if the sky had leaked down over Houghton. She smelled the stars through the glass, mellow and sweet, as she tried to focus on her reflection. It struck her then; she had completely forgotten about her scar.

Chapter 41
Heave-ho!

From the sea-stacks, Basil heard the happiness at the Murray house echoing up. Though it pained him that he wasn't there wishing the young couple well, offering them a heartfelt blessing, he knew he didn't belong. Over the years, the folks of Bellwether had learned to honor his need to be alone, and for that, he was grateful. The contact with Uriah, preparing him to take over as teacher—and the here and there visits from Hiram—that was all he needed, all he could handle. It was during an unexpected parley after school that Uriah shared how fond of Eva he was becoming and that their time together was more than just courting. It's a good day for such an occasion, he thought.

But for Basil, springtime was harder than all other seasons, always brought with it bigger tides of Stella's memory. He can hear her soft voice, crystal clear, telling him how April and May are God's special months. "That's when all hope is restored, when life rises up from the breathless winter," she'd say. That's Stella. Always speaking songlike as if Elizabeth Barrett Browning was perched on her tongue. Basil felt her in the house even more on those spring nights. He'd sit at the table, sip coffee and talk to her, in his head mostly, but out loud, too. He had stopped saying sorry years ago, it felt daft, irrelevant. The time for that was when she was still taking air into her precious lungs. Or those times she stepped outside, pretending she had a task to do whenever something brought their childlessness to the forefront, like the mention of birth in a bible passage or the sound of a baby crying in a passing carriage. From the window, Basil would watch her cry, head against a tree, knowing she was begging the Lord to make her fertile.

The night of Uriah's and Eva's wedding, Stella's presence was too strong. Basil stayed awake the whole night through. It started the usual way, him telling her about his day, the mundane things—brisk winds and beautiful sky; the piny perfume of evergreens sharpening the air; and the loose gate on the chicken coop—but when the small hours came, he shared his decisive plan. It was like she knew he was close to joining her, like she was giving him permission, maybe even an invitation. Like she, too, felt the time was consecrated. The answers were coming easy, give Uriah and Eva the house, bless them with a big start on their new life. *You've been done with this life for so long.* A strange repose swept through the house like a cool springtide.

Basil had fallen asleep with the side of his face atop his forearm. The coffee fell onto the floor, but there wasn't much left to spill. With his socked foot, he soaked up the few black beads and said sorry out loud—Stella used to hate it when he mopped with his foot. Then, he went to work packing the open chest, the one he'd been preparing for months. Or more accurately, the one in which he'd shifted the contents, over and over, arranging them, then rearranging them, searching for the perfect grouping. Inside, there were gifts and letters he'd received from students over time; some empty bottles of verbena that had been sitting on the mantle since Stella died; and his tattered Wordsworth collection. Atop all of the keepsakes, he placed a special hardcover of *A View of the Evidences of Christianity*, the Hillsdale College stamp on the front cover. Before the reminiscence could flare up, overtake his head and heart, he closed the book, then the lid. Next, he took a blank envelope from his desk and across the top, he wrote:

To Eva and Uriah, I leave my home and all my belongings. Have a blessed life.

Mr. Brandt

He placed the envelope squarely atop his journal and headed to the barn.

* * *

Should someone happen to pass by at this early hour, it would be an odd sight indeed, he thought, Mr. Brandt dragging a cedar chest through the field. But most likely, they'll just think, *poor ol' Basil, he's finally gone mad,* and let him be. He had considered just taking the buggy, but what if days pass before anyone notices he's gone? Or before Hiram thinks to search for him at their meeting place? Can't do that to my horse, he decided. So, at one end of a piece of rope, he made a shackle knot just big enough to put his hands through and tied it around his waist. Then he tied a second rope through the hole on the lock hasp of the chest, pulled each end over his shoulders and started hauling the precious load like a pack mule.

Though unwieldy, he managed to tow it to the sea-stacks unseen and with only stopping for a couple of breaks. He was sad to see how badly the stones had chipped the bottom wood pieces. After having traveled the mile to the church, he dragged it across the familiar stretch of cliffs. Once he reached the base of the lofty precipice leading to Hiram's and his special spot, he turned backward, dug his heels into the limestone and arched his spine against the chest, pushing with all his might. He could feel the grooves between the slats making imprints on his skin while he ascended the slope. "God, help me," he petitioned, just before giving a final stalwart thrust.

Once atop the sea-stack, Basil looked out over the great lake, combed his grassy beard with his fingers and ran a sleeve across his forehead, the sweat was cold upon his skin as the brisk wind passed over. He unbuttoned the top two buttons of his shirt and sat down on the chest. When he lifted his hat from his wet head and brushed back a lock of hair, a hapless caw escaped his lips. It was unexpected and ugly, rattling out across the water. Then he crinkled up his boxy face like paper, cupped his mouth and sobbed like a child.

* * *

It was dusk when Hiram scaled the limestone crags and stepped across the cliffs to Basil. Though night was upon them, there was enough light left that they could see one another. Basil had spent the entire day up high—praying, sleeping, wondering, regretting. He did not bother to call out as Hiram rustled and crackled nearer. He simply sat upright and watched his friend approach. "Therefore, if anyone is in Christ, he is a new creation," Hiram said in customary fashion. "The old has gone, the new has come. That's Second Corinthians—"

"Chapter 5, verse 17," Basil inserted.

"Nicely done," Hiram quipped as he stepped in front of him and the cedar chest.

Silently, Basil paid homage to his friend as even in the shadows of sundown, he could see that the spiritual burdens of Bellwether had taken a toll, the deep lines on Hiram's face were distinct. "How did you know I was here?" he asked.

"Happy coincidence."

"No, really. How?"

"I had a good day. Thought I'd try to share it with my ever-witty companion. When you didn't answer, I looked inside, didn't like what I saw. Too empty. And with your horse and wagon still there, I knew there was only one other place." Basil didn't move when Hiram sat down next to him, the closeness was consoling. "Last time we were here together, things got a bit sour. Must be something in the limestone."

"What made this day better than the rest?" Basil asked. "The wedding?"

"Well, sure. Bringing together a godly young couple is always joyous. But what's more, the Lord brought someone back to me today, even though I'm undeserving of such a blessing."

"I'm glad for you." From Hiram's roving eyes and flattening tone, Basil knew that his friend figured out his intentions for being there.

"You know, Basil, I can't let you do this."

"It's not your place." Though their time together had grown rare, they still loved as brothers do. And for a second time, they argued as brothers, too.

"It most certainly is," Hiram snapped. "You did not fail your wife."

Basil felt his face wrench again as if he'd bitten a lime, felt his eyes sheen like ice, the tears teetering. He jerked his head toward Hiram as if he'd been slapped. Then, his cheeks went lax. "Didn't I?" he choked, then held up his hand with fanned fingers, beseeching Hiram to stop.

"That was God's will, friend." Hiram pulled a wicker wrapped flask from his pocket, unscrewed the cap and took a long draught. He sighed and smacked his lips. "There's another joyous thing about weddings, friend. It's an excuse to savor some fine spirits." A strong wind carried up mist from below, and both men turned their faces into the spray. "Hell, teacher, what would you have me do?" Hiram asked.

Basil reached for the flask that Hiram was extending, took a nip of Mount Vernon. The fiery rye burned, making him cough. After he cleared his throat, he said, "You weren't supposed to be here."

"That was God's will, too."

"Not this time, Hiram. Not sure I can take too much talk about faith or mercy right now. I can't keep trying to piece together God's puzzles. It has made me tired."

"Fair enough," Hiram replied. "Let's get on with it. Tell me, what was the next part of your plan?"

Basil knew Hiram was only pacifying him for the time being, until he could figure out another way to approach the circumstances. But a truce was good, even if only for a minute. He pulled up his shirt, showed him the rope with the shackle knot.

"Quite a scheme you've hatched, fine sir. Tie yourself to the chest, push it over the side. Give yourself to our beloved Lake Superior." Hiram shook his head. "Not sure she should have to hold a story like this one."

Basil closed his eyes and pictured the sea-stacks in broad daylight. How the bits of foliage always burst through the stony cracks this time of year. And how, from a distance, the cliffs looked ablaze. And on cloudy days, the water always showed green, almost florid, like the leafy head of a rhubarb stalk. In a gusty wind, the waves would rush through the caves below and slap against their walls, glugging with abandon. And the scars on the bluff meandered in a colorful helix—coral, cornmeal and peach.

"For what it's worth," Hiram interrupted his muse, "I agree with half of your design. If that chest is full of painful memories, then by all means, let's sink it forever. Our dear lake can keep those kind of secrets like no other. You've been plagued for too long, friend. God didn't put you here to bend beneath the guilt of a few bad decisions. This isn't fair to—"

"So the chest goes over without me? That's your amendment?"

"Yes."

A quiet spell followed, then Basil stepped behind the chest. "Well, come on then. Heave-ho."

"You have not changed your heart that quickly, Basil. I fear this is a trick."

"No trickery, Hiram. You've earned the right to convince me that my life matters. And that there's an end point in atoning for my gutless ways. But I'm only promising a delay, and an open ear."

"Will you stand back then, let me do the pushing?"

"I gave my word. That's enough. Besides, it's a heavy son of a gun."

Under the gravity of Hiram's discerning eye, Basil felt small, like a boy standing next to a man. He focused his attention on turning the chest width ways so they could push it together. At the lip of the high point, they decided not to rock it over the edge as they might not be able to stop their momentum and could tumble over with it. Instead, they sat in front of it and kicked the bulky coffer with their feet, sporadically at first, then harder and more rhythmically. With a final, heedless shove, they sent it plunging over the side, listened to it crash against the stone then drop into the water with a thwack. They lay on their backs. It was darker now, the stars were starting to show, though thin and faint. They drained the rest of the flask in silence.

Eventually, Hiram said he'd feel better about pleading his case if they were in the rectory. "It's warmer and besides, Miss Murray sent me home with the leftover pies."

Basil conceded and the two of them headed off the sea-stack.

"I might be a sheet or so in the wind, fine minister," Basil said. And as Hiram turned to offer a hand, Basil met his eyes, just before slipping over the edge.

* * *

That Sunday, Hiram dedicated the sermon to Bellwether's learned recluse, Mr. Brandt, speaking about mercy and idle tongues, nimbly quoting Psalms and warning the congregation about the dangers of wallowing in hearsay. And it seemed his counsel was not in vain. As days passed, many of the parishioners made it a point to tell him there wasn't much prattling about Basil's death. "No buzzing, Father, just grief and pity," Ada told him.

A month later, Uriah and Eva were moved into the Brandt home. Neither of them had much, their own clothes and some donations from the Lovetts and Ma Murray—bedding, linens and cookery. Pa Lovett gave up some basic tools as well as a cider press and carving table. Basil had sold most of his land, so there wasn't any need for a grain reaper or fanner just yet.

Though the house was alive with busy hands and talk of the young couple's hereafter, there was a strange feeling of intrusion that Eva could not push aside. She knew that Ma, the Lovetts, and Uriah all felt it, too, but for her, it was almost strangling. This is what Mr. Brandt wanted, she thought. Meddlesome or not, it was his wish. Eva sat at the table a moment, watching everyone she loved fluttering about like hummingbirds while she remembered how he made her love poetry and stories and all things deeply human. Because of her beloved teacher, Eva knew that many lives were made more bountiful. If she hadn't learned from books what strength and endurance could do, she would have never left. And, though the trials in Chicago were nearly insufferable, staining her for life, she could not imagine the horror of having stayed.

She had hidden Basil's journal on the kitchen shelf, behind the metal canisters—coffee, sugar, tea and flour—and would wait until everyone had gone and Uriah was asleep to read it. She wondered if Basil would still be alive had she ever told him of his influence, but that was not a millstone she was willing to carry. No room for supposing in her new life, only hope, love and the here-and-now.

As soon as Uriah began to snort and snuffle in his sleep, Eva crept to the kitchen and pulled the journal from the shelf. She lit a lamp and made herself some tea. One by one, she poured over Basil's entries and letters, piecing together his life. All the doubt and shame and silence—

...one thing is for certain, my love. I'm the reason you're dead. That is my only true claim. Every night, I imagine your fair face,

for fear I will forget your kind eyes. Then, after I can see them clearly, I force myself to remember how brown the blood was after it dried on your skin, in your hair. Only then do I feel I've earned the right to blunder my way through another punishing slumber.

Eva folded the journal into her lap, took a deep breath, rubbed her lips together. Then she brought it to her face again—

After all, if I'm not the man letting Stella down, then who am I?

Eva began to cry, the quiet kind, where tears roll steady but there's no choking or gasping, just calm, simple sadness. Then she read through letters Basil had written to the children he'd never have, addressed to his unborn son and daughter, apologizing for his inability to bring them to life. She didn't finish, just closed the journal, held it tight, and mourned the children as if they had lived, gamboled in the big water, fished for perch and bluegill, pestered one another the way siblings do. She told Basil of her own hope for children. It would be my honor to bring little ones into your home, she told him.

And though it felt like she might be tempting fate, Eva asked God to bless her again, just one more time. So much grace had been given her as of late, yet still, she pleaded for the chance to bear a child. As it was intended to be, not by wicked lust and a treacherous father but from a loving, devoted husband. Let Uriah be the remarkable father that he could be, she implored. Let us bring more life to this place. This has been an unhappy home for too long.

* * *

It was just a few weeks later that Eva started feeling sick in the mornings like she had years before. She was hopeful. Then her time of the month passed with an unstained sanitary belt. And she thanked God. Though she was heaving in the outhouse and her feet and thighs were already starting to crick and ache, she chortled and began to ponder baby names.

There was something Eva had to do before she shared the good news. Having Basil's secrets in her possession was pulling on her conscience. She didn't like being the keeper of someone else's skeletons. After much pondering, she decided that the journals must die with him. Though most were disappointed that he sidestepped his patriotic duty, in death, his devotion to the children of Bellwether should ring loudest. As for deceiving his wife, should that go beyond their marriage? she asked herself. Wasn't that between him and the Lord? What good would come of the village knowing such a thing?

Didn't feel right just tossing his history in the stove one night, making supper from its heat. He deserved more. Eva found her copy of *The Scarlet Letter*, which Ma had kept safe for her through the years. Though it took some time, she found the quotes she would offer her dear teacher in private. Next, she fetched one of Uriah's fishing creels from the barn and headed the mile or so to Mill's Creek.

Sitting on the dewy bank, Eva bent the leather cover of the journal back so the papers fanned out, making sure each page would fully burn. The water was as gray as the morning. And in the mist and chill, she managed to light a match, set the wicker basket on fire. She lay the story of Basil Brandt into a swell, the spring currents swallowing his shame forever. She flipped to the first marked passage, whispered it aloud—

"I have laughed, in bitterness and agony of heart, at the contrast between what I seem and what I am."

The final words jumbled in her mouth. For a moment, she focused on the tiny pyre, praying Basil was weeping with abandon at the face of Christ. After she tempered herself, Eva flipped to the second passage, spoke that one aloud, too—

"We dream in our waking moments, and walk in our sleep."

The burning wicker spun and roiled in the stony water. The blue devils in her heart were thinning to a softer shade as she watched the papery heap. It smoldered to nothingness, black wisps of smoke dissolving into the sunless sky. The space between the living and the dead shrunk to naught, and Eva knew that Basil heard her loud and clear when she vowed, "Your legacy will be one of goodwill."

Then she stood to go but emptied her stomach on the damp ground. Basil's approval was touchable, even rapturous.

* * *

Roman was born on January 19, 1874. Eva watched Uriah cradling their newborn son in his good arm, staring down at him with full, lit up eyes. She knew he was thinking about the power of parenthood, how the boy he was holding was his own. His safety, happiness, and wellbeing, it all depended on him. Uriah started to snivel as he beheld the tiny, pink babe, then brought his artificial hand to his mouth, bridling the emotion. Why he felt the need to stifle his joy, Eva did not understand. But it was not the time to say so.

Baby Roman kicked at the air, exploring his newfound freedom, and piped loud and shrill, like a warrior's battle cry. Eva looked at each of the faces of her loved ones, the grandparents, and Ada, Hiram and Sarah, marking the glint in their eyes. Her labor had been just under twelve hours and through it all, she cudgeled her brains around the agony of childbirth—the anguish of fighting the instinct to run from pain, and instead, bear down on it, push through the stretching and seizing of her womanhood. But watching her husband and son meet, seeing all the love, the already unbreakable union, her soreness faded into the background.

After being passed from Ma Murray and the Lovett's, then to Ada, baby Roman was finally handed to Sarah. It was only then that the boy stopped wailing. The quiet was loud in the room.

"Would you lean over the bed so I can see Roman's face in a state of peace. I have yet to see what that looks like," Eva quipped to Sarah, her voice tired to her own ears.

Sarah bent down, held Roman out for his mother to see, yet his eyes stayed riveted on Sarah, spellbound. Still, he did not cry. Hiram broke the silence when he said, "I understand, child. Sometimes, I stare at her for hours, too."

Chapter 42
No Bones

Eva dressed Roman in her own christening gown. Ma had surprised her with it the day she told her she was with child. It was extraordinarily big. "More like a prairie schooner bonnet than a garment," Eva said. "But he'll have plenty of room to flail and wriggle like he does." In garb so white, she knew that he'd spit up or mess himself, it would be like a rite of passage for both parent and child. So, when Roman did both before they even arrived at the church, she laughed. And when Uriah tried changing the diaper and smeared things further, she laughed even harder.

All those who had gathered for the birth were at the baptism, too, as well as Oscar and Ruby Lee and their sons and wives. Mr. and Mrs. Lovett were to be Roman's godparents. It made sense for a married couple to do the job, Uriah suggested. Eva agreed, and there were no words to the wiser. Hiram held Roman lengthwise along the underside of his arm, the baby's head down near the pool of water. It wasn't until the affusion that Roman began to cry. Though she'd experienced other sacraments many times before, Eva had never felt an almighty presence, never felt the darkness shifting to light. As the holy water dripped down the sides of Roman's face and shaded the thatch of hair atop his head, she savored the grace and freedom.

"I baptize you," Hiram announced. "In the name of the

Father, and of the Son, and of the Holy Spirit." A gentle warmth came over her, and a kind of balancing happened, as if Roman becoming a child of God kindled a final alignment inside her—heart and body. Any lopsidedness that still existed was set right with Hiram's words. More sublime than any birdsong or breeze or hymn, the clapping of those assembled was the purest sound she could recall ever hearing.

After the sermon, everyone flocked around the wood stove for coffee and slices of Ada's tangy rhubarb pies. The praises for her baking talents were ardent and having eaten all that was offered, the disappointment was just as enthusiastic. When Sarah took baby Roman, Eva chose that moment to motion Ma close, tell her about the wish to build her a fresh start, one free of old haunts. "And now that Basil has given us his home, there's no reason to wait any longer. I saved money while I was away, enough to start—"

"A selfless gesture, Eva. One that I'll carry in my heart till the day I die," Ma said, clutching her chest. "But I don't want it. Scratching out the past, why, that only prunes down all that's coming. We don't need to rub out our history. That'll leave us floating, nothing to hold on to. We're not a bunch of balloons."

From a distance, Hiram called out to Ada. "Miss Williams, what's a man have to do to get more pie? I'd pay you handsomely." Then, Sarah chimed in, too, begged for the recipe, for any hints she was willing to share. Oscar admitted that he couldn't spare much for pie but said he'd do just about anything if she'd tell Ruby Lee what was in it.

Ma Murray turned to Eva and said, "There it is, my dear. You're gonna build Ada a place to make her pies. That's money better spent." Eva couldn't let go of the dream that quickly, a new house for Ma had been the purpose, the incentive, the life force. A home free of wickedness and betrayal, that's why she suffered through the whoredom. That's what was going to make the scar on her face more bearable. Yet giving Ada a livelihood, a way to contribute, even out the score on the village that lynched her daughter, then shut its eyes on her, that notion had instant charm. The to-do about Ada's pies was still coming to pass and Eva joined in, "With your sweet treats, Ada, you could bait an outlaw straight into a jail cell."

* * *

It only took one more conversation for Eva to know that Ma would never change her mind, never leave her home for another. "That would mean blinking away my own sins," Ma said. "All those years, something in my guts told me Pa was looking at you in a bad way and still, I did nothing. I even left you alone with him, too afraid to face it. That's a wrong that can only be righted in this house. And it has to happen every day of my life, till the Lord finally takes me." And in all the hearkening, Eva began to let the thrill of Ada's bakery spread out some, take hold. The thought of Ada coming full circle, rising from Bellwether's darkest hours and living out her days in plentitude and pride, that was a trade-off she could accept.

Eva felt it best to offer Ada the money in private, just the two of them. And baby Roman. However, when she arrived at Ada's house, Hiram and Sarah were there, all of them sipping coffee and eating cookies. Ada pointed to an empty chair and Hiram rose to greet them while Sarah motioned with her hand to give Roman over, reaching out her arms. Eva laughed at her insistence and gave her the bundled child. Then she eyed the plate of cookies—the smell of vanilla and cocoa was verdant and the cherries were full and lumpy. "You gonna eat one? Or just stare at 'em like a rattle-boned bobcat?" Ada asked.

"Thought you'd never ask," Eva said. She stepped to the table, lifted a cookie and bit it all the way to the middle. The tartness of the cherries leapt in her mouth and she relished the smooth, buttery texture, chewing slow and long. She wondered if it was best to wait for another time when it was more private, but soon decided it was right that Hiram and Sarah were there. They were trailblazers to a better Bellwether and the best of companions. Eva swallowed the last bit of cookie and said with a questioning air, "You know, Ada, lots of folks would pay a thundering heap for your pastries and pies."

"Amen," Hiram said.

"Mighty kind of you to say, Eva. But there's just as many who still think me a blister. They'd be too afraid to eat anything I made, scared there was some kind of devilish potion inside. Just the other day, Mr. Turner crossed my path and said real heavy that he'd never set foot in the church again, not till I was dead and gone. And I swear someone's been trapping skunks and letting 'em loose on my porch. I've got a slew of them rascals like never before, stealing eggs, making a mess of the yard. And the other night, I heard men's voices outside. They were whispering, but it was that rowdy kind of whisper that drunk people do, trying to be quiet but jabbering even louder. I couldn't get to my door fast enough to catch 'em, but I'll have a boiling pot of water ready next time. I'll scald the spite right out of 'em."

"Not sure the Lord would approve of that," Hiram said. "But a foot-hold trap, now that might garner His blessing. I'll loan you mine." Everyone chuckled, including Hiram.

"So let's build a place for you to bake your goodies," Eva said. "Those who want to buy them will come. Those who don't can pass on by, hearts full of hate and grudges. And their bellies rumbling, wishing for your toothsome pastries."

"That all sounds good, dear Eva, but unless you hunted down that rook husband of mine and got back all the tin he pinched from the church, we've got an empty purse."

"Well, as much as I'd like to watch the good minister squirm like a grub on a hook, I think our purse is fuller than you think." Eva stepped to Sarah, put her hand inside Roman's blanket and pulled out a sheaf of greenbacks. A smile spread across her face, her scar folding into the creases as she fanned the money with her thumb then offered up the abundance. Ada's eyes grew big and she curled her fingers over the bills, staring at her hand as if it had six fingers. Slowly, she turned her gaze to Sarah, then Hiram, who shrugged his shoulders, his bewilderment plain.

"What is this about, Eva?" he asked.

"I was in Chicago for fourteen years, friends. Working and saving. I wasn't going to the music halls or hobnobbing at the theater. Now, it's not enough to build a new place and furnish it, too. But I was thinking, what if we buy *The Lumberjack* and fix it up? That nasty old saloon is an eyesore, kind of hair-raising, too, knowing all the bad stories that come from there. Folks will thank us."

"We could get it for next to nothing, I'll bet." Hiram began to catch on, joining Eva in the bulwark. "All the floor joists have to be replaced. And the roof is pretty bad. Needs new windows, too. But we'll do the work ourselves."

"You bet we will," Sarah spliced in. Roman wiggled in her lap, let out a grunt. "Tell you what. While you folks are building Miss Ada's shop, I'll take care of this beautiful child, that'll be my part." All three of them laughed, loud enough to make Roman twist again before falling back into a slumber.

Ada was shaking her head, no, but Eva nodded with vehemence in a once-and-for-all gesture. Everyone watched as Ada's hand that gripped the money began to tremble. Soon the tears dropped down one after another. There was a silence in her lament, seemed like even the house could feel the tangle of emotions—gladness of redemption, and the mourning of lost years. Eva understood that just because Ada was partly reconciled didn't mean the damage would magically disappear. The moment was only a valve, letting some of the decades of cruelty pour out, as if someone had pierced the house's sides and the blood and water were spilling over its walls, levitating everything close-at-hand for now.

"That day on the church steps, when you first came home,

Eva. Everyone was shuffling past me like they always did." She shook her head and sucked in deep, then let it out. "But you stood still. Folks were bumping and chattering away, and you just kept steady, refusing to turn away from me. I knew right then that the light of God was in you. And now, you've gone and made me start hoping and dreaming again." Ada's voice was drawn tight. "Who knows if it will work. Not too sure it'll let me down all that much if it don't, though. This moment right here is what I'll remember. Nothing or nobody can go one better."

* * *

Ada called her shop Elinor's Place and it opened for business in the spring of '74. For the first week or two, Ada's clientele consisted of just Uriah, the Lovetts, Hiram and Sarah, and every other day or so, the Lee family. Sarah and Eva had become mainstays, one of them helping bake while the other held, bounced and burped baby Roman. Come July, she was selling bread and pasties in addition to the pies and cakes. Then, on a warm Saturday morning, Mr. Miller opened the front door. All heads turned when he said, "Good morning." His gruff voice was undeniable.

None of them returned the greeting. Ada and Sarah froze, their hands buried in mounds of dough. Eva pulled Roman close to her chest and stared the man down. After a few seconds of silence, Mr. Miller said, "I don't blame you for not speaking to me. I wouldn't either." He took another step forward, pushed the door closed then leaned against it, his head hanging low. "Lord, I knew this wasn't gonna be easy," he said. "Just hear me out. It's a gruesome story but my point for being here comes from telling it."

"We're listening," Eva said.

He pulled off his hat, pinched the crown with his fingers and pushed it against his chest. "See, my grandson was helping me pull a dead foal from its mother. Poor thing died in the womb. Mare was too give-out to deliver it. Had to get the saw wire, cut it in pieces while—" He stopped. "You ladies don't need to hear all them details. It's what happened after, that's what opened my eyes to all the wrong I been doing. So, my grandson and me, we was standing in the barn. The mare was breathing heavy, fighting for her life, and the foal's carved up pieces were lying at our feet. Blood everywhere. In all my live-long days on a farm, I ain't never seen more blood—" He stopped again.

Eva looked to Ada and Sarah, both of them put their fingers to their lips at the same time. She heeded their request and turned back to Mr. Miller. With his head still down, he continued, slow and strained. "So the boy, well, he starts laughing. And before I can stop him, he starts kicking the foal's severed head like a ball, its little white splotch of fur showing through the slick afterbirth. I couldn't say nothing. No words would come out. I was sad and angry and sick to my belly. I ought not tell you what he said next, Miss Ada, but I feel like I have to. That's the only way me being here makes any sense."

"You okay, Ada?" Eva asked. "If you don't want to hear no more, just tell him. This is your shop. You say who comes and goes."

Ada nodded her head. "Go on, Mr. Miller, tell me."

"Well, as my grandson is looking at the dead filly's insides, he says, 'Is this what hanging the Williams girls looked like? Bleedin' body parts and all?' Then he laughs, and says, 'Only missin' the broken rope, ain't we?' Even made a wisecrack about Elinor being, you know, slow." He drew in air through his nose then let it bubble out through his lips like a horse, cheeks rippling. "And for the first time ever, I hit one of my own. My knuckles cracked against his jawbone. Think I broke my thumb. But that didn't hurt near as much as telling him to leave my house. That was months ago now. And he's obeyed, hasn't come to visit again. Fact is, I don't miss him much."

Eva looked at the two women again. By then, Sarah had

pulled her hands from the dough and placed them on Ada's shoulders, the flour showing fingerprints on her dress. Eva patted Roman's back as she stepped to Mr. Miller. "I'm sad for you. Truly, I am. But I'm still not sure why you're telling us your troubles."

"'Cause I saw the hate in my grandchild that day. How could he watch all of us treating Ada the way we do, listen to all the lies at the supper table, and not be burning up with spite? I got to thinking, all of Bellwether's young ones have shot up that way. Filled to the brim with gall."

Ada stepped from around the counter, limped her way to Mr. Miller and put her hand on his heart. He covered it with his own. "I called on Mr. Turner," he said, his voice cracking, "begged him to come with me—" A sob caught in his throat. "But I think some folks might just keep on hating forever. Maybe it's all they got to hold on to."

"Don't you worry none about that," Ada said. "You can't be taking the blame for others. You're here, that's all that counts."

"I'm sorry, Miss Ada. I've been a blue-ribbon mudsill. And I should've—"

"Enough. Pull up a chair and fill your mouth with this here strudel, that'll keep you from getting too soppy on us." Ada took in a quick breath and let it out in jerks then fetched a pastry from the counter. "It's something new we're trying here at Elinor's Place." All of them watched as he wolfed it down in three bites, picked a bit of apple from his teeth with his fingernail and moaned with overdone satisfaction.

He stood to go, reached in his pocket. Before he could pull up any money, Eva held up her hand. "It's on the house. Just spread the word about Ada's vittles, how they make a mouth water like the Tahquamenon."

"Done," he said, putting his hat back on, adjusting it some. "There's something else I aim to say. Not sure it matters too much now, but hell, after all I've blabbed already this morning." He let out a heavy sigh. "All those years ago—" He stopped, rubbed the back of his neck and kept his hand there. "Good Lord, Ada, how old are we now? I've lost track. You and me, we've gotta be nearing seventy."

"Turning sixty-eight this winter," she said.

"Jesus, Mary and Joseph," he whispered. Then he sucked in, looked her in the eyes and spoke fast. "It was my wife who dropped your baby girl that Godforsaken mornin'. Seems someone passed Elinore to her, then there was a bit of a tangle, too many ladyfolk trying to help. Well, she tottered some and—"There was a bout of quiet before Mr. Miller headed for the door. He turned back around, beheld the three women a moment. "She told me that story a thousand times, Ada. Every retelling ending with tears. God rest her soul."

"That was long ago, Mr. Miller. Now get on out of here. Your loitering is bad for business." Ada took a couple of gimp steps forward and shooed him out the door with the back of her hand. She rested her head against the door a moment. Then with a lurch, told the women to get back to work. "Looks like we have more strudel to make."

* * *

Two weeks after Mr. Miller's visit, on a Friday, mid-afternoon, Ada sold out of baked goods and had to close early. Eva held a broom overhead, taking swipes at a black fly while glancing down at Roman in the bassinet, here and there, his eyes still smoky and wandering, surveying the scene like a bird-dog. After missing the fly several times, she took a break and rested her hand and chin on the broom handle, watched Sarah wiping down the counter, listened to her mellow voice as she hummed the tune to "I Gave My Love a Cherry." Soon enough, Sarah began singing the words aloud. And when she came to the last verse, Eva joined in, the two of them crooning together—"Well, a cherry when it's blooming, it has no stone. A chicken when it's pippin', it has no bone."

Ada stepped out from the kitchen, pulled the kerchief

from her head and plunked down at the closest of the two tables. She patted her forehead with the washrag in her hand then leaned her face into the bassinet. Sarah and Eva stopped singing, and she could feel them looking at her. The room grew quiet, nothing but Roman's gurgling and the faint rattle and clank of breeching straps of a carriage passing by.

END

About The Author

Chad V. Broughman was the recipient of the Rusty Scythe Prize Book Award and the Adobe Cottage Writers Retreat honor in New Mexico. As well, Chad was awarded two chapbook contracts for his short story collections—"the forsaken" and "slighted"—both published by Etchings Press. His fiction can be found in journals nationwide, such as Carrier Pigeon, East Coast Literary Review, River Poets Journal, Burningword, Pulp Fiction, Sky Island Journal, and From Whispers to Roars, and he is anthologized in Write Michigan Short Story Anthology, On Loss, and Scribes Valley Anthology. He is a Best of the Net and Pushcart Prize nominee, holds an MFA from Spalding University and served as co-editor for the fiction/poetry blog "Cafe Aphra" based out of the United Kingdom. Chad teaches English and Creative Writing at the secondary and post-secondary levels but is most proud of his roles as a husband and devoted father to two rambunctious young sons.

Other Books You Might Enjoy From Anamcara Press Llc

ISBN: 9781941237-88-5
$21.99

ISBN: 9781941237-31-1
$21.99

ISBN: 9781941237-32-8
$18.95

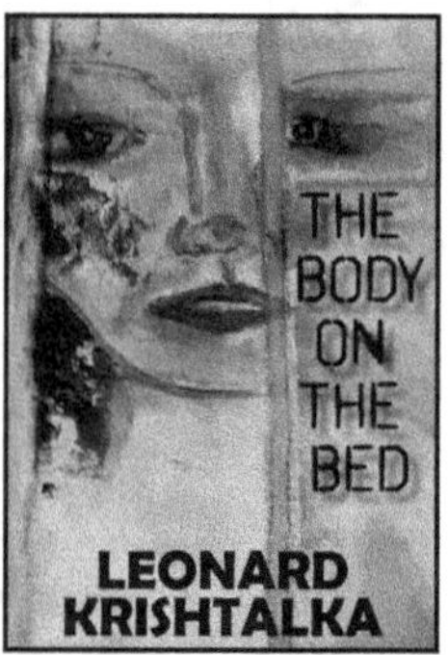

ISBN: 9781941237-82-3
$21.99

ISBN: 9781941237-18-2
$21.99

ISBN: 9781941237-08-3
$24.95

Available wherever books are sold and at:
anamcara-press.com

Thank you for being a reader! Anamcara Press publishes select works and brings writers & artists together in collaborations in order to serve community and the planet. *Your comments are always welcome!*

Anamcara Press
anamcara-press.com

www.ingramcontent.com/pod-product-compliance
Lightning Source LLC
Chambersburg PA
CBHW072038190726
48294CB00005B/1311